The
IMMORTAL
Rules

Books by Julie Kagawa
from Harlequin TEEN

The Iron Fey series (in reading order)

THE IRON KING
WINTER'S PASSAGE (ebook)
THE IRON DAUGHTER
THE IRON QUEEN
SUMMER'S CROSSING (ebook)
THE IRON KNIGHT

Blood of Eden series

THE IMMORTAL RULES

The
IMMORTAL
Rules

Julie Kagawa

A legend begins.

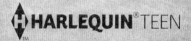

HARLEQUIN® TEEN

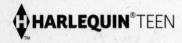 **HARLEQUIN**®TEEN

ISBN-13: 978-0-373-21051-0

THE IMMORTAL RULES

Copyright © 2012 by Julie Kagawa

Recycling programs
for this product may
not exist in your area.

This edition published by arrangement with Harlequin Books S.A.

For questions and comments about the quality of this book please contact us at Customer_eCare@Harlequin.ca.

® and TM are trademarks of the publisher. Trademarks indicated with ® are registered in the United States Patent and Trademark Office, the Canadian Trade Marks Office and in other countries.

www.HarlequinTEEN.com

Printed in U.S.A.

To Nick, who will always slay vampires with me.

PART I

HUMAN

CHAPTER 1

They hung the Unregistereds in the old warehouse district; it was a public execution, so everyone went to see.

I stood at the back, a nameless face in the crowd, too close to the gallows for comfort but unable to look away. There were three of them this time, two boys and a girl. The oldest was about my age, seventeen and skinny, with huge frightened eyes and greasy dark hair that hung to his shoulders. The other two were even younger, fourteen and fifteen if I had to guess, and siblings, since they both had the same stringy yellow hair. I didn't know them; they weren't part of my crowd. Still, they had the same look of all Unregistereds; thin and ragged, their eyes darting about like trapped animals. I crossed my arms tightly, feeling their desperation. It was over. The trap had closed; the hunters had caught them, and there was no place for them to run.

The pet stood on the edge of the platform, puffed up and swaggering, as if he had caught the kids himself. He was walking back and forth, pointing to the condemned and rattling off a list of crimes, his pale eyes gleaming with triumph.

"…assaulting a citizen of the Inner City, robbery, trespassing and resisting arrest. These criminals attempted to steal Class One foodstuffs from the private warehouse of the Inner City. This is a crime against you, and more important, a crime against our benevolent Masters."

I snorted. Fancy words and legal mumbo jumbo didn't erase the fact that these "criminals" were just doing what all Unregistereds did to survive. For whatever reasons, fate, pride or stubbornness, we nonregistered humans didn't have the mark of our vampire masters etched into our skin, the brands that told you who you were, where you lived and who you belonged to. Of course, the vampires said it was to keep us safe, to keep track of everyone within the city, to know how much food they had to allow for. It was for our own good. Yeah, right. Call it what you wanted, it was just another way to keep their human cattle enslaved. You might as well be wearing a collar around your neck.

There were several good things about being Unregistered. You didn't exist. You were off their records, a ghost in the system. Because your name wasn't on the lists, you didn't have to show up for the monthly bloodletting, where human pets in crisp white coats stuck a tube in your vein and siphoned your blood into clear bags that were placed into coolers and taken to the Masters. Miss a couple lettings and the guards came for you, forcing you to pony up the late blood, even if it left you empty as a limp sack. The vamps got their blood, one way or another.

Being Unregistered let you slip through the cracks. There

was no leash for the bloodsuckers to yank on. And since it wasn't exactly a crime, you'd think everyone would do it. Unfortunately, being free came with a hefty price. Registered humans got meal tickets. Unregistereds didn't. And since the vamps controlled all the food in the city, this made getting enough to eat a real problem.

So we did what anyone in our situation would do. We begged. We stole. We scraped up food wherever we could, did anything to survive. In the Fringe, the outermost circle of the vampire city, food was scarce even if you weren't Unregistered. The ration trucks came twice a month and were heavily guarded. I'd seen Registered citizens beaten just for getting out of line. So while it wasn't exactly a crime to be Unregistered, if you got *caught* stealing from the bloodsuckers and you didn't have the Prince's cursed brand gracing your skin, you could expect no mercy whatsoever.

It was a lesson I'd learned well. Too bad these three never did.

"…eight ounces of soy, two potatoes, and a quarter loaf of bread." The pet was still going on, and his audience had their eyes glued to the gallows now, morbidly fascinated. I slipped into the crowd, moving away from the platform. The smug voice rang out behind me, and I clenched my hands, wishing I could drive a fist through his smiling teeth. Damn pets. In some ways, they were even worse than the bloodsuckers. They'd chosen to serve the vamps, selling out their fellow humans for the safety and luxury it brought. Everyone hated them, but at the same time everyone was jealous of them, as well.

"The rules regarding Unregistered citizens are clear." The

pet was wrapping up, stretching out his words for the greatest effect. "According to clause twenty-two, line forty-six of New Covington law, any human found stealing within city limits, who does not have the mark of protection from the Prince, shall be hanged by the neck until they are dead. Do the accused have any last words?"

I heard muffled voices, the oldest thief swearing at the pet, telling him to do something anatomically impossible. I shook my head. Brave words wouldn't help him. Nothing would now. It was fine and good to be defiant to the end, but it was better not to get caught in the first place. That was his first mistake and, ultimately, his last. *Always leave yourself an out;* that was the first rule of the Unregistereds. Do whatever you want—hate the vamps, curse the pets—but never get caught. I picked up my pace, hurrying past the edge of the crowd, and broke into a jog.

The clunk of the trapdoors releasing echoed very loudly in my ears, even over the gasp of the watching crowd. The silence that followed was almost a living thing, urging me to turn, to glance over my shoulder. Ignoring the knot in my stomach, I slipped around a corner, putting the wall between myself and the gallows so I wouldn't be tempted to look back.

LIFE IN THE FRINGE is a simple thing, like the people who live here. They don't have to work, though there are a couple "trading posts" set up around the Fringe, where people collect what they find and exchange it for other things. They don't have to read; there are no jobs that require it, and besides, owning books is highly illegal—so why risk it? All they have to worry about is feeding themselves, keeping their clothes mended, and patching up whatever hole or box or gutted out building they call home well enough to keep the rain off them.

The secret goal of almost every Fringer is to someday make it into the Inner City, past the wall that separates the civilized world from the human trash, into the glittering city that looms over us with its great starry towers that had somehow resisted crumbling into dust. Everyone knows someone who knows someone who was taken into the city, a brilliant mind or a great beauty, someone too unique or special to be left here with us animals. There are rumors that the vampires "breed" the humans on the inside, raising the children to be their thralls, completely devoted to their masters. But since none who are Taken into the city ever come out again—except the pets and their guards, and they aren't talking—no one knows what it's really like.

Of course, this only feeds the stories.

"Did you hear?" Stick asked as I met him at the chain-link fence that marked the edge of our territory. Beyond the fence, across a grassy, glass-strewn lot, stood a squat old building that my gang and I called home. Lucas, the de facto leader of our gang, said it used to be a "school," a place where kids like us gathered every day in huge numbers to learn. That was before the vamps had it gutted and burned, destroying everything on the inside, but it was still a refuge for a gang of skinny street rats. Three stories high, the brick walls were beginning to crumble, the top floor had fallen in, and the halls were filled with mold, rubble and little else. The charred halls and empty rooms were cold, damp and dark, and every year a little more of the walls fell away, but it was our place, our safe haven, and we were fiercely protective of it.

"Hear what?" I asked as we ducked through the gap in the rusty fence, striding through weeds and grass and broken bottles to where home beckoned invitingly.

"Gracie was Taken last night. Into the city. They say some vampire was looking to expand his harem, so he took her."

I looked at him sharply. "What? Who told you that?"

"Kyle and Travis."

I rolled my eyes in disgust. Kyle and Travis belonged to a rival gang of Unregistereds. We didn't bother each other, usually, but this sounded like something our competitors would concoct just to scare us off the streets. "You believe anything those two say? They're screwing with you, Stick. They want to scare you."

He trailed me across the lot like a shadow, watery blue gaze darting about. Stick's real name was Stephen, but no one called him that anymore. He was taller than me by several inches, but my five-foot nothing didn't make this feat all that impressive. Stick was built like a scarecrow, with straw-colored hair and timid eyes. He managed to survive on the streets, but just barely. "They're not the only ones talking about it," he insisted. "Cooper said he heard her scream a few blocks away. What does that tell you?"

"If it's true? That she was stupid enough to go wandering around the city at night and probably got herself eaten."

"Allie!"

"What?" We ducked through the broken door frame into the dank halls of the school. Rusty metal lockers were scattered along one wall, a few still standing, most dented and broken. I headed toward an upright one and yanked the door open with a squeak. "The vamps don't stay in their precious towers all the time. Sometimes they go hunting for live bodies. Everyone knows that." I grabbed the brush that I kept here to go with the mirror that was stuck to the back, the only useable one in the building. My reflection stared at me, a dirty-faced girl with straight black hair and "squinty eyes," as Rat put it. At least I didn't have teeth like a rodent.

I ran the brush through my hair, wincing at the snags. Stick was still watching me, disapproving and horrified, and I rolled my eyes. "Don't give me that look, Stephen," I said, frowning. "If you're out past sundown and get tagged by a bloodsucker, that's your fault for not staying put or not paying attention." I replaced the brush and shut the locker with a bang. "Gracie thought that just because she's Registered and her brother guards the Wall, she was safe from vampires. They always come for you when you think you're safe."

"Marc is pretty torn up about it," Stick said almost sullenly. "Gracie was his only family since their parents died."

"Not our problem." I felt bad for saying it, but it was true. In the Fringe, you looked out for yourself and your immediate family, no one else. My concern didn't extend beyond myself, Stick and the rest of our small gang. *This* was my family, screwed up as it was. I couldn't worry about the trials of everyone in the Fringe. I had plenty of my own, thanks.

"Maybe…" Stick began, and hesitated. "Maybe she's…happier now," he continued. "Maybe being Taken into the Inner City is a good thing. The vampires will take better care of her, don't you think?"

I resisted the urge to snort. *Stick, they're vampires,* I wanted to say. *Monsters. They only see us as two things: slaves and food. Nothing good comes from a bloodsucker, you know that.*

But telling Stick that would only upset him more, so I pretended not to hear. "Where are the others?" I asked as we walked down the hall, picking our way over rubble and broken glass. Stick trailed morosely, dragging his feet, kicking bits of rock and plaster with every step. I resisted the urge to smack him. Marc was a decent guy; even though he was Registered, he didn't treat us Unregistereds like vermin, and even spoke to us on occasion when he was making his rounds at the Wall. I also knew Stick had feelings for Gracie, though he would never act on them. But I was the one who shared most of my food with him, since he was usually too scared to go scavenging by himself. Ungrateful little snot. I couldn't watch out for everyone; he knew that.

"Lucas isn't back yet," Stick finally mumbled as we came to my room, one of the many empty spaces along the hall. In the years I had been here, I'd fixed it up the best I could. Plastic bags covered the shattered windows, keeping out the rain and damp. An old mattress lay in one corner with my blanket and pillow. I'd even managed to find a folding table, a couple chairs and a plastic shelf for various clutter, little things I wanted to keep. I'd built a nice little lair for myself, and the best part was my door still locked from the inside, so I could get some privacy if I wanted.

"What about Rat?" I asked, pushing on my door.

As the door squeaked open, a wiry boy with lank brown hair jerked around, beady eyes widening. He was older than me and Stick, with sharp features and a front tooth that stuck out like a fang, giving him a permanent sneer.

Rat swore when he saw me, and my blood boiled. This was *my* space, my territory. He had no right to be here. "Rat," I snarled, bursting through the doorway. "Why are you snooping around my room? Looking for things to steal?"

Rat held up his arm, and my stomach went cold. In one grubby hand, he held an old, faded book, the cover falling off, the pages crumpled. I recognized it instantly. It was a made-up story, a fantasy, the tale of four kids who went through a magic wardrobe and found themselves in a strange new world. I'd read it more times than I could remember, and although I sneered at the thought of a magical land with friendly, talking animals, there were times when I wished, in my most secret moments, that I could find a hidden door that would take us all out of this place.

"What the hell is this?" Rat said, holding up the book. Having been caught red-handed, he quickly switched to the offensive. "Books? Why are you collecting garbage like that? As if you even know how to read." He snorted and tossed the book to the floor. "Do you know what the vamps would do, if they found out? Does Lucas know about your little trash collection?"

"That's none of your business," I snapped, stepping farther into the room. "This is my room, and I'll keep what I want. Now get lost, before I tell Lucas to throw you out on your skinny white ass."

Rat snickered. He hadn't been with the group long, a few months at most. He claimed he'd come from another sector and that his old gang had kicked him out, but he'd never said why. I suspected it was because he was a lying, thieving bastard. Lucas wouldn't even have considered letting him stay if we hadn't lost two members the previous winter. Patrick and Geoffrey, two Unregistered brothers who were daring to the point of stupidity, who bragged the vampires would never catch them. They were too quick, they claimed. They knew all the best escape tunnels. And then one night they went out looking for food as usual…and never came back.

Kicking the book aside, Rat took a threatening step forward and straightened so that he loomed over me. "You got a big mouth, Allie," he snarled, his breath hot and foul. "Better watch out. Lucas can't be around to protect you all the time. Think about that." He leaned in, crowding me. "Now get out of my face, before I bitch slap you across the room. I'd hate for you to start crying in front of your boyfriend."

He tried pushing me back. I dodged, stepped close and slammed my fist into his nose as hard as I could.

Rat shrieked, staggering backward, hands flying to his face. Stick yelped from behind me. Blinking through tears, Rat screamed a curse and swung at my head, clumsy and awkward. I ducked and shoved him into the wall, hearing the thump of his head against the plaster.

"Get out of my room," I growled as Rat slid down the wall, dazed. Stick had fled to a corner and was hiding behind the table. "Get out and stay out, Rat. If I see you in here again, I swear you'll be eating through a straw the rest of your life."

Rat pushed himself upright, leaving a smear of red on the plaster. Wiping his nose, he spat a curse at me and stumbled out, kicking over a chair as he left. I slammed and locked the door behind him.

"Bastard. Thieving, lying bastard. Ow." I looked down at my fist and frowned. My knuckle had been cut on Rat's tooth and was starting to well with blood. "Ew. Oh, great, I hope I don't catch something nasty."

"He's going to be mad," Stick said, venturing out from behind the table, pale and frightened. I snorted.

"So what? Let him try something. I'll break his nose the other way." Grabbing a rag from the shelf, I pressed it to my knuckle. "I'm tired of listening to his crap, thinking he can do anything he wants just because he's bigger. He's had it coming for a while."

"He might take it out on *me*," Stick said, and I bristled at the accusing tone, as if I should know better. As if I didn't think of how it might affect him.

"So kick him in the shin and tell him to back off," I said, tossing the rag on the shelf and carefully picking up the abused book. Its cover had been ripped off, and the front page was torn, but it seemed otherwise intact. "Rat picks on you 'cause you take it. If you fight back, he'll leave you alone."

Stick didn't say anything, lapsing into sullen silence, and I bit down my irritation. He wouldn't fight back. He would do what he always did—run to me and expect me to help him. I sighed and knelt beside a plastic box by the back wall. Normally, it was hidden by an old sheet, but Rat had ripped that off and tossed it in the corner, probably looking for food or other things to steal. Sliding back the top, I studied the contents.

It was half full of books, some like the paperback I held in my hand, some larger, with sturdier covers. Some were moldy, some half charred. I knew them all, front to back, cover to cover. This was my most prized, most secret, possession. If the vamps knew I had a stash like this, they'd shoot us all and raze this place to the ground. But to me, the risk was worth it. The vamps had outlawed books in the Fringe and had systematically gutted every school and library building once they'd taken over, and I knew why. Because within the pages of every book, there was information of another world—a world before this one, where humans didn't live in fear of vampires and walls and monsters in the night. A world where we were free.

Carefully, I replaced the small paperback, and my gaze shifted to another well-worn book, its colors faded, a mold stain starting to eat one corner. It was larger than the others, a children's picture book, with brightly colored animals dancing across the front. I ran my fingers over the cover and sighed. *Mom.*

Stick had ventured close again, peering over my shoulder at the tote. "Did Rat take anything?" he asked softly.

"No," I muttered, shutting the lid, hiding my treasures from view. "But you might want to check your room, as well. And return anything you borrowed recently, just in case."

"I haven't borrowed anything for months," Stick said, sounding frightened and defensive at the thought, and I bit down a sharp reply. Not long ago, before Rat came to the group, I would often find Stick in his room, huddled against the wall with one of my books, completely absorbed in the story. I'd taught him to read myself; long, painstaking hours of us sitting on my mattress, going over words and letters and sounds. It had taken a while for Stick to learn, but once he did, it became his favorite way to escape, to forget everything right outside his door.

Then Patrick had told him what vampires did to Fringers

who could read books, and now he wouldn't touch them. All that work, all that time, all for nothing. It pissed me off that Stick was too scared of the vamps to learn anything new. I'd offered to teach Lucas, but he was flat-out not interested, and I wasn't going to bother with Rat.

Stupid me, thinking I could pass on anything useful to this bunch.

But there was more to my anger than Stick's fear or Lucas's ignorance. I wanted them to learn, to better themselves, because that was just one more thing the vampires had taken from us. They taught their pets and thralls to read, but the rest of the population they wanted to keep blind, stupid and in the dark. They wanted us to be mindless, passive animals. If enough people knew what life was like…before…how long would it be until they rose up against the bloodsuckers and took everything back?

It was a dream I didn't voice to anyone, not even myself. I couldn't force people to want to learn. But that didn't stop me from trying.

Stick backed up as I stood, tossing the sheet over the box again. "You think he found the other spot?" he asked tentatively. "Maybe you should check that one, too."

I gave him a resigned look. "Are you hungry? Is that what you're saying?"

Stick shrugged, looking hopeful. "Aren't you?"

I rolled my eyes and walked to the mattress in the corner, dropping to my knees again. Pushing the mattress up revealed the loose boards underneath, and I pried them free, peering into the dark hole.

"Damn," I muttered, feeling around the tiny space. Not much left—a stale lump of bread, two peanuts and one potato that was beginning to sprout eyes. This was what Rat had probably been looking for: my private cache. We all had them somewhere, hidden away from the rest of the world. Unregistereds didn't steal from each other; at least, we weren't supposed to. That was the unspoken rule. But, at our hearts, we were all thieves, and starvation drove people to do desperate things. I hadn't survived this long by being naive. The only one who knew about this hole was Stick, and I trusted him. He wouldn't risk everything he had by stealing from me.

I gazed over the pathetic items and sighed. "Not good," I muttered, shaking my head. "And they're really cracking down out there, lately. No one is trading ration tickets anymore, for anything."

My stomach felt hollow, nothing new to me, as I replaced the floorboards and split the bread with Stick. I was almost always hungry in some form or another, but this had progressed to the serious stage. I hadn't eaten anything since last night. My scavenging that morning hadn't gone well. After several hours of searching my normal stakeouts, all I had to show for it was a cut palm and an empty stomach. Raiding old Thompson's rat traps hadn't worked; the rats were either getting smarter or he was finally making a dent in the rodent population. I'd scaled the fire escape to widow Tanner's rooftop garden, carefully easing under the razor-wire fence only to find the shrewd old woman had done her harvest early, leaving nothing but empty boxes of dirt behind. I'd searched the back-alley Dumpsters behind Hurley's trading shop; *sometimes,* though rarely, there would be a loaf of bread so moldy not even a rat would touch it, or a sack of soybeans that had gone bad, or a rancid potato. I wasn't picky; my stomach had been trained to keep down most anything, no matter how disgusting. Bugs, rats, maggoty bread, I didn't care as long as it faintly resembled food. I could eat what most people couldn't stomach, but today, it seemed Lady Luck hated me worse than usual.

And continuing to hunt after the execution was impossible. The pet's continued presence in the Fringe made people nervous. I didn't want to risk thievery with so many of the pet's guards wandering about. Besides, stealing food so soon after three people had been hanged for it was just asking for trouble.

Scavenging in familiar territory was getting me nowhere. I'd used up all resources here, and the Registereds were getting wise to my methods. Even if I crossed into other sectors, most of the Fringe had been picked clean long, long ago. In a city full of scavengers and opportunists, there just wasn't anything left. If we wanted to eat, I was going to have to venture farther.

I was going to have to leave the city.

Glancing at the pale sky through the plastic-covered window, I grimaced. The morning was already gone. With afternoon fading rapidly, I'd have only a few hours to hunt for food once I was outside the Wall. If I didn't make it back before sundown, other things would start hunting. Once the light dropped from the sky, it was *their* time. The Masters. The vampires.

I still have time, I thought, mentally calculating the hours in my head. *It's a fairly clear day; I can slip under the Wall, search the ruins and be back before the sun goes down.*

"Where are you going?" Stick asked as I opened the door

and strode back down the hall, keeping a wary eye out for Rat. "Allie? Wait, where are you going? Take me with you. I can help."

"No, Stick." I turned on him and shook my head. "I'm not hitting the regular spots this time. There are too many guards, and the pet is still out there making everyone twitchy." I sighed and shielded my eyes from the sun, gazing over the empty lot. "I'm going to have to try the ruins."

He squeaked. "You're leaving the city?"

"I'll be back before sundown. Don't worry."

"If they catch you…"

"They won't." I leaned back and smirked at him. "When have they ever caught me? They don't even know those tunnels exist."

"You sound like Patrick and Geoffrey."

I blinked, stung. "That's a bit harsh, don't you think?" He shrugged, and I crossed my arms. "If that's how you feel, maybe I won't bother sharing anything I bring back. Maybe you should hunt for your own food for a change."

"Sorry," he said quickly, giving me an apologetic smile. "Sorry, Allie. I just worry about you, that's all. I get scared that you'll leave me here, alone. Promise you'll come back?"

"You know I will."

"Okay, then." He backed away into the hall, the shadows closing over his face. "Good luck."

Maybe it was just me, but his tone almost implied that he was hoping I'd run into trouble. That I would see how dangerous it really was out there, and that he'd been right all along. But that was silly, I told myself, sprinting across the empty lot, back toward the fence and the city streets. Stick needed me; I was his only friend. He wasn't so vindictive that he'd wish me harm just because he was pissed about Marc and Gracie.

Right?

I pushed the thought from my mind as I squeezed through the chain-link fence and slipped into the quiet city. I could worry about Stick some other time; my priority was finding food to keep us both alive.

The sun teetered directly above the skeletal buildings, bathing the streets in light. *Just hang up there a little longer,* I thought, glancing at the sky. *Stay put, for a few more hours at least. Actually, feel free to stop moving, if you want.*

Vindictively, it seemed to drop a little lower in the sky, taunting me as it slid behind a cloud. The shadows lengthened like grasping fingers, sliding over the ground. I shivered and hurried into the streets.

CHAPTER 2

People will tell you that it's impossible to leave New Covington, that the Outer Wall is impenetrable, that no one can get in or out of the city even if they want to.

People are wrong.

The Fringe is a massive concrete jungle; canyons of broken glass and rusting steel, skeletal giants choked by vines, rot and corrosion. Save for the very center of the city, where the looming vampire towers gleam with dark radiance, the surrounding structures look diseased, hollow and perilously close to collapse. Below the jagged skyline, with few humans to keep it in check, the wilderness outside creeps closer. Rusted shells of what were once cars are scattered about the streets, their rotted frames wrapped in vegetation. Trees, roots and vines push up through sidewalks and even rooftops, splitting pavement and steel, as nature slowly claims the city for its own. In recent years, a few of the looming skyscrapers finally succumbed to time and decay, tumbling to the ground in a roar of dust and cement and breaking glass, killing everyone unlucky enough to be around it when it happened. It was a fact of life anymore. Enter any building nowadays, and you could hear it creaking and groaning above your head, maybe decades away from collapse, or maybe only seconds.

The city is falling apart. Everyone in the Fringe knows it, but you can't think about that. No use in worrying about what you can't change.

What *I* was worried about, more than anything, was avoiding the vamps, not getting caught, and getting enough to eat to survive one more day.

Sometimes, like today, that called for drastic measures. What I was about to do was risky and dangerous as hell, but if I was worried about risk, I wouldn't be Unregistered, would I?

The Fringe was divided into several sections, sectors as they called them, all neatly fenced off to control the flow of food and people. Another device built "for our protection." Call it what you want; a cage is still a cage. As far as I knew, there were five or six sectors in a loose semicircle around the Inner City. We were Sector 4. If I had a tattoo that could be scanned, it would read something like: *Allison Sekemoto, resident number 7229, Sector 4, New Covington. Property of Prince Salazar.* Technically, the Prince owned every human in the city, but his officers had harems and thralls—bloodslaves—of their own, as well. Fringers, on the other hand—Registered Fringers anyway—were "communal property." Which meant any vampire could do anything they wanted to them.

No one in the Fringe seemed bothered by their tattoo. Nate, one of the assistants at Hurley's trading post, was constantly trying to get me to Register, saying the tattooing didn't hurt very much and the whole giving blood part wasn't so bad once you got used to it. He couldn't understand why I was being so stubborn. I told him it wasn't the scanning or the giving blood that I hated the most.

It was the whole "Property of" bit that bothered me. I was no one's property. If the damn bloodsuckers wanted me, they'd have to catch me first. And I wasn't going to make it easy for them.

The barrier between sectors was simple: chain-link topped with barbed wire. The steel curtains ran for miles and weren't well patrolled. There were guards at the iron gates in each sector that let the food trucks in and out of the Inner City, but nowhere else. Really, the vamps didn't particularly care if some of their cattle slipped back and forth between sectors. The majority of the deadly, lethal force was dedicated to protecting the Outer Wall every night.

You had to admit, the Outer Wall was pretty impressive. Thirty feet high, six feet thick, the ugly monstrosity of iron, steel and concrete loomed over the perimeter of the Fringe, surrounding the entire city. There was only one gate to the outside, two doors of solid iron, barred from the inside with heavy steel girders that took three men to remove. It wasn't in my sector, but I'd seen it open once, while scavenging far from home. Spotlights had been placed along the Wall every fifty yards, scanning the ground like enormous eyes. Beyond the Wall was the "kill zone," a razed strip of ground littered with barbed-wire coils, trenches, spiked pits and mines, all designed to do one thing: keep rabids away from the Wall.

The Outer Wall was feared and hated throughout New

Covington, reminding us that we were trapped here, like penned-in sheep, but it was greatly revered, as well. No one could survive the ruins beyond the city, especially when darkness fell. Even the vamps disliked going into the ruins. Beyond the Wall, the night belonged to the rabids. No sane person went over the Wall, and those who tried were either gunned down or blown to bits in the kill zone.

Which was why I planned to go beneath.

I PUSHED MY WAY THROUGH the waist-high weeds that filled the ditch, keeping one hand on the cement wall as I maneuvered puddles and shattered glass. I hadn't been here in a while, and the weeds had covered all traces of previous passing. Circling the rock pile, ignoring the suspicious-looking bones scattered about the base, I counted a dozen steps from the edge of the rubble, stopped and knelt down in the grass.

I brushed away the weeds, careful not to disturb the surroundings too much. I didn't want anyone knowing this was here. If word got out—if the vampires heard rumors that there was a possible exit out of their city, they would have every square inch of the Fringe searched until it was found and sealed tighter than a pet's hold on the food warehouse key. Not that they were terribly concerned about people getting out; there was nothing beyond the Outer Wall except ruins, wilderness and rabids. But exits were also entrances, and every few years, a rabid would find its way *into* the city via the tunnels that ran beneath. And there would be chaos and panic and death until the rabid was killed and the entryway found and blocked off. But they always missed this one.

The weeds parted, revealing a circle of black metal sunk

into the ground. It was insanely heavy, but I kept a piece of rebar nearby to pry it up. Letting the cover thump into the grass, I gazed into a long, narrow hole. Rusty metal bars were set into the cement tube beneath the cover, leading down into the darkness.

I glanced around, making sure no one was watching, then started down the ladder. It always worried me, leaving the tunnel entrance wide open, but the cover was too heavy for me to slide back once inside the tube. But it was well hidden in the long grass, and no one had discovered it yet, not in all the years of me sneaking out of the city.

Still, I couldn't dawdle.

Dropping to the cement floor, I gazed around, waiting for my eyes to adjust to the darkness. Putting a hand in my coat pocket, I closed it around my two most prized possessions: a lighter, still half full of fluid, and my pocket knife. The lighter I'd found on my previous trip into the ruins, and the knife I'd had for years. Both were extremely valuable, and I never went anywhere without them.

As usual, the tunnels beneath the city reeked. The old-timers, the ones who had been kids in the time before the plague, said that all of the city's waste was once carried away through the pipes under the streets, instead of in buckets emptied into covered holes. If that was true, then it certainly explained the smell. About a foot from where I stood, the ledge dropped away into sludgy black water, trickling lazily down the tunnel. A huge rat, nearly the size of some of the alley cats I glimpsed topside, scurried off into the shadows, reminding me why I was here.

With one last glance through the hole at the sky—still sunny and bright—I headed into the darkness.

PEOPLE USED TO THINK rabids lurked underground, in caves or abandoned tunnels, where they slept during the daylight hours and came out at night. Actually, most everyone still thought that, but I'd never seen a rabid down here, not once. Not even a sleeping one. That didn't mean anything, however. No one topside had ever seen a mole man, but everyone knew the rumors of diseased, light-shy humans living beneath the city, who would grab your ankles from storm drains and drag you down to eat you. I hadn't seen a mole man, either, but there were hundreds, maybe thousands of tunnels I'd never explored and didn't plan to. My goal, whenever I ventured into this dark, eerie world, was to get past the Wall and back up to the sunlight as quickly as possible.

Luckily, I knew this stretch of tunnel, and it wasn't completely lightless. Sunlight filtered in from grates and storm drains, little bars of color in an otherwise gray world. There were places where it *was* pitch-black, and I had to use my lighter to continue, but the spaces were familiar, and I knew where I was going, so it wasn't terrible.

Eventually, I wiggled my way out of a large cement tube that emptied into a weed-choked ditch, almost sliding on my stomach to get through the pipe. Sometimes there were perks to being very skinny. Wringing nasty warm water from my clothes, I stood up and gazed around.

Over the rows of dilapidated roofs, past the barren, razed field of the kill zone, I could see the Outer Wall rising up in its dark, deadly glory. For some reason, it always looked strange from this side. The sun hovered between the towers in the center of the city, gleaming off their mirrored walls. There were still a few good hours left to hunt, but I needed to work fast.

Past the kill zone, sprawled out like a gray-green, suburban carpet, the remains of the old suburbs waited for me in the fading afternoon light. I vaulted up the bank and slipped into the ruins of a dead civilization.

Scavenging the ruins was tricky. They say there used to be massive stores that had rows and rows of food, clothes and all kinds of other things. They were enormous and easily identified by their wide, sprawling parking lots. But you didn't want to look there, because they were the first to be picked clean when everything went bad. Nearly sixty years after the plague, the only things left behind were gutted-out walls and empty shelves. The same was true of smaller food marts and gas stations. Nothing was left. I'd wasted many hours searching through those buildings to come up empty-handed every time, so now I didn't bother.

But the normal residences, the rows of rotting, dilapidated houses along the crumbling streets, were a different story. Because here's something interesting I've learned about the human race: we like to hoard. Call it stockpiling, call it paranoia, call it preparing for the worst—the houses were far more likely to have food stashed away in cellars or buried deep in closets. You just had to ferret it out.

The floorboards creaked as I eased through the door of my fifth or sixth hopeful—a two-story house surrounded by a warped chain-link fence and nearly swallowed up by ivy, windows broken, porch strangled under vines and weeds. The roof and part of the upper floor had fallen in, and faint rays of light filtered through the rotten beams. The air was thick with the smell of mold, dust and vegetation, and the house seemed to hold its breath as I stepped inside.

I searched the kitchen first, rummaging through cupboards, opening drawers, even checking the ancient refrigerator in the corner. Nothing. A few rusty forks, an empty tin can, a broken mug. All stuff I'd seen before. In one bedroom, the closets were empty, the dresser overturned, a large oval mirror shattered on the floor. The blankets and sheets had been stripped from the bed, and a suspicious dark blot stained one side of the mattress. I didn't wonder what it might be. You don't wonder about things like that. You just move on.

In the second bedroom, which was not quite as ravaged as the first, an old crib stood in the corner, filmy and covered in cobwebs. I eased around it, deliberately not looking inside the peeling bars, to the once-white shelves on the wall. A shattered lamp stood on one shelf, but beneath it, I saw a familiar, dust-covered rectangle.

Picking it up, I wiped away the film and cobwebs, scanning the title at the top. *Goodnight, Moon,* it read, and I smiled ruefully. I wasn't here for books, and I needed to remember that. If I brought this home instead of say, food, Lucas would be furious, and we'd probably fight about it, again.

Maybe I was being too hard on him. It wasn't that he was stupid, just practical. He was more concerned with survival than learning a skill that was useless in his eyes. But I couldn't give up just because he was being stubborn. If I could get him to read, maybe we could start teaching other Fringers, kids like us. And maybe, just maybe, that would be enough to start…something. I didn't know what, but there had to be *something* better than just survival.

I'd tucked the book under my arm, filled with a new resolve, when a soft clink made me freeze. Something was in the house with me, moving around just outside the bedroom door.

Very carefully, I laid the book back on the shelf without disturbing the dust. I'd come back for it later, if I survived whatever was coming.

Slipping my hand into my pocket, I gripped my knife and slowly turned. Shadows moved through the sickly light coming from the living room, and the faint, tapping steps echoed just outside the doorway. I flipped the knife blade open and stepped backward, pressing myself against the wall and the dresser, my heart thudding against my ribs. As a dark shape paused just outside the door, I heard slow, labored panting, and held my breath.

A deer stepped into the frame.

My gut and throat unclenched, though I didn't immediately relax. Wildlife was common enough in the city ruins, though why a deer would be wandering around a human house, I didn't know. Straightening, I blew out a slow breath, causing the doe to jerk her head up, peering in my direction, as if she couldn't quite see what was there.

My stomach growled, and for a moment, I had visions of sidling up to the deer and plunging the blade into her neck. You almost never saw meat of any kind in the Fringe. Rat and mouse were highly prized, and I've seen nasty, bloody fights over a dead pigeon. There were a few stray dogs and cats running around the Fringe, but they were wild, vicious creatures that, unless you wanted to risk an infected bite, were best left alone. The guards also had leave to shoot any animal found wandering about the streets, and usually did, so meat of any kind was extremely scarce.

A whole deer carcass, cut into strips and dried, would feed me and my crew for a month. Or I could trade cuts for meal tickets, blankets, new clothes, whatever I wanted. Just thinking about it made my stomach growl again, and I shifted my weight to one leg, ready to ease forward. As soon as I moved, the deer would probably bolt out the door, but I had to try.

But then, the doe looked right at me, and I saw the thin streams of blood oozing from her eyes, spotting the floor. My blood ran cold. No wonder she wasn't afraid. No wonder she had followed me here and was watching me with the flat, glazed stare of a predator. She had been bitten by a rabid. And the disease had driven her mad.

I took a quiet breath to slow my heartbeat, trying not to panic. This was bad. The doe was blocking the door, so there was no way I could go through her without risking an attack. Her eyes hadn't turned completely white yet, so the sickness was still in its beginning stages. Hopefully if I kept calm, I could get out of here without being trampled to death.

The doe snorted and tossed her head, the jerky movement causing her to stumble into the door frame. Another effect of the sickness; diseased animals seemed confused and uncoordinated one moment but could switch to hyper-aggressive fury in the blink of an eye. I gripped my knife and eased to the side, toward the broken window along the wall.

The doe raised her head, rolling her eyes, and gave a raspy

growl unlike anything I'd ever heard from a deer. I saw her muscles bunching up to charge, and I bolted for the window.

The deer lunged into the room, snorting, hooves flailing in deadly arcs. One of them caught my thigh as I darted past, a glancing blow, but it felt like someone had hit it with a hammer. The doe crashed into the far wall, overturning a shelf, and I threw myself out the window.

Scrambling through the weeds, I ran for a partially collapsed shed in the corner of the backyard. The roof had fallen in, and vines completely covered the rotting walls, but the doors were still intact. I squeezed through the frame and ducked into a corner, panting, listening for sounds of pursuit.

For the moment, everything was silent. After my heartbeat returned to normal, I peered through a crack between boards and could just make out the doe's dark form still in the room, stumbling about in confusion, occasionally attacking the mattress or broken dresser, blind in her rage. Okay, then. I would just sit tight until psycho deer calmed down and wandered away. Hopefully, that would be before the sun went down. I needed to head back to the city soon.

Easing away from the wall, I turned to observe the shed, wondering if anything useful was still intact. There didn't seem to be much: a few collapsed shelves, a handful of rusty nails that I quickly pocketed, and a strange, squat machine with four wheels and a long handle that looked like you'd push it around. To what end, I hadn't a clue.

I noticed a hole in the planks beneath the strange machine and shoved it back, revealing a trapdoor underneath. It had been sealed with a heavy padlock, now so rusty a key would've been useless, but the floorboards themselves were rotten and falling apart. I easily pried up several planks to make a big enough hole and found a set of folding steps leading down into the darkness.

Gripping my knife, I descended into the hole.

It was dark in the basement, but at least an hour of broad daylight remained, enough to filter in through the hole and the cracks in the ceiling above me. I stood in a small, cool room, concrete lining the walls and floor, a lightbulb with a string dangling overhead. The walls were lined with wooden shelves, and on those shelves, dozens upon dozens of cans winked at me in the dim light. My heart stood still.

Jackpot.

Lunging forward, I snatched the nearest can off the shelf, sending three others clattering to the floor in my excitement. The can had a faded label wrapped around it, but I didn't bother trying to figure out the words. Digging out my knife, I jammed the blade into the top and attacked the tin furiously, sawing at the metal with shaking hands.

A sweet, heavenly aroma arose from inside, and my hunger roared to life in response, making me slightly dizzy. *Food! Real food!* Prying back the lid, I barely took the time to glance at the contents—some kind of mushy fruit in a slimy liquid—before I dumped the whole thing back and into my mouth. The sweetness shocked me, cloyingly thick and pulpy, unlike anything I'd tasted before. In the Fringe, fruit and vegetables were almost unheard of. I drank the entire thing without pause, feeling it settle in my empty stomach, and grabbed another can.

This one contained beans in more glistening liquid, and I devoured that, too, scooping the red mush out with my fingers. I went through another can of fruit slime, a can of creamed corn, and a small tin of sausage links the size of my finger, before I finally slowed down enough to think.

I'd stumbled upon a treasure trove, one so vast it was staggering. These kinds of hidden caches were the stuff of legends, and here I was, standing in the middle of one. With my stomach full—a rare sensation—I started exploring, taking stock of what was here.

Nearly one whole wall was dedicated to cans, but there was so much *variety,* according to the different labels. Most were too faded or torn to read, but I was still able to pick out a lot of canned vegetables, fruit, beans and soup. There were also cans containing strange foods I'd never heard of. *Spa Gettee Ohs,* and *Rah Vee Oh Lee,* and other weird things. Shelved in with the cans were boxes containing squarish bundles of something wrapped in shiny, silvery paper. I had no idea what they were, but if the answer was more food, I wasn't complaining.

The opposite wall had dozens of clear gallon water jugs, a few propane tanks, one of those portable green stoves I'd seen Hurley use, and a gas lantern. Whoever set this place up sure wasn't taking any chances, for all the good it did them in the end.

Well, thanks, mysterious person. You sure made my life a lot easier.

My mind raced, considering my options. I could keep this place a secret, but why? There was enough food here to feed my whole gang for months. I scanned the room, pondering how I wanted to do this. If I told Lucas about this place, the four of us—me, Rat, Lucas and Stick—could come back and take everything in one fell swoop. It would be dangerous, but for this amount of food, it would be worth it.

I turned slowly, regretting that I didn't have anything to carry the food back in. *That was intelligent of you, Allison.* I usually took one of the backpacks the crew kept in a hall closet when venturing into the ruins—that's what we kept them for, after all—but I hadn't wanted to run into Rat again. Still, I had to take something back. If I was going to convince Lucas to risk a very dangerous trip out of the city, I'd need some kind of proof.

Scanning the room, I paused. A pair of bulging garbage bags lay on the top shelf, shoved against the wall. They looked like they might hold blankets or clothes or other useful things, but right now, I was more concerned with food.

"That'll work," I muttered and walked up to the shelves. Without a ladder or a box or anything to stand on, I was going to have to climb. Putting a foot between the cans, I heaved myself up.

The board creaked horribly under my weight but held. Gripping the rough wood, I pulled myself up another foot, then another, until I could reach my arm over the top shelf and feel around for the bags. Gripping a corner of filmy plastic in two fingers, I pulled it toward me.

The wood suddenly groaned, and before I knew it, the entire shelf tipped backward. Panicked, I tried to jump clear, but dozens of cans rushed forward, slamming into me, and I lost my grip. I struck the cement floor, the ring and clatter of metal tins all around me, and had a split-second glance of the shelves filling my vision before everything went black.

CHAPTER 3

A pounding in my skull brought me back to reality. My ears rang, and when I opened my eyes, darkness greeted me. For a moment, I didn't know where I was or what had happened. Something heavy pressed on my chest and legs, and when I shifted, several small, metal things rolled off me and pinged to the ground.

"Shit," I whispered, remembering. Frantically, I wiggled out from beneath the shelf and limped to the steps, gazing up. Through the hole in the roof, the night sky was hazy and starless, but a sickly yellow moon peered through the clouds like a swollen eye.

I was in trouble.

Careless, stupid mistake, Allie. Creeping up the steps, I scanned the darkness and shadows, my heart crashing against my ribs in the silence. Below me, the cans made soft metallic sounds as they rolled across the floor, but I couldn't worry about the wealth I was leaving behind. I had to get back to the city. I couldn't stay here. I'd heard stories of rabids tearing through walls and floors to get to their prey; they never gave up once they sensed you. I couldn't let anything slow me down.

Carefully, I eased myself out of the hole and crept to the door, reaching out to push it open. Froze.

Along the side of the shed, something was moving.

Weeds hissed against the wall as footsteps shuffled over the ground, and low growling that might've belonged to an animal slithered through the cracks. Withdrawing my hand, I silently eased into a corner and put my back to the wall, squeezing my knife to stop my hands from shaking. Outside the shed, it was nearly pitch-black, but I caught glimpses of a pale, emaciated figure through the cracks in the wood, listened to its steps as it moved along the outer wall...and stopped at the door.

I held my breath, counting the seconds with every frantic heartbeat, biting my cheek to keep from panting.

The door creaked and swung slowly inward.

I didn't move. I didn't breathe. I felt the rough wood at my back and imagined myself a part of the wall, part of the shadows that cloaked me, hiding me from everything. On the other side of the door between us, the slow, raspy growls grew louder as the shadow turned its head from side to side, scanning the walls.

An eternity passed.

Finally, the door slowly creaked shut, and the shadow turned away, slouching off into the weeds. I listened to the shuffling footsteps as they moved away, growing fainter, until the only sounds were the buzz of insects in the night.

It was a moment before I could move or even breathe properly. Once the shaking stopped, I slipped out of the shed and hurried through the weeds, following the same path I'd taken to get there. With a chill I noted that my trail wasn't the only one cutting through the tall grass; a few other paths now crisscrossed the yard, showing I hadn't been alone in my time belowground. If it had found the stairs…

I shuddered and hurried onward, stumbling through the empty streets. In the moonlight, the ruins looked even more foreboding, stark and hostile to the intruder in their midst. After dark within the city walls, people vanished off the streets and vampires walked the night, but the shadows were familiar, the darkness comforting. Here in the ruins, the darkness was alien, and the shadows seemed to creep closer, reaching out for you.

Something shrieked in the night, a scream of animalistic fury, and I began to run.

IT WAS THE LONGEST FEW MINUTES of my life, but I made it back to the tunnels. Wriggling through the drain pipe, I'd almost convinced myself that something was behind me and sharp claws would close around my ankles, dragging me back. Mercifully, that didn't happen, and I leaned against the wall, gasping in short, frantic breaths until my heart stopped racing around my rib cage.

In the tunnel, I couldn't see my hand before my face, and no amount of waiting would help my eyes adjust to the pitch blackness. Digging in my pocket, I brought out the lighter, clicking a tiny flame to life. It barely illuminated the ground at my feet, but it was better than nothing.

With the flickering light held up before me, I started down the tunnels.

Strange how a few short hours could change your view of the world. The once familiar tunnels were menacing now, the darkness a living thing, pressing in on all sides, suffocating me. My footsteps seemed too loud in the quiet, and several times I held my breath, listening for phantom noises I was certain I'd heard over my quiet panting.

The tunnels went on, and despite all my fears and imaginings, nothing leaped out at me. I was nearly home, just another turn and a few hundred yards to the ladder that led topside, when a splash echoed in the darkness.

It wasn't loud, and in the daylight hours, with sunlight slanting in through the grates, I might've blamed a rat or something similar. But in the looming silence and blackness, my heart nearly stopped, and my blood turned to ice. I doused my flame and ducked into a corner, holding my breath, straining my ears to listen. I didn't have to wait long.

In the darkness of the tunnel ahead, a single flashlight beam flickered over the ground, and low, guttural voices echoed off the walls.

"...what've we got here?" a voice wheezed, as I pressed myself into the wall. "A rat? A big rat, come creeping out of the darkness. You sure picked the wrong night to go wandering the undercity, friend."

Holding my breath, I risked a quick peek around the corner. Four men blocked the exit of the tunnel, thin and ragged, in filthy clothes and unkempt hair. They stood slightly hunched over, their shoulders bent and crooked, as if they spent all their lives in small cramped spaces and weren't used to standing up straight. They clutched jagged, rusty blades in their hands and grinned maniacally at a lone figure in the center of the tunnel, their eyes gleaming with anticipation and something darker.

I ducked behind the corner again, heart pounding. *You've got to be kidding,* I mused, sinking farther into the concealing shadows, hoping they didn't hear me. *This just isn't my night. Deer, rabids, and now freaking mole men in the tunnels. No one is going to believe this.* I shook my head and huddled lower, clutching the handle of my knife. *Now all I need is a vampire to come sauntering through and it'll be perfect.*

The mole men chuckled, and I heard them ease forward, probably surrounding the poor bastard who'd walked into their ambush. *Run, you idiot,* I thought, wondering what he thought he was doing, why I didn't hear footsteps pounding frantically away. *Don't you know what they'll do to you? If you don't want to be on a stick over the fire, you'd better run.*

"I want no trouble," said a low voice, calm and collected. And even though I couldn't see him, didn't dare peek around the corner again, it sent shivers up my spine. "Let me pass, and I'll be on my way. You don't want to do this."

"Oh," one mole man purred, and I imagined him sidling forward, grinning, "I think we d—"

His voice abruptly changed to a startled gurgle, followed by a wet splat, and the faint, coppery stench of blood filled the air. Enraged cries rang out, the sound of a scuffle, blades cutting through flesh, agonized screams. I crouched in my shadowy corner and held my breath, until the final shriek died away, until the last body fell and silence crept into the tunnels once more.

I counted thirty seconds of quiet. Sixty seconds. A minute and a half. Two. The tunnel remained silent. No footsteps, no shifting movements, no breathing. It was as still as the dead.

Warily, I peered around the corner and bit my lip.

The four mole men lay in heaps, weapons scattered about, the flashlight shining weakly against a wall. Its beam pointed to a vivid splash of red, trickling down the cement to a motionless body. I scanned the tunnel again, looking for a fifth heap, but there were only the mole men, lying dead in the pale flashlight beam. The dark stranger had disappeared.

I sidled closer. I didn't want to touch the bodies, but the flashlight was a valuable find. One that would keep me fed for several days if I could find the right trader. Edging around a pale, dirty arm, I snatched my trophy and rose—

—shining the light right into the face of the stranger. Who didn't wince. Didn't even blink. I scrambled back, nearly tripping over the arm I'd stepped around, bringing my knife up before me. The stranger remained where he was, though his eyes, blacker than pitch, followed me as I retreated. I kept both the blade and the flashlight pointed in his direction until I reached the edge and tensed to bolt into the shadows.

"If you run, you'll be dead before you take three steps."

I stopped, heart pounding. I believed him. Gripping my knife, I turned around, staring at him over the bodies of the dead, waiting for his next move.

There was no doubt in my mind. I knew what I faced, what stared at me across the tunnel, so still he might've been a statue. I was down here, alone, with a vampire. And there was no one who could help me.

"What do you want?" My voice came out shakier than I'd

wanted, but I planted my feet and glared defiantly. Show no fear. Vampires could sense fear, at least that's what everybody said. If you ever ran into a hungry bloodsucker alone at night, not looking like prey might give you an edge in surviving the encounter.

I didn't believe that, of course. A vampire would bite you whether you were scared of him or not. But I wasn't going to give him the satisfaction, either.

The vamp tilted his head, a tiny movement that would've gone unnoticed, save the rest of him was so very, very still. "I am trying to decide," he said in that same low, cool voice, "if you are a simple scavenger, eavesdropping on the conversation, or if you are about to scuttle off to tell the rest of your clan I am here."

"Do I look like one of them?"

"Then...you are a scavenger. Waiting until your prey is dead to feed, instead of killing it yourself."

His tone hadn't changed. It was the same, cool and detached, but I felt myself bristle through my fear. Anger, hate and resentment bubbled to the surface, making me stupid, making me want to hurt it. Who did this murdering, soulless bloodsucker think he was, lecturing *me?* "Yeah, well, that's what happens when you let the cattle starve," I snapped, narrowing my eyes. "They start turning on each other, or didn't you know that?" I gestured to the dead mole men, scattered at my feet, and curled a lip. "But I'm not one of them. And I sure as hell don't eat people. That's *your* thing, remember?"

The vampire just looked at me. Long enough for me to regret taunting him, which was a stupid thing to do from the start. I almost didn't care. I wouldn't grovel and beg, if that's what he was looking for. Vampires had no souls, no emotions and no empathy to appeal to. If the bloodsucker wanted to drain me dry and leave me here to rot, there wasn't anything I could say that would stop him.

But I'd give him one hell of a fight.

"Interesting," the vamp finally mused, almost to himself. "I forget, sometimes, the complexities of the human race. We've reduced so many of you to animals—savage, cowardly, so willing to turn on each other to survive. And yet, in the darkest places, I can still find those who are still, more or less, human."

He wasn't making any sense, and I was tired of talking, of waiting for him to make his move. "What do you want, vampire?" I challenged again. "Why are we still talking? If you're going to bite me, just get on with it already." *Though don't expect me to lie down and take it. You'll have a pocketknife shoved through your eye socket before I'm done, I swear.*

Amazingly, the vampire smiled. Just a slight curl of pale lips, but in that granite face, he might as well have beamed from ear to ear. "I have already fed tonight," he stated calmly, and took one step backward, into the shadows. "And you, little wildcat, I suspect you have claws you wouldn't hesitate to use. I find I am in no mood for another fight, so consider yourself lucky. You met a heartless, soulless bloodsucker and lived. Next time, it might be very different."

And just like that, he turned on his heel and walked away into the darkness. His final words drifted out of the black as he disappeared. "Thank you for the conversation." And he was gone.

I frowned, utterly confused. What kind of vampire killed

four people, had a cryptic conversation with a street rat, thanked the street rat for talking with him, and then walked off? I swept the flashlight around the tunnel, wondering if it was a trick to get me to lower my guard, and the bloodsucker was lying in ambush just ahead, laughing to himself. That seemed like something a vampire would do. But the tunnel was empty and silent in the flashlight beam, and after a moment, I picked my way over the still-bleeding corpses, hurried to the ladder and scaled the tube as fast as I could.

Aboveground, the city was silent. Nothing moved on the streets; the crumbling stores and houses and apartments lay quiet and dark. Overhead, looming above everything, the vampire towers glittered in the night, cold and impassive like their masters. It was still the predator's time, this silent hour before dawn, and everyone was off the street, huddled in their beds with their doors and windows barred. But at least on this side of the Wall, the darkness didn't conceal savage, mindless horrors that had once been human. Here, the predators were more complex, though just as dangerous.

A cold wind blew down the street, stirring up dust and sending an empty can skittering over the ground. It reminded me of what I'd left behind, on the other side of the Wall, and anger burned its way into my stomach, killing the last of the fear. So much food! So much wealth, to have to leave it all behind.... The thought made my gut boil, and I kicked a rock into a dead car, the stone clanking off the rusty frame.

I had to get back there. No way was I going to huddle behind the Wall, eating cockroaches, fantasizing about shelves and shelves of real food rotting away in someone's basement.

One way or another, I was going to return to that place and reclaim what I'd lost.

But right now, my stomach was full, I ached from my fall, and I was damn tired. The flashlight beam shone weakly in the darkness, and I clicked it off, not wanting to waste valuable battery life. I didn't need artificial light to navigate the Fringe, anyway. Slipping my single prize into a back pocket, I headed for home.

"Oh, my God, you're alive."

I gave Stick a disdainful look as I slipped into my room, kicking the door shut behind me. He scrambled off my mattress, gaping, as if I was a hallucination. "What's that look for?" I frowned at him. "And why are you here, anyway? Have you been waiting up for me all night?"

"You didn't hear?" Stick's eyes darted about, as if someone could be lurking in the shadows, listening. "Lucas didn't tell you?"

"Stick." I sighed and collapsed on the mattress. "I just got back from a rather hellish night out," I muttered, putting an arm over my eyes. "I'm tired, I'm cranky, and unless someone is on the verge of death or the vampires are breaking down our doors, I want to go to sleep. Whatever this is, can it wait till morning? I need to talk to Lucas, anyway."

"The vampires were out tonight," Stick continued, as if I hadn't said a word.

I removed my arm and sat up to face him, a chill crawling up my spine. His face was pale in the shadows of the room, thin mouth tight with fear. "I saw them. They were going from sector to sector with their pets and guards and everything, breaking down doors, going into people's houses. They didn't come here, but Lucas moved us all into the basement until he was sure they had moved on. I heard…I heard someone was killed…trying to run away."

"Was anyone Taken?"

Stick shrugged bony shoulders. "I don't think so. They just came through, went into several buildings and left. Lucas said they were looking for something, but no one knows what it is."

Or some*one*. I thought back to the vampire in the tunnels below the city. Was he part of that search party, exploring the underworld for whatever item the bloodsuckers wanted? Or…was *he* the mysterious thing they were all searching for? But that didn't make much sense. Why would the vampires be hunting one of their own?

And if they were, why couldn't they do it more often?

"There are rumors of a citywide lockdown," Stick went on in a low, frightened voice. "Curfews, guards, area restrictions, everything."

I muttered a curse. Lockdowns were bad news and not just for Unregistereds. There had been two in the past, once when gang warfare swept through the Fringe, clogging the streets with dead bodies, and once when an infestation of rabid rats created a citywide panic. Lockdowns were the vampires' last resort, their answer when things got out of control. Everyone was required to stay in their homes during curfew hours, while armed guards swept the streets. If you were caught outside during lockdown, they would shoot you, no questions asked.

"Allie, what are we going to do?"

"Nothing," I said, and he stared at me. I shrugged. "Nothing tonight. It'll be dawn in a few hours. The bloodsuckers will go back to their towers, and nothing will be done until this evening. We can worry about it then."

"But…"

"Stick. I. Am. Tired." I rose from the mattress and, taking his elbow, steered him to the door. "If Lucas is still up, tell him I need to speak to him tomorrow. It's important. *Really* important." He started to protest, but I firmly pushed him over the threshold. "Look, if you want to stay up and worry about vampire hunts, you can do it for both of us. I'm going to sleep while I still can. Wake me when it's dawn, okay?" And before he could make any more excuses, I shut the door in his face.

Collapsing on the mattress, I turned my face to the wall and closed my eyes. Stick's news was troublesome, but I'd learned that worrying about things you couldn't change was useless and just kept you from getting sleep. Tomorrow, I'd talk to Lucas and tell him about the food cache I'd found, and he could convince the others to go after it. Before the city went into lockdown, of course. Working together, we could probably clear that whole room in two or three trips and not have to worry about the coming winter. Rat was a dick and a bully, but he was part of my crew, and we looked out for each other. Besides, it would take a single person forever to clear that place, and I didn't want to be in the ruins any longer than I had to be.

With plan firmly in mind, I dismissed all thoughts of that night—of rabids and manhunts and vampires in the sewers—and drifted into oblivion.

CHAPTER 4

"Allison," Mom said, patting the cushion beside her, "come up here. Read with me."

I scrambled onto the threadbare couch that smelled of dust and spoiled milk, snuggling against her side. She held a book in her lap, bright happy animals prancing across the pages. I listened as she read to me in a soft, soothing voice, her slender hands turning the pages as if they were made of butterfly wings. Except, I couldn't see her face. Everything was blurry, like water sluicing down a windowpane. But I knew she was smiling down at me, and that made me feel warm and safe.

"Knowledge is important," she explained patiently, now watching an older version of me from across the kitchen table. A sheet of paper lay in front of me, marked with scrawling, messy lines. "Words define us," Mom continued, as I struggled to make my clumsy marks look like her elegant script. "We must protect our knowledge and pass it on whenever we can. If we are ever to become a society again, we must teach others how to remain human."

The kitchen melted away, ran like water down a wall, and turned into something else.

"Mom," I whispered, sitting beside her on the bed, watching the slow rise and fall of her chest under the thin blanket. "Mom, I brought some soup for you. Try to eat it, okay?"

The frail, white form, surrounded by long black hair, stirred weakly. I couldn't see her face, though I knew it should be somewhere within that dark mass. "I don't feel well, Allison," she whispered, her voice so faint I barely caught it. "Will you...read to me?"

That same smile, though her face remained blurry and indistinct. Why couldn't I see her? Why couldn't I remember? "Mom," I said again, standing up, feeling the shadows closing in. "We have to go. They're coming."

"A is for apple," Mom whispered, falling away from me. I cried out and reached for her, but she slipped away, into the dark. "B is for blood."

Something boomed against the door.

I JERKED AWAKE, THE DOOR TO MY ROOM still rattling from the sudden blow. On my feet, I glared at the door, heart pounding. I was already a light sleeper, hypersensitive to footsteps and people sneaking up on me while I slept, so the first bang nearly made me jump through the ceiling. By the fourth, I had wrenched the door open, even as Lucas was pulling his fist back to knock again.

Lucas blinked at me. Dark and muscular, he had large hands and a curiously babylike face, except for his thick, serious eyebrows. When I first joined the group, Lucas had been intimidating; a serious, no-nonsense figure even as a twelve-year old. Over the years, the fear had lessened, but the respect had not. When our old leader started demanding a food tax—a portion of everything we scavenged—Lucas had stepped in, beaten him to a pulp and taken over the gang. Since then, no one had challenged him. He was always fair; survival was his priority, regardless of feelings. Like me, he'd watched members of our gang die of starvation, cold, sickness, wounds, or just vanish off the face of the earth. We'd burned more "friends" than anyone should ever have to. Lucas had to make hard, unpopular decisions sometimes, and I didn't envy him the job, but everything he did was to keep us alive.

Especially now that the group was so small. Fewer people meant fewer mouths to feed, but that also meant fewer bodies to hunt for food and to protect us from rival gangs if they ever got the notion to invade our turf. It was just the four of us—me, Rat, Lucas and Stick, not enough protection if Kyle's gang decided they wanted us gone. And Lucas knew it.

Lately he confused me. We'd always been friends, but this past year his interest in me had changed. Maybe because I was the only girl in the group, maybe something else; I didn't know and I wasn't going to ask. We'd kissed last summer, more out of curiosity on my part, but he had wanted more and I wasn't sure if I was ready. He hadn't pressed the issue when I'd stopped him, saying I needed time to think about it, but now it hung between us, unresolved, like a big flag. It wasn't that Lucas was ugly or undesirable; I just didn't know if I wanted to get that close to someone. What if he disappeared, like so many of our kind did? It would just hurt that much more.

Lucas was still frozen in the doorway, broad shoulders filling most of the frame. I glanced past him and saw sunlight streaming in the broken windows of the school, casting jagged spots of light over the cement. By the looks of the sky, it was early to midafternoon. Damn. I'd slept far too long. Where was Stick and why hadn't he woken me?

"Allison." The relief in Lucas's voice was palpable. Stepping forward, he surprised me by pulling me into a tight hug. I returned it, feeling the hard muscles of his back, his breath against my skin. Closing my eyes, I relaxed into him, just for a moment. It was nice, having someone *I* could lean on for a change.

We drew back quickly, not wanting the others to see just yet. This was still new for both of us. "Allie," Lucas muttered, sounding embarrassed. "Stick told me you came back. Were you out all night?"

"Yeah." I gave him a crooked smile. "Sounds like things got exciting after I left."

He glared at me. "Rat started telling everyone you'd been Taken. Stick was freaking out. I had to tell both of them to shut up or I'd put a fist in their face." His glare grew sharper, almost desperate. "Where the hell *were* you all night? The bloodsuckers were all over the streets."

"The ruins."

Lucas's dark eyes bulged. "You went outside the Wall? At night? Are you crazy, girl? You *want* to get eaten by rabids?"

"Believe me, I didn't mean to get stuck there after sunset." I shivered, remembering what had almost happened in the shed that night. "Besides, rabids or no, I found something that made it all worth it."

"Yeah?" He raised a thick, bristling eyebrow. "This I gotta hear."

"A whole basement of food." I smirked as both of Lucas's eyebrows shot up. "Canned goods, packaged stuff, bottled water, you name it. I'm serious, Luc—wall-to-wall shelves, full of food. And no one's guarding it. We'd be set for months, maybe the whole winter. All we have to do is get out there and grab it before anyone else does."

Lucas's eyes gleamed. I could almost see the wheels in his brain turning. The thought of going into the ruins was scary as hell, but the promise of food trumped that easily. "Where is it?" he asked.

"Just past the kill zone. You know the drainage pipe that empties out near the old—" He gave me a confused look, and I shrugged. "Don't worry about it. I can get us there. But we should leave now, while there's daylight."

"Now?"

"You wanna wait to see if there's a lockdown?"

He sighed and jerked his head down the hall. I followed him toward the common room. "No, but it'll be risky. Lots of patrols today—pets and guards combing the streets, still looking for something. It'll get worse tonight, though."

We entered the common room, where Rat lounged in a moldy chair playing with his knife, his legs dangling over the arm.

"Oh, hey, the lost bitch returns," he drawled. His voice was honking and nasal, as if his nose was still full of blood. "We were sure you'd been Taken, or had your throat torn out in some dark alley. Sure was nice and quiet without you. Except for your wuss boyfriend, bawling in the corner." He sneered at me, mean and challenging. "I had to shove his pasty head into a doorjamb to get him to stop mewling."

Lucas pretended to ignore him, though I saw his jaw tighten. We'd kept our...thing...a secret from the others, which meant Lucas couldn't show favoritism by leaping to my defense. Fortunately, I could take care of myself.

I smiled sweetly at Rat. "I'm sure you did. How's that busted nose treating you, by the way?"

Rat's sallow cheeks reddened, and he held up his rusty knife. "Why don't you come over here and take a look?"

Lucas kicked the back of his chair, making him yelp. "Make yourself useful and get the backpacks from the hall closet," he ordered. "Allie," he continued, as Rat pulled himself to his feet, scowling, "find Stick. If we're going to do this now, we need all the help we can get."

"With what?" Stick asked, coming into the room. Seeing the three of us, his eyes widened, and he edged closer to me. "Are we going somewhere?"

"Oh, there you are." Rat smiled like a dog baring its fangs. "Yeah, we were just talking about how we don't have enough food and that the weakest link, the one that doesn't do anything around here, should be fed to the vampires. And hey, it's you. No hard feelings, right?"

"Ignore him," I said, locking eyes with Rat as Stick cringed away. "He's being an ass, as usual."

"Hey." Rat held up his hands. "I'm only being honest. No one else has the guts to say it, so I will."

"Aren't you supposed to be doing something?" Lucas asked in a warning voice, and Rat left the room with a leer, waggling his tongue in my direction. I made a note to break his nose the other way as soon as I got the opportunity.

Stick frowned, looking back and forth at both of us. "What's going on?" he asked warily. "You guys aren't..." He trailed off, looking at me. "You aren't *really* discussing what Rat said, right? I'm not that pathetic…am I?"

I sighed, ready to brush it off as being stupid, but Lucas spoke up before I got the chance. "Well, now's your chance to prove him wrong," he said. "Allison, in her insane night-time wandering, found something important. We're going to get it."

Stick blinked, glanced nervously at Rat coming into the room again, four dusty, tattered backpacks slung over his shoulders. "Where?"

"The ruins," I answered as Rat instantly dropped the packs in horror and disbelief. "We're going into the ruins."

WE SPLIT INTO TWO TEAMS, partly to avoid notice with the patrols still wandering about the Fringe, and partly because I would've strangled Rat if I had to hear him complain one more time that I was going to get us killed. Stick wasn't happy, either, but at least he shut up after the first round of protests. Lucas finally gave Rat a choice: either help out, or get out and don't come back. Personally, I was hoping Rat would choose the latter, swear at us all and stalk out of our lives in a huff, but after a murderous look at me, he grabbed a pack from the floor and finally shut up.

I gave Lucas directions to the tunnel entrance before we split into two groups, taking different routes in case we met with any patrols. Guards didn't look kindly on street rats and Unregistereds, and because we "didn't exist," this gave some the idea that they could do anything they wanted to us, including beatings, target practice and…other things. I'd seen enough to know it was true. It was almost better to be caught by the hungry, soulless vampires; the most they would probably do was drink your blood and leave you to die. Humans were capable of far, far worse.

Stick and I reached the ditch first and descended into the tunnels. I had the flashlight, but it was more of a "just-in-case" item. I didn't want to be spoiled by artificial light or, more important, use up all the battery life. The sun peeking in through the grating up top was still more than enough to see by.

"Rat and Lucas better get here soon," I muttered, crossing my arms and gazing up at the cracks overhead. "We have a lot of stuff to move, and there's not much daylight left. I'm not doing a repeat of yesterday, that's for sure."

"Allie?"

I glanced at Stick, huddled against the wall, an oversize pack hanging from his skinny shoulders. His face was tight with fear, and his hands clutched the straps so hard his knuckles were white. He was trying to be brave, and for a moment, I felt a stab of guilt. Stick hated the dark.

"Do you think I'm useless?"

"Are you obsessing over what Rat said?" I snorted and waved it off. "Ignore him. He's a greasy little rodent with a security problem. Lucas will probably kick him out soon, anyway."

"But he has a point." Stick kicked at a loose bit of pavement, not meeting my eyes. "I'm the weakest link in the gang. I'm not good at stealing like Rat or fighting like Lucas, and I'm not brave enough to go scavenging outside the Wall by myself like you. What am I good for, if I can't even take care of myself?"

I shrugged, uncomfortable with this conversation. "What do you want me to say?" I asked, my voice coming out sharper than I'd intended. Maybe it was the fight with Rat, maybe I was still tense from last night. But I was tired of listening to excuses, of him wishing for things to be different. In this world, you were either strong, or you were dead. You did what you had to if you wanted to survive. And I could barely take care of myself; I couldn't worry about someone else's insecurities. "You don't like the way you are?" I asked Stick, who shrank back from my tone. "Fine—then don't be that way. Grow some balls and tell Rat to piss off. Punch him in the nose if he tries to bully you. Do *something,* but don't just roll over and take it." He seemed to collapse in on himself, looking miserable, and I sighed. "You can't depend on me forever," I said in a softer voice. "Yeah, we look out for each other, mostly. Yeah, Lucas preaches family and all-for-oneness and whatever, but that's a load of crap. You think any of them would jump in front of a vampire for you?" I sneered at the thought. "Lucas would be the first one out the door, with Rat right behind him. And me."

Stick turned away, hunching his shoulders. It was an old tactic of his, avoid the problem and hope it went away, and that only pissed me off more. "I know that's not what you wanted to hear," I continued ruthlessly, "but, God, Stick, wake up! This is the way things are. Sooner or later, you're going to learn that it's everyone for themselves out here, and the only person you can depend on is you."

He didn't answer, just continued staring down at the pavement. I turned away as well, leaning against the wall. I wasn't worried. Give him a few minutes, and he'd be back to normal, talking and pretending that nothing had happened. If he wanted to keep burying his head in the sand, I wouldn't stop him. But I wasn't going to keep holding his hand anymore, either.

After several long minutes, Rat and Lucas still hadn't showed. I fidgeted and glanced at the sky through the grate. *Hurry up, you two.* Cutting it this close to evening was already making me jumpy. But I wanted that food. I was hungry again, and knowing there was a whole stash of food out there, just beyond the wall, was driving me crazy. I'd almost forgotten what it was like *not* to be starving all the time. Not feeling your stomach cramp so badly you wanted to puke, only there was nothing in it to throw up. Not having to eat roaches and spiders, just to stay alive. Or share a crust of stolen bread with Stick, because if I didn't take care of him, he would curl up somewhere and die. If we could get to that food, I wouldn't have to worry about any of that for a long, long time. If Rat and Lucas ever got their sorry butts down here.

And then, I had another thought, one that the cynical street rat in me hadn't had before. If we could get all that food, I wouldn't have to worry about Stick as much. Lucas would probably be happier and less stressed, and might agree to learn how to read. Even Rat might go for it—if I could stomach teaching him, anyway. Again, I had no idea where it would lead, but every revolution had to start somewhere.

The vampires have taken everything from us, I thought, angrily kicking a pebble into a wall. *Well, I'm going to make sure we take something back.*

First things first, though, and that was surviving.

Several minutes later, Rat and Lucas finally showed up. Both were panting, and Rat glared daggers at me as he dropped from the ladder, his beady eyes filled with fear and hate.

"What happened?" I asked, narrowing my eyes as Lucas came down the tube.

"Ran into a couple pets near the broken statue," he muttered as he dropped beside me, wiping sweat from his brow. "They followed us several blocks before we lost them in the park. Everyone up there is twitchy. Wish I knew what was going on."

"This is stupid," Rat broke in, his gaze darting up and down the tunnel, as if it was about to close on him. "We shouldn't be going...out there."

"Should we go back?" Stick whispered.

"No," I snapped. "If we don't do this now, who knows when we'll get another chance."

"How do we even know she's telling the truth?" Rat continued, switching tactics now that he couldn't scare me into giving up. "A whole basement of food? Gimme a break." His lips twisted. "Girls don't know what to look for out there. Maybe she saw a few empty cans and jumped to conclusions. Maybe she's too scared to go by herself and needs a big strong guy to keep her safe."

"Keep talking, moron. I think it's funny when you use big words."

"Will you two shut up?" Lucas snapped, showing how on edge he was. "We're wasting time! Allie, you know the way, right?" He motioned me down the tunnel. "After you."

The sky was considerably darker when we crawled out

of the drainage ditch into the open, gazing around warily. Overhead, slate-gray clouds massed together, and a flicker of lightning lit up the ground.

"There's a storm coming," Lucas muttered unnecessarily, as a growl of thunder followed his statement. I muttered a curse. Back in New Covington, the rain would fill the wells and cisterns of the sectors, but it also drew more things out into the open. "And the sun is going down. We have to do this *now*."

"Come on," I said, pushing through weeds and brush and chest-high grass to reach the top of the bank. They followed, scrambling up the ditch until we came to the edge and the tangled, empty ruins sprawled out before us, silent and menacing in the fading light.

Rat swore and Stick was breathing hard, almost hyperventilating. "I can't do this," he whispered, edging away toward the ditch. "I can't go in there. I have to go back. Let me go back."

"I knew it," Rat sneered. "Pissing little coward. Totally useless. Let him run home, but he sure ain't getting *my* share of the food."

Lucas grabbed Stick's arm before he could run away. "Rat's right. You do this, don't expect a share of anything we bring back."

"I don't care," Stick panted, his eyes wide. "This is crazy. The sun is about to go down. You're all going to be killed."

"Stick," I said, trying to be reasonable, "you don't know the way back. Are you going to go through the tunnels in the dark? Alone?"

That seemed to get through to him. He stopped fighting

Lucas and cast a fearful glance at the dark entrance to the sewers. Shoulders sagging, he looked up at me, pleading. "I don't want to," he whispered. "Let's go back, Allie, please. I have a bad feeling about this."

Rat made a disgusted noise, and my annoyance flared. "No," I said flatly. "We keep moving. There's still some light left. We're not going back without that food." I looked at Stick with an encouraging smile. "Wait till you see how much there is—it'll be worth it."

He still looked terrified but followed silently as we sprinted through the cracked, tangled streets, leaping over roots and weaving between rusty cars to beat the coming storm. A small herd of deer scattered before us as we hurried down the sidewalk, and a flock of crows took to the air with startled, screaming cries. But other than that, the ruins were still except for our footsteps pounding over the cement and our own raspy breathing.

As I led them through the overgrown yard to the crumbled shed, the first raindrops began to fall. By the time we had crowded into the tiny building, a deluge was drumming the tin roof and pouring in through the holes. I clicked on the flashlight as I descended the ladder into the basement, half-terrified that when we got there the food would be gone. But everything was as I had left it: a section of shelf lay broken on the cement, and cans were scattered everywhere, glinting in the flashlight beam.

"Holy shit." Rat shoved past me, stumbling into the room. His mouth dropped open as he scanned the wall of tins, his eyes gleaming hungrily. "The bitch wasn't kidding. Look at all this."

"Is that...all food?" Stick asked timidly, picking up a can. And before I could reply, Rat shocked me with a wild, high-pitched laugh.

"It sure is, piss-wad!" Snatching the can from Stick's fingers, he pried the top open and shoved it back at him. "Check that out! Tell me that's not the greatest thing you've ever seen!" Stick blinked in astonishment, nearly dropping the opened can, but Rat didn't seem to notice. Grabbing two more tins from the floor, he wrenched the tops away and started digging into them with long dirty fingers.

"We don't really have time for this," I cautioned, but not even Lucas was listening now, busy tugging the lid off his own can. Stick gave me an apologetic look before scooping out handfuls of beans, devouring them with as much gusto as Rat, whose face was now smeared with a slimy coating.

"Guys!" I tried again. "We can't stand around stuffing our faces all night. We're almost out of time." But they were deaf to my arguments, drunk on the amount of food and the prospect of filling their stomachs. That's what being Unregistered teaches you; when you find food, you eat as much of it as you can, because you don't know when your next meal might be. Still, all I could think of was how they were fattening themselves up for the things that wanted to eat *us*.

Outside, the storm had picked up, howling against the walls of the shed, and water began to drip through the trapdoor. It was very dark up top, a dimming twilight, the clouds hiding what little sun remained. I peered up the steps, narrowing my eyes. The spaces between the slats were almost impossible to see in the darkness, but I thought I saw something move outside the wall. It could've been a tree branch, blowing in the wind, or it might've been my imagination.

I clicked off the flashlight. The room plunged into shadow. There was a startled yelp from Stick, and then a moment of silence as everyone finally realized what was happening.

"Something is out there," I said into the stillness, very aware of my own heartbeat thudding against my ribs. And, for just a moment, I wondered why I'd been stupid enough to lead everyone here. Stick was right. This had been a mistake. In the darkness, with the rain screaming outside, the piles of food didn't seem important enough to die for. "We have to get out of here now."

"Get the packs." Lucas's voice was gruff, embarrassed, as he wiped his mouth with the back of his hand. I shot him a glance, and it was difficult to see his face in the shadows, but he must've seen my expression. "We're not leaving empty-handed," he said, "but let's do this as quickly as possible. Take as much as you can, but don't pack so much it slows you down. We're not going to get it all in one trip, anyway." I started to say something, but he cut me off with a sharp gesture. "Let's move, people!"

Without arguing, Rat and Stick knelt and began stuffing their packs with cans, moving as quietly as they could. After a moment, I unzipped my bag and joined them. For several minutes, the only sounds were the scuffle of hands in the dark, the clink of metal on metal and the rain beating the roof overhead.

I could hear Stick's frightened breathing, Rat's occasional curses as he dropped cans in his haste to stuff them into the packs. I said nothing to anyone as I worked, only looking up when my bag was full. Zipping it up, I hefted it onto my shoulders, wincing at the weight. It might slow me down a bit, but Lucas was right; we'd come too far to leave empty-handed.

"Everyone ready?" Lucas asked, his gruff voice sounding low and small in the darkness. I looked around as Rat and Stick finished zipping their packs and stood up, Stick grunting a little under the weight of his half-full bag. "Let's get out of here, then. Allie, lead the way."

We left the basement, inching up the steps to the ruined shed. Water poured in from the storm, running in streams from the roof, splashing over everything. Somewhere in the darkness, droplets kept striking a metal bucket with a rhythmic *ping-pinging* sound. It sounded like my heartbeat; rapid, frantic.

A gust of wind blew open the door with a creak, knocking it into the side of the building. Beyond the frame, the ruins were blurry and dark.

I swallowed hard and stepped out into the rain.

Water drenched me in half a second, sliding down my neck and flattening my hair. I shivered and hunched my shoulders, striding through the tall, wet grass. Behind me, I heard the others following my steps as I pushed through the weeds. Lightning flickered overhead, turning everything white for a split second, showing rows of ruined houses side by side before plunging everything into darkness once more.

Thunder boomed. As the rumble faded, I thought I heard another sound, somewhere to my left. A faint rustle that didn't come from my friends behind me.

Something brushed against my jeans in the grass, something

hard and pointy. I jerked away and clicked on the flashlight, shining it at whatever snagged me in the darkness.

It was a hoof, small and cloven, attached to a hind leg that led to the gutted carcass of a doe lying on her side in the weeds. Her stomach had been torn open, and intestines spilled from the hole like pink snakes. Her eyes, glazed and dark, stared sightlessly up at the rain.

"Allie?" Lucas whispered, coming up behind me. "What's going— Oh, shit!"

I swung the light around, taking a breath to shout a warning to the others.

Something pale and terrible rose from the grass behind Rat, all limbs and claws and shining teeth. Before he knew what was happening, it yanked him off his feet. I didn't even have time to shout before he vanished into the weeds and darkness with a yelp.

Then he began to scream.

We didn't pause. We didn't waste breath to scream out the word. The grass around us started to move, rustling madly as they came toward us, and we just ran. Behind us, Rat's agonized shrieks abruptly cut off, and we didn't look back.

I reached the chain-link fence surrounding the yard and vaulted over it, landing unsteadily as the bag's weight nearly toppled me over. Lucas was right behind me, using both hands to launch himself over the top. Stick scrambled over and fell in the dirt on the other side but bounced to his feet in an instant and followed me as we ran.

"Allie!"

Lucas's scream made me look back. His backpack had caught on the prongs at the top of the fence, and he was yanking at

it madly, his eyes huge and frantic. I glanced at Stick, sprinting away into the darkness, and swore.

"Just leave the damn bag!" I shouted, stepping toward
Lucas, but my voice was drowned in a roar of thunder overhead, and Lucas continued to yank on it, terrified. "Lucas,
leave the pack already! Just get out of there!"

Understanding dawned on his face. He shrugged out of
the straps, just as a long white arm whipped over the links
and grabbed his shirt, dragging him back against the fence.
Lucas screamed, yanking and thrashing, trying to free himself, but another claw reached over and sank into his neck,
and his screams became gurgles. My gut heaved. I watched,
dazed, as Lucas was dragged, kicking and wailing, back over
the fence, and vanished under the pale mass of creatures on
the other side. His screams didn't last as long as Rat's, and
by that time, I was already running after Stick, ignoring my
twisting insides and not daring to look back.

I could barely make out Stick's lanky form in the distance,
running down the middle of the road, weaving between cars.
Stripping off my pack, I followed, feeling highly exposed on
the open street. The rain was slowly letting up, the brunt of
the storm passing on, toward the city. Over the fading rain,
I heard the cans clanking against his back with every step he
took. In his panic, he hadn't thought to take off his pack, either. I sprinted after him, knowing he couldn't keep up that
pace for long.

Two blocks later, I found him leaning against the rusty hulk
of an overturned car, next to a tree growing out of the sidewalk. He was gasping so hard he couldn't speak. I crouched

down beside him, breathing hard, seeing Lucas's and Rat's deaths over and over again, their screams echoing in my mind.

"Lucas?" Stick's voice was so soft I barely heard him.

"Dead." My voice sounded as if it belonged to someone else. It didn't seem real that I'd lost him. My stomach threatened to crawl up my throat, and I forced it down. "He's dead," I whispered again. "The rabids got him."

"Oh, God." Stick's hands went to his mouth. "Oh, God, oh, God, oh, God!"

"Hey," I snapped, and shoved him, halting the string of words before they got even more frantic. "Stop it. We have to keep our heads if we're going to get out of here, okay?" There would be time later to shed tears, to mourn what I'd lost. But right now, the most important thing was figuring out how to stay alive.

Stick nodded, his eyes still glazed and terrified. "Where do we go now?"

I started to look around to get my bearings but suddenly noticed something that turned my blood to ice. "Stick," I said softly, looking down at his leg, "what happened?"

Blood was oozing from a gash in his knee, spreading through the thin fabric of his pants. "Oh," Stick said, as if he'd just noticed it himself. "I must've cut it when I fell off the fence. It's not very deep..." He stopped when he saw my face. "Why?"

I stood slowly, carefully, my mouth going dry. "Blood," I murmured, backing away. "Rabids can smell blood if they're close enough. We have to go n—"

It leaped atop the car with a howl, lashing out at the space I'd been a moment before, ripping through the metal with its claws. Stick yelled and dove away, skittering behind me, as the thing atop the car gave a chilling wail and looked right at us.

It had been human once, that was the most horrible thing about it. It still had a vaguely human face and emaciated body, though its skin, nearly pure white and stretched tightly across its bones, looked more skeleton than human. The tattered threads of what had been clothes hung on its frame, and its hair was tangled and matted. Its eyes were white orbs with no irises or pupils, just a blank, dead white. It hopped off the car and hissed at us, baring a mouthful of pointed teeth, the two oversize fangs extending outward like a snake's.

Behind me, Stick was whimpering, soft choked noises that made no sense, and I caught the sharp ammonia smell of urine. Heart pounding, I eased away from him, and the rabid's hollow gaze followed me before returning to Stick. Its nostrils flared, and bloody foam dripped from its jaws as it took a lurching step forward.

Stick was frozen in terror, watching the rabid like a cornered mouse would a snake. I had no idea why I did what I did next. But my hand reached into my pocket and grabbed the knife. Pulling open the blade, I closed my fist around the edge and, before I thought better of it, sliced it across my palm.

"Hey!" I yelled, and the rabid snapped its horrible gaze to me, nostrils flaring. "That's right," I continued, backing away as it followed, leaping atop another car as easily as walking. "Look at me, not him. Stick," I called without taking my eyes from the rabid, keeping a car between it and myself, "get out of here. Find the drain—it'll take you back to the city. Do you hear me?"

No answer. I chanced a sideways glance and saw him still frozen in the same spot, eyes glued to the rabid stalking me. "Stick!" I hissed furiously, but he didn't move. "Dammit, you spineless little shit! Get out of here now!"

With a chilling shriek like nothing human, the rabid lunged.

I ran, ducking behind a truck, hearing the rabid's claws screech off the rusty metal as it followed. I dodged and wove my way through the vehicle-littered street, keeping the cars between myself and the pursuing rabid, glancing back to gauge how close it was. It snarled and hissed at me over the vehicles, hollow eyes blazing with madness and hunger, its claws leaving white gashes in the rust.

Dodging behind another car, I gazed around frantically for a weapon. A pipe, a branch I could use as a club, anything. The rabid's shriek rang out behind me, horrifyingly near. As I reached down and grabbed a chunk of broken pavement from the curb, I glimpsed a pale form in the corner of my eye and turned quickly, swinging with all my might.

The jagged concrete hit the rabid square in the temple as it lunged for me, grasping claws inches from my face. I heard something crack beneath the stone as I knocked the creature aside, smashing it into the door of a car. The rabid collapsed to the pavement, trying to get up, and I brought the stone down again, smashing the back of its skull. Once, twice and again.

The rabid screamed and twitched, limbs jerking sporadically, before collapsing to the sidewalk. A dark puddle oozed from beneath its head and spread over the street.

Trembling, I dropped the stone and sank to the curb. My hands shook, my knees shook, and my heart was doing its best to hammer its way through my ribs. The rabid looked smaller in death than in life, all brittle limbs and protruding bones. But its face was as horrible and terrifying as ever, fangs frozen in a snarl, soulless white eyes staring up at me.

And then a hiss behind me made my heart stop a second time.

I turned slowly as another rabid slid out from behind a car, arms and mouth smeared with wet crimson. It clutched a branch in one claw...only the branch had five fingers, and the tattered remains of a shirt clung to it. Seeing me, the rabid dropped the arm to the pavement and crept forward.

Another rabid followed. And another leaped to the roof of a car, hissing. I spun and faced two more, sliding from beneath a truck, pale dead eyes fastened on me. Five of them. From all directions. And me, in the center. Alone.

Everything grew very quiet. All I heard was my pulse, roaring in my ears, and my ragged breathing. I gazed around at the pale, foaming rabids, not ten yards from me in any direction and for just a moment I felt calm. So this was the knowledge that you were about to die, that no one could help you, that it would all be over in a few short seconds.

In that brief moment between life and death, I looked between cars and saw a figure striding toward me, silhouetted black against the rain. Something bright gleamed in its hand, but then a rabid passed through my field of vision, and it was gone.

Survival instincts kicked in, and I ran.

Something hit me from behind, hard, and warmth spread over my neck and back, though there was no pain. The blow knocked me forward, and I stumbled, falling to my knees. A weight landed on me, screeching, tearing at me, and bright strips of fire began to spread across my shoulders. I screamed and flipped over, using my legs to shove it away, but another pale creature filled my vision, and all I could see was its face and teeth and blank, dead eyes, lunging forward. My hands shot out, slamming into its jaw, keeping those snapping teeth away from my face. It snarled and sank its fangs into my wrist, chewing and tearing, but I barely felt the pain. All I could think about was keeping the teeth away from my throat, though I knew its claws were ripping open my chest and stomach—*I had to keep it away from my throat.*

And then the others closed in, screaming, ripping. And the last thing I remembered, before the bloody red haze finally melted into blackness, was a flash of something bright and the rabid's body dropping onto my chest while its head continued to bite my arm.

Then there was nothing.

WHEN I WOKE UP, I knew I was in hell. My whole body was on fire, or at least it felt that way, though I couldn't see the flames. It was dark, and a light rain was falling from the sky, which I found strange for hell. Then a dark figure loomed over me, jet-black eyes boring into mine, and I thought I knew him from…somewhere. Hadn't I met him before…?

"Can you hear me?" His voice was familiar, too, low and calm. I opened my mouth to reply, but only a choked gurgle escaped. What was wrong with me? It felt as if my mouth and throat were clogged with warm mud.

"Don't try to speak." The soothing voice broke through my agony and confusion. "Listen to me, human. You're dying. The damage the rabids did to your body is extreme. You have only a few minutes left in this world." He leaned closer, face intense. "Do you understand what I'm telling you?"

Barely. My head felt heavy, and everything was foggy and surreal. The pain was still there, but seemed far away now, as if I was disconnected from my body. I tried raising my head to see the extent of my wounds, but the stranger put a hand on my shoulder, stopping me. "No," he said gently, easing me back. "Don't look. It's better that you do not see. Just know that, whatever you choose, you will die today. The manner of your death, however, is up to you."

"Wha—" I choked on that warm wetness, spat it out to clear my throat. "What do you mean?" I rasped, my voice sounding strange in my ears. The stranger regarded me without expression.

"I'm giving you a choice," he said. "You are intelligent enough to know what I am, what I'm offering. I watched you draw the rabids away to save your friend. I watched your struggle to fight, to live, when most would have lain down and died. I see...potential.

"I can end the pain," he continued, smoothing a strand of hair from my eyes. "I can offer you release from the mortal coil, and I promise that you will not spend eternity as one of them." He nodded to a pale body, crumpled against a tire a few yards away. "I can give you that much peace, at least."

"Or?" I whispered. He sighed.

"Or…I can make you one of us. I can drain you to the point of death, and give you my blood, so that when you die you will rise again…as an immortal. A vampire. It will be a different life, and perhaps not one that you would suffer through. Perhaps you would rather be dead with your soul intact than exist forever without one. But the choice, and the manner of your death, is up to you."

I lay there, trying to catch my breath, my mind reeling. I was dying. I was dying, and this stranger—this *vampire*—was offering me a way out.

Die as a human, or become a bloodsucker. Either way, the choice was death, because the vampires *were* dead, they just had the audacity to keep living—walking corpses that preyed on humans to survive. I hated the vampires; everything about them—their city, their pets, their domination of the human race—I despised with my entire being. They had taken everything from me, everything that was important. I would never forgive them for what I had lost.

And I'd been so close, so close to changing something. To *maybe* making a difference in this stupid, screwed-up world. I'd wanted to know what it was like not to live under vampire rule, not to be starving all the time, not having to shut everyone out because you were afraid they would die in front of you. Such a world had existed, once. If I could only make others realize that as well…but that choice was gone. My world would remain as it always was: dark, bloody and hopeless. The vampires would always rule, and I couldn't change anything.

But the other choice. The other choice…was to die for real.

"You are running out of time, little human."

I wished I could've said I would rather die than become a bloodsucker. I wished I had the courage, the strength, to stick with my convictions. But in reality, when faced with death and the great unknown that came after, my survival instinct snatched wildly at whatever lifeline was offered. I didn't want to die. Even if it meant becoming something I loathed, my nature was, first and always, to survive.

The stranger, the vampire, still knelt beside me, waiting for my answer. I looked up into his dark eyes and made my decision.

"I want...to live."

The stranger nodded. He didn't ask if I was sure. He only moved closer and slid his hands under my body. "This will hurt," he warned and lifted me into his arms.

Though he was gentle, I gasped as pain shot through my broken body, biting down a scream as the vampire drew me to his chest. He lowered his head, close enough for me to see his cold pale skin, the dark circles beneath his eyes.

"Be warned," he said in a low voice, "even if I turn you now, there is still a chance for you to rise as a rabid. If that happens I will destroy you permanently. But I will not leave you," he promised in an even softer voice. "I will stay with you until the transformation, whatever it may be, is complete."

I could only nod. Then the vampire's lips parted, and I saw his fangs grow, lengthen, become long and sharp. It was nothing like the rabid's teeth, jagged and uneven, like broken glass. The vampire's fangs were surgical instruments, precise and dangerous, almost elegant. I was surprised. Even living so close to the bloodsuckers, I had not seen a vampire's killing tools until now.

My pulse throbbed, and I saw the vampire's nostrils twitch, as if smelling the blood coursing through my veins, right below my skin. His eyes changed, growing even darker, the pupils expanding so they swallowed all of the white. Before I could be terrified, before I could change my mind, he lowered his head in one smooth, quick motion, and those long, bright fangs sank into my throat.

I gasped, arching my back, my hands fisting in his shirt. I couldn't move or speak. Pain, pleasure and warmth flooded my body, coursing through my veins. Someone once told me there was some kind of narcotic in the vampire's fangs, a soothing agent; that was why having two long incisors in your neck wasn't the blinding agony one thought it should be. Of course, that was only speculation. Maybe there wasn't a scientific explanation. Maybe the bite of a vampire just felt like this: agony and pleasure, all at the same time.

I could feel him drinking, though, feel my blood leaving my veins at an alarming rate. I felt drowsy and numb, and the world started to blur at the edges. Abruptly, the vampire released me, brought a hand to his lips and sliced his wrist open on his fangs. As I watched, dazed and nearly insensible, he pressed the bleeding arm to my mouth. Thick, hot blood spread over my tongue, and I gagged, trying to pull away. But the hand pressing against my mouth was as immovable as a wall.

"Drink," a voice commanded, low and stern, and I did, wondering if it would come right back up. It didn't. I felt the blood slide down my throat, burning a path all the way to my stomach. The arm didn't move, and hot liquid continued to flow into my mouth. Only when I had swallowed three or four times did the wrist pull away and the vampire lay me back down. The pavement was cold and hard against my back.

"I don't know if I got to you in time," he murmured almost to himself. "We shall have to wait and see what becomes of you. And what you will become."

"What...happens now?" I was barely conscious enough to force out the words. Sleepily, I gazed at him as the pain faded to a distant throbbing that belonged to someone else. Blackness crawled at the edges of my vision like a million ants.

"Now, little human," the vampire said, placing a hand on my forehead. "Now, you will die. And hopefully I will see you again on the other side."

Then, my eyes flickered shut, darkness pulled me under and, lying in the rain, in the cold embrace of a nameless vampire, I exited the world of the living.

Part II

Vampire

CHAPTER 5

Fragments of nightmare plagued my darkness.

Lucas and Rat, pulled under by grasping white hands.

The dead deer, rising from the grass to stare at me, her gaping ribs shining in the moonlight.

Running through aisles of rusty cars, thousands of pale things following me, shrieking and hissing at my back.

Ripping the tops off metal cans, finding them filled with dark red liquid, and drinking it furiously...

I BOLTED UPRIGHT, SHRIEKING, clawing at the darkness. As I opened my eyes, a searing light blinded me, and I cringed away with a hiss. All around me, strange noises assaulted my eardrums, familiar yet amplified a hundredfold. I could hear the scuttle of a cockroach as it fled up the wall. A trickle of water sounded like a waterfall. The air felt cold and damp against my skin, but in a strange way—I could feel the chill, but it wasn't cold at all.

I felt waxy and stiff, empty as a limp sack. Gingerly I turned my head and fire spread through my veins, hot and searing, nearly blinding me with pain. I arched back with a scream as the flames spread to every part of my body, liquid agony shooting through my skin. My mouth ached, my upper jaw felt tight, as if something sharp was pressing against my gums, trying to burst out.

Flashes of emotion, like the shards of someone else's life, flickered through my head. Pity. Empathy. Guilt. For a split second, I saw myself, my own body, writhing on the floor, clawing at the cement and the walls. But then a bolt of pain turned my stomach inside out, doubling me over, and the strange image was lost.

The pressure against my jaw grew unbearable, and I screamed again, sounding like a snarling animal. And suddenly, something did burst through my gums, relieving the awful pain. The heat through my veins flickered and died, and I slumped to the hard cement, shuddering with relief. But there was a new pain inside me, a hollow, throbbing ache radiating somewhere from my middle. I pushed myself to my hands and knees, shaking, growling deep in my throat. Hungry. I was hungry! I needed food!

Something pressed against my face, cold and wet. Plastic? I recoiled with a snarl. Wait, the bag smelled of food, it was food! I lunged forward, sinking my teeth into the bag, tearing it from the air. Something flooded my mouth, cold and thick, cloying. Not warm, like it should be, but it was still food! I sucked and tore at the flimsy plastic, freeing the food within, feeling it slide down my throat into my stomach.

And then, as the awful Hunger faded and the ache inside was filled, I realized what I was doing.

"Oh, God." Dropping the mangled bag, I looked at my hands, covered in blood. The ground I lay on was splattered with it, dark stains against the cement. I could feel it around my mouth, on my lips and chin, the scent of it filling my nose. "Oh, God," I whispered again, scrambling away on my butt. I hit a wall and stared in horror at the scene before me. "What...what am I doing?"

"You made a choice," came a deep voice to my right, and I looked up. The vampire loomed over me, tall and solemn. A flickering candle sat behind him on an end table—the light that had blinded me earlier. It was still painfully bright, and I turned away. "You wanted to survive, to become one of us." He looked to the torn blood bag, lying a few feet away. "You chose this."

I covered my mouth with a shaking hand, trying to remember, to recall what I'd said. All I could see was blood, and me in an animal rage, tearing at it, ripping it open. My hand dropped to my lips and jaw, probing my teeth where the ache had been. I drew in a quick breath.

There they were. Fangs. Very long and very, very sharp.

I snatched my hand back. It was true, then. I really had done the unthinkable. I'd become that which I hated most in the world. A vampire. A monster.

I slumped against the wall, trembling. Looking down at myself, I blinked in surprise. My old clothes were gone. Instead of my thin, faded patchwork shirt and pants, I wore black jeans and a dark shirt without a single hole or tear. The filthy, torn and probably bloodstained jacket had been replaced with a long black coat that looked almost new.

"What...what happened to my clothes?" I asked, touching

the sleeve of the coat, blinking at how thick it was. Frowning suddenly, I looked up at the vampire. "Did you dress me?"

"Your clothes were torn to pieces when the rabids attacked you," the vampire informed me, still not moving from where he stood. "I found you some new ones. Black is the best color for us—it hides the bloodstains rather well. Do not worry." His deep, low voice held the faintest hint of amusement. "I did not see anything."

My mind spun. "I—I have to go," I said shakily, getting to my feet. "I have to...find my friends, see if they made it back to the hideout. Stick is probably—"

"Your friends are dead," the vampire said calmly. "And I would abandon all attachments to your life before. You are not part of that world any longer. It is better to simply forget about it."

Dead. Images flashed through my mind—of rain and blood and pale, screeching things, hands pulling someone over a fence. With a hiss, I shied away from those thoughts, refusing to remember. "No," I choked out, shuddering. "You're lying."

"Let them go," the vampire insisted quietly. "They're gone."

I had the sudden, crazy urge to snarl and bare my fangs at him. I stifled it in horror, keeping a wary eye on the stranger, who watched me impassively. "You can't keep me here."

"If you want to leave, you may go." He didn't move, except to nod to a door on the other side of the small room. "I will not stop you. Though you will be dead within a day, if it takes that long. You have no idea how to survive as a vampire, how to feed, how to avoid detection, and if the vampires of this city discover you, they will most likely kill you. Alternatively, you could remain here, with me, and have a chance of surviving this life you have chosen."

I glared at him. "Stay here? With you? Why? What do you care?"

The stranger narrowed his eyes. "Bringing a new vampire into the world is something I do not take lightly," he said. "Turning a human only to abandon it without the skills it needs to survive would be irresponsible and dangerous. If you stay here, I will teach you what you need to know to live as one of us. Or—" he turned slightly, gesturing to the door "—you can leave and try to survive on your own, but I wash my hands of you and whatever blood comes after."

I slumped back to the wall, my mind racing. Rat was dead. Lucas was dead. I'd seen them, pulled under by rabids in the old city, torn apart before my eyes. My throat closed up. Stick, much as I hated to admit it, was most likely dead as well; he couldn't survive the trek back to the city on his own. It was just me now. Alone. A vampire.

My chest felt tight, and I bit my lip, imagining the faces of my friends staring at me, pale and accusing. My eyes burned, but I swallowed hard and forced back the tears. I could cry and scream and curse the world and the rabids and the vampires later. But I would not show weakness in front of this stranger, this bloodsucker who might have saved me, but about whom I knew nothing. When I was alone, I would cry for Rat and Lucas and Stick, the family I'd lost. Right now, I had larger issues to deal with.

I was a vampire. And, despite everything, I still wanted to live.

The stranger waited, as unmoving as a wall. He might be a bloodsucker, but he was the only familiar thing I had left. "So," I said softly without looking up. Resentment boiled, an old, familiar hate, but I shoved it down. "Do I call you 'master' or 'teacher' or something else?"

The vampire paused, then said, "You may call me Kanin."

"Kanin? Is that your name?"

"I did not say it was my name." He turned as if to leave, but crossed the room and sank into a rusty folding chair on the other side. "I said it was what you could call me."

Great, not only was my new teacher a vampire, he was one of those cryptic, mysterious ones, too. I crossed my arms and eyed him warily. "Where are we?"

Kanin considered this. "Before I disclose anything about myself," he said, leaning forward and resting his elbows on his knees, "I would like to know a bit more about you. I will be teaching you, after all, and that means we will be spending a great deal of time together. I want to know what I am up against. Are you amenable to this?"

I shrugged. "What do you want to know?"

"Your name, first off."

"Allie," I said, then elaborated. "Allison Sekemoto."

"Interesting." Kanin straightened, watching me with intense black eyes. "You know your full name. Not many humans do, anymore."

"My mom taught me."

"Your mother?" Kanin leaned back, crossing his arms. "Did she teach you anything else?"

I bristled. I suddenly didn't want to discuss my mom with this bloodsucker. "Yeah," I said evasively.

He drummed his fingers on his biceps. "Such as?"

"Why do you want to know?"

He ignored the question. "If you wish for me to help you, you will answer me."

"Reading, writing and a little math," I snapped at him. "Anything else?"

"Where is your mother now?"

"Dead."

Kanin didn't seem surprised, or shocked at my bluntness. "And your father?"

"I never knew him."

"Siblings?"

I shook my head.

"So you have nothing on that side to go back to." Kanin nodded. "Good. That will make things easier. How did she die?"

I narrowed my eyes, about fed up with this interrogation. "That's none of your business, vampire," I snapped, wanting some emotion to cross his impassive face. Except for a raised eyebrow, his expression remained the same. "Besides, what's it to you? Why should you care about the lives of a couple humans, anyway?"

"I don't," the vampire said and shrugged. "Like I said before, I want to evaluate my chances of success. Humans have a tendency to cling to the past, which can make teaching them difficult. The more attachments a person has, the harder it is to learn to let go when becoming a vampire."

I clenched my hands, trying to calm the sudden rage. I would have been tempted to leap up and punch him, ungrateful as that was, if I didn't know he could tear my head off without blinking. "Yeah, well, I'm beginning to regret that decision."

"It's a little late now, don't you think?" Kanin asked softly as he rose. "Take a moment," he said, walking to the door on the opposite wall. "Mourn your past life if you wish, for you will not see it again. When you are ready to learn what it means to be a vampire, come find me."

He opened the door and strode through without a backward glance, leaving me alone.

AFTER KANIN LEFT, I sat on the chair, scraped the dried blood off my hands and thought about what I was going to do next.

So. I'm a vampire now. I bristled, trying not to dwell on it—it was either that or die in the rain. Kanin was right, it was my decision, after all. I'd chosen this. I'd *chosen* to become undead, to never see the sunlight again, to drink the blood of the living.

I shuddered and kicked the empty bag away. That was the part that bothered me—well, besides the whole undead, soulless-monster thing. I shoved that thought to the back of my mind. Vampires were predators, but maybe there was a way *not* to feed on humans. Maybe I could survive on animal blood, though the thought of biting into a live, squirming rat was disturbing. Did vampires *have* to drink human blood, or did they just prefer it? How often did they have to feed? Where and how did they sleep during the day? I realized that, even living in this city for seventeen years, I knew virtually nothing about its most famous citizens except that they drank blood and came out at night.

Well, there is one person who could tell you all about it.

I struggled with myself a moment longer. He was a vampire, but if I was going to survive, then I needed to learn. Perhaps later, when I had all I needed to know, I would take my revenge for my mom, for Stick, Lucas and everyone else who was taken from me. But right now, I could swallow my pride and start learning how to be undead.

Reluctantly, I pulled myself to my feet and went looking for my new mentor.

The door led into another room that might've been an office once. A few broken chairs were tossed carelessly to the side, and several long metal cabinets lay on the floor, spilling paper everywhere. Against the far wall, Kanin sat behind a large wooden desk covered in dust and scratches. He glanced up from a stack of folders and raised an eyebrow as I came in.

"I have a few questions," I said, wondering if it was improper to ask and then deciding I didn't care. "About vampires, and this whole drinking-blood thing in general."

Kanin shut the folder, put it aside and nodded to one of the chairs. I pulled it upright and sat down, resting my arms over the back.

"Let me guess," he said, lacing his hands together. "You're wondering if you have to prey on humans, if you can survive by drinking the blood of animals or other creatures. You're hoping you won't have to kill people to live. Am I right?"

I nodded. Kanin smiled bitterly.

"You cannot," he said in a flat voice, and my heart sank. "Let me give you your first and most important lesson, Allison Sekemoto—you are a monster. A demon who feeds on human beings to survive. The vampires at the center of the city may look and act and pretend to be civilized, but do not let that fool you. We are monsters, and nothing will change that. And do not think that you can cling to your humanity by drinking the blood of dogs or rats or sheep. It is junk food—garbage. It will fill you for a time, but it will never sate the Hunger. And you will soon crave the blood of humans so badly that the mere sight of one will send you into a frenzy, and that human will die, because you will be unable to stop yourself from draining them completely. That is the single most important thing you must understand, before we go any further. You are no longer human. You are a predator, and the sooner you accept that, the easier this life, this existence, will become."

My heart sank even lower. It seemed everything I'd thought about vampires was proving to be right. But I still said, "I'm not going to kill humans to feed on them, I can tell you that now."

"It always starts out that way," Kanin said, and his voice was distant, as if remembering. "Noble intentions, honor among new vampires. Vows to not harm humans, to take only what is needed, to not hunt them like sheep through the night." He smiled faintly. "But it becomes harder and harder to remain on their level, to hold on to your humanity, when all you can see them as is food."

"I don't care." I thought of Stick, of Lucas and even Rat. They had been friends. People. Not walking blood bags. "I'll be different. I'm sure as hell going to try."

Kanin didn't argue. Rising, he stepped around the desk and beckoned with a large pale hand. "Come here."

Wary, I stood, edging toward him. "Why? What are we doing?"

"I said I would teach you how to survive as a vampire."
He took a single step forward, and I now stood a foot or two
away from him, gazing up at his chin. Geez, he was big. His
presence was overwhelming. "To live, you must understand
the vampire body, how it works, how it endures. Take off
your coat."

I did, dropping it on the chair behind me, wondering what
he was getting at. In one blindingly quick motion, he grabbed
my wrist, yanked my arm up, and slashed it open with that
long, bright dagger he carried. Blood welled and streamed
from the wound, a second before the pain hit like a hammer.

"*Ow!* What the hell are you *doing?*" I tried yanking back,
but it was like pulling on a tree. Kanin didn't even twitch.
"Let go, you psychopath! What kind of sick game are you
playing?"

"Wait," Kanin ordered, giving my arm a little shake. I gritted my teeth as the vampire held up my wrist. "Look."

My arm was a mess, blood everywhere, oozing down my
elbow. I could see the wound, the deep, straight gash that
probably went to the bone. *Psychotic vampire.* But as I watched,
panting, the wound started to heal, the gaping flesh drawing together, turning from red to pink to white until only a
faint, pale scar remained. And then nothing at all.

I gaped as Kanin released my arm. "We are very difficult
to kill," he explained to my shocked expression. "Stronger
than humans, faster than humans, and we heal from most
anything. This is why we are the perfect predator, but be
warned, we are not invincible. Fire harms us, as does any massive trauma. The strongest vampire will not walk away from
a bomb going off under his feet. But bullets, knives, clubs,

swords—it will hurt, being struck by one, but it will not usually kill us. Although…" He touched my chest. "A wooden
stake driven through the heart will not instantly kill us, but
it will paralyze and usually send us into hibernation. That is
our body's last-ditch effort to survive—it shuts down completely and we are forced into sleep, sometimes for decades,
until we can rejoin the living world again." He withdrew his
hand. "But to completely destroy a vampire, beheading it or
burning it to ash is the only sure way. Are you getting this?"

"Kill a vampire, aim for its head," I muttered. "Got it."
The pain was gone now, and there was a gnawing ache in
my gut, though I still wanted to learn more. "But why am I
bleeding at all?" I wondered, looking up at him. "Do I even
have a heartbeat? I thought…I thought I was dead."

"You *are* dead."

I scowled. "I suppose this is a case of death taking a while
to kick in, then."

Kanin's expression didn't change. "You are still thinking
like a human," he said. "Listen to me, Allison, and keep
your mind open. Mortals view death in terms of black and
white—you are either alive, or you are not. But between
them—between life and death and eternity—there is a small
gray area, one that the humans have no knowledge of. That is
where we reside, vampires and rabids and a few of the older,
inexplicable creatures that still exist in this world. The humans cannot understand us, because we live by a different set
of rules."

"I'm still not sure I understand."

"We have no heartbeat," my mentor continued, lightly
touching his own chest. "You wonder how the blood can

pump through your veins, right? It doesn't. You have no blood. None that is your own, anyway. Think of it as our food and drink—it is absorbed into the body the same way. Blood is the core of our power. It is how we live, it is how we heal. The longer we go without, the farther we slip from humanity, until we resemble the cold, empty, living corpses the humans think us to be."

I stared at Kanin, looking for any sign that he wasn't human. His skin was pale, and his eyes were hollow, but he wasn't corpselike. Unless you looked really hard, you wouldn't know he was a vampire at all.

"What happens if we don't...uh...drink blood?" I asked, feeling a pang in my stomach. "Can we starve to death?"

"We're already dead," Kanin replied in that same infuriatingly cool tone. "So, no. But go long enough without human blood, and you will start to go mad. Your body will shrivel, until you are nothing but an empty husk wandering around, very much like the rabids. And you will attack any living creature you come across, because the Hunger will take over. Also, because your body has no reserves to draw upon, any damage that doesn't kill you could drive you into hibernation for an indefinite amount of time."

"You couldn't have told me all this without slicing my arm open?"

"I could have." Kanin shrugged unrepentantly. "But I had another lesson in mind. How do you feel?"

"Starving." The ache in my gut had grown more painful; my body was crying out for food. I thought longingly of the once-full blood bag, lying empty on the floor. I wondered if there was anything left that I could suck out, before I caught myself in horror.

Kanin nodded. "And that is the price of such power. Your body will heal itself from most anything, but it will draw upon its own reserves to do so. Look at your arm."

I did and gasped. My skin, especially the area where Kanin had cut me, was chalk-white, definitely paler than before, and cold. Dead flesh. Bloodless flesh. I shuddered and tore my gaze away, and felt the vampire's smile.

"If you do not feed soon afterward, you will fall into a blood frenzy, and someone will die," he announced. "The greater the wound, the more blood you need to replenish it. Go too long without feeding, and the result will be the same. And this is why vampires do not become attached to humans, or anyone. Sometime in your life, Allison Sekemoto, you will kill a human being. Accidentally or as a conscious, deliberate act. It is unavoidable. The question is not *if* it will happen, but *when*. Do you understand?"

"Yeah," I muttered. "I got it."

He watched me with depthless black eyes. "Be sure that you do," he said quietly. "Now, from here, you must learn the most important part of being one of us—how to feed."

I swallowed. "Don't you have any more of those bags?"

He chuckled. "I procured that from one of the guards at this week's bloodletting. It's not something I'd normally do, but you needed food immediately upon waking. But you and I are not like the vampires in the city, with their slaves and pets and cellars of 'wine.' If you want to feed, you must do it the old-fashioned way. I'll show you what I mean. Come, follow me."

"Where are we going?" I asked as he opened the door, and we stepped out into a long, narrow hallway. Once-white paint was peeling from the walls, and glass crunched under my feet as we walked. Every few yards, a doorway opened into another room, the remains of beds and chairs and odd machines I didn't recognize scattered about and broken. A strange chair with wheels lay on its side in one doorway, covered in dust and cobwebs. I realized I could see perfectly in the dark corridor, though there was no light, and it should've been pitch-black down here. Kanin looked back at me and smiled.

"We're going hunting."

WE TURNED A CORNER, and the hallway opened into what looked like an old reception area with another big wooden desk in the middle of the room. Above the desk, tarnished gold letters hung on the wall, most of them skewed or broken, so it was impossible to make out what it had once said. There were a lot of smaller signs, too, on walls and at the entrances to hallways, all difficult to make out. Glass, debris and sheets of paper were scattered about the cracked tile floor, rustling where we walked.

"What is this place?" I asked Kanin. My voice echoed weirdly in the open chamber, and the silence of the room seemed to press down on me. The vampire didn't answer for a long moment.

"At one time," he murmured, leading me across the room, "this was the sublevel of a hospital. One of the busiest and most well established in the city. They did more than treat patients—there was a team of scientists here, researchers committed to ending disease and discovering new cures. Of

course, when the Red Lung virus hit, the hospital was over-run—they couldn't keep up with the amount of patients pour-ing through their doors. A lot of people died here." He gazed at the desk, his eyes hooded and far away. "But then, a lot of people died everywhere."

"If you're trying to creep me out, congratulations. So, how do we get out of here?"

He stopped at a large, square hole in the wall and gestured at the opening. I peered through the gap and saw a long shaft, leading up into darkness, with thick metal ropes dangling from somewhere up top.

"You're kidding, right?" My voice echoed up the tube.

"The stairs to ground level are collapsed," Kanin replied calmly. "There is no other way in or out. We have to use the elevator shaft."

Elevator shaft? I frowned and looked back at him. "There's no way I can climb that."

"You aren't human anymore." He narrowed his eyes. "You're stronger, you have unlimited endurance and you can do things humans cannot. If it puts your mind at ease, I will be right behind you."

I looked at the elevator tube and shrugged. "All right," I muttered, reaching out to grab the cables. "But if I fall, I ex-pect you to catch me."

Tightening my hold, I pulled.

To my surprise, my body rose off the ground as if I weighed nothing at all. I shimmied up the tube, going hand over hand, feeling a thrill I'd never known. My skin didn't tear, my arms didn't burn, and I wasn't even breathing hard. I could've done this forever.

I paused, my rhythm stumbling to a halt. I wasn't breathing. At all. My pulse didn't race, my heart didn't pound... because I wasn't alive. I was dead. I would never age, never change. I was a parasitic corpse who drank the lifeblood of others to survive.

"Having problems?" Kanin's deep, impatient voice echoed from below me.

I shook myself. Empty elevator tubes were not the best places for personal revelations. "I'm fine," I answered and started climbing again. I would sort all this out later; right now, my dead-corpse stomach was telling me I was starving. I found it very strange that my heart and lungs and other organs didn't work, but my stomach and brain were still functioning. Or maybe they weren't—I had no idea. Everything about vampires, I was learning, was a complete mystery.

A cold breeze hit my face as I scrambled out of the shaft, gazing around warily.

There had been a building here once. I could see the remains of steel beams and girders surrounding us, along with maybe half a wall, falling to pieces in the long yellow grass. The plaster was blackened and scorched, and charred bits of furniture—beds, mattresses, chairs—were strewn about and half hidden in the grass spreading across the floor. The tube we'd just come through was nothing more than a dark hole in the tile, hidden among the rubble and weeds. If you weren't standing directly above it, you might never see the gaping hole until you tumbled down the shaft and broke your spine at the bottom.

"What happened here?" I whispered, gazing around at the devastation.

"A fire," Kanin said, starting across the empty lot. He moved quickly, and I scrambled to keep up with him. "It started on the ground floor of the hospital. It quickly grew out of control and destroyed the building and most everyone inside. Only the lower levels were...spared."

"Were you there when it happened?"

Kanin didn't answer. Leaving the hospital ruins, we crossed an empty lot where nature had risen up to strangle everything it could get its green-and-yellow claws around. It pushed up through the once-flat parking lots and curled around several outbuildings, choking them with vines and weeds. When we reached the edge of the lot and looked back, you could barely see the hospital remains through the vegetation.

It was dark on the streets of the Fringe. Clouds scuttled across the sky, blocking the moon and stars. But I still saw everything clearly, and even more amazing, I knew exactly what time it was and how long we had until dawn. I could sense the blood on the air, the lingering heat of warm-blooded mammals. It was an hour past midnight, long after the bravest humans closed their doors against the dark, and I was starving.

"This way," Kanin murmured and glided into the shadows.

I didn't argue, following him down a long, dark alleyway, subtly aware that something was different, though I couldn't put my finger on it.

Then it hit me. The smell. All my life, I had grown up with the smells of the Fringe: the garbage, the waste, the aroma of mold and rot and decay. I couldn't smell any of that now. Perhaps because smelling and breathing were so closely linked. My other senses were heightened: I could hear the scuttle of a mouse, scrambling into its hole a dozen yards away. I could feel the wind on my arms, cold and clammy, though my skin didn't respond as it should and pucker with goose bumps. But when we passed an ancient Dumpster and I felt the buzz of flies from within, heard maggots writhing through dead, rotting flesh—of an animal I hoped—I still couldn't smell anything.

When I mentioned this to Kanin, he gave a humorless chuckle.

"You can smell, if you want to," he replied, weaving around a pile of shingles that once belonged to a roof. "You just have to make a conscious effort to take a breath. It's not a natural thing anymore because we don't need to do it. You'll want to remember that if there's a situation where you're trying to blend in. Humans are usually unobservant, but even they will know something is wrong if you don't appear to be breathing."

I took a breath and caught the stench of decay from the Dumpster. I also smelled something else on the wind: blood. And then I saw a splash of paint across a crumbling wall—a skull with a pair of red wings on either side—and I realized where we were.

"This is gang territory," I said, horrified. "That's the sign for the Blood Angels."

"Yes," said Kanin calmly.

I resisted the instinct to scramble away from him, to flee into the nearest alleyway and head for home. Vampires weren't the only predators to roam the city streets. And scavengers weren't the only groups to stake their territories in the Fringe. While some Unregistereds were simply thieves, bands of kids looking to survive, there were other, more sinister groups.

Reapers, Red Skulls, Blood Angels: these were only a few of the "other" gangs that had carved out certain parts of the Fringe for themselves. In this world, the only law was to obey the Masters, and the Masters didn't care if their cattle occasionally turned on each other. Run into a bored, hungry gang, and you'd be lucky if all they did was kill you. I'd heard stories of certain gangs who, after having their "fun" with a trespasser, would slice them up and eat them, as well. Urban legends, of course, but who was I to say they weren't true? That was why venturing out of familiar territory was a bad idea at best, suicidal at worst. I knew which parts of the Fringe were gang turf and had avoided them like the plague.

And now we were walking right into their territory.

I eyed the vampire at my side. "You know they're going to kill us for being here."

He nodded. "I'm counting on it."

"You know that they *eat* people, right?"

Kanin stopped, turning to me with intense black eyes. "So do I," he said evenly. "And now, so do you."

I felt slightly sick. *Oh, yeah.*

The smell of blood was getting stronger, and now I could hear the familiar sounds of a fight: cursing, shouting, the smacks of fists and shoes on flesh. We turned a corner and entered the back lot between several buildings, surrounded by chain-link, broken glass and rusting cars. Graffiti covered the crumbling bricks and metal walls, and several steel drums burned around the perimeter, billowing a thick, choking smoke.

In the center of the arena, a group of ragged, similarly dressed thugs clustered around a crumpled form on the pavement. The body was curled into a fetal position, covering its head, while two or three thugs broke away from the circle to punch or kick at it. Another body lay nearby, disturbingly still, its face smashed beyond recognition. My gut twisted at the sight of the broken nose and staring eyes. But then the scent of blood came to me, stronger than ever, and I growled low in my throat before I realized I'd made a sound.

The gang members were laughing too loud to hear and were too focused on their sport to notice us, but Kanin kept walking forward. Calmly, as if out for a late-night stroll, he approached the ring of humans, making no sound whatsoever. We could've sauntered right past them and continued into the night, but as we neared the circle of thugs, who still hadn't noticed us, he deliberately kicked a broken bottle, sending it clinking and tumbling over the pavement.

And the Blood Angels looked up.

"Good evening," Kanin said, nodding cordially. He continued to walk past them, moving at a slower pace, I noted. I followed silently, trying to be invisible, hoping the gang would just let us go without a challenge.

But part of me, the strange, alien, hungry part, watched the humans eagerly and hoped they would try to stop us.

It got its wish. With muffled curses, the whole group moved to block our path. Kanin stopped and watched impassively as a thug with a scar over one pale eye stepped forward, shaking his head.

"Look at this," he said, grinning at Kanin, then me. "Lucky night for us, ain't it, boys?"

Kanin didn't say anything. I wondered if he was afraid

speaking to them would clue them in to what he was; he didn't want to scare away our food.

"Look at him—so scared he can't even talk." Derisive laughter all around. "Shoulda thought of that before you came through our turf, pet." Scar-face stepped forward, the jeers and insults of his gang backing him up. "Gonna drop your pants so we can kiss your shiny ass, is that what you want, *pet?*" He spat the word, before his gaze flicked to me, and his leer turned ugly. "Or maybe I'll just save it for that sweet little Asian doll. We don't get many whores through here, do we, boys?"

I snarled, feeling my lips curl back. "Bring your cesspit mouth anywhere near me and I'll tear it off," I spat at him. The gang hooted and edged closer.

"Ooh, she's a feisty one, ain't she?" Scar-face grinned. "I hope there's enough of that to go around. You don't mind sharing, do you, pet?"

"Be my guest," Kanin said and stepped away from me. I gaped at him as Scar-face and his gang exploded with eager, taunting laughter.

"Pet's so scared, he pissed his pants!"

"That's a real man, hiding behind a girl!"

"Hey, thanks, pet," Scar-face called, his mouth split into a truly evil grin. "I'm so touched, I'm gonna let you go this time. Thanks for the Asian doll! We'll try not to break her, *too* quickly."

"What are you doing?" I hissed, betrayed. The thugs stalked forward, grinning, and I backed up, keeping them in my sights while glaring at the vampire. "What about all that talk of 'teaching' and 'preparing' me and all that crap? What, you're just going to throw me to the wolves now?"

"Your sense of predator and prey is backward," the vampire said in a low voice, so that only I could hear. I wanted to throw something at him, but the approaching gang members were more of a problem. The raw lust in their eyes made me feel sick, and I felt a snarl rising in my throat. "This will show you exactly where you stand on the food chain."

"Kanin! Dammit, what am I supposed to do?"

Kanin shrugged and leaned against a wall. "Try not to kill anyone."

The thugs rushed me. I tensed as one grabbed me around the waist, trying to lift me off my feet and push me to the ground. I hissed as his arms touched me, planted my feet, and shoved him away as hard as I could.

He flew backward as if he weighed nothing at all, crashing onto the hood of a car twenty feet away. I blinked in astonishment, but the next thug came rushing up with a howl, swinging a fist at my face.

Instinctively, I raised a hand and felt the meaty fist smack into my palm, surprising us both. He tried pulling back, but I squeezed hard, feeling bones crunch and grind together, and gave it a sharp twist. His wrist snapped with a popping sound, and the thug screamed.

Two more Blood Angels came at me from different directions. They moved slowly, like they were running through water, at least that's how it looked to me. I easily sidestepped the first lunge and kicked the thug in the knee, feeling it snap under my ankle. He jerked sideways and smashed to the ground. His friend swung at me with a lead pipe; I grabbed it, wrenched it from his grasp, and backhanded him across the face with it.

The scent of blood from the gang member's cheek misted on the air, and something inside me responded. I pounced on him with a roar, feeling my teeth burst through my gums.

The bark of gunfire shattered the night and something small whipped past my head. I felt the wind from its passing rip at my hair, and I spun into a crouch, hissing and baring my fangs. Scar-face's eyes went wide, a string of swearwords falling from his lips as he pointed a smoking pistol at me.

"Vampire!" he shrieked, amid a flurry of cussing. "Oh, shit! Shit! Get away from me! Get away—!"

He took aim, and I tensed to fling myself across the pavement, to pounce on my prey and drive my fangs deep into his throat. But suddenly, his eyes went wide, and he was lifted off his feet, kicking helplessly as Kanin picked him up as easily as a cat, wrenched the gun away, and threw him into a wall.

The crack of the Blood Angel's head against the brick pierced my wild, foaming rage and brought everything into focus again. I shook free of the bloodlust, the consuming Hunger, and gazed around in both horror and amazement. Five bodies lay on the ground, moaning, broken and bleeding. By my hand. I looked at Kanin, who tossed the gun almost disdainfully and raised an eyebrow as I approached.

"You knew," I said softly, glancing at one dazed Blood Angel. "You knew what I would do—that's why you let them attack me." He didn't answer, and I realized I wasn't shaking with fear or adrenaline or anything. My heart was still and cold. I glared up at Kanin, furious at his manipulation. "I could have killed them all."

"How many times must I tell you?" Kanin said, peering down at me. "You are a *vampire* now. You are no longer human. You are a wolf to their sheep—stronger, faster, more savage than they could ever be. They are *food,* Allison Sekemoto. And deep down, your demon will always see them as such."

I looked at Scar-face lying in a heap beside the wall. Though his forehead was cut open and a large purple bruise had already begun to form, he groaned and tried to get up, only to slump back again, dazed. "Then why didn't you kill him?" I asked.

Kanin's stare went cold. Turning, he walked stiffly over to the gang leader, grabbed him by the scruff and dragged him back to me, throwing him at my feet.

"Drink," he ordered in a steely voice. "But remember, take too much, and you will kill the host. Take too little, and you will have to feed again very soon. Find the balance, if you care whether you drain them or not. Usually five or six swallows will suffice."

I looked down at the gang leader and recoiled. Chomping through a blood bag was one thing, but biting the neck of a living, breathing person? I had been so eager to do it a moment ago, when my Hunger and fury were raging, but now I felt nauseated.

Kanin continued to stare at me. "You will do this, or you will starve yourself to the point of frenzy and kill someone," he said in a flat voice. "This is what being a vampire is about, our most basic, primal need. Now..." With one hand, he hauled the thug up and grabbed his hair with the other, wrenching his head back and exposing his throat. "Drink."

Reluctantly, I stepped forward. The human moaned and tried fending me off, but I easily slapped his arms away and bent close to the hollow at the base of his throat. My fangs lengthened as I inhaled and sensed the warm blood coursing just below the surface of the skin. The scent of life was overwhelmingly strong in my nose and mouth. Before I could even think about what I was doing, I lunged forward and bit down hard.

The Blood Angel gasped and jerked, twitching weakly. Warm thickness flowed into my mouth, rich and hot and strong. I growled and bit down harder, eliciting a strangled cry from my prey. I felt heat spreading through my body, filling me with strength, with power. It was intoxicating. It was…I couldn't describe it. It was bliss, pure and simple. I let my eyes slip shut, almost in a trance, consumed with wanting more, more…

Someone took my hair, pulling me back from my prey, breaking the connection. I snarled and tried to lunge forward again, but an arm barred my way, moving me back. The thug's body collapsed bonelessly to the ground. I snarled again and tried to reach it, fighting the arm that held me back.

"Enough!" Kanin's voice rang with authority, and he shook me, hard. My head snapped back like a rag doll's, making me dizzy for a moment. "Allison, enough," he repeated as my vision slowly cleared. "Any more and you'll kill him."

I blinked and backed off a step, the Hunger slowly ebbing away into something that wasn't frantic and raging. Horrified, I stared at the Blood Angel crumpled on the pavement. He was pale, barely breathing, two dark puncture wounds oozing crimson from his throat. I'd almost killed him. Again. If

Kanin hadn't stopped me, I would've drained him dry. Self-loathing curled my stomach. For all my hatred of vampires, all my resolve not to be like them, I was no better than the worst bloodsucker to stalk the streets.

"Seal the wound," Kanin ordered, pointing to the gang leader. His voice was cool, unsympathetic. "Finish what you started."

I wanted to ask how, but suddenly I knew. Bending down, I pressed my tongue against the two small punctures and felt them close. Even then, I could sense the blood slowly pumping beneath the skin, and it took all my willpower not to bite him a second time.

Standing up, I turned to Kanin, who nodded his head once, watching me. "Now," he said, his voice dark and unyielding, "you understand."

I did. I gazed at the bodies scattered about the lot, at the destruction I'd caused, and I knew. I was truly inhuman. Humans were prey. I craved their blood like the worst addict on the street. They were sheep, cattle, and I was the wolf, stalking them through the night. I had become a monster.

"From here on," Kanin said, "you will have to decide what kind of demon you will be. Not all meals will come to you so easily, ignorant and seeking to do you harm. What will you do if your prey invites you inside, offers you a place at the table? What will you do if they flee, or cower down, begging you not to hurt them? How you stalk your prey is something you must come to terms with, or you will quickly drive yourself mad. And once you cross that threshold, there is no coming back from it."

"How do you do it?" I whispered. Kanin shook his head with a chuckle.

"My method would not help you," he said as we started to leave the lot. "You will have to find your own way."

As we entered the alley, we passed one of the thugs who was just starting to come around. He groaned and swayed as he staggered to his feet, gasping with pain, and though my Hunger was sated, something inside me reacted to the sight of a wounded, helpless creature. I half turned with a growl, fangs lengthening, before Kanin grabbed my arm and dragged me away into the darkness.

CHAPTER 6

When I awoke next, I was alone, lying on a dusty cot in one of the old hospital rooms. It was night once more, and I knew the sun had set about an hour ago. Kanin had kept me out last night until it was nearly dawn, explaining that, as a vampire, I needed to know when the sun approached and how much time I had to seek shelter. Despite the legends, he explained, we wouldn't immediately burst into flames, but our body chemistry had changed now that we were, technically, dead. He likened it to a human disease called porphyria, where toxic substances in the skin caused it to blacken and rupture when exposed to ultraviolet sunlight. Caught outside with no shelter, the direct rays of the sun would burn our exposed skin until it did, eventually, catch fire. It was a messy and extremely painful way to die, he said to my horrified expression, and something you wanted to avoid at all costs.

Despite this, we almost didn't make it back. I remembered approaching the ruined hospital, growing more sleepy as the sky went from pitch-black to navy blue. But even through the lethargy, I had felt a growing panic and desperation, urging me on to find shelter. As I'd fought desperately against the sluggishness weighing me down, Kanin had scooped me up, holding me close as he strode through the grass and weeds, and I had drifted off against his chest.

The events of the previous night came back to me, and I shivered. It still felt unreal, as if everything I'd been through had happened to someone else. Experimentally, I tried growing my fangs and felt them lengthen immediately, pushing through my gums, sharp and lethal. I wasn't hungry, though, which was both a relief and a disappointment. I wondered how often I would have to...feed. How soon before I could plunge my fangs into someone's throat and have that rush of heat and power flow into me—

I shook myself, furious and disgusted. One night as a vampire, and I was already slipping, giving in to the demon.

"I'm not like them," I seethed to the darkness, to the coiling thing inside me. "Dammit, I *will* beat this. Somehow. I will not become a soulless monster, I swear it."

Pushing myself off the bed, I ducked into the dark, narrow hallway in search of Kanin.

He was sitting at the desk in the office, sifting through a large stack of papers. His eyes flicked to me as I came in, then he continued to read.

"Um." I perched on one of the overturned cabinets. "Thanks. For not letting me burn this morning. I suppose that's what would happen if I get stuck outside in the sun, right?"

"It's something I wouldn't wish on my worst enemy," Kanin

replied without looking up. I watched him, remembering how he'd carried me inside, and frowned.

"So, why were you able to stay awake when I fell asleep?"

"Practice." Kanin turned over one sheet and started on another. "All vampires must sleep in the daytime," he went on, still not looking at me. "We are nocturnal creatures, like owls and bats, and something in our body makeup makes us lethargic and tired when the sun is high overhead. With practice and a great deal of willpower, we can fight off the need to sleep for a little while. It just grows more difficult the longer we stay awake."

"Well...thank you." I stared at the top of his head and wrinkled my nose. "I guess I'm glad you're extremely stubborn, then."

He finally looked up, raising an eyebrow. "You are welcome," he said, sounding amused. "How are you feeling now?"

"Okay, I guess." I picked at a sheet of paper on the cabinet. No one ever asked me how I was feeling, not since I was young. "I'm not hungry, anyway."

"That's normal," Kanin explained as he started on a new stack of paper. "Typically, barring wounds and overexertion, one needs to take blood every fortnight to remain fed and sated."

"Fortnight?"

"Every two weeks."

"Oh."

"Though it is not unusual for a vampire, if he has the means, to feed every night. The Prince of the city and his council, you can be sure, indulge far more often than that.

But two weeks is the safest amount of time one can go without human blood. After that, you will get hungrier and hungrier, and nothing will satisfy you until you feed again."

"Yeah, you might've mentioned that once or twice."

He eyed me over his paper and set it down, coming around the desk to lean against the front. "Do you want me to continue teaching you?" he asked. "Or would you like me to leave so you may figure everything out yourself?"

"Sorry," I muttered, looking away. "Still getting used to this whole being-dead thing, I guess." A thought came to me, and I looked back, frowning. "So, what am I supposed to do, once this 'training' is over?"

"I suspect you will continue to live as a vampire."

"That's not what I mean, and you know it, Kanin." I gestured vaguely at the ceiling. "Will I be allowed into the Inner City? Will the other vampires let me past the gates now that I'm one of them?"

Now that I'm one of them. That was a disgusting thought. *I'll never be one of them,* I promised myself. *Not completely. I'm not like them. I won't sink to their level, won't think of humans as nothing more than animals.*

"Unfortunately," Kanin said, "there is more to it than that."

It sounded as if he was going to give another lecture, so I dropped into the chair from the night before, resting my chin in my hands. Kanin paused, watching me a moment, before he continued. "You're a vampire now, so, yes, you'll be allowed past the gates into the Inner City. That is, if you do not bring up your association with me. But you need to understand the politics of your undead brethren before you can strike out on your own. There is a hierarchy among city vampires, a chain of rank and command, that you must be aware of if you hope to fit in."

"Fit in," I repeated and snorted. "I've been a street rat and a Fringer my whole life. I don't think I'll be cozying up to the vampires of the Inner City anytime soon."

"Regardless." Kanin's voice didn't change. "This is something you need to know. Not all vampires are created equal. Are you aware of the differences between the Prince of this city and his followers?"

I frowned. To me, all bloodsuckers were the same; they had fangs, they were dead, they drank blood. But Kanin wouldn't accept that for an answer, and I really didn't want him to leave yet, so… "I know the city has a Prince," I replied. "Salazar. And all the other vamps listen to him."

"Yes." Kanin nodded approval. "Within every city, there is a Prince, a Master Vampire, the strongest and most powerful of them all. He, or she, heads the council, commands the lesser vampires, and makes most of the decisions within the Inner City. That's how most vampire cities work, though there are a few that are set up differently. I've heard of territories where only one vampire rules over everything, though that type of city is extremely rare and usually doesn't last long. The Prince would have to be very strong, to keep his city from falling to other vampires or even his own humans."

"How many vampire cities are there?"

"Worldwide?" Kanin shrugged. "No one really knows. It's constantly in flux, you see, especially within the smaller regions. Cities rising and falling, attempts to take over another's territory, disease or rabids wiping out whole populations. But the largest vampire cities, like New Covington, have survived since the plague, and there are perhaps a few dozen, worldwide."

"All ruled by a Master."

"Usually. Like I said before, there are exceptions, but, yes, most cities are ruled by a Master."

That meant there were several very strong, probably very old, vampires out there. That was something to keep in mind, though it sounded as if most of them stayed in their cities, like Salazar, and never ventured beyond the Wall.

"Beneath the Prince," Kanin continued, "are the Type-2s, the vampires who have been sired by a Master. They are not as powerful as the Prince, but they are formidable in their own right, and usually make up the council, the elite guard and the Prince's trusted seconds. Are you following so far?"

"Type-2s?" I bit down a smirk. "I was expecting something a little more…exotic, and vampirey-sounding. Type-2 sounds like the symptoms of a disease."

Kanin shot me an exasperated look. "The bloodlines of certain old families are extremely long and complex," he explained in a sharper voice. "It would be pointless to explain them to a new vampire, so I am giving you the simplified version."

"Sorry. Go on."

"Beneath them," Kanin continued, "are the Type-3s, the mongrels, and these are the most common and least powerful in the hierarchy. They have been sired by either a Type-2 or another mongrel, and they are the type of vampire you will most likely encounter wandering the streets. Mongrels make up the vast majority of the population, and they're the weakest of us all, though still stronger and faster than any human.

"So, the stronger the vamp who sired you, the stronger you're likely to be?"

"To a point." Kanin leaned back, resting his palms on the desk. "Before the virus, vampires were spread across the world, hidden from mankind, blending into society. Most of them were mongrels, Type-3s, and if they occasionally sired another vampire, they would always create a mongrel. The Masters and their covens were few and far between, secluded from the rest of the world, until the Red Lung virus hit. When the humans began to die from the virus, our food source disappeared, and we were in danger of starving or going mad.

"Then rabids started to appear, and things grew even more chaotic. At that time, we didn't know whether the rabids were the final effect of the Red Lung virus or if they were something new, but there was mass panic for both humans and vampires. Eventually a few ingenious Masters devised a way to keep the few remaining, noninfected humans close, creating a never-ending food supply in exchange for protection from outside threats. And so the vampire cities were born. But there are so few Masters now." He paused and looked away. "And that means fewer vampires every year. It's only a matter of time before our race disappears completely."

He didn't sound sad about it. More…resigned. I blinked. "What do you mean?" I asked. "I thought you said mongrels or Type-2s or whatevers could create other vampires. What do you mean, you're dying out?"

He was silent, his eyes dark and far away. Finally, he looked up, staring right at me. "Do you know how the rabids were created?" he asked in a soft voice. "Do you know what they are?"

I swallowed. "You mean, besides the obvious?"

"They're vampires," Kanin continued, as if I hadn't said anything. "Originally, rabids were vampires. In the early stages of the plague, a group of scientists discovered that vampires were immune to the virus that was killing the human race. Up until that point, our race was virtually unknown, hidden and scattered throughout the world. We were happy to remain the monsters of Halloween and horror films. It was better that way."

"So what happened?"

Kanin made a disgusted sound in the back of his throat. "A fool of a Master vampire went to the scientists himself, exposing our kind, wanting to 'save the human race.' Apparently, he thought—and rightly so—that if mankind went extinct, vampires would soon follow. The scientists told him that vampire blood was the key to finding a cure, that they could beat the Red Lung virus if they only had live samples to work with. So, the Master tracked down and captured other vampires for the scientists to experiment on, betraying his own kind for a cure that would save the world." Kanin shook his head. "Unfortunately, what they created, what they turned those vampires into, was far worse than anything anyone had anticipated."

"The rabids," I guessed.

He nodded. "They should have destroyed them all when they had the chance. Instead, the rabids escaped, carrying inside them the mutated Red Lung virus that had killed most of humanity. Those same pathogens spread rapidly across the world, infecting both human and vampire. Only now, instead of dying from Red Lung, the infected humans *changed*. They became like the original rabids themselves: vicious and mindless, craving blood, unable to come out in the daytime. Over five billion people succumbed to the mutated virus and went rabid. And whenever a vampire came into contact with someone who carried the virus, he became infected as well. Most of us didn't turn, but the virus spread through our ranks just as quickly as the humans'. And now, over the course of six generations, *all* vampires have become carriers of Rabidism. Unlike humans with Red Lung, our bodies adapted more quickly to the virus, and we were able to fight it off. But our race is still in decline."

"Why?"

"Because the virus prevents the creation of new vampires," Kanin said gravely. "Masters can still sire Type-2s, and on the very, very rare occasion, other Masters. But for every new vampire he creates, there is the chance he won't sire a vampire at all, but a rabid. Type-2s sire rabids more than ninety percent of the time, and mongrels?" Kanin shook his head. "Mongrels will always create a rabid. They cannot sire anything else. Most Masters have sworn not to create new offspring. The risk of Rabidism inside the city is too great, and they are very protective of their remaining food supply."

I thought of the sick deer, flailing blindly about, the absolute viciousness of the rabids themselves, and shuddered. If this was the world outside the city walls, it was a wonder anyone could survive out there. "So," I mused, looking up at Kanin, "I suppose I'm a carrier now, too, right?"

"That is correct."

"So, why didn't I turn into a rabid?"

He shook his head. "Think about it," he said quietly. "Think about what I told you. You're bright enough to fig-ure it out."

I thought about it. "I didn't turn into a rabid," I said slowly, "because…you're a Master vampire." He gave me a humor-less smile, and I looked at him with new eyes. Kanin was a Master vampire; he could be a Prince. "But, if you're a Mas-ter, why don't you have a city of your own? I thought—"

"Enough talking." He pushed himself off the desk. "We have somewhere to be tonight, and it is a long way through the undercity. I suggest we get moving."

I blinked at his sudden change of mood. "Where are we going this time?"

Kanin spun so gracefully I didn't even know he'd moved until he had me pinned against the wall, the long, curved blade of his dagger pressed against my throat. I froze, but a split second later the pressure on my neck was gone and the knife disappeared into the folds of his black coat. Kanin gave me a faint, tight smile, and stepped away.

"If I was an enemy, you'd be dead now," he said, walking down the hall again like nothing had happened. I clutched my chest, knowing that if I'd still had a heartbeat, it would have been pounding through my ribs. "The city can be a danger-ous place. You're going to need something bigger than that two-inch blade you keep in your pocket to defend yourself."

As A STREET RAT, I'd had the underground tunnels below the city as my turf, my secret passageways, the hidden road that let me slip through the districts unseen. I'd been proud of my knowledge of the city's underworld. But my vampire mentor either had a near-perfect memory, or he'd been through the dark, twisty underground many, many times before. I followed him through passageways I'd never seen, never known existed. Kanin never slowed down or appeared to be lost, so keeping up with him was a challenge sometimes.

"Allison." There was a hint of exasperation in his voice as he turned, pausing to wait for me. "The night is waning, and we still have a good ways to cover before we reach our destination. Would you kindly get a move on? This is the third time I've had to wait for you."

"You know, you could slow down a little." I leaped down from a dead subway car and jogged back to him, ducking a pipe that dangled above the tracks. "In case you haven't noticed, short people have short legs. I have to take three steps to one of yours, so stop griping."

He shook his head and continued down the cement tunnel, walking a bit slower now, so it was a small victory. I hurried to keep pace. "I had no idea there was another railway system down here," I said, gazing at the hulk of a rusty car, overturned on the tracks. "I knew the one that ran below the third and fourth districts, but it was blocked when a building collapsed above it. Where does this one go?"

"This one," Kanin said, his voice echoing down the dark tunnel, "runs straight through the heart of the Inner City, right between the towers themselves. The station that leads down to it has long been closed off, and the tunnels have been sealed, but we're not going all the way to the towers."

"We're below the Inner City?" I glanced up at the ceiling as if I could see the looming vampire buildings through the concrete and cement. I wondered what it was like up there; glass towers and sparkling lights, well-dressed humans, and even vehicles that still worked. A far cry from the dirty, hopeless, starving existence of the Fringe.

"Don't be too enamored," Kanin warned, as if reading my thoughts. "The humans of the Inner City might be better dressed and better fed, but only because they are useful. And what do you think will happen to them, once their master grows bored or displeased?"

"I'm guessing they don't have a retirement plan."

Kanin snorted.

"And you want me to eventually live up there?"

He glanced down at me, his expression softening. "Allison, how you live your life is up to you. I can only give you the skills you need to survive. But eventually, you will have to make your own decisions, come to your own terms about what you are. You are Vampire, but what kind of monster you become is out of my hands."

"What if I don't want to live up there?" I gave him a sideways look, then focused on the tracks at my feet, watching them glimmer as we passed. "What if I wanted to…go with you?"

"No." Kanin's voice was sharp, booming down the tunnel, making me wince. "No," he said again, softer this time. "I would not suffer anyone to endure the path I walk. My road must always be traveled alone."

And that was the end of it.

The subway went on, but Kanin took me down another, narrower tunnel, through a dozen more twists and turns, until I was completely lost. We passed under storm drains and metal grates, where I could look up and finally see the city above, gleaming and bright. But the streets seemed empty, abandoned. I'd been expecting crowds of people out walking the streets, unafraid of the night and the predators surrounding them. Maybe I would even catch a glimpse of a vampire, surrounded by his pets and thralls, strolling down the sidewalk. A vehicle passed overhead, making a manhole cover clink, filling the quiet with the growl of its engine. I gaped at the sight of a real, working car, but other than that, the city was as silent as the Fringe.

And, as we continued under the quiet streets, the lights revealed other things, too.

You didn't notice it at first, being dazzled by the lights and the tall buildings, but the Inner City was just as broken and damaged as the worst parts of the Fringe. There were no rows of gleaming mansions, no buildings overflowing with food and clothes and everything you'd need, no cars for every family. There *were* a lot of broken, half-decayed buildings that looked slightly more taken care of than the rest of the city. There were flickering streetlamps and rusty cars and weeds growing through walls and concrete. Except for the trio of gleaming vampire towers in the distance, the Inner City looked like a brighter, well-lit version of the Fringe.

"Not what you expected, is it?" Kanin mused, as we ducked into another cement tube and the lights faded above us. I followed, not knowing if I was vindicated or disappointed.

"Where are all the people?" I wondered. "And the vampires?"

"The humans who are awake are all working," Kanin said. "Keeping the electrical grid up and running, managing the remains of the sewer systems, repairing broken machinery. That's why the vampires look for those who are talented or knowledgeable or skilled and take them into the city— they need them to keep it running. They also have humans to man their factories, clean and repair their buildings, and grow the food needed for the rest of the population. The rest of them, guards, thralls, pets and concubines, serve them in other ways."

"But...*everyone* can't be working."

"True," Kanin agreed. "Everyone else is behind closed, locked doors, keeping off the streets and out of sight as much as they can. They are much closer to the monsters than the people of the Fringe, and they have just as much reason to be afraid."

"Wow," I muttered, shaking my head. "Wouldn't everyone back home be surprised to learn how it really is up there."

Kanin didn't say anything to that, and we traveled in silence for a while.

He finally stopped at a steel ladder that went up to a metal grate on the ceiling. Pushing it aside with the ease of vampire strength, he climbed through the hole and beckoned me to follow.

"Where are we now?" I asked, trailing him down another long cement hallway. At the end of this one, we hit a rusty metal door, locked, of course, but Kanin put his shoulder to the metal and bashed it open.

"We," he replied, stepping back for me to take in my surroundings, "are in the basement storage of the city's old museum."

I gazed around in wonder. We were standing at the edge

of the largest room I'd ever seen in my life, a warehouse of cement and steel that stretched farther than even my vampire vision reached. Rusting metal shelves created a labyrinth of aisles, hundreds of narrow corridors that vanished into the back of the room. The contents of those shelves were covered in sheets or stored in wooden boxes, wrapped in a thick film of spiderwebs and dust. If I took in a breath I could smell the choking stench of mold and fungi, growing everywhere, but surprisingly, the shelves seemed fairly intact.

"I can't believe this place is so...unbroken," I said, as we started down one of the narrow aisles. Under a filthy sheet, I caught a glimpse of yellow bone and lifted the corner to reveal the skeleton of some kind of enormous cat, frozen in a crouch. I stared at it, amazed, wondering why anyone would want to keep the dead bones of an animal. It was kind of creepy, seeing it like that, without skin and fur. "What the heck is this place anyway?"

"Before the plague, museums were places of history," Kanin explained as I hurried away from the cat to catch up. His voice echoed in the vastness. "Places of collected knowledge, places where they stored all the items, memories and artifacts of other cultures."

I paused, catching sight of a mannequin dressed in furs and animal hide. Feathers poked out of its hair, and it held some kind of stone ax. "Why?"

"To remember the past, to not let it fade away. The customs, histories, religions and governments of a thousand cultures are stored here. There are other places like this one all around the world, hidden and forgotten by man. Places that still hold their secrets, waiting to be discovered again."

"I can't believe the vamps haven't burned this place to the ground."

"They tried," Kanin replied. "The building above us has been destroyed, no trace of it remains. But the city vampires are mostly concerned with what happens on the surface—they rarely venture down into the tunnels and the secrets below the earth. If they knew about this place, you can be sure they would have burned it to ashes."

I scowled, hating the vampires again. "And humans will never know about it, will they?" I muttered, following Kanin down an aisle, feeling morose. "All this knowledge, right under their feet, and they'll never know."

"Maybe not today." Kanin stopped at a shelf holding a long, narrow wooden box. Faded red letters were printed on the side, below all the cobwebs and dust, but it was difficult to read. "But there will come a time when man is no longer concerned only with survival, when he will once more be curious as to who came before him, what life was like a thousand years ago, and he will seek out answers to these questions. Maybe it won't happen for a hundred years or so, but humans' curiosity has always driven them to find answers. Even our race cannot keep them in the dark forever."

He broke the box open and rummaged through the contents. I heard the clink and scrape of metal, and then he pulled something out.

It was a sword, a long, double-edged blade with a black metal hilt that looked like a cross. Kanin held it in one hand, but the blade itself was huge, probably close to five feet. With the hilt, it was a few inches taller than me.

"Two-handed German greatsword," he said, giving me,

and it, a scrutinizing look, sizing us up. "Probably too big for
you."

"You think?"

He replaced it and opened another box from the shelf overhead, this time pulling out a large, spiked ball on a chain. It
looked extremely nasty, and I was intrigued, but he let it drop
with barely a second glance.

"Hey, what was that?" Easing forward, I tried peering into
the box on tiptoe, but he shouldered me away. "Oh, come
on. I want to see the big-spiky-ball thing."

"You do *not* need a flail." Kanin scowled, as though imagining what I could do with it. I tried peeking into the box
again, and he gave me an exasperated look, warning me back.
I glared at him.

"Fine. Then tell me, oh, great one. What are we looking
for? What *do* I need?"

He pulled out another weapon, a spear with a long metal
tip, and put it back with a shake of his head. "I'm not sure."

I peeked under another cloth, where a stuffed-dog-looking
thing stared back sightlessly. "Why are we looking for ancient
weapons, anyway?" I muttered, dropping the cloth. "Wouldn't
it be easier to use, oh, I don't know…a gun?"

"Guns require ammunition," Kanin replied without looking up. "Ammunition is difficult to find, even if the Prince
did not have a stranglehold on the automatic weapon distri-
bution in the city. And an empty gun is about as useful as a
large paperweight. Besides, guns are impractical for dealing
with our kind. Unless you can somehow tear off our head,
bullets will only slow us down at best. To adequately protect
yourself from a vampire, you're going to need a blade. Now…"

He moved to the next box, tearing off the lid, nails and all. "Why don't you make yourself useful and look through a few of these yourself? See if anything jumps out at you. Remember, you're looking for a *blade*. Not a mace or a maul or a huge spiked chain that you'd probably hurt yourself with trying to learn."

"Fine." I wandered down the aisle, looking at random articles. "But I still say the flail looked like it could bash in a vamp's head pretty efficiently."

"Allison—"

"I'm going, I'm going."

More wooden boxes lined the aisle to either side, covered in dust. I brushed back a film of cobwebs and grime to read the words on the side of the nearest carton. *Longswords: Medieval Europe, 12th century.* The rest was lost to time and age. Another read: *Musketeer Rapie...*something or other. Another apparently had a full suit of gladiator armor, whatever a gladiator was.

A clang from Kanin's direction showed him holding up a large, double-bladed ax, before he laid it aside and moved on to another shelf.

One box caught my attention. It was long and narrow, like the other boxes, but instead of words, it had strange symbols printed down the side. Curious, I wrenched off the lid and reached in, shifting through layers of plastic and foam, until my fingers closed around something long and smooth.

I pulled it out. The long, slightly curved sheath was black and shiny, and a hilt poked out of the end, marked with diamond pattern in black and red. I grasped that hilt and pulled the blade free, sending a metallic shiver through the air and down my spine.

As soon as I drew it, I knew I had found what Kanin wanted.

The blade gleamed in the darkness, long and slender, like a silver ribbon. I could sense the razor sharpness of the edge without even touching it. The sword itself was light and graceful, and fit perfectly into my palm, as if it had been made for me. I swept it in a wide arc, feeling it slice through the air, and imagined this was a blade that could pass through a snarling rabid without even slowing down.

A chuckle interrupted me. Kanin stood a few yards away, arms crossed, shaking his head. His mouth was pulled into a resigned grin.

"I should have known," he said, coming forward. "I should have known you would be drawn to that. It's very fitting, actually."

"It's perfect," I said, holding up the sword. "What is it, anyway?"

Kanin regarded me in amusement. "What you're holding is called a *katana*. Long ago, a race of warriors known as the samurai carried them. The sword was more than a weapon—to the samurai, their blades were an extension of their souls. It was the symbol of their culture and their most prized possession."

I didn't really need the history lesson, but it was pretty cool to think that there was an entire race of people who'd carried these once. "What happened to them?" I asked, sheathing the sword carefully. "Did they all die out?"

Kanin's grin grew wider, as if he was enjoying his own private joke. "No, Allison Sekemoto. I would say not."

I frowned, waiting for him to explain, but he stepped back and motioned me to follow. "If you're going to carry that blade," he said as we headed back through the maze of aisles and shelves, "you'll have to learn how to use it. It is not a pocketknife you can just swing in circles and hope it hits the target. It is an elegant weapon and deserves better than that."

"I don't know, swinging it in a circle sounds like a pretty good trick to me."

He gave me another of his exasperated looks. "Having a weapon you do not know how to use is better than not having one at all, but not by much," he said, ducking through the door and entering the narrow hallway. "Especially when dealing with vampires. *Especially* when dealing with older vampires who already know how to fight—they're the most dangerous. They'll cut off your head with your own blade, if you're not careful."

We came to the metal grate he'd pulled up earlier, and Kanin dropped out of sight, back into the sewers. I clutched my new prize to my chest and followed.

"So, are you going to teach me, then?" I asked as I hit the ground.

"Oh, I'm afraid he won't be teaching you anything, girl," a cool voice said from the darkness. "Except, perhaps, how to die a horrid and painful death."

I froze, and in that second, two figures melted out of the darkness of the tunnel, smiling as they came to stand before us. I knew instantly that they were vampires; pale skin and hollow eyes aside, I could sense, in a strange, unexplainable way, that they were just like me. In the dead, bloodsucking sense, at least. The woman's dark, curly hair tumbled elegantly down her back; she wore heels and a business suit that hugged her body like snakeskin. The man was lean and pale, all sharp points and angles, but he still managed to fill out his suit jacket. And he stood over six feet tall.

Kanin went rigid. A tiny movement, and the knife appeared in his hand.

"You've got some nerve to show your face here, Kanin," the female vampire said in a conversational tone, smiling and showing perfectly white teeth. "The Prince knows you're here, and he wants your head on a platter. We've been sent to oblige him." She stepped toward us, oozing forward like a snake. Her bloodred lips parted in a smile, showing fangs, and she turned her predatory gaze on me. "But who's this little chick, Kanin? Your newest protégé? How charming, continuing your cursed bloodline. Does she know who you really are?"

"She's no one," Kanin said flatly. "She doesn't matter—the only thing you need to worry about is me."

The vampiress's grin grew savage. "Oh, I don't think so, Kanin. After we remove your head, we'll drag your little spawn back to the Prince and watch him take her apart, piece by piece. Isn't that right, Richards?"

The male vampire still didn't say anything, but he smiled, showing his fangs.

"How does that sound, chicky?" the female vamp said, still smirking at me. "Don't you feel special? You can have your heart removed and eaten by the Prince of the city himself."

"He can try," I shot back and felt my own fangs lengthen as I bared them in a snarl. Both vampires laughed.

"Oh, she is a firebrand, isn't she?" The female vamp gave me a patronizing look. "One of those disgusting Fringers, I take it? I simply love your affection for hopeless cases. But then, that's what got you into this mess in the first place, isn't it?"

Her companion reached into his suit jacket and pulled out a thin, foot-long blade. It was a delicate weapon, slender and razor sharp, made for precision. Somehow, it seemed more frightening than if the vampire had drawn an ax or even a gun.

"Allison," Kanin muttered, stepping in front of me, "stay back. Don't engage them. Don't try to help me, understand?"

I growled, gripping the sheath of my katana. "I'm not afraid of them. I can help."

"Promise me," Kanin said in a low, tense voice. "Promise me you will not get involved."

"But—"

He turned, pinning me with a cold, frightening glare. His eyes had darkened to pure black, hollow and depthless, with no light behind them. "Your word," he almost whispered. I swallowed.

"All right." I looked down, unable to meet that unnerving gaze. "I promise."

He reached down and grasped the hilt of my katana, drawing it in one smooth motion as he turned to face his attackers. "Go," he told me, and I backed away, retreating behind a cement pillar as Kanin gave the katana a wicked flourish and stepped forward.

The female vamp hissed and sank into a crouch, stretching the fabric of her suit. I saw her nails then, very long and red and sharp, like giant talons, digging into the pavement. She hissed again, looking more like a beast than anything remotely human, and sprang forward.

Kanin met her in the center of the room, the katana whirling through the air. They moved faster than I could follow, slashing, whirling, leaping back and lunging forward again. The female vamp moved like some kind of mutant cat, springing at Kanin on all fours, even in high heels, raking at him with her claws. She was insanely fast, ducking the sword, leaping over it, teeth flashing as she shrieked and screamed and danced around him. Watching them fight, a cold feeling spread through my gut. I'd seen brawls before, even participated in a few. This wasn't a brawl; this was a brutal, screaming free-for-all between two monsters. I couldn't have beaten her, I realized with a sick feeling in my gut. Kanin was doing fine, fending off her attacks and striking back, vicious blows that barely missed the snarling whirlwind of death, but she would've torn me apart.

I was so focused on the female vamp, I didn't see the other vampire until he was behind Kanin, that thin, sharp blade moving to take off his head. I started to yell a warning, cursing myself for not seeing him sooner: the female was a colorful, lethal distraction while her partner moved in silently for the kill. But before I could say two words, Kanin's hand shot out, grabbed the female by the hair as she shrieked and clawed at his face, and threw her into her partner. They hit each other with a sickening crack. The male vampire stumbled backward, wincing, while the female vampire crumpled to the ground.

I thought that was it for her. The force Kanin had generated could've put a hole through a brick wall. But a half second later, the vampiress stirred and rose to her feet, shaking her head. She didn't even look dazed.

Now I was scared. I was certain the fight had been half over, but both enemy vamps approached Kanin again, smiling. Kanin waited patiently, the sword at his side. Blood streamed down the side of his face where the vampiress had clawed him, but he didn't seem to notice it. As they got closer, they split off, circling him from different directions. He raised the sword, circling with them, but he couldn't watch them both at the same time.

As expected, the vampiress attacked first, bounding in with a growl, and Kanin spun toward her. But halfway there, she stopped, leaping away, and the male vampire lunged at Kanin's open back.

Faster than thought, Kanin whirled, slashing at the second attacker, a blow that was vicious and powerful, but also left his back unprotected again. The male vampire ducked away, grinning, as the vampiress turned on a heel and flew at Kanin once more, silent and deadly. I saw the triumph in her eyes as she leaped at him, fangs bared, claws slashing down at his neck.

Kanin didn't move. But I saw the point of the blade turn as he spun it around and stabbed *backward,* passing it against his ribs, and the vampiress's lunge carried her right onto the tip, which went out through her back.

The vampiress screamed, equal parts fury and pain, and

ripped at Kanin's shoulders. He stepped forward and in one quick motion, drew his other blade, yanked the sword out of the vamp's stomach and spun, cutting off her head.

The head bounced twice, then rolled toward me and stopped a few feet away, glaring up with a frozen snarl. I shuddered and looked back toward the fight, where Kanin was still facing the remaining vampire. It roared, fangs bared, and lunged at him with the knife stabbing at his chest. Kanin took one step back, sweeping both arms forward in a scissoring motion as the vampire came within reach, cutting through its head and chest. The head fell away and the body split open, and the vampire crumpled to the pavement, nearly cut in two.

I bit my cheek, pressing my face against the pillar to avoid being sick. I didn't have much time to recover, as Kanin swept up and hauled me away, thrusting the sword back into my arms.

"Hurry," he ordered, and I didn't need encouragement this time. We raced back to the hospital, where Kanin told me to stay put and not leave the underground until I heard from him again.

"Wait. Where are you going?" I asked.

"I have to go back and dump the bodies," he replied. "Somewhere on the surface, to lead the Prince away from the tunnels. Also, I'm going to have to feed before the night is out. Stay here. I'll be back before dawn."

He leaped up the elevator shaft, vanishing into the darkness, leaving me alone. I drew my sword, staring at the blood marring the once-pristine blade, and wondered what demons Kanin was running from.

Chapter 7

In the weeks that followed, my nights settled into a routine. I would wake up at sundown, grab my sword and find Kanin in the office. For a few hours, he would lecture me on vampire society, history, feeding habits, strengths and weaknesses. He would ask me questions, testing my knowledge of things I'd learned the night before, pleased when I remembered what I was supposed to. He also insisted on teaching me math, writing down simple and then more complex equations for me to solve, patiently explaining them when I couldn't. He made up logic puzzles for me to struggle through and gave me complex documents to read, asking me what they meant when I was done. And though I hated this, I forced myself to concentrate. This was knowledge, something I might be able to use against the vampires someday. Besides, Mom would've wanted me to learn, though I wasn't sure when long division would ever come in handy.

While I worked, Kanin read, shuffling through documents,

sometimes bringing in more boxes of papers to sift through. Sometimes, he would read an entire stack of paper, carefully setting each aside when he was done. Sometimes he would only glance at a pile of documents before crumpling them impatiently and shoving them away. As the days passed, he grew more impatient and agitated with every sheet he crumpled in his fist, every wad he threw across the room. When I got up the nerve, once, to ask him what he was looking for, I received an annoyed glare and a terse command to keep working. I wondered why he hadn't left the city yet; the vampires were obviously out there, looking for him. What was so important that he would risk staying down here in this dark little ruin, going through endless files and half-burned documents? But Kanin kept me so busy with learning everything he thought was important—vampire history and reading and math—that I didn't have the time or brain capacity to wonder about other things.

And really, I could respect that. He had his secrets, and I had mine. I wasn't about to go poking around his private life, especially when he didn't ask *me* anything about my past, either. It was sort of an unspoken truce between us; I wouldn't pry, and he would keep teaching me how to be a vampire. Anything that didn't have to do with survival wasn't that important.

After midnight was my favorite time. After several hours of straining my brain, getting bored and irritated and feeling as if my head was about to explode, Kanin would finally announce that I could stop for the night. After that, we would make our way to our floor's reception area, which he had cleared of debris and chairs and broken furniture, and he would teach me something different.

"Keep your head up," he stated as I lunged at him, swinging my sword at his chest. At first, I was a little worried, fighting him with a live blade. It shocked me, how quickly I could move, so fast that sometimes the room blurred around me, the sword weighing next to nothing in my hands. But Kanin made it clear that he was in no danger, after the first lesson left me crumpled in my bed for the rest of the night, bruised and aching, freaky vampire healing or not.

Stepping aside, Kanin rapped me on the back of the head with a sawed-off mop handle, not lightly. My skull throbbed, and I turned on him with a snarl.

"You're dead," Kanin announced, waggling the dowel at me. I bared my fangs, but he wasn't impressed. "Stop using the blade like an ax," he ordered, as we circled each other again. "You're not a lumberjack trying to hack down a tree. You're a dancer, and the sword is an extension of your arm. Move with the blade and keep your eyes on your enemy's upper body, not their weapon."

"I don't know what a lumberjack is," I growled at him. He gave me an annoyed look and motioned me forward again.

I gripped the hilt, relaxing my muscles. *Don't fight the sword,* Kanin had told me on countless occasions. *The sword already knows how to cut, how to kill. If you're tense, if you only use brute strength, your strikes will be slow and awkward. Relax and move with the blade, not against it.*

This time, when I attacked, I let the blade lead me there, darting forward in a silver blur. Kanin stepped aside, swatting at my head with the dowel again, but I half turned, catching the stick with my weapon, knocking it aside. Pushing forward, I let the sword slide up toward Kanin's neck, and he instantly fell backward to avoid being cut in the throat.

I froze as he rolled to his feet, looking mildly surprised. I blinked at him, just as shocked as he was. Everything had gone by so fast; I hadn't even had time to think about my actions before they were done.

"Good!" Kanin nodded approval. "You can feel the difference now, can't you? Let your strikes be smooth and flowing—you don't have to hack at something to kill it."

I nodded, looking at my blade and feeling, for the first time, that we had worked together, that I wasn't just swinging a random piece of metal around the room.

Kanin tossed the dowel into a corner. "And, on that note, we should stop for the night," he announced, and I frowned.

"Now? I was just getting the hang of this, and it's still early. Why stop?" I grinned and brandished the sword, shooting him a challenge down the bright metal. "Are you scared that I'm getting too good? Is the student finally surpassing the master?"

He raised an eyebrow, but other than that, his expression remained the same. I wondered if he had ever laughed, really laughed, in his entire unlife. "No," he continued, motioning me out of the room. "Tonight we're going hunting."

I slipped the katana into its sheath on my back and hurried after, excitement and uneasiness fighting within me. Ever since the encounter with the vampires, over three weeks ago, we hadn't left the hospital grounds. It was too dangerous to roam the tunnels now, too risky to venture up top, where anyone could see us. I had fed about two weeks ago, when

Kanin had given me a thermos half filled with cooling blood when I woke up. He hadn't said where he'd gotten it, but the blood tasted thin and grimy and somehow reeked of mole men.

I was eager to leave the hospital, with its dank rooms and claustrophobic hallways. I grew more restless with every passing night. The thought of hunting sent a thrill through me, but I was also scared that I would turn into that snarling, hungry creature from the night with the Blood Angels. I was afraid I wouldn't be able to control myself, and I would end up killing someone.

And, deep down, a part of me didn't care. That was the scariest thing of all.

We went up the elevator shaft and moved quickly through the neighborhoods, wary and suspicious of roaming vampires or guards. Several times, Kanin turned off the street and pulled us into an alley or abandoned building, blending into a dark corner. A trio of guards passed us once, so close that I could see the pockmarks marring one guard's cheek. If he'd turned his head and pointed his flashlight into the alleyway, he would've spotted us. Another time, a pet surrounded by two well-armed soldiers stopped and stared at the doorway we had ducked into seconds before. I could see his eyes narrow, trying to pierce the darkness, listening for any sound of movement. But, one thing about being a vampire, I discovered, was that you could go perfectly still and remain that way for as long as you needed. Kanin even had me practice this little talent back in the hospital. I would stand in a corner for hours, never moving, never breathing, having no need to shift or cough or blink. Even when he started lobbing his dagger at me, thunking it in the wall inches from my head, I wasn't supposed to twitch an eyelash.

After a couple close calls, Kanin led me onto the roof of a building, over the chain-link fence separating the districts, and into a familiar neighborhood. I recognized these streets, the shape of the buildings crumbling on the sidewalks. I saw old Hurley's Trading Shop, the scraggly, weed-choked park with its rusty, sharp playground that nobody went near, the lot between the warehouses where they'd hung the three Unregistereds what felt like ages ago. And I knew if we took *that* shortcut through the alley and crawled through a rusty chain-link fence, we'd find ourselves at the edge of a cracked, deserted lot with an empty, abandoned school in the distance.

This was Sector Four. I was home.

I didn't mention this to Kanin. If he knew where we were, he might make us leave, and I wanted to see my old neighborhood again, in case I ever needed to come back. So I followed him silently through familiar streets, past familiar buildings and landmarks, feeling the school lot get farther and farther away. I wondered if my room was still intact, if any of my old possessions were still there. My mom's book came to mind; was it still safely hidden in its crate? Or had the school been claimed by another, all my stuff stolen or traded away?

Kanin finally led me toward an empty-looking warehouse on the outskirts of the neighborhood, an ancient brick building with smashed windows and a roof that had partially fallen in. I knew this place; it was Kyle's turf, the rivals of my old crew. We'd competed for food, shelter and territory, but in a mostly friendly way, one group of scavengers to another. There was an unspoken truce among the Unregistereds; life was hard enough without violence and fighting and blood-shed. On the streets, we acknowledged one another with a nod or quick word, and occasionally warned each other about guard sweeps and patrols, but for the most part we left the other groups alone.

"Why are we here?" I asked Kanin as we crept along the crumbling walls, stepping between glass and nails and other things that could clink and give us away. "Why don't we just head into Blood Angel or Red Skull territory and take out another gang?"

"Because," Kanin said without looking back, "word spreads on the streets. Because we left those men alive, other gangs will be on the lookout for a young girl and a lone male who happen to be vampires. They will be wary, but more im-portant, the Prince's guards will be watching gang territory closely now. There are always consequences for your actions. Also—" he paused and turned to me, eyes narrowing "—how did you know where we are?" A moment of silence, and he nodded. "You've been here before, haven't you?"

Damn. The vampire was way too perceptive. "This was my sector," I confessed, and Kanin frowned. "I lived not very far from here, at the old school." *With my friends,* I added in my head. Lucas and Rat and Stick, all gone now, all dead. A lump caught in my throat. I hadn't thought of them much before this, willing myself to bury the pain, the guilt that still clawed at me. What would've happened if I had never found that basement of food, if I'd never insisted we go after it? Would they still be alive? Would *I* still be alive?

"Stop it," Kanin said, and I blinked at him. His face and expression were cold. "That part of your life is gone," he continued. "Put it behind you. Do not make me regret giving you this new life, when all you can do is cling to the old one."

I glared at him. "I wasn't clinging," I snapped, meeting his steely gaze. "I was remembering. It's this thing people do when they're reminded of the past."

"You were clinging," Kanin insisted, and his voice dropped several degrees. "You were thinking of your old life, your old friends, and wondering what you could've done to save them. That sort of remembering is useless. There was nothing you could have done."

"There was," I whispered, and my throat unexpectedly closed up. I swallowed hard, using anger to mask the other emotion, the one that made me want to cry. "I led them there. I told them about that basement. They're dead because of me."

My eyes stung, which was a complete shock. I didn't think vampires could cry. Angrily, I swiped at my eyes, and my fingers came away smeared with red. I cried *blood*. Fabulous. "Go on, then," I growled at Kanin, feeling my fangs come out. "Tell me I'm being stupid. Tell me I'm still 'clinging to the past,' because every time I close my eyes, I can see their faces. Tell me why I'm still alive, and they're all dead."

More tears threatened at the corners of my eyes, bloody and hot. I whispered a curse and turned away, digging my nails into my palms, willing them back. I hadn't cried in years, not since the day my mom died. My vision tinted red, and I blinked, hard. When I opened my eyes again, my sight was clear, though my chest still felt as if it had been squeezed in a vise.

Kanin was silent, watching me as I composed myself, a mo-

tionless statue with empty, blank eyes. Only when I looked
up at him again did he move.

"Are you finished?" His voice was flat, his eyes a depthless
black.

I nodded stonily.

"Good. Because the next time you throw a tantrum like
that, I will leave. It is no one's fault that your friends are dead.
And if you keep holding on to that guilt, it will destroy you,
and my work here will be for nothing. Do you understand?"

"Perfectly," I replied, matching my tone to his. He ignored
my coldness and nodded to the building, gesturing through
a shattered window.

"A group of Unregistereds live here, though I suspect you
already know that," he continued. "As to your previous question, I chose this spot because Unregistereds are off the system and no one will notice if one or two go missing."

True, I thought, trailing him through the weeds. *No one
ever misses us, because we don't exist. No one cares if we disappear,
or cries for us when we're gone.*

We slipped through one of the many broken windows,
vanishing into the darkness of the room. Rubble had piled
everywhere in large drifts, creating a small valley of open
space in the center of the building.

A fire flickered in an open pit, and wisps of greasy smoke
rose from burning wood and plastic, settling hazily over the
room. There were more of them than I had expected. Card-
board boxes, cloth tents and lean-tos had been hastily constructed and were scattered around the fire like a miniature
village. I could see dark shapes huddled within, ignorant of
the predators watching them sleep from just a few yards away.

I could smell their breath and the hot blood pumping beneath their skin.

I growled and eased forward, but Kanin put a warning hand on my arm. "Quietly," he said, a whisper in the dark. "Not all feedings have to be violent and bloody. If you are careful, you can feed from a sleeping victim without rousing them. The old Masters used this technique a lot, which was why strings of garlic around the bed and on the windowsills were so popular in certain regions, futile as they were. But you must be careful, and very patient—if your victim wakes up before you bite them, things can get ugly."

"*Before* I bite them? Won't they wake up when they feel... I don't know...a couple long teeth in their neck?"

"No. The bite of a vampire has a tranquilizing effect on humans when they're asleep. At best, they'll remember it as a vivid dream."

"How does *that* work?"

"It just does." Kanin sounded exasperated again. "Now, are you going to do this or should we go somewhere else?"

"No," I muttered, staring down at the camp. "I think I can do this."

Kanin released my arm but then pressed a small package into my hands, wrapped in greasy paper. "When you are finished, leave this where your prey will find it."

I frowned, lifting a corner of the paper, finding a pair of shoes inside, fairly new and sturdy. "What's this?"

"An exchange," Kanin replied and turned away as I continued to stare at him. "For the harm our actions will bring them tonight."

I blinked. "Why bother? They won't even know we were here."

"I'll know."

"But—"

"Don't question it, Allison," Kanin said, sounding weary. "Just go."

"All right." I shrugged. "If you say so." Tucking the package under one arm, I started toward my sleeping prey.

I was maybe halfway to the cluster of lean-tos, the scent of blood and sweat and human grime getting stronger each time I breathed in, when I caught movement from the other side of the room. I ducked behind a corroded metal beam as two ragged figures slowly picked their way toward the camp, murmuring back and forth. With a start, I recognized one of the boys, Kyle, the leader of our rival gang. Snippets of their conversation drifted to me over the rubble pile, talk of food and patrols and how they were going to have to scavenge in other territories soon. It filled me with an odd sense of déjà vu, hearing pieces of my old life played back to me.

When they reached the camp, however, one of them gave a shout and lunged forward, reaching into a box and dragging something out by the ankle. The figure pulled out of his shelter gave a feeble cry and tried crawling back into the box but was yanked into the open by the other two.

"You again! Dammit, kid! I told you, this is my box! Find your own!"

"Look at that," said the other boy, peering into the box, scowling, "he went through your food bag, too, Kyle."

"Son of a bitch." Kyle loomed over the cringing boy, still sprawled out at his feet, and gave him a vicious kick to the

ribs. "You miserable little shit!" Another blow, and the cringing boy cried out, curling into a fetal position. "I swear, pull
another stunt like that, and I won't just throw you out, I'll
kill you. You got that?" One last solid kick, eliciting another
cry of pain, and the larger boy shoved him aside with his foot.
"Go crawl away and die already," he muttered and ducked
into his shelter, pulling the curtain shut.

In the wake of the outburst, the rest of the camp was stirring, faces squinting out of their shelters with bleary, confused frowns. I remained motionless behind the beam, but
after gauging what had happened, the rest of the camp lost
interest and vanished back into their individual homes. I heard
disgruntled murmurs and complaints, most of them directed
at the boy lying on the ground, but no one went forward to
help him. I shook my head, pitying the boy but not blam-
ing the others for being angry. In a gang like this, you pulled
your own weight and contributed to the rest of the community or you were considered dead weight. Stealing, sneaking
around and using other people's things was the quickest way
to getting a beating or worse, being shunned and exiled from
the gang. I had been a loner in my old gang, but I had always
pulled my own weight. And I'd *never* stolen from the others.

Then the boy stood up, brushing at his clothes, and I nearly
fell over in shock.

"Stick," I whispered, unable to believe my eyes. He blinked,
gazing around the camp, sniffling, and I blinked hard to make
sure it was really him. It was. Thin, ragged and dirty, but
alive. "You got out. You made it back, after all."

I started toward him, unthinking, but something clamped

my arm in a viselike grip and pulled me back, into the shadows.

"Ow! Dammit, Kanin," I said in a snarling whisper. "What are you doing? Let go!" I tried yanking back, but he was much too strong.

"We're leaving," he said in an icy voice, continuing to pull me away. "Now. Let's go."

Planting my feet didn't work. Neither did jerking my arm back; his fingers just tightened painfully on my arm. With a hiss, I gave up and let him drag me through the room and out another window. Only when we were several yards from the warehouse did he finally stop and let me go.

"What is *wrong* with you?" I snarled, biting the words off through my fangs, which had sprouted again. "I'm getting a little tired of being dragged, cut, hit, yanked and ordered around whenever you please. I'm not a damn pet."

"You knew that boy, didn't you?"

I curled a lip defiantly. "What if I did?"

"You were going to show yourself to him, weren't you?"

I should've been afraid, especially when his eyes went all dark and glassy again, but I was just pissed now. "He was my *friend*," I spat, glaring up at him. "I know that's impossible for you to understand, seeing as you don't have any, but I knew him years before you came along."

"And what," Kanin asked in his cold, cold voice, "were you intending to do once he saw you? Go back to your old gang? Join this new one? A vampire among the sheep? How long do you think you would last without killing them all?"

"I just wanted to talk to him, dammit! See if he's doing all right without me!" The rage was fading now, and I slumped against a wall. "I left him alone," I muttered, crossing my arms and looking away. "I left him, and he was never good at taking care of himself. I just wanted to see if he was doing all right."

"Allison." Kanin's voice was still hard, but it had lost its frosty edge, at least. "This is why I told you to forget your human life. Those people you knew before you were turned, they will continue living, surviving, without you. You are a monster to them now, and they will never take you back, they will never accept you for what you were. And eventually, whether from age or starvation or sickness or their fellow man, they will all die. And you will continue to live, assuming you don't decide to meet the sun or get your head torn off by another vampire." He gazed down at me, his face softening just a touch, almost pitying. "Immortality is a lonely road," he murmured, "and it will only be made worse if you don't release your attachments to your old life. To that boy, you are the enemy now, the unseen monster that haunts his nightmares. You are the creature he fears the most. And nothing in your previous life, not friendship or loyalty or love, will ever change that."

You're wrong, I wanted to tell him. I had looked after Stick almost half my life. He was the closest thing I had to family now that everyone else was dead. But I knew arguing with Kanin was useless, so I shrugged and turned away.

Kanin was not pleased. "Don't go after that boy, Allison," he warned. "No matter what you think you've left behind. Forget about him and your old life. Do you understand?"

"Yeah," I growled. "I hear you."

He stared at me. "Let's go," he said at last, walking away. "We'll have to find somewhere else to feed tonight."

I gave the warehouse one last look and turned away. But before trailing after Kanin, I unwrapped the shoes and placed them on the ground in plain sight, hoping that Stick would stumble upon them the next morning. We left Sector Four, wandered back into gang territory and were eventually set upon by two Red Skulls who apparently didn't get the note about rogue vampires. They then proceeded to have a very bad night. We returned to the hospital with full stomachs, though Kanin and I didn't speak to each other for the rest of the evening. Mister Broody Vampire vanished into his office, and I wandered back to the reception area to swing my katana at imaginary enemies with Kanin's face.

At least he didn't ask me about the shoes. And I never told him.

FOR THE NEXT FEW NIGHTS, everything was normal. I continued my lessons, suffering through math and English and vampire history before moving on to training. As I got better with my katana, Kanin would give me various patterns to work on and then leave me alone to practice. He never told me where he went, but I suspected he'd searched everything on this floor and had moved to the lowest floor of the building, past a large red door at the bottom of a stairwell. The one marked with the faded sign that read, Danger! Employees Only. I'd stumbled across it one night, wandering the hospital in a rare moment of leisure. But I'd left it alone when Kanin called me back.

I was curious, of course. I wanted to know what was on

the other side of that door, what Kanin was really looking for. The one time I followed him down the stairwell, the metal door was shut, and I didn't want to risk going inside and having him find me. Ever since that night in Sector Four, there was a wall between us. Kanin never said anything about it and never went out of his way to check up on me, but we were cooler toward each other now and didn't speak much beyond training. He probably wouldn't care if I ventured down to the lowest floor, but I wanted to lie low for a few days, let things smooth over.

I didn't want to give him any reason to suspect that I was planning to do something stupid.

CHAPTER 8

One night I woke up, alone as usual, and wandered down the hall to Kanin's office, only to find him gone. A note sat in the middle of the desk in neat, spidery handwriting: *Down on the lowest floor. Practice patterns 1-6 on your own. You've learned all I can teach you about vampire society.—K.*

A strange flutter went through my stomach. This was it. Kanin was absent, and tonight I could do what I wanted. I wouldn't get a better chance.

I left the office and walked to the reception area with my katana, as the note instructed me to do. But I didn't stop there. Without pausing to think, I hurried to the elevator shaft, grasped the cables and pulled myself up the tube as fast as I could go.

On the surface, the sun had just set over the jagged horizon, and the sky was dark blue with bloodred clouds. It had been a long time since I'd seen anything but darkness and night, and for a brief moment I stared at the splashes of color across the sky, marveling at how quickly I'd forgotten what a sunset looked like.

So you're going to stand there gaping at some pretty clouds like a moron until Kanin finds you outside, then? With an annoyed mental slap, I wrenched my gaze from the horizon and hurried away from the hospital, not daring to look back.

I felt a strange thrill, creeping through the shadows and alleyways on my own, the same feeling I'd gotten while exploring beyond the wall: excited and terrified at the same time. I wasn't supposed to be out here. There was no doubt in my mind that Kanin was going to be *pissed,* but it was too late to worry about that now. I'd been planning this moment for days, and I needed to discover some things for myself. Besides, he couldn't keep me in that old hospital forever, like some sort of prison guard. Before we'd met, I went where I wanted when I wanted, and no one could stop me. I wasn't going to start submitting now, just because some moody, evasive vampire told me I had to forget.

I slipped through the sectors, remembering the paths Kanin had used but also my own knowledge from when I was a Fringer. It was much easier, now that I was dead, to move like a ghost through the darkness, to be able to leap onto the roof of a two-story building to avoid the guards, to freeze and become part of the stones and shadows. Unseen and unheard, I crept through the streets, weaving around buildings, until I reached a familiar chain-link fence. Slipping under the links, I crossed the empty lot quickly and walked into the shadowy halls of my old home.

It seemed much emptier than before, silent and deserted. I found my old locker, opened it with a creak and sighed.

Empty, as I'd feared. The scavengers had already found this place.

Halfheartedly, I walked toward my old room, knowing I'd probably find it stripped clean. It never took long for scavengers to move in; I only hoped that *maybe* they'd left a certain crate alone, having no use for something that could get them killed.

I turned the knob, swung open the door and stepped inside, not realizing until too late that someone was already there.

A body looked up from where it crouched in the corner, leaning against the wall. I started, automatically going for my sword, thinking for one terrifying moment that it was Kanin. It wasn't, but it was another vampire, a lean, bony male with white skin and a head as bald as an egg. He smiled, showing perfect teeth, and the moonlight shining through the broken windows fell across his pale features and the vivid web of scars slashed across his face.

"Evening, little bird." His voice, soft, raspy and somehow very, very wrong, made me shiver. "Out for a midnight flight, on wings of blood and pain? Like razor blades across the moon, they cut the night and make the sky bleed red." He chuckled, sending chills down my back. I drew away, and the stranger cocked his head at me. "Oh, don't mind me, love. I get a little poetic sometimes. The moonlight does that to me." He shook himself, as if shaking off the crazy, and rose to his feet.

I noticed the book in his long, bony hands, then, and stepped forward. "Hey! What are you doing with that? Those are mine."

"Are they?" The vamp moved, coming away from the wall.

I tensed, but he only crossed the room to set the book gently on a shelf. "Then perhaps you should have taken better care of them, love," he purred, staring at me with soulless black eyes. "The rats here were using them to keep their skinny hides warm."

He nodded to the corner. I looked over and saw a pair of human bodies sprawled out on my old mattress, pinched and ragged-looking—the scavengers that had moved in. From their unnatural stillness and the scent of old blood, they were obviously dead. I looked closer and saw their throats were gone, the skin around them dark and stained, as if they'd been torn out. Horror crept over me, and I nearly fled the room, away from the vampire who was truly a monster.

But there was a spot on the cement floor next to the mattress that was blackened and charred, and I had to know what it was. As I studied the remains of book pages, scattered among the ashes, my heart sank. All that time, all that work, and in the end my collection had been burned to keep two strangers warm.

The strange vampire chuckled. "They won't need words now," he mused. "Not to read, not to burn, not to nibble on. Always nibbling, the rats. Creeping into dark places to get warm, spreading their filth. No more words for them. No more anything." He chuckled again, the empty sound making my skin crawl.

I resisted the urge to draw my weapon. He wasn't making any threatening moves, but I felt as if I was standing close to a coiled, venomous snake. "Who are you?" I asked, and his blank gaze switched to me. "What's your business in New Covington?"

"Just looking for something, little bird." Another of his eerie smiles, and this time his fangs showed, just the tips. "And if you want my name, you'll have to give me yours. It's only polite, and we're a polite society, after all."

I hesitated. For whatever reason, I did not want this creepy bloodsucker to know my name. Not that I was worried that he would report it to the Prince who, according to Kanin, did *not* instantly know the name of every vampire in the whole city, especially the Type-3 riffraff. The Prince was concerned only about those in his immediate circle; the common vampires were below his notice.

But I did not want *this* vampire to know me, because I knew, somehow, that he *would* remember, and that seemed like a very bad idea.

"No?" The vampire smiled at my silence, unsurprised. "Not going to tell me? I guess I can't blame you. I am a stranger and all. But you'll have to forgive me if I don't disclose my identity, then. Can't be too careful these days."

"I want you to leave," I told him, feigning a bravado I really didn't feel. "This is my sector, my hunting grounds. I want you out. Right now."

He gave me a long, eerie stare, as if sizing me up. He was perfectly still, but I could sense those tendons coiling beneath his pale skin, ready to unleash. And suddenly, I was terrified of this stranger. This thin, motionless vampire whose eyes were as dark and soulless as Kanin's. My hands shook, and I crossed my arms to hide them, knowing the stranger would see the smallest detail. I knew I stood in the presence of a killer.

Finally, he smiled. "Of course," he said, nodding as he

stepped away, and my knees nearly buckled with relief. "Terribly sorry, love. Didn't mean to intrude. I'll be leaving now."

He stepped aside, moving toward the door, but paused, giving me a thoughtful stare. "Little bird, your song is so different than his," he crooned, to my utter confusion. "Don't disappoint me."

I didn't say anything. I just held his gaze, hoping he would go away. The vampire gave me one last terrible smile, then turned and vanished through the door. I listened for his footsteps, walking away, but heard nothing.

The world seemed to breathe again. I waited several minutes, unmoving, wanting the creepy vampire to get as far away as he could, before I finally strode to the open crate, lying against the wall, and peered inside.

Two books. That was all that was left. Two books out of a lifetime of effort, and neither was the one that mattered. I sank to my knees, feeling my throat close up, my stomach twisting. For a moment, I wished the two greedy scavengers were still alive so I could hurt them, make them feel the same pain. I had nothing left now, nothing to remind me of my past. My mom's book, the only thing I had to remember her by, was lost forever.

I didn't cry. Numbly, I pulled myself to my feet and turned away, stifling my anger and despair, letting cold indifference settle over me. Loss was nothing new. Those two strangers only had done what anyone would to survive. Nothing lasted in this world; it was everyone for himself. Allie the Fringer knew that; Allison the vampire just needed the reminder.

I left the school without looking back. There was nothing there for me anymore, and I was already putting it from my mind, shoving it down into the deepest parts where I kept all the memories I didn't want to remember. You don't dwell on what you've lost, you just move on. The night was waning, and I had something else to do, one more piece of my past to check on, before Kanin discovered I was missing.

I MADE MY WAY to the old warehouse with a growing sense of urgency. Slipping inside the building, I scanned the room and the boxes in the center of the rubble piles, looking for a familiar face. It seemed most of the gang had returned already, for there were about a half-dozen young people bunched together around the fire, talking and laughing. I looked closely at each of them, but Stick was not among them.

And then I saw him, huddled off to the side, his thin frame curled around himself. He was shivering, hunched over and miserable, and I felt a flare of anger and disgust. Anger for these people who shunned him, who weren't taking care of their own, who would let him slowly die from starvation and cold right in front of them. But I also felt a sudden contempt toward Stick, who still hadn't learned to take care of himself, who was still relying on others to save him, when it was obvious that they didn't care.

Quietly, I made my way through the rubble, keeping to the shadows, until Stick was just a few yards away. He looked even thinner than usual, a near-skeleton of a boy with pinched skin and greasy hair and dull, dead eyes.

"Stick," I whispered, casting a quick glance toward the group by the fire. They all had their backs to me, or to Stick, more likely, and didn't notice us. "Stick! Over here! Look this way!"

He jerked and raised his head. For a few seconds, he looked confused, gazing around blearily, his eyes staring right through my hiding spot. But then I waved to him, and his eyes nearly bugged out of his head.

"Allie?"

"Shh!" I hissed, drawing back into the shadows as some of the gang members half turned their heads, frowning. I gestured for him to follow, but he just sat there, staring at me as if I was a ghost.

In a sense, I suppose I was.

"You're alive," he whispered, but his voice lacked the excitement, the relief, I was expecting. It sounded dull, almost accusing, though he wore a confused expression. "You shouldn't be alive. The rabids…I heard…" He shuddered violently, curling into himself. "You didn't come back," he said, and now there was a definite note of accusation in his voice. "You didn't come back for me. I thought you were dead, and you left me alone."

"I didn't have a choice," I said through gritted teeth. "Believe me, I would have come here sooner if I could, but I didn't know you were alive, either. I thought the rabids got you, like Rat and Lucas."

He shook his head. "I went back home and waited for you, but you never came. I stayed there, alone, for days. Where were you? Where have you been all this time?"

He sounded like a pensive toddler, and my frustration increased. "Near an old hospital in Sector Two," I snapped, "but that doesn't matter now. I came here to see if you're all right, if you're taking care of yourself."

"What do you care?" Stick muttered, fiddling with his

tattered sleeve. His watery gaze eyed my coat and narrowed darkly. "You never really cared what happened to me. You always wanted me gone. You and everyone else. That's why you never came back."

I swallowed a growl, barely. "I'm here now, aren't I?"

"But you're not staying, are you?" Stick looked up at me, his eyes hooded. "You're going to leave again, leave me alone with these people. They hate me. Just like Rat and Lucas did. You hated me, too."

"I didn't, but you're sure pushing me in that direction," I grumbled. This was crazy. I had never seen Stick like this and had no idea where the sullen rage was coming from. "God, Stick, stop being a baby. You can take care of yourself. You don't need me around to look after you, I've always told you that."

"Then...you're *not* staying." Stick's voice trembled, and his anger melted away into real panic. "Allie, please. I'm sorry! I was just scared when you didn't come back." He scrambled forward, pleading, and I cast a nervous look at the group around the fire. "Please, don't go," Stick begged. "Stay with us. This place isn't so bad, really. Kyle won't mind another person, especially someone like you."

"Stick." I shushed him with a sharp gesture, and he fell silent, his eyes still begging me to stay. "I can't," I told him, and his expression crumpled. "I wish I could, but I can't. I'm... different now. I can't be seen aboveground. So you'll have to survive without me."

"Why?" Stick crept forward. His chin trembled; he was near tears. "Why can't you just stay? Do you hate me that much? Am I that pathetic, that you can just leave me alone to die?"

"Stop being dramatic." I half turned, embarrassed and angry, both at myself and him. Kanin was right, I should never have come here. "You're not helpless," I said. "You've been Unregistered just as long as me. It's time you learned to fend for yourself. I can't help you anymore."

"No, that's not a reason," Stick protested. "There's something you're not telling me."

"You don't want to know."

"Why are you keeping secrets? Don't you trust me? We never kept anything from each other before."

"Stick, leave it alone."

"I thought we were friends," he insisted, leaning forward. "No one here likes me, no one understands me like you. I thought you were dead! But now you're back, and you won't tell me what's going on."

"All right!" I turned to face him fully, narrowing my gaze. "All right, you really want to know why?" And before he could answer, before I could reflect on the absolute stupidity of my actions, I opened my mouth and bared my fangs.

Stick went so pale, I thought he would faint. "Don't scream," I told him urgently, retracting my fangs, knowing it had been a mistake the second I showed him. "I'm not going to hurt you. I'm still me, just...different now."

"You're a vampire," Stick whispered, as if he'd just figured it out. "A *vampire*."

"Yeah." I shrugged. "I was pulled down by rabids and would've died, but a vampire happened to be in the area and Turned me instead. But the other vamps are looking for us now, that's why I can't stay. I don't want them to come after you, too."

But Stick was edging away, every muscle in his body tight with fear. "Stick," I tried again, holding out my hand. "It's still me. Come on, I'm not going to bite you or anything."

"Stay away from me!" Stick's frantic cry finally roused the others around the fire, and they looked toward us, muttering and rising to their feet. I felt my lips curl back, my fangs lengthen, even as I gave my old friend one last, desperate look.

"Stick, don't do this."

"Vampire!" he shrieked and lunged backward, sprawling in the dirt. "Vampire, over here! Get away from me! Help! Someone, help!"

I growled and drew back as the group around the fire leaped to their feet, shouting and cursing. Stick half ran, half crawled back to the fire, shouting and pointing in my direction, and the rest of the camp exploded into terrified chaos. Screams of *"Vampire"* echoed through the warehouse as the small group of Unregistereds scattered to every corner of the room, diving through windows and shoving each other aside to escape. Stick gave one last cry and fled into the darkness, out of sight.

The noise from the panicked Unregistereds was almost deafening, stirring something primal within, something that urged me to give chase, to slip into the crowd and start tearing out throats. For just a moment, I watched the humans scramble to escape a predator they didn't even see, who could kill them before they knew it was there. I could sense the terror, smell the hot blood and sweat and fear, and it took all my willpower to turn away, to draw back into the shadows and leave them alone. They fled before me, but in the mass confusion, I slipped through a window, and I didn't look back until the howls and screams of terror had faded into the night.

HE WAS SITTING AT THE OFFICE DESK when I crept back down the elevator shaft into the hospital. I didn't see him in the reception area or the halls, and thought I was home free as I tiptoed back to my room. But then I passed his office door.

"Did you enjoy your time with your friend?"

I winced, freezing midstep. Kanin sat behind the desk with a stack of files, scanning another document. He didn't look up as I slipped warily into the room.

"I had to," I told him softly. "I had to know if he was all right."

"And how did that work out for you?"

I swallowed hard, and Kanin finally put down the paper, watching me with unreadable black eyes.

"Did he scream?" he asked calmly. "Did he curse you and flee in terror? Or was he 'understanding' and promised nothing would change, only you could see how terrified he was?" I didn't answer, and Kanin's mouth twitched in a humorless smirk. "I'm guessing there was screaming and running."

"You knew," I accused. "You knew I would go after him."

"You aren't the most pliable student in the world." Kanin didn't sound amused or angry or resigned. He just stated it as a fact. "Yes, I knew, eventually, you would seek out the last remnants of your old life. Everyone does. You aren't one to listen to advice you don't agree with—you had to see it for yourself. That said…" His voice went cold, and his eyes glittered in that blank, terrifying stare. "Our time together is drawing to a close. If you disobey me again, I will take that as a sign that you don't need a teacher any longer. Is that understood?"

I nodded, and Kanin's expression softened, even if his voice did not. "What did the boy say?" he asked. "After you showed him?"

"Nothing," I said miserably. "He just screamed 'vampire' and ran. After everything I did for the ungrateful little…" I stumbled to a halt, not wanting to think about it, but Kanin raised his eyebrows, silently telling me to go on. "I knew him for years," I growled. "I shared my food with him, looked out for him, stood up for him when he would've gotten his ass kicked—" My chest felt tight, and I crossed my arms. "And after all that…" I paused, not knowing if I wanted to cry or rip a door off its hinges and fling it through the wall. "After all that…" I tried again.

"He still saw you as nothing more than a monster," Kanin finished.

With a cry, I turned and drove my fist through the wall. The plaster flew inward, leaving a six-inch hole behind. "Dammit!" I slugged the wall again, feeling it give way with a satisfying crunch. "I was his *friend*. I was the only thing that kept him alive, all those years of picking up his slack, all those years of going hungry so he wouldn't starve!" I slammed a fist into the wall once more, then leaned into it, feeling chalky plaster against my forehead. My eyes burned, and I squeezed them shut, willing the pain to go away. "He should've known better," I whispered through clenched teeth. "He should've known *me* better."

Kanin hadn't moved, letting me rip apart his wall without

comment. Finally, he rose, coming to stand just behind me. "Did you tell him where we were?" he asked in a low voice.

"No." I shook my head against the wall and finally pulled back. "I didn't...wait. Yes, I might've...mentioned the hospital. But he doesn't know where it is." I half turned, looking up at Kanin, who watched me gravely. "He wouldn't come looking for it, anyway," I said, hearing the bitterness in my voice. "He's too scared to leave the hideout most of the time, much less the sector."

"You're still being naive." Kanin rubbed a hand over his eyes, stepping back. "Stay here. Don't leave the hospital. I'll be back soon."

"Where are you going?" I said, suddenly on edge. A thought entered my mind, and my stomach went cold. "You're not...going after him, are you?"

"No," Kanin said, pausing in the doorway, and I sagged in relief. "But I need to set up alarms around the area. The few already in place won't be enough, I fear."

"For what?" Frowning, I followed him down the hall. He didn't answer, and I gaped at him as I realized. "You think Stick will tell someone," I guessed, hurrying to keep pace with his long strides. "That's not going to happen. I'm telling you, Kanin, you don't have to worry about that. He's too much of a coward to go to anyone."

"Perhaps." Kanin strode into the reception area and stopped me at the desk. "And perhaps he will surprise you. Wait here. Practice your sword techniques. Don't leave the hospital grounds, understand? After tonight, you won't be able to go anywhere without triggering an alarm unless I'm with you."

"I still think this is pointless, Kanin."

The look he gave me was pitying. "Maybe it will be as you say. Maybe this boy will surprise me. But I've lived far too long to leave anything to chance, particularly when it comes to human betrayal. If there is nothing to lose, and even very little to gain, you can almost count on it. Now, give me your word that you won't try to leave."

"What if I need to go outside?"

"Either stay here or leave now and don't come back. Your choice."

"Fine." I glared at him. "I won't try to leave."

"Forgive me if I don't take your immediate word," Kanin deadpanned in a cold voice. "I want your promise. Do you swear?"

"Yes!" I bared my fangs at him. "I swear."

He nodded curtly and turned away. I watched him shimmy up the elevator tube, trying to work my way through a jumble of swirling emotions: anger, frustration, disappointment, hurt. One second I hated Stick, and the next I could almost understand his instant terror. I despised it and thought it sucked, especially after all I'd done for him, but I could understand. After all, he'd reacted to a vampire appearing suddenly in his home. If he'd suddenly disappeared and shown up as a bloodsucker, I might have reacted the same way. Or I might have attempted to see through my knee-jerk reaction and actually tried to talk to him, for friendship's sake. I didn't know. I *did* think Kanin was overreacting, setting up alarms and forbidding me to leave the hospital when there was no need.

Only when he was gone did I remember the strange vampire I'd met in my old room earlier, the one with the dead eyes and terrible smile. I considered climbing the shaft and hurrying after Kanin to warn him, but I'd just promised him I wouldn't leave the hospital. Besides, Kanin was a big, capable vampire. He could take care of himself.

I practiced my sword drills, thought of Stick and what I could have done differently, and wandered the halls, waiting for my mentor to come back.

But Kanin did not return that night.

CHAPTER 9

I jerked awake, hissing and baring my fangs, the nightmare ebbing away into reality. I'd been dreaming, for the first time since I'd become a vampire, about dark tunnels and twisting corridors and something terrible lurking within them, stalking me. I remembered the cold fear, sensing the unknown evil drawing closer, and then a blinding flare of pain as the creature finally pounced, though I never saw its face. It was enough to wake me up, and upon reflection, I thought it was very strange. How did the dead dream, exactly? I'd have to ask Kanin about that.

Kanin. Rising, I grabbed my sword and hurried to his office, hoping I would see his calm, efficient form sitting behind the desk with a stack of documents, as always.

The office was empty. Nor was there any note on the desk, telling me my assignments for the night. I prowled the halls, peering into every room, every corner I might've overlooked. Nothing. No sign of him anywhere. He was truly gone.

For a moment, I wondered if he had left on purpose, if last night, he'd had no intention of coming back. Had he gotten tired of his stubborn, moody, impossible student and decided it was time to be free of her? I shook my head. No, Kanin wasn't like that. He was cold, unsympathetic, jaded and sometimes scary as hell, but he was not a liar. If he wasn't here, then he was out there, somewhere. Was he hurt? Captured?

Dead?

Stop that, I told myself. Just because Kanin wasn't in the hospital was no reason to panic. Maybe he was in the tunnels, setting up traps or alarms. Or maybe he *was* somewhere in the hospital still, in a room I hadn't checked or...

Wait. There *was* one more place I could look.

At the bottom of the stairs, the red metal door groaned and swung open reluctantly as I pushed on it, revealing a long corridor. I caught a glimpse of a broken security camera mounted above the red door and another at the end of the hall. As I slipped into the hallway, the door groaned shut behind me, closing with a bang and plunging the narrow space into darkness.

My new vampire sight let me see even in pitch-blackness, however, and I made my way to the end of the hall, where another door was set firmly into the wall. It was stainless steel, barred from the outside and heavy enough to stop a train. It didn't have a normal handle or doorknob but a wheel set in the very center, rusty with age.

What were they keeping back here? I wondered, turning the wheel to the right. It spun reluctantly, then with a faint hiss, the door swung outward.

Past the frame, I stepped into yet another dark, claustrophobic hallway. Only this time, large windows ran along the wall, looking into isolated rooms. Though some of the windows were smashed and broken, the glass was extremely thick, and more than a few were still intact. I looked closer, and a chill skittered down my spine.

Thick steel bars ran vertically across the windows, like cages. The doors on the rooms were the same thick, heavy metal, and they all locked from the outside. Within each room, the walls were white and crumbling, but I saw gouges in the tile, as if something had clawed at it, all the way down to the metal beneath.

"What the hell is this place?" I whispered.

My voice slithered into the room, unnaturally loud in the silence. The darkness seemed to reach for me, trying to draw me in. I could smell blood and pain and death, worked into the very walls, seeping from the cracks in the floor. Movement flickered at the corners of my eyes, faces peering out of the glass, ghostly images of things not there.

My skin crawled. Whatever had happened here, whatever secrets lay beyond those doors, it was something I didn't want to uncover.

There was a thump on the stairwell, soft footsteps padding into the corridor.

I shivered with relief. "Kanin," I called, striding up to the thick metal door. It was halfway shut, and I pushed it open. "Where the hell have you been?"

And the vampire with the terrible smile grinned down at me.

"Hello, love," the vampire purred, smiling as I backed away, drawing my blade as he eased into the room. "What a surprise to run into you again. Some little birdie has been lying to me."

I kept my blade between me and the vampire, circling with him as he prowled the edges of the room. His eyes weren't on me, however, but rather staring blankly at the walls and glass windows lining the hall. "What are you doing here?" I growled, trying to control my fear. "How did you find this place?"

"Ahhhh..." the vampire breathed, the air rasping through a windpipe that hadn't been used in years. "That is a fine question, little bird." He reached out and put one pale claw against the glass, pressing his cheek against it. I noticed a splash of old, dry blood on his neck, as if something had slashed at him recently. "Did you know these walls will talk to you? If you ask them. They'll tell you their secrets, though sometimes you have to beat it out of them, yes. Sometimes it was necessary." He straightened and turned to me, his eyes empty black holes in his smiling face. "Where's Kanin?" he asked in a patient, understanding voice. "Tell me now, and save me the trouble of pulling off your fingers."

"He's not here," I said. The vampire didn't look surprised.

"Not back yet then? I must've hit him harder than I thought. Very well, we can wait for him. I have all the time in the world."

"What did you do to him?" I snarled.

He chewed a fingernail, ran a tongue along his thin lips, and smiled at me. "Have you ever filleted a fish?"

"What?" God, this freak was creeping me out. "What the hell are you talking about?"

"No? It's quite easy." There was a flash of metal, and the vampire was suddenly holding a thin, bright blade. I jumped; he was so quick I hadn't even seen his hand move. "The trick is to start skinning them as soon as you pull them out of the water, before they have a chance to die. You just slip the knife beneath the flesh and pull..." He demonstrated with the blade, making a long, slow cut in the air, "and the skin peels right off." He looked me in the eye, and his grin stretched wider, showing fangs. "That's what I did to Kanin's last little fish. He screamed, oh, did he scream. It was glorious." He waggled the knife at me. "I wonder if you will be so obliging?"

My arms shook, making the sword tremble, and I squeezed the hilt to stop them. I could barely move, frozen with a terror unlike any I'd known before. An image came to mind before I could stop it: a body hanging from the ceiling, raw muscles exposed to the air as it writhed and screamed in agony. I slammed that thought away before I was sick.

"Why...why do you hate him so much?" I asked, mostly to keep him talking, to buy myself some time. My voice wavered, making me furious with myself. Dammit, I could not show fear in front of this psycho. I bit my cheek, tasting blood, and that was enough to rouse the demon inside. My next words were stronger. "Why do you want to kill him?"

"I don't want to kill him," the vampire explained, sounding surprised. "That would be too good for Kanin. Surely he's told you. What he is? What he's done? No?" He chuckled, shaking his bald head. "Always keeping your spawn in the dark, hmm, old friend? They don't even know why they must suffer for you." He moved toward me, and I jerked backward, muscles tightening, but the vampire only crossed the room, running his fingers down one of the metal doors. He was no longer smiling, his face as empty as a blank sheet, making him a thousand times more terrible.

"I remember," he mused, his voice a cold whisper in the darkness. "I can't ever get it out of my head. The screams. The blood on the walls. Watching everyone around me turn into those *things*." He shivered, curling his lips back, and suddenly his resemblance to the creatures in the ruins was unmistakable. "They stuck me with the same needles, pumped the same sickness into me. But I never turned. I've always wondered about that. Why I never turned."

My eyes flickered to the exit, judging the distance between me and the heavy metal door. Not enough time. Psycho vamp was probably just as fast as Kanin, which meant he was much faster than me. I'd have to buy myself more time, a few seconds at least.

Keeping one hand on the sword, I slowly reached down, into my jeans, and closed my fingers around the familiar handle of my knife. Pulling it out slowly, flicking open the tiny blade, I cupped it in my palm, hiding it from view.

"But I know now." Psycho vamp turned, and that awful grin was back on his face. "I know why I was spared. To punish the one responsible for our pain. Every scream, every drop of blood, every strip of flesh and shattered bone, I will revisit upon him tenfold. He will know the pain, and fear and despair of every life within these walls. I will scour the earth of his blood, I will raze his lineage from existence. And only when his screams and the screams of his offspring replace the ones in my mind, when I can no longer see their faces and hear their cries of anguish, only then will I grant him leave of this world."

"You're a freaking psychopath," I said, but he only chuckled.

"I don't expect you to understand, little bird." He turned toward me fully, fingering his blade and smiling. "I expect you only to sing. Sing for me, sing for Kanin, and make it a glorious song."

He lunged at me, coming in fast and catching me off guard, even though I was expecting it. I swung the katana at him one-handed, aiming for his neck, but he slithered aside, stepped within my guard and slammed me into the wall. My head struck the glass, and I felt something crack beneath me, either my head or the glass itself. Before I could react, a cold, dead hand clamped around my sword arm, threatening to snap it, and the point of a blade pierced my jaw.

"Now, little bird," psycho vamp whispered, pressing his lean body against mine. I tried throwing him off, but it was like steel cables, pinning me to the wall. "Sing for me."

I bared my fangs in his face. "Sing yourself," I hissed and thrust my free hand up, jamming the pocket knife into one crazy black eye.

Psycho vamp screamed and reeled away, clutching his face. I sprang from the wall and rushed for the door, but I hadn't taken three steps when the vampire's scream turned into a chilling roar of fury that made my hair stand on end. Fear made me quick. I reached the exit and lunged through the opening, dropping my blade and spinning around to push it shut. I saw psycho vamp racing toward me, his face a mask of rage, fangs bared, eyes bloody and murderous, and shoved hard on the door. It groaned as it swung shut, and I wrenched the wheel to the left, sealing it tight as a thunderous *boom* echoed from the other side.

My arms shook as I grabbed my katana and backed away from the door. It was strange; I felt my heart should be pounding a mile a minute, my breath coming in short, panicked gasps. But of course, there was none of that. Only the slight tremble in my arms and legs showed how very close I had come to death again.

Another hollow boom against the steel door made me wince. How long would it be before psycho vamp got out? Could he get out? If he did, he would be coming for me, no question about it. I had to put as much distance between me and murderous psycho vamp as I could.

I took another step back, turned to flee, and ran into a body in the hallway.

"Kanin!" I nearly fainted with relief, putting out my arms to steady him. Kanin staggered back a step, leaning heavily against the wall. He looked even paler than usual, and his shirt was stained with dried blood. His own. "You're hurt!"

"I'm all right." He waved me off. "It's old. I've already fed, so don't worry about me." His eyes scanned the hallway, narrowing to slits. "Did Sarren come down here?"

"Sarren? You mean psycho vamp with the messed-up face? Yeah. Yeah, he did." I jerked my thumb toward the steel door, just as another thud echoed down the hallway, followed by a desperate screech. "Friend of yours, Kanin? He seemed very interested in peeling my skin off."

"You're lucky to be alive," Kanin muttered, shaking his head, and I thought I heard the faintest note of admiration in his voice. "He surprised me last night. I didn't think he would find me here so soon."

"Are you all right?"

He shook himself, pushing off the wall. "We have to get out of here," he continued, staggering away. "Hurry. There's not much time."

"You think Smiley can get out of there?" I glanced back at the door. "Really? It's like two feet of solid steel."

"No, Allison." Kanin looked back at me, his face darkening. "Your friend went to the authorities this evening. He told them that two unauthorized vampires are hanging around the old hospital grounds. The Prince's men are coming. We have to move now."

I stared at him in horror, hardly believing what I'd just heard. "No," I said as he turned away, walked back down the hall. "You're wrong. Stick wouldn't do that to me. That's the one rule everyone understands—we don't sell each other out to the bloodsuckers."

"You *are* a bloodsucker now." Kanin's voice echoed back, dull and weary. "And it doesn't matter. Someone tipped them off, and they're on their way. If they catch us here, they'll kill us. We have to get out of the city."

"We're leaving?" I hurried after him, feeling my stomach twist. "Where are we going?"

"I don't know." Kanin suddenly slammed a fist into the wall, making me jump. "Dammit," he growled, bowing his head. "Dammit, I was so close. If I only had a little more time…." He smashed his fist into the wall again, leaving a gaping hole, and I shifted uncomfortably. It occurred to me that whatever he'd been looking for, whatever he had been researching all this time, was lost. Either he hadn't found it, or it wasn't here in the first place. Weeks of searching, reading endless files and documents, all for nothing in the end.

And then everything—the research, the hospital rooms, the crazy vampire with a vendetta against Kanin—clicked into place. And I felt like an idiot for not realizing it sooner.

"It was you." I stared at the hunched figure against the wall. And I couldn't be sure, but I thought I saw his shoulders flinch, just a little, at the words. "You were the vampire, the Master, that sold out the other vampires for a cure to Red Lung. You were the one working with the scientists. And this place—" I glanced back at the steel door "—this was where it all happened. That was what Smiley was talking about. The experiments, the screaming. You're the one responsible for the rabids!"

Kanin straightened, though he didn't look at me. "That vampire is gone," he said in the coldest voice I'd ever heard. "He was foolish and idealistic, and his faith in mankind was horrendously misplaced. It would've been better had he let the virus run its course—some humans would have survived, they always survive. And if our kind had starved, if vampires all went extinct, maybe that would have been preferable to this."

I was silent, not knowing what to say. I thought I would hate him; this was the vampire whose actions had created something horrible, who was responsible for the spread of the rabids, who had inadvertently caused the enslavement of the entire human race. But even in my darkest, angriest moments, I could not match the depth of loathing I heard in Kanin's voice, the absolute hatred for the vampire who had doomed both species, and the desperate need to make things right.

"Let's go," he finally said, starting forward again. "We have to keep moving. Take nothing you don't need, we'll want to travel light, and we have only a few hours to clear the wall and get out of the ruins."

"I'm good to go," I said, holding up my sword. "I don't have anything except this." It was kind of sad, really. That I'd lived in a place for seventeen years and had nothing to show for it but a sword and the clothes on my back. And they weren't even mine. For a second, I wished I had some keepsake of my mom's, something to remember her by, but the vampires had taken even that.

And then it really hit me. I was leaving. I was leaving the only place I'd ever known, the place that had been home my entire life. What lay beyond the Wall, beyond the ruins, I had no idea. From what Kanin told me, I knew there were other vampire cities, scattered about the wilderness, but I had no idea where any of them were located. Kanin always seemed reluctant to talk about his travels, about the world outside, so it rarely came up. Were there humans out there, scorning vampire protection, living free? Or was the world beyond a wasteland of dead buildings and forests teeming with rabids and other horrors?

I guessed I would find out, because Kanin was giving me no time to consider. "Hurry," he snapped as we jogged to the elevator shaft. This would be the last time we used it. "Get up there now. They're probably almost here."

I scurried up the dark tube and came out in the hospital ruins, stepping aside so Kanin could follow me up. Around us, the blackened remains stood silent, but across the empty lot, slithering like the wind through the grass, I could hear footsteps. Lots of footsteps. Coming this way.

And then, over the tops of the grass and weeds, I saw them. Vampires. A whole lot of them, their skin pale under the glowing moon, moving in tandem over the lot. Surrounding and flanking them were several human guards carrying very large weapons—assault rifles. The vampires looked unarmed, but the sheer number of them, gliding noiselessly through the weeds like an army of corpses, made me bite my lip until I tasted blood.

Kanin gripped my shoulder, and I glanced up at him, trying to hide my fear. He pressed a finger to his lips and pointed silently into the city. We slipped away into the darkness, as voices and the steady march of footsteps drew closer to our location.

I'D NEVER RUN SO FAST in my life, or death, for that matter.

Kanin was relentless, leading me through the city, down side streets, into alleyways, under and through old buildings on the verge of collapse. It was a good thing I never got winded or tired anymore, running along behind Kanin as we fled the army at our backs. Frighteningly, our pursuers didn't get tired, either, and had apparently called in reinforcements once they discovered we were on the run. Vehicles and armored trucks scoured the once empty streets, bright spotlights piercing the darkness, armed guards ready to open fire at anything that moved. All humans had wisely moved indoors; not even the gangs were roaming the alleyways tonight. A citywide manhunt, where even the vampires were out in the open, in large numbers, was cause enough for the bravest thug to stay off the street.

The streets rapidly became too dangerous for us to cross, but Kanin wasn't planning on staying aboveground for long and took us into the undercity as quickly as he could. Prying up a manhole cover, he motioned me down the hole, and I dropped into the belly of the city without hesitation.

"We can't slow down," Kanin cautioned after he'd landed noiselessly beside me. "They'll be searching the tunnels, as well. Perhaps even more extensively than the streets. But at least down here we'll be out of the open, away from the trucks."

I nodded. "Where to now?"

"We head for the ruins. Past the edge of the city, they probably won't follow us."

I felt my stomach clench at the thought of going into the ruins, and the rabids that waited there, in the place that I'd died. But I squashed down my fear. It was either face the threat of rabids, who might kill us, or stay here and wait for the Prince's men, who definitely would. Between the two, I'd rather have a fighting chance.

"Not much night left, Kanin," I said, feeling the hours slip away from us. He gave a curt nod.

"Then we'll have to pick up the pace."

We did, running madly through the tunnels, hearing the echo of voices around and above us.

THEY WERE WAITING FOR US at the edge of the old city.

The ruins were crawling with soldiers and guards, more than I'd seen before in my life. Whether through testament to Kanin's infamy or Prince Salazar's hatred, we had barely come out of the tunnels when there was a shout in the darkness and machine-gun fire ricocheted around us, sparking off the pavement and walls. We fled, ducking through overgrown lots and between buildings, but the alert was sounded, and they all knew we were here. Gunfire and shouts echoed from all directions. A trio of snarling dogs came at us and Kanin had to cut them down before we could move on.

"This way," Kanin hissed, ducking around an old brick building half covered in vines. "We're not far from the city limits now. See those trees?" He pointed over the rooftops to where a blanket of leaves crowded the horizon. "If we can get into the forest, we'll be able to lose—"

A roar of gunfire erupted from a line of cars in front of us, making little explosions of blood erupt from Kanin's chest, and he jerked back with a painful hiss. I cried out in terror. Staggering away, Kanin turned and dived through the window of the old building, shattering the glass and dropping from sight. Ducking bullets, I scrambled through after him.

"Kanin!"

The interior of the building smelled of oil, grease and rust, and the skeletons of several cars sat on the cement floor as I rolled to my feet, glancing around wildly. The vampire lay a few feet from the window, surrounded by broken chips of glass, and I dropped beside him as he pushed himself to his knees. He was grimacing, teeth clenched tightly together, his fangs smeared with blood. Blood also spattered his clothes, fresh stains against the old ones, and pooled from holes in his chest and stomach, the gunshot wounds he had taken head-on. As I watched, horrified and fascinated at the same time, he dug his thumb and two fingers into the holes, clenching his jaw, and pulled out three lead slugs, dropping them to the pavement with a clink. The gaping wounds sealed, though the blood on his shirt, chest and hands remained.

Kanin shuddered, slumping against the wall. Voices echoed around us, men shouting, calling for backup. Through the window, the sky against the horizon was a dark blue, and a faint orange glow signaled the approach of the sun.

"Allison." Kanin's voice was soft; I barely heard it against the backdrop of shouting and gunfire. "Our time together has come to an end. This is where we have to part."

"What? Are you crazy?" I stared at him wide-eyed. "Screw that! I'm not leaving you."

"I've brought you as far as I can." Kanin's eyes were glassy; I realized he was probably starving, after taking those shots to the chest. But he still tried to speak calmly. "You know almost everything you need to survive. There's just one more thing I have to tell you." A bullet ricocheted off a car, sparking in the shadows, and I flinched. Kanin didn't seem to notice. "One last skill every vampire should know," he went on in a near whisper. "When you're caught outside with no shelter, you can burrow deep into the earth to escape the sun. It's something we do instinctively. It's also how the rabids sleep during the day, so be careful, because they're known for appearing right under your feet. You have to find a strip of natural earth, not rock or cement, and you must cover yourself completely. Do you understand? You might need it very, very soon."

I shook my head, barely listening to him, as the shouts and

wild barking drew even closer. "Kanin," I began, feeling my eyes start to burn, "I can't! I can't leave you here to die."

"Don't underestimate me, girl," Kanin replied with the faintest of smiles. "I've lived a long, long time. You think this is the worst situation I've encountered?" The smile got bigger, more evil, before he became serious again. "You, however. You will not survive this. Not now, not as you are. So you go out there, and you live, and get stronger. And someday down the road, we might meet again."

A howl of discovery, and a hail of gunfire peppered the wall, as we ducked down even farther. Kanin snarled, fangs springing to light, the glassy look in his eyes getting brighter. He looked at me and curled his lip. "Go! Head for the forest. I'll keep them busy for a while yet." A bullet hit the wall, spraying us with grit, and he growled, "Go! Leave me."

"Kanin—"

He roared, his face turning demonic, the first real glimpse of what he could become, and I shrank back in terror. "Go! Or so help me, I will tear your heart out myself!"

I bit back a sob. Turning, I crawled across the floor and slipped through a broken window on the far wall, half expecting a bullet in the spine at any second. I didn't look back. Kanin's howl rose into the air, a chilling sound of defiance and rage, followed by a frantic burst of gunfire and a desperate scream.

Reaching the edge of the lot, I fled into the ruins, hot bloody tears streaming down my face, blinding me. I ran until the sounds of battle faded behind me, until I left the ruins and entered the forest, until the lightening sky forced my limbs to a sluggish crawl.

Finally, I collapsed, snarling and crying, at the roots of several old trees. Dawn was seconds away from touching the earth and turning me into a fiery inferno. Half blinded by red tears, I buried my fingers in the cool, damp ground, scraping away dirt and leaves, wondering if I could really burrow fast enough to escape the sun. It was hot, so very hot. I scraped faster, frantic, wondering if smoke really was rising from my skin.

The earth rippled and seemed to melt beneath me, swallowing me up. I dropped into a black hole, cold dirt settling around me like a cocoon, and the heat vanished immediately. Cool, blessed darkness flooded in, and then there was nothing.

WHEN I WOKE AGAIN, the world was quiet, and I was alone.

Shaking free the dirt that clung to my hair and clothes, I gazed around, listening for gunfire, for any signs of life in the darkness. Nothing moved except the leaves, rustling in the trees above me. Through the branches, the sky blazed with stars.

Kanin was gone. I searched the area halfheartedly, backtracking toward the edge of the ruins, but I knew finding him was impossible. If he was dead, there would be nothing left behind but ash. I did stumble across a couple of human corpses, torn apart and savaged by what looked like a vicious beast. One of them still clutched an assault rifle in one bloody hand. I examined it, but the gun was empty, the rounds spent, and it was too useless and awkward to take with me.

Only when I was certain I was truly alone did I wonder what I would do next.

Damn you, Kanin, I thought, trying to stifle the fear, the uncertainty, threatening to smother me. Where could I go now? What was I going to do? I didn't dare go back to the city; the Prince would certainly have me killed for my association with the vampire world's Most Wanted. But whatever lay beyond the ruins was a mystery. What was out there, really? Another vampire city, perhaps. But maybe not. Maybe it was all wilderness, as far as the eye could see. Maybe nothing existed out there but rabids, crawling over everything, killing any human they came across.

But I wasn't human anymore. And I wasn't as afraid of them as I once was. I was part of *their* world now, part of the darkness.

I was still scared. I hated the thought of leaving home and the relative safety of the city. But there was a part of me that was a tiny bit excited, as well. Maybe everything in my short miserable life had led up to this. I was outside the walls. I was far from vampire influence. True, I was dead, but there was a strange freedom in that. Everything in my other life was gone. I had nothing to go back to.

Go out there, and live, and get stronger.

"All right then, Kanin," I muttered. "Guess I'll just go see what's out there."

Turning, I gazed through the trees, back toward the ruins and the city, sparing one last look at the lights of my old home. Then, with nothing but my sword and the clothes on my back, I put New Covington behind me and stepped forward, into the wilderness. And I didn't stop until I was certain I would see nothing but trees if I looked back.

PART III

MONSTER

Chapter 10

That first night, I walked through trees and brush and tangled undergrowth, shaking my head at the vastness of it all, wondering if it would ever end. There was no road to follow, at least, not where I had come out. After spending my entire life within the city walls, this alien, green-and-brown world felt hostile and dangerous, like it was trying to drag me down and swallow me whole. I did stumble upon a few leftovers of human civilization—old houses crumbling under carpets of weeds and moss, a few rusty car skeletons choked with vines—but the farther I got from the city, the wilder the forest became. I'd had no idea it was this big, that trees could just stretch on forever and ever. I thought of New Covington and wondered how many years it had left, how long until nature crawled up its walls and smothered it completely.

And unlike the empty city, with its silent streets and cold, dead buildings, the wilderness was alive. Everything moved out here. Branches sighed in the wind. Insects buzzed through the air. Things rustled in the bushes just out of sight. At first, it was unnerving; I'd grown up on the street where every noise or sudden movement made you flinch and tense to run. But after a couple nights of this, listening to things flee from *me,* I came to the conclusion that there was nothing beyond the city that could really put me in any danger. I was a vampire. I was the scariest thing out here.

I was dead wrong, of course.

Just after dusk one evening, I stumbled upon a slow-moving stream and followed it for a while, wondering if it led anywhere. I caught glimpses of several deer and a raccoon at the water's edge, and figured more animals would be drawn to the water. But I'd grown so used to seeing wildlife by now that I didn't think much about it.

There was a low growl in the shadows ahead, and I froze.

Something massive and dark lumbered out of the trees, coming to a stop a few yards away at the edge of the water. It was the biggest animal I'd ever seen, with shaggy brown fur, huge shoulders and enormous yellow claws. It snuffed at me, then raised its lip, revealing a set of huge teeth, some as long as my fingers.

My stomach dropped. I'd heard the stories the old-timers of the city would throw around sometimes, of the wild creatures that lived beyond the walls, breeding and populating without restraint. But the word *bear* didn't do the real animal justice. This thing could tear a rabid in two without thinking about it. It could probably give a vampire a run for its money.

Which meant I might be in a bit of trouble here.

The bear stared at me with beady black eyes, huffing softly, shaking its huge head as if confused. I stood rigidly still and tried to remember what you were supposed to do if you met a bear out in the woods. Fall down? Play dead? Yeah, *that* didn't sound like a good idea at all. Slowly, I reached back and grasped the hilt of my sword, ready to draw it if the bear charged. If I landed one good, solid blow on the neck, behind its head, maybe that would be enough to kill it. Or at least slow it down. And if that didn't work, I could always climb a tree...

The bear snorted at me, nostrils twitching. It swayed back and forth, making low groaning sounds in its chest, scraping the dirt with its claws. I got the distinct impression that it was confused. Maybe I didn't smell like prey. Maybe I didn't smell alive at all. But it turned and, with one last grunt in my direction, lumbered away into the woods. I waited until I could no longer hear it plowing through the undergrowth, then hurried away in the opposite direction.

Okay, so there were bigger, scarier things out here than rabids. Good to know. I wondered why it hadn't attacked me. Had it sensed another predator, like itself, and decided to look for easier prey? I didn't know. But I could guess that the bear thought I was something unnatural, something that didn't belong in this leafy world with its endless trees. The wildlife out here probably didn't meet many vampires. I also wondered what the rest of New Covington would say if a bear came waddling down the street into the city. I smirked at the thought. They'd probably crap their pants. If Stick saw one, he'd faint dead away.

My smile faded. Where was he now? I wondered. Was he still living in the warehouse with the other Unregistereds?

Or had he sold me out to move into the vampire towers, to be fed and taken care of, beginning a new life as a pet?

I growled and grabbed a branch, tearing it away from the trunk. He wouldn't do that to me, I told myself angrily. It couldn't have been him. We looked out for each other, watched each other's backs. I had saved his life countless times. He wouldn't just throw all that away, as if all those years meant nothing to him, as if I was dead to him now. The enemy. A vampire.

Stop kidding yourself, Allie. Who else could it have been? I sighed and kicked a rock, sending it flying into the undergrowth. The way Stick had looked at me that night in the warehouse, that was true terror. I'd seen it in his eyes: Allison Sekemoto, the girl who looked after him for years and years, was dead. My emotions still held a stubborn hope that humans could be loyal, that they could hold out against the promise of an easy life. But I knew better. Unregistered or not, if offered a way out of being hungry and cold and dumped on, Stick would take it in a heartbeat. It was just human nature.

The wilderness went on, and I wandered for several nights, not knowing or caring where I was going. When dawn tinted the skies pink, I burrowed into the earth, only to awake the following night with no sense of where I was or where I should go next. I met no one in my travels, human or vampire, though the woods were teeming with wildlife, most of which I had never seen before and knew their names only through stories. Fox and skunk, rabbit and squirrel, snakes, raccoons and endless herds of deer. I saw larger predators, too: a wolf pack loping silently through the trees one evening, the tawny form of a huge cat, its eyes glowing in the darkness.

They never bothered me, and I gave them a wide berth as well, one predator to another.

On the sixth night, I climbed out of my shallow grave with a sense of purpose, feeling my fangs pressing against my bottom lip. I was hungry. I needed to hunt.

The small herd of deer feeding in the meadow scattered when they saw me, but I was faster, pouncing on a stag and bringing it, kicking and bleating, to the ground. The blood that flowed into my mouth was hot and gamey, but though I felt it spread through my stomach, the gnawing ache was still there. I ran down another deer and gorged myself on its blood, to the same effect. I was still hungry.

Other animals couldn't fill the Hunger, either. I went to sleep famished, and each night, rising from the earth, I went hunting, chasing down and draining anything I came across. Nothing helped. My stomach was full, sometimes overly so; I could feel it pressing against my ribs. But the Hunger only got stronger.

Until, one night, starving and desperate, I chased a doe out of the briars, lunged forward to grab it, and landed on a stretch of pavement.

Blinking, I stood, letting the deer bound away into the trees. I was in the middle of a road, or what had been a road. Most of it was covered in weeds and brush, and grass was pushing up through numerous cracks in the pavement. Forest was closing in on either side, threatening to swallow it whole, but it was still there, a narrow strip cutting through the trees, vanishing into the darkness in both directions.

I stifled a flare of excitement. There was no guarantee the road led anywhere now. But following it was a lot more promising than wandering aimlessly through the wilderness, and right now, I'd take what I could get.

Picking a direction, I began walking.

I SLEPT ONE MORE DAY, burrowing into the earth on the side of the road and waking the next night completely starved. My fangs kept slipping out on their own, and I found myself perking at every rustle, every movement in the darkness around me. The urge to hunt was almost overwhelming, but I'd only be wasting time and energy, and it wouldn't stop the awful Hunger gnawing at my insides. So I kept walking, following the road, my mouth as dry as grit and my stomach threatening to eat its own lining.

A few hours from dawn, the woods finally began to thin out. Not long after that, they turned into rolling grasslands, with barely a tree to be seen. I was relieved, for I had seriously started to think the woods went on forever.

The road widened as it cut across the plains. It was quiet out here, unlike the forest, with its constant rustle of small creatures in the brush, the hiss of wind moving through the leaves. Except for my soft footsteps against the pavement, the world was silent and still, and the stars blazed overhead, stretching on forever.

So I heard the rumble of engines a very long ways off, probably several miles in the distance. At first, I thought I was hearing things. Coming to a stop in the middle of the road, I watched, fascinated, as headlights appeared and the rumbles grew louder.

Gliding over a rise were two short, sleek machines. They weren't cars or trucks or any type of vehicle I'd seen before;

they had two wheels and moved faster than a car, but it was difficult to see anything else beyond the headlights. Watching them approach, I felt a ripple of excitement. If there were strange vehicles like these on the road, then maybe humans lived outside the Wall, after all.

The headlights drew closer, shining in my eyes, nearly blinding me. Somewhere in the back of my mind, the old Allison, the wary, cautious street rat, was telling me to get off the road, to hide, to let them go by without knowing I was there. I ignored the voice. My gut told me that whatever powered these strange machines was human. I was curious. I wanted to see it for myself. I wanted to see if humans could live outside the city, away from vampire influence.

And…I was hungry.

The vehicles pulled to a stop a few feet away and the rumble of engines kicked off, though the lights remained, shining in my eyes. Raising a hand to shield my gaze, I heard a rusty squeak as something stepped off the machine, coming to stand beside it.

"Well, well." The voice was deep and mocking, and a large, rough-looking man stepped forward, silhouetted against the light. He was tall and barrel-chested, with tattoos covering his arms like sleeves. Another covered half his face, the image of a grinning dog or wolf or coyote, baring its fangs at me. "What do we have here?" he mused. "You lost, little girl? This is a bad place for you to be stranded, all alone, at night."

A second man joined the first, smaller and skinnier, but no less threatening. Unlike the first, he seemed more eager, less cautious than his companion. He had the same dog tattoo on one shoulder, and a bright, hungry gleam in his eyes.

"We don't see many bitches out here," he agreed, running a tongue along his bottom lip. "Why don't you keep us company for a while?"

I bristled, backing up a step, fighting the urge to snarl at them. This had been a mistake. They were human and, worse, they were men. I knew what they wanted; I'd seen it on the street countless times, and it made my gut tense. I should've stayed hidden, should've let them go by. But it was too late. I could taste the violence on the air, smell the lust and sweat and blood pumping below their skin. Something inside me responded, rising eagerly, the Hunger a dancing flame in my gut.

There was a metallic click, and the first man drew a gun, pointing the barrel at my face. "Don't even think of running," he crooned, baring yellow, uneven teeth in a wide grin. "Just come over here and make it easy on yourself."

When I didn't move, he nodded at his companion, who stepped forward and grabbed my arm.

The second his hand touched my skin, something inside me snapped.

Prey! Food! With a wild screech, I turned on the human, fangs bared, and he jerked back with a screaming curse. I snatched at him, sensing the heat and hot fluids below his skin, pumping in time with his heart. I could smell his blood, hear his frantic heartbeat, and my vision went red with Hunger.

A howl and a roar behind me. The vivid scent of fresh blood, and the human jerking against me, gasping. I spun, furious now, searching for my prey. It stood against the light, smelling of blood and fear, the gun leveled at my chest. I roared, dropping the limp human, and lunged. The gun barked twice, missing, and I slammed into the prey's chest, driving him to the ground. He swung wildly at my face, elbows glancing off my cheek, as I yanked him up and sank my fangs into his neck.

The prey stiffened, going rigid, and I sank my fangs in deeper, piercing the vein and causing the blood to flow more freely. Warmth filled my mouth and throat, flowing down to my stomach, easing the horrible ache that had been there so long. I growled in pleasure and tore impatiently at the surrounding flesh, causing even more blood to flow. I drew that power into myself, easing the pain in my stomach and shoulder, feeling my wounds close and the Hunger fade. The rest of the world disappeared, all sounds vanished, all sensations shrank down to this—this perfect, intoxicating moment where nothing mattered but power.

Beneath me, the human made a choking, shuddering sound, like a whimper, and I suddenly realized what I was doing.

Shaking, I released him, staring down at the man, the human who, for a few insane moments, had been nothing but prey to me. His neck was a mess of blood; in my eagerness, I'd done more than simply bite his throat—I'd shredded it. Red soaked his collar, but the wound wasn't oozing blood. Experimentally, I shook his shoulder.

His head lolled to the side, and his eyes stared ahead, unseeing and glassy. He was dead.

No. I put both hands to my mouth, shaking so hard I thought I would puke. It had happened, just like Kanin had said it would. I had killed someone. I had murdered a human being. The second I'd tasted blood, the demon had taken over, and I'd lost my mind. I'd lost control to the Hunger. And in those mad few heartbeats, with the blood flowing hot in my mouth and through my veins, I had loved every second of it.

"Oh, God," I whispered, staring at the body, the corpse that, a few minutes ago, had been a living, breathing being. I'd killed him. I'd *killed* him. What did I do now?

An agonized groan interrupted me. I looked fearfully to where the other human lay sprawled on the pavement, gazing up at the sky. He was breathing in short, panicked gasps, and his eyes widened as I stood and walked toward him.

"You!" he gasped. His legs twitched as he tried to get up. Blood seeped from his chest, where he'd taken a bullet meant for me. He didn't have long, even I could see that. But he didn't seem to notice, staring up at me with glazed eyes. "Didn't know...you were a vampire."

The man gagged, blood spilling out of his mouth, running down to the pavement. His blank stare cut me like a thousand knives. "I'm sorry," I whispered, not knowing what else to say. But that only seemed to push him over the edge, for he started to laugh.

"Sorry," he repeated, as his head lolled to the side. "Vampire kills my mate, then says she's sorry." He collapsed into uncontrollable giggles, choking on his own blood. "This is...a joke, right?" he whispered, as his eyes rolled up in his head. "A vampire...joke? Jackal...would've...laughed..."

He didn't move again.

I might've stayed there, kneeling in the cold grass, the smell of blood clogging my nose and mouth, except the sky over the hills was lightening, and my internal clock warned me dawn wasn't far away. For a moment, I wondered what it would be like if I just...stayed aboveground. Met the sun, as

Kanin once said. Would it burn me to ash? Would it take very long, be very painful? I wondered what lay beyond; I'd never been very religious, but I'd always believed vampires had no souls, and no one knew what happened to them when they finally left the world. It didn't seem possible that I, a monster and a demon, could ever have a shot at heaven or eternity or whatever happened when humans died. If such a thing existed.

But if heaven existed, then so did...the other place.

Shuddering, I crawled into the grass and burrowed deep into the earth, feeling it close around me like a grave. I might be a demon and a coward, and I might deserve to burn, but in the end, I didn't want to die. Even if it damned me to hell, I would always choose to live.

Though, for the first time since the attack that terrible night in the ruins, I wished Kanin hadn't saved me, after all.

CHAPTER 11

The bodies were still there, stiff and waxy, when I rose the next evening. They had already attracted a flock of crows and other carrion birds. I shooed the scavengers away and, feeling it was the least I could do, dragged the bodies off the road into the tall grass, leaving them to nature. The vehicles they'd been driving had run out of fuel or electricity or whatever powered them, for their lights were dead, and they were cold and still. I wondered if I could've ridden one of them, but I'd never driven anything in my life, and the machines seemed very complicated even if they still worked. So I left them sitting on the side of the road as I continued my journey to wherever I was going.

Another night or two passed with no distractions. I walked through towns and settlements, all dead, all overgrown and empty. I came upon several crossroads, where other roads stretched away in opposite directions until they were lost to the darkness, but I kept to the road I was walking. I became used to the silence, the emptiness and the vastness of the sky above. The stars were my only constant companions, though I did see deer and small animals and herds of shaggy horned beasts roaming the plains. When the sun threatened the horizon, I burrowed into the earth and slept, only to rise and repeat the same thing the following night. Everything I did became habit: rise, shake the dirt out, face the same direction as the night before and walk. I didn't think of the city. Or Kanin. Or anything behind me on the road. Instead, I occupied myself with what I might find over the next rise, the next hill. I sometimes imagined a distant city, sparkling with lights, or the glow of a vehicle, coming toward me. Or even the silhouette of another traveler, walking toward me in the darkness. Of course, nothing like that ever appeared; no lights, no vehicles, no humans. Only empty flatlands and the skeletons of what had been houses or farms. The encounter with the two men seemed a hazy, half-remembered dream, something that hadn't really happened to me, as it soon felt as if I was the only person left in the entire world.

I didn't run into any rabids, which was surprising at first. I'd been expecting to fight my way past at least a few by now. But maybe rabids only hung around cities and towns where their human prey would be. Or perhaps, like the bear, they didn't bother hunting vampires. Maybe their prey had to be alive and breathing to catch their attention.

Maybe they thought vampires were just like them.

Finally the road took me through another dead town. It was much like the few others I'd seen—empty and overgrown, buildings crumbling to rubble, abandoned cars rotting in the streets. As I passed the remains of an old gas station, I wondered if it had already been raided for food and supplies. Then I realized I didn't need to check, which I found ironic and a little sad. The old Allie would've seen a place like that as a potential treasure trove. Old buildings, abandoned stores, empty gas stations—there were a ton of supplies out here just waiting to be scavenged. I didn't need food or water or any of that anymore. The only thing I needed was the one thing that wasn't here.

I sighed, just for the hell of it, and continued into the town.

As I passed a tree growing through the hood of a car, I caught a faint rustle in the grass and a quiet whimper. Not an animal noise, either. This sounded human.

I paused. It had been four days since the…incident…with the men on the road. Was I still a danger to humans? Could I control myself in the presence of my prey? The Hunger seemed sated for now, held in check, but I'd still have to be very careful.

The sound came again. Wary of rabid wildlife, I drew my sword and eased around the car, ready to slash at anything that came flying out of the weeds. When I saw what was hiding behind the tree, however, I relaxed.

A small, frightened face gasped and recoiled, wide-eyed, tears streaking his cheeks. He had dark hair, smudged, dirty skin, and was probably no more than six years old.

A kid? What's a kid doing way out here, alone?

Still wary, I lowered my sword. The child sniffled and gazed up at me, teary-eyed but silent. I looked for wounds on his small body, bite marks or scratches, but he was clean. There wasn't any blood, though he was frightfully thin, a trait that was all too common where I came from. "W-who are you?" he sniffled, pressing himself against the trunk. "I don't know you. You're a stranger."

"It's all right. I'm not going to hurt you." Sheathing the blade, I knelt beside the kid, holding out my hand. "Where do you live?" I asked gently, stunned that someone would let a child roam around these streets at night. Did they *want* him eaten by rabids? "Where's your mom and dad?"

"I d-don't live here," he whispered, hiccuping with the effort not to cry. "I don't h-have a mom or a dad. I live with e-everyone, but now I can't find them!"

He wasn't making much sense, and the last sentence had finally dissolved into a frightened wail, setting my teeth on edge. We'd never get anywhere like this, and his howling could attract rabid animals at the least. They might ignore me, but if they sensed this child, we'd have a problem.

"It's okay," I said quickly as the child stuffed his small fist into his mouth. "It's all right, we'll find everyone else. There are other people here, right? In the town?"

He nodded. "They were looking for food and stuff," he said, pointing a grubby finger in an indiscriminate direction. "Over there, I think. I had to go potty, but when I came back they were gone."

So, hopefully, they'd be close. Whoever *they* were. Probably an aunt or a relative or something, since the kid didn't have any parents. His bottom lip trembled, and I scrubbed my eyes. "Let's go look for them," I said, standing up. "Come on. I'm sure they're looking for you, too."

What? The Fringer street rat in me recoiled, aghast. *What are you doing, Allison? You don't know this kid. Why are you getting involved?*

I ignored the voice. What was I supposed to do? I certainly couldn't leave a child out here alone. Not even I was that callous. I'd drop him off with his parents or guardians or whomever, and then...

I repressed a shiver. When was the next time I might run into humans? If I returned this child to his guardians, they would probably be relieved. They might ask me inside, offer to let me spend the night. It would be easy enough, while they were sleeping, to slip up beside them, to...

Horrified, I shut those thoughts away. But what could I do? I was a vampire, and if I didn't keep the Hunger in check, I would revert to that snarling, mindless creature on the road. If I had to feed, at least it would be on my terms now. "Well," I asked the boy, holding out my hand, "are you coming or not?"

The kid brightened. Standing up, he reached for my hand and clung tightly to my fingers as I led him away. He didn't cry or even sniffle as we wove through dark alleys, between rotting buildings, and around smashed, rusty cars. Either he was too frightened to say anything, or he was used to walking around scary, unfamiliar places in the middle of the night.

"What's your name?" he asked as we made our way down another sidewalk, stepping over glass and fallen streetlights. He seemed calm now, relieved to be in the presence of a grown-up, even if she was a stranger.

"Allison," I muttered back, scanning the darkness and shadows for any signs of movement, human or otherwise. A gray fox glanced up from where it scavenged along a wall and darted into the weeds, but other than that the night was still.

"I'm Caleb."

I nodded and turned down another road, finding the edge of what was once a plaza. Moss covered the remains of benches along the cracked sidewalks, and the stone fountain in the center of the square was dry and crumbling to gravel. Leaves crunched under our feet as we followed one of the paths past a gazebo with a fallen roof, toward the other edge of the plaza.

Suddenly, I paused, pulling Caleb to a halt. Behind us, amid the broken wreckage of the gazebo, I heard the quiet thump of a heartbeat.

"Why are we stopping?" whispered Caleb.

"Turn around," said a voice, somehow, impossibly, at my back. "Slowly."

Still keeping a tight grip on Caleb's hand, I turned.

A human stood behind us, a few yards from the gazebo. He was lean, a few inches taller than me, with blond hair, and his eyes—a bright, piercing blue—never left my face.

Neither did the barrel of the pistol trained on my head.

"Zee!" Caleb cried and rushed forward. I let him go, and he hurled himself at the stranger, who bent down, hugged the child to his neck and stood. All without taking his eyes, or his gun, off me.

"Hey, rug rat," he murmured, speaking to Caleb but still watching me intently. "*You* are in a ton of trouble, little man. Your sister and I have been looking everywhere for you." His eyes narrowed. "Who's your friend?"

"Caleb!"

A scream interrupted him, and a slender, dark-haired girl of maybe sixteen rushed up to us, holding out her hands. "Caleb! Oh, thank God! You found him!" She took the child from "Zee," hugged him tightly, and set him on the ground to glower at him. "Where did you go? You scared us all to death, wandering off like that! Don't ever, *ever* do that again, do you understand?"

"Ruth," the blond boy said quietly, still keeping me in his sights. "We have company."

The girl's head jerked up, her eyes widening when she saw me. "Who…?"

"That's Allison," Caleb chirped, turning to smile at me. I smiled back, but my gaze was still on the boy with the gun. "She helped me find you when I was lost."

"Is that so?" The boy frowned, shifting forward to put himself between me and his charges. "And what is she doing out here, wandering the town all alone in the middle of the night?"

"That's what I'd like to know," the girl, Ruth, added, glaring at me over the boy's shoulder. "And just what were you planning to do with my brother?" she demanded—very brave, I thought, for someone hiding behind a gun. "Who are you, anyway?"

I ignored her, knowing the boy was the one I'd have to convince. He watched me calmly, blue eyes taking in my every move. Now that I saw him clearly, I realized he was probably no older than me, with dusty jeans, a tattered jacket, and jagged blond hair that fell into his eyes. He returned my smirk with the unmistakable air of someone who knew how to handle himself. But maybe that was due to the weapons he was carrying. Besides the gun, still pointed at me, he wore a hatchet on one hip, a dagger on the other, and a strap across his chest, the hilt of a machete poking up behind his shoulder. I had no doubt he had a couple other weapons hidden somewhere, a knife in his boot or up his sleeve. I also suspected he knew how to use each and every one of them. A small silver cross dangled from a chain around his neck, glimmering against his ragged shirt.

His eyes flicked to the hilt over my shoulder, then to my waist, looking for weapons. I kept very still, wondering if I could reach him and yank the pistol away without getting shot in the face. If it came to that. The strange boy seemed wary but not openly hostile. I suspected he didn't want a fight, and I didn't, either. Not after...

I shoved that memory down and focused on the humans, still eyeing me cautiously. "So, are you going to shoot me?" I asked after we spent a moment sizing each other up. "Or are we going to stand around looking at each other all night?"

"Depends," the boy said with an easy smile, not lowering the gun. "Who are you? There aren't many people who go wandering around at night with the rabids. And you're not from around here, I know that much. Where did you come from?"

"New Covington."

He frowned, not recognizing the same. "One of the vampire cities," I elaborated without thinking better of it.

Ruth gasped. "A vampire city! Zeke, come on!" She tugged at his sleeve. "We should get back to the others, warn them!" Her dark glare stabbed at me behind his arm. "She could be one of those pets Jeb told us about! She could be out hunting for new blood slaves."

"I'm not a pet," I snapped at her. "And pets don't bother hunting for blood slaves—they let the raiding parties do that. Do you see anyone else around here?"

The boy, Zeke, hesitated, shaking off Ruth's arm. "If you came from a vampire city, what are you doing here?" he asked in a reasonable voice.

"I left." I raised my chin and stared him down defiantly. "I got tired of being hunted, of watching the vamps do whatever they want to us, because we're just animals to them. Better to take my chances outside the Wall and free than stay in the city as a slave to some bloodsucker. So I got out. And I'm never going back. If you want to shoot me for that, you go right ahead. It's better than what I left behind."

The boy blinked and seemed about to say something, when Caleb let out a soft cry and rushed forward, hitting his leg.

"Don't shoot her, Zee!" Caleb ordered as the boy flinched, more in surprise than pain. "She's nice! She helped me find you." He pounded the leg again with his small fists. "If you shoot her, I'll be mad at you forever. Leave her alone!"

"Ow. Okay, okay. I won't shoot her." Zeke winced and lowered his pistol, as Ruth grabbed Caleb by the arm, dragging him away. "I wasn't going to, anyway." He sighed and sheathed the gun in a back holster, turning to me with a resigned shrug. "Sorry about that. We were all freaking out when we couldn't find the rug rat, and we don't run into many people out here. I didn't mean to scare you."

"It's fine," I said, and the tension diffused. Ruth was still glaring at me, with Caleb in her arms now, squirming to get down. But she seemed petty and unimportant compared to the boy across from me.

He smiled and suddenly looked younger, far less threatening. "Let's try this introduction thing again," he offered with a rueful look. "Thank you for bringing Caleb back. I'm Zeke

Crosse. This is Ruth—" he nodded to the girl, who narrowed her eyes even more "—and you've already met Caleb."

"Allison. Or Allie." I nodded at them, looking around for other humans besides the trio, finding none. "What are *you* doing out here? Is it just the three of you all alone?"

He shook his head, raking bangs out of his eyes. "Just passing through, like you said. We stopped here to look for supplies before we move out again."

"How many of you are there?"

"About a dozen." He blinked, regarding me intently. I raised an eyebrow and gazed back. "You really came from a vampire city?" he asked in an awed voice. "And you've been traveling since then, all alone? Do you know how dangerous it is out here?"

"Yes." I reached back and touched the hilt of my katana. "And you don't have to worry. I can take care of myself."

Zeke whistled softly. "I don't doubt it," he muttered, and I thought I caught a hint of respect below the quiet surface. He blew out a breath and smiled at me. "Listen, I have to get these two," he nodded at Caleb and Ruth, "back to the others before Jeb goes through the roof. Do you need anything? We don't have much, but I'm sure we can spare a bag of chips or a can of beans or something. You don't look like you've eaten much lately."

I blinked in shock. His offer seemed genuine, which caught me off guard, making me wary again. Humans never gave food away to complete strangers. But before I could say anything, Ruth put Caleb down and stalked forward, eyes blazing.

"Zeke!" she hissed, tugging his sleeve again. He sighed as

she bent close. "We don't know anything about her," she said in a whisper, though I could hear every word. "She could be a thief, or a pet or a kidnapper for all we know. What will Jeb say if we come back with a complete stranger? Especially one who lived with *vampires?*"

"She just helped us find Caleb," Zeke replied, frowning. "I don't think she was going to spirit him off to New Covington or wherever she's from. Besides, you weren't worried when we let Darren join us, and he was from a bandit camp. What are you afraid of?"

"I want her to come," Caleb said, clinging to Zeke's pant leg. "Don't make her leave. She should come with us."

Well, this was entertaining, but it was probably time I left. There was no way I could travel with a group during the daylight hours. Though if I hung back and waited until they went to sleep...

"I really don't need anything," I told the trio in a flat voice. "Thanks, anyway. I was just leaving."

Caleb pouted. Zeke glared at Ruth, and she flushed, backing away. "It's up to you, Allison," Zeke said, glancing at me again. "But it's not any trouble, really. We're sort of used to picking up strays, isn't that right, rug rat?" He tousled the kid's hair, making Caleb giggle, before looking seriously back at me. "You're welcome to join us, at least for tonight. Jeb doesn't turn away anyone in need. In fact, if you want," he continued, cocking his head in a thoughtful manner, "you can even travel with us for a little while. We seem to be going the same direction. You'll have to get used to our weird hours, though. We sleep during the day and head out at night."

I blinked, hardly believing my ears. "You travel *at night?*" I asked, just to confirm it, and he nodded. "Why?"

A shadow crossed Zeke's face, and Ruth paled, glancing at Caleb. Both of them got very quiet for a moment. "That's…a long story," Zeke muttered, sounding uncomfortable, or sad. "Ask me again later." He jerked his head toward the child clinging to his leg, indicating: *ask me when Caleb isn't around to hear it.*

Definitely a story there. The grim look on his face spoke louder than words and made me curious. *I wonder what happened to them? What was so terrible that he doesn't want Caleb to hear?*

"So," Zeke continued as Ruth scowled, "the offer still stands, Allison. Are you coming or not?"

I shouldn't. I should just turn around and walk away without looking back. According to Zeke, there were at least a dozen humans wandering around, smelling like prey and blood, blissfully ignorant of the vampire lurking so close to their little community. If I accepted his offer, how long before they realized I wasn't human, especially with Ruth hovering like a suspicious vulture, waiting to expose me? And how long could I possibly go without wanting to eat them?

But then, if I stayed away from humans, isolating and starving myself, I'd eventually lose control again. And then I *would* kill someone. Maybe a child, like the boy on Zeke's leg. What if I had found *him* first, instead of those two men? The thought made me sick. I couldn't do that again. I couldn't.

Maybe…maybe if I took just a little blood at a time, I could keep the demon bottled up. There had to be a way. No one could find out, of course, and I'd have to be really, really careful, but that seemed a better plan than stalking them through the darkness, waiting for the Hunger to overcome me again.

"Please, Allie?" Caleb looked at me with large, pleading eyes as I still hesitated. "Please come with us? Pleeeaaase?"

"You heard him." Zeke smiled, handsome and charming in the moonlight. "You have to come now, or you'll make him cry."

Ruth pressed her lips together, glaring at me with darkest hate, but she was no longer important. I sighed, both because I felt like it and to give the impression that I still breathed. "All right," I said, shrugging. "You win. Lead the way."

Caleb grinned, skipped up to me, and took my hand. Ruth made a disgusted noise and stalked away into the shadows, muttering to herself. Shaking his head, Zeke gave me an apologetic glance and motioned us forward.

As I followed them, my fingers clutched firmly in the child's grip, I couldn't help but feel uneasy. This was probably an insanely bad idea, but I couldn't stop now. The cards had been dealt, and I was going to have to bluff my way through.

Besides, I didn't want to admit it, but I missed talking to someone. Those long, silent nights in the wilderness made me realize how much of a social creature I really was. Talking to Zeke was easy, and I wasn't quite ready to be alone again.

Even though, just a few minutes into our trek, he started to ask the hard questions.

"So, Allison," Zeke said quietly, as we picked our way over a stretch littered with nails, boards and shards of glass, sparkling in the moonlight. Caleb was in his arms, clinging tightly to his neck as he maneuvered through the debris, and

Ruth lagged a few steps behind, her glare burning into my back. "How long did you live in a vampire city?"

"All my life," I muttered. "I was born there."

"What was it like?"

"What do you mean, what was it like?"

"I mean, I've never been to one," Zeke answered, shifting Caleb to his other side, shaking out his arm. "I've never seen the inside of a vampire city—I've just heard the stories and rumors. And of course, no two are the same, you know?"

"Not really." I looked away, wondering how I could get him off the subject. "What have you heard? What kind of stories?"

He gave me a crooked grin. "I could tell you, but I think it would be too scary for certain little ears." He used his free hand to point at Caleb, who seemed blissfully unaware. "Let's just say a few of them involve giant freezers and hooks on the ceiling."

I wrinkled my nose. "It's not like that," I said, giving in. "Basically it's a big city with lots of old buildings, vampires and poor people. There's a big wall that keeps rabids out, and a wall surrounding the Inner City, where the vampires live, and in between there are the humans. Or, at least, the ones that haven't been Taken into the Inner City to work for the vamps." I paused to kick a broken bottle, which went clinking over the pavement into the weeds. "Nothing special about it."

"Have you ever seen a vampire?"

I winced. That was another question I didn't want to answer. "They really didn't leave the Inner City very often," I said evasively. "Why, have you?"

"I've never seen one," Zeke admitted. "Rabids, yeah, I've

seen a ton of those. But never a real vampire. Jeb has, though.
He says they're vicious, soulless demons that can tear a man
in half and punch through steel walls. If you ever meet a real
vampire, the only thing you can do is pray and hope it doesn't
notice you."

My apprehension grew. "You keep talking about this Jeb
person," I said, not liking the sound of him at all. "Is he like
your leader or something?"

"My father," Zeke replied.

"Oh. Sorry."

"Not my real one." Zeke smiled, easing my embarrassment.
"He died when I was three. My mom, too. Killed by rabids."
He shrugged, as if telling me it was a long time ago and that
I didn't need to act sympathetic. "Jeb adopted me. But, yeah,
I guess he is our leader. He was the minister of our church,
anyway, before we all decided to leave to find Eden."

"Say *what?*"

I nearly tripped over a broken crate. For a second, I didn't
think I'd heard him right. Did he just say they were looking
for Eden? I wasn't religious at all, but even I knew what Eden
was. What it was supposed to be.

I stared at the boy walking casually at my side, wondering
if delusions could strike someone so young and handsome.
Zeke rolled his eyes.

"Yeah, I know." He gave me a sideways look, cocking an
eyebrow. "It sounds insane. Crazy fanatics off looking for
the Promised Land—I've heard it all before. No need to rub
it in."

"It's none of your business, anyway," Ruth added sharply.
"We don't need you to tell us how stupid it sounds."

"I wasn't going to say anything," I said, though that's exactly what I'd been thinking.

"But we're not looking for the biblical place," Zeke continued, as if I hadn't said anything. "Eden is a city. A huge city. One with the technology of the old days, before the plague. And it's run completely by humans. There are no vampires in Eden."

I stopped to face him. "You're joking."

He shook his head. "No. According to rumor, Eden lies somewhere on a huge island, surrounded by an enormous lake. The lake is so big and vast, no rabids would dare cross it, and the vampires don't know it exists."

"A magical island with no rabids or vampires." I curled my lip in disdain. "Sounds like a fairy tale to me."

I heard the bitterness in my voice, though I wasn't sure where it came from. Perhaps it was because the news that a city completely made up of humans, with no vampire influence and no threat of rabids, had come just a little too late for me. If I had heard this rumor earlier, when I was still alive, I might've gone looking for it, too. Or...maybe not. Maybe I would've laughed it off as a wild fantasy and continued life as I knew it. But at least I would've heard about it. I'd want the chance to know, to decide for myself. Eden didn't do me any good now.

Behind us, Ruth gave a disgusted snort. "If you don't believe him, leave," she challenged, stepping beside Zeke to glare at me. "No one is stopping you."

I resisted the urge to snap at her, focusing on Zeke, instead. "Is it really out there?" I asked, trying to give the notion of a vampire-free utopia the benefit of the doubt. "You really think you'll find it?"

Zeke shrugged, unconcerned, as if he'd heard it all before. "Who knows?" he said. "Maybe it doesn't exist, after all. Or maybe it's out there somewhere and we'll never find it. But that's what we're looking for."

"We'll find it," Caleb chimed in, nodding seriously. "We'll find it soon, Jeb says so."

I didn't want to crush his expectations, so I didn't say anything to that. A few minutes later, we walked past a rusting iron gate into the courtyard of a small apartment complex. Another human, a few years older than me, black-haired and lean like a wolf, stood guard near the entrance. He nodded and smiled at Zeke, but his eyes widened when he saw me.

"Zeke! You found him. But...who's this?"

"Another stray, wandering in the wilderness," Zeke replied with a wry grin at me. "Allison, this is Darren, our other stray. You two will have a lot to talk about."

"Ezekiel!"

Everyone straightened. We all turned as another human came striding up, dressed in black, his entire frame locked into a sense of determined purpose. Everything about him seemed sharp and hard, from the pinched, angled face to the bony shoulders, to the jagged white scar running from temple to chin. His long hair might've been jet-black once, but it was now the color of steel, tied behind him in a neat tail. His eyes, the same color as his hair, took stock of us all in a glance, before turning to Zeke.

"You found him, then." The clipped voice fit the man. It wasn't a question.

"Yes, sir. Actually—" and Zeke nodded to me "—she found him. I was hoping we could…let her stay with us for a while."

Those sharp gray eyes raked over me, missing very little. "Another stray?" he asked. "You've spoken to her then, Ezekiel?"

"Yes, sir."

"And does she know our situation? What we are searching for?"

"I've told her, yes."

I expected Ruth to pipe up, voicing her suspicions to what was obviously the leader of the group. But Ruth was quiet and still as she stood beside Darren, staring at the ground. Caleb, too, clung to her hand and remained silent. Only Zeke seemed truly at ease, though he stood straight and tall with his hands clasped behind him, like a soldier awaiting orders.

What have you gotten yourself into, Allison?

The human continued to observe me, betraying no emotion. "Your name?" he asked, like a pet barking orders to his underlings. I swallowed a growl and met his piercing stare head-on.

"Allison," I replied, giving him a smirk. "And you must be Jeb."

"I am Jebbadiah Crosse," the man continued with a slightly offended air. "And Ezekiel knows I turn away none in need, so you are welcome here. However, if you choose to stay, there are rules everyone must follow. We travel at night, and we move fast. Those who fall behind will be left. Everyone contributes—there are no free meals here, so you will be expected to work: hunting, gathering, cooking if there is need.

Thievery of any sort will not be tolerated. If you think you can follow these rules, then you are welcome to stay."

"Can I now?" I said as sarcastically as I could. "Thanks so much." I couldn't help it. Throwing rules in my face, expecting me to follow just because someone said so, never sat well with me. Ruth and Darren blinked at me, shocked, but Jebbadiah didn't so much as twitch an eyebrow.

"Ezekiel is my second—any problems you have, you take up with him," he continued and turned to Zeke, giving him a curt nod. "Good work finding the boy, son."

"Thank you, sir."

A very faint, proud smile crossed Jebbadiah's lips before he turned sharply to Ruth, who cringed under his stare. "I expect you to keep a better eye on young Caleb in the future," he said. "Such carelessness is unforgivable. Had Ezekiel not found him tonight, he would've been left behind. Do you understand?" Ruth's lower lip trembled, and she nodded.

"Good." Jeb stepped back, nodded at me, his steely eyes unreadable. "Welcome to the family, Allison," he stated and strode away, hands clasped behind him. I was tempted to make a face at his retreating back, but Zeke was watching me, so I resisted.

Darren slapped Zeke on the shoulder and returned to his post. Caleb beamed at us, but Ruth took his hand and dragged him off. I shot Zeke a sideways look, raising an eyebrow.

"Ezekiel?"

He winced. "Yeah. It's the name of an archangel, but only Jeb calls me that anymore." Raking a hand through his hair, he turned away. "Come on, I'll introduce you to everyone."

Not long after, I met nearly everyone in the small congregation, though I forgot most of their names as soon as I heard them. Of the dozen or so skinny, half-starved people, about half were adults; the rest were kids my age and younger. I suspected, from the amount of children running around with no parents, that the group had been larger once. I wondered how long they had been wandering, following a fanatical old man, looking for some mythical city that probably didn't exist. I wondered how many hadn't made it this far.

Initially, the adults were cool toward me; I was a stranger, new and untried, and yet another mouth to feed. It was the same back in the Fringe. But after Zeke told my story, with even more hatred and anger for the vampires than I had first embellished, they regarded me with newfound sympathy, awe and respect. I was relieved; in one fell swoop, I had won over this group of strangers without having to say or prove anything at all. Well, actually, it was Zeke who did the winning, but I wasn't going to complain. Staying with these people would be hard enough without immediate suspicion and distrust.

"All right, listen up, everyone!" Zeke called after introductions were made. "Dawn is about two hours away, and it's too late to continue on tonight. So we're setting up camp here. Now, listen, I need the first and second watch doubled until sunrise. Darren and I didn't see any rabids in the area, but I don't want to take chances. Allison…" He turned in my direction, surprising me. "Did you see any rabids when you first came in?"

"No," I replied, thrilled at what he was doing. Including me, making me a part of the group. "The road was clear."

"Good." Zeke turned back to the others. "Most of the

apartment rooms are fairly clear and have concrete floors, so we'll be safe there. Everyone get some rest while they can. Jeb wants an early start tomorrow night."

The group broke into organized chaos, moving slowly into the apartment complex. I stood beside Zeke, watching them, and caught several curious glances, especially from the kids and young people. Ruth glared daggers as she led Caleb into the apartment ruins, and I smiled back nastily.

"Ezekiel." Jeb appeared again, coming from nowhere to stand before us.

"Sir."

Jeb put a hand on his shoulder. "I want you to take first watch tonight with the others. At least until dawn. It's not that I don't trust Jake and Darren, but I want someone more experienced in a town like this. Make sure the demons don't creep up on us in our sleep."

"Yes, sir."

Jeb's gaze shifted to me and back again. "Take Allison with you. Tell her how things are done here. She can start contributing to the group today."

Oh, great. I hope they don't expect me to take watch in the daylight hours. How am I going to get out of this?

Jeb suddenly looked right at me, and something in those flinty eyes made me want to back away, snarling. "You don't mind, do you girl?"

"Not at all," I replied, staring him down, "if you ask me nicely."

Jeb's eyebrow twitched. "Ezekiel, will you excuse us a moment?" he asked in his not-really-a-question voice. Zeke gave me a helpless look but immediately nodded and left, walking back toward the gate.

I raised my chin and faced Jebbadiah Crosse, defiant smirk firmly in place. If this crazy old man wanted to lecture me, he was in for a surprise. I wasn't afraid of him, I wasn't part of his flock, and I was more than ready to tell him what he could do with his lecture.

Jeb regarded me with no expression. "Do you believe in God, Allison?"

"No," I said immediately. "Is this the part where you tell me I'm going to hell?"

"This is hell," Jebbadiah said, gesturing to the town around us. "This is our punishment, our Tribulation. God has abandoned this world. The faithful have already gone on to their reward, and he has left the rest of us here, at the mercy of the demons and the devils. The sins of our fathers have passed on to their children, and their children's children, and it will continue to be so until this world is completely destroyed. So it doesn't matter if you believe in God or not, because He is not here."

I blinked at him, speechless. "That's…"

"Not what you were expecting?" Jeb gave a bitter smile. "It is useless to offer words of hope when you have none yourself. And I have seen things in this world to make me certain that God is no longer watching us. I am not here to preach His message or to convert the entire world—it is far too late for that.

"However," he continued, giving me a hard stare, "these people expect me to lead them to our destination. I expect Ezekiel has already told you about Eden. Know this—I will allow nothing—*nothing*—to keep us from our goal. I will do whatever it takes to reach it, even if it means leaving a few behind. Those who cannot contribute, or those who cause problems, will be cast out. I give you this warning now. Make of it what you will."

"You're still hoping to reach your Promised Land even though you don't believe in it?"

"Eden is real," Jeb said with utter confidence. "It is a city, nothing more. I have no illusions of a Promised Land or Paradise. But there *is* a human city, one with no vampires, and that is enough to keep us searching.

"I cannot offer them God," Jebbadiah continued, looking back toward the apartments. "I wish I could, but He is far from our reach. But I can give them hope of something better than this." His expression hardened. "And perhaps, when we reach Eden, I can offer something more."

Once again, his gaze flicked to me, becoming sharp and cold. "This world is full of evil," he said, peering at me as if he was trying to see inside my head. "God has abandoned it, but that does not mean we should submit to the devils who rule it now. I know not what waits beyond this hell. Perhaps this is a test. Perhaps someday, we will cast the devils out for good. But first, we have to reach Eden. Nothing matters but that."

He might not be a true religious fanatic, but he was still scary, with that determined, obsessive gleam in his eyes. "Well, you can relax," I told him. "If you want to look for Eden, by all means, go right ahead. I'm not about to stop you."

"No, you will not." Jebbadiah stepped back as if that was the end of it. "Go to Ezekiel," he said, dismissing me with a wave of his hand. "Tell him to find you a tent and a back-pack—we have a few left over from those who have passed on. And be ready to move out as soon as the sun sets. We have a lot of ground to cover."

As soon as he was gone, I seriously considered leaving. Walking away from this insane cult with its fanatic leader who already had it in for me. How was I going to feed with ol' Crazy-eyes watching my every move? Something told me Jeb wasn't the understanding type. If he ever discovered what I was, I could see torches and angry mobs and stakings in my future.

For a second, I wondered if I shouldn't just vanish into the night. It was stupid and risky to be around so many humans, anyway. Maybe I *should* turn into a predator lurking on the fringes of their small society, hunting them through the darkness. But then Zeke came around a corner, a green knapsack over one shoulder, and I felt my convictions disappear.

"Heads up," Zeke said, tossing the pack at me. "There's a tent and a few supplies," he explained as I caught it, surprised that it was so light. "It's not big, but at least it'll keep the rain off you when we're camping out in the open. You know how to put up a tent, right?"

"Not really."

"I can show you," Zeke said, smiling again. "Tomorrow, I promise. But right now, I have first watch until dawn. Come sit with me a few minutes, and then I'll let you sleep—you probably need it after today."

As I smiled back and followed him to where he had set up

watch, I couldn't help thinking that this boy—this helpful, friendly, genuinely nice human being—was probably going to get me killed.

CHAPTER 12

The next evening, I woke up groggy and a bit disoriented. I wasn't in the cool, comforting earth; I'd taken shelter in a top room of the old apartment complex the previous night, well away from the group below. I'd had to climb a few flights of broken stairs, and I'd spent the daylight hours in a windowless hole of a room, lying on hard concrete, but it was necessary. I didn't want anyone tripping over my body in the daytime and realizing I slept like the dead.

Dropping back to the ground floor, I found most of the group just beginning to stir, as well. In the middle of the room, Ruth and an older woman with graying hair were starting to lay out food, opening cans of fruit and pouring them into metal bowls and cups. They seemed efficient as they opened a can, poured half the contents into a bowl, and handed it to a waiting child. Caleb, after receiving his share, trotted away with cup in hand, picking out yellow slices with his fingers. He stopped short when he saw me.

"Hi, Allie." Beaming, he held up his cup. "Look at what Zeke and Darren found yesterday! It's sweet. Are you going to get some?"

"Um." I glanced at the women and found Ruth glaring at me again. What the hell was the girl's problem? "Not now. I'm not really that hungry."

His eyes widened, as if he couldn't believe what I had just said. "Really? But, we hardly ever get food like this! You should try it, at least a little bit."

I smiled wistfully, remembering when I had taken such pleasure in a can of fruit. I wished I could've tried some, but Kanin had warned me that normal food would make me sick, and my body would expel it almost immediately. Meaning I would hurl it back up, something I did not want to do in front of a group of strangers.

"Here." Caleb held up a dripping yellow slice, and abruptly, the sweet, cloying smell made me slightly nauseated. "Have one of mine."

"Maybe later." I shifted uneasily and took a step back, feeling Ruth's never-ending glare at the base of my skull. "Have you seen Zeke?"

"He's always with Jeb when we first wake up." Caleb stuffed the whole slice into his mouth, then gave me a yellow-orange smile. "We usually don't see him until after breakfast."

"Here, dearie." An older woman stepped in front of me, holding out a bowl. It was half full of slimy, colorful fruit chunks, and my stomach recoiled at the sight of it. "We never got to thank you for finding Caleb last night. I know you must be hungry—go ahead and eat. We won't tell the others you skipped your place in line."

I stifled a sigh and took the bowl. "Thank you," I told her, and she smiled.

"You're one of us now," she said and hobbled back to the others, favoring her left leg. I tried to remember her name and failed.

Taking the bowl with me, I walked outside, looking for Zeke.

I found him talking to Darren near the broken gate, discussing plans for the night. Physically, Darren and Zeke were similar, all lean muscle and wiry strength, though Darren was dark where Zeke was pale and fair. Between them, the pair probably did most of the harder physical tasks, since the majority of the group were women, kids and old people. There was a middle-aged black man—Jake, I think his name was—who helped out as well, but he had a bad shoulder so the harder tasks fell to the two boys.

"I think we should spend some more time scavenging, too," Zeke was saying as I came up, "but Jeb wants everyone to move out as soon as they've finished eating. He already thinks we've wasted too much time here. You want to argue, you take it up with him. Oh, hey, Allison." He nodded pleasantly, and Darren scowled at me and walked off. I jerked my thumb at his back.

"What's with him?"

"Darren?" Zeke shrugged. "He's just being sulky, don't worry about it. He thinks we should wait another night before moving on, search the rest of the town for food and supplies. We got lucky yesterday. Found a mini-mart that hadn't been picked clean, and Dare thinks there could be more nearby."

He sighed and shook his head. "He has a point. Unfortunately, once Jeb says it's time to go, it's time to go."

"That's insane. Here." I handed him the bowl. He blinked in surprise but took it with a murmur of thanks. "He won't even stop for food? What's the hurry?"

"He's always been like that," Zeke replied with a careless shrug, and picked out a chunk of white fruit, tossing it back. "Hey, don't look at me. I don't make the rules. I just carry them out. But Jeb has our best interests at heart, always, so don't worry about it. Speaking of which, did you get any-thing to eat? We're not going to stop for several hours, and you should have something for the march."

"I'm good," I told him, avoiding his eyes. "I already ate."

"Ezekiel!" called a familiar voice. Jeb walked out of the apartments and motioned to him. "Are we almost ready?"

"Yes, sir!" Zeke called back and headed in his direction. But he stopped and gave the bowl to the elderly man sitting on the fountain ruins before continuing toward Jeb. "Every-one is packing up. As soon as we're all finished eating, we're ready to go."

They walked off, still discussing. I turned and came face-to-face with Ruth.

The other girl held my gaze. We were about the same height, so I could see right into her dark brown eyes. Oh, man, she didn't just dislike me, she *loathed* me. Which was pretty ungrateful, I thought. Especially since I had saved her darling little brother. *Especially* since I had no idea why she hated me so much.

"Can I help you?" I asked, arching an eyebrow at her.

She flushed. "I know who you are," she huffed, making my

stomach lurch. "I know why you're here, why you're hanging around."

Narrowing my eyes, I regarded her intently, wondering if she knew what a dangerous position she was in. "Is that so?"

"Yes. And I'm here to tell you to forget it. Zeke isn't interested."

Ah, *now* it all made sense. I almost laughed in her face. "Look, you don't have to worry," I said, trying to be reasonable. "I'm not interested that way, either."

"Good," she said, watching me intently. "'Cause there's something about you that isn't…right."

My amusement vanished. My senses prickled a warning, and the vampire within urged me to attack, to silence her before she became a problem. I shut it down, hard. "Aren't you taking this 'don't talk to strangers' thing a little far?" I asked.

Ruth's lips tightened. "You're hiding something," she said, taking a step back. "I don't know what it is, and I don't care, but Zeke is too good to be ruined by someone like you. He has the unfortunate habit of seeing the good in everyone, and he's too nice to realize he's being taken advantage of. So I'm warning you now, keep your dirty claws away from him. I'll make you sorry you ever came here if you don't." Before I could respond, she flounced off, dark curls bouncing. "And stay away from Caleb, too," she called back over her shoulder.

"Charming," I muttered under my breath and felt my fangs poking my gums. "Well, we know who's going to get bitten first now, don't we?"

Not long after that, fed, packed up and ready to march, the small group of eleven people gathered around the fountain, talking quietly with each other and shooting curious glances at me, hanging back in the shadows. Then, as if prodded by an invisible signal, we started moving out; three teens, five adults, three children and a vampire, weaving silently through town and onto the road. They walked quickly—even the kids and the two elderly people moved with a sense of purpose— and soon the town faded behind us.

"SO, ALLISON, WAS IT? You came from a vampire city. Did you see many of the soulless devils wandering about?"

I repressed a sigh. That was the question of the night, it seemed. I'd already been asked something similar by Teresa, the old woman with the bad leg; Matthew, a freckly ten-year-old; and Ruth, who inquired with a perfectly straight face if I had been a vampire's whore. Of course, then Caleb had to ask what a whore was, and Ruth gave him a very vague and watered-down explanation, all the while smiling at me over his head. If Zeke and Jeb hadn't been nearby, out of earshot of course, I might've punched the smug bitch in the nose.

This time, the question came from Dorothy, a middle-aged blond woman with vacant green eyes and a smile to match. She would often wander a little behind the rest of the group, staring down the road or toward the horizon, always smiling. Sometimes she waved to things in the distance—things that were never there. Other times she would randomly break into song, belting out "Amazing Grace" or "On a Hill Far Away" at the top of her lungs until someone told her, very nicely, to shush.

I suspected she was a few bricks short of a full load. But there were also times where she seemed perfectly coherent and normal. Times like now, unfortunately, when she was sane enough to ask questions I really didn't want to answer.

"No," I muttered, keeping my gaze on the road ahead. *Don't make eye contact with the crazy woman; don't look at her and maybe she'll go away.* "I didn't see many vampires 'wandering about.' I didn't see many vampires, period."

"How do you know?" Dorothy asked, and I gave her a suspicious look, forgetting not to make eye contact. She smiled emptily. "Vampire devils are masters of disguise," she went on, to my extreme discomfort. "People think they're slavering monsters with red eyes and fangs, but that's what they want you to think. Really, they can look like anyone else." Her voice dropped to a whisper. "That's what makes them so dangerous. They can look perfectly human. They can look just like Teresa. Or me. Or you."

I felt a flutter of panic and squashed it down. "I don't know, then," I told her with a shrug. "I saw lots of people in the city. Maybe they were all vampires—I couldn't tell."

"Oh, there are other ways to tell if a person is really a devil," Dorothy continued, nodding seriously. "Devils hate the sun. They burst into flame in the light. Devils can't resist the sight of blood, and they don't breathe like we do. But most important..." She leaned in, and I felt my fangs pressing through my gums, wanting to bite, to silence her. "Most important," she whispered, "devils are surrounded by this red glow, this aura of evil that only a few can see. You have to know what to look for, and it's difficult to see at a distance, but that is how you can tell a devil from a real person. Just like the white glow around the angels that walk down the road sometimes." She broke off, smiling dreamily at the horizon, where the pavement met the sky. "Oh, there's one now! Can you see him? He's walking away from us, so it might be hard to tell."

There was no one on the road. There was nothing ahead of us at all, except a large brown bird, perched on a fence post. I gave her a wary look and edged away, as she waved both arms in the air, making the bird fly off with a startled *whoo-whooing* sound.

"Is that Gabriel? Or Uriel?" She signaled frantically, then pouted. "Oh, he disappeared! They're so shy. It might've been Gabriel, though."

"Dorothy." Zeke was suddenly there, smiling as I shot him a desperate look over the crazy woman's shoulder. "Allison doesn't know us very well yet. She might be nervous around your angels—not everyone can see them as well as you."

"Oh, right! Sorry, love." Dorothy squeezed his shoulder, beaming crazily, but he only grinned back. "I forget sometimes. You're an angel yourself, you know that? Ezekiel. The angel of death."

Now Zeke looked faintly embarrassed, giving me an apologetic glance as Dorothy patted his arm and turned to me. "He thinks he can fool me," she whispered, loud enough for everyone to hear, "but I know he's an angel in disguise. You can tell. When you've seen as many angels as I have, you can always tell."

She tried patting my arm but missed as I slid smoothly away. Unconcerned and humming softly to herself, she wandered to the side of the road and peered into the distance, probably looking for her bashful angels. Zeke sighed and shook his head.

"Sorry about that," he said with a rueful grin. "Forgot to warn you about Dorothy—she's a little touched in the head, if you hadn't figured it out by now. Sees angels every other day."

My body uncoiled in relief. For a second, I'd thought I was in real trouble. "Has anyone here seen a real vampire?" I asked, wondering whom I should be wary of. "Forget fangs and claws and red beady eyes, does anyone here really know what they look like?"

"Well, Dorothy swears she's seen one, though she can't remember exactly when or where, so who knows if it was real. Beyond that..." He shrugged. "Jeb. Jebbadiah's whole family was slaughtered by a vampire when he was a kid, and he's never forgotten what it looked like. He says he's always remembered, so he can kill the vampire if they ever meet again."

I looked at Jebbadiah, at the head of the group, walking briskly down the road without looking back. And I wondered what a lifetime of anger, resentment and hatred could do to someone like him.

A few hours later, my internal clock was giving me the two-hour warning when Jeb held up a hand, calling the group to a stop. Zeke jogged up beside him, leaned in as Jeb spoke quietly, then turned to face the rest of us.

"Set up camp!" he called, sweeping his arm to the side, and the group immediately began shuffling off the road into the dry grass that surrounded us. "Jake, Silas, you're on first watch. Teresa—" he nodded at the old woman "—Darren will help Ruth with dinner tonight. You should rest your leg. Keep off it for a few hours at least." Darren muttered something as he passed, and Zeke rolled his eyes. "Yes, poor Darren, forced to cook and clean and do other unmanly things. Next thing you know he'll be wearing an apron and popping out babies." He snorted as Darren turned and did something with his hand. "We're friends, but we're not that close, Dare."

I hung back, watching as Zeke cleared away a patch of earth, built a tent of sticks over a bundle of dry grass, and started a fire. Quick. Efficient. Like he'd done this many times before. As I was wondering how long the group had been traveling, Ruth suddenly broke away from her tent and glanced up at me, raising an eyebrow.

"What's the matter, city girl?" she called, smiling sweetly. "Don't know how to set up a tent? A three-year-old could do it. Want Caleb to teach you how?"

I stifled the urge to strangle her, especially with Zeke nearby. "No, I'm fine, thanks." Hefting the bag on my shoulder, I marched past her, past the circle of tents around the campfire, to a spot about a hundred yards away. Dumping the tent onto the ground, I studied it fiercely.

All right. I can do this. How hard can it be, really? Kneeling, I picked up a long metal spike, frowning. *What in the world? Are you supposed to stab someone with these? Do tents come with vampire-slaying kits?*

Actually, it was fairly simple, once you figured it out. The metal stakes pinned the corners to the ground, and a couple plastic rods held it upright from inside. I was feeling fairly proud of myself, setting up a tent on the first try, when I fumbled with the rods and the whole thing collapsed on top of me.

Laughing, Zeke slipped into the small interior as I cursed

and struggled, shoving at the canvas. Grabbing the plastic frame, he maneuvered it into place with the ease of familiarity, snapping the tent upright.

"There," he said, still chuckling. "That should do it. You got one of the flimsy tents, sadly. Not bad, though, getting it up on your first try. You should've seen Ruth the first few times she tried setting hers up. I've never heard such language coming from our delicate flower."

I smirked, feeling vindicated. "It doesn't seem very sturdy," I admitted, gently shaking the plastic tube holding up the wall. Zeke chuckled again. He had a nice laugh, I decided, even if it was directed at me.

"Just don't hit the frame, and it'll be fine. Unless it's really windy outside. Or if someone accidentally bumps it. Or if an ant crawls on it." Zeke grinned. "Actually we're all used to the tents falling on top of us. Most of us don't even wake up when it happens."

I snorted. "So, if a big storm comes through—"

"At least you'll be dry as you go rolling across the plains."

I laughed. It felt strange; I hadn't done that in a while. Then I realized how close we were, huddled together beneath this tiny dome of canvas. I could see the details of his face, even in the darkness: the lines around his mouth and eyes, the faint scar on his forehead, nearly hidden by his pale hair. I could hear his heartbeat, sense the blood pulsing in his veins, right below the skin. For a moment, I wondered what Zeke tasted of, how it would feel to draw him close and sink into that oblivion.

It scared me, and I drew back. If I had been the slightest bit hungry...

Zeke blushed, raking his fingers through his hair, and I realized I'd been staring. "I should go," he muttered, backing out of the tent. "The others…I should probably help them." He pushed himself to a crouch at the entrance, balanced on the balls of his feet. "If you need anything, just let me know. Dinner should be ready soon. Oh, yeah. And this is for you."

Reaching off to the side, Zeke grabbed something and tossed it into the tent. It landed with a poof of dust: a thick blue-and-white quilt with only a tiny hole in one corner.

Stunned, I looked up at him. A blanket like this could be traded for a month of meal tickets back in the Fringe, and he was just *giving* it to me? That couldn't be right. "I…I can't take this," I muttered, holding it back to him. "I don't have anything to trade."

"Don't be silly." Zeke smiled, a little puzzled. "You don't have to give me anything for it. It's yours." Someone shouted to him across the camp, and he raised his head. "Be right there!" he called back, and nodded to me. "Gotta go. See you at dinner."

"Zeke," I called softly, and he paused, peeking back into the tent. "Thanks."

One corner of his mouth quirked up. "Don't worry about it. We look out for each other out here." He flicked the canvas wall, lightly. "And like I said, if the tent falls on you in the middle of the night, don't panic. You'll get used to it. No one really worries about keeping things erect around here, and… Wow, that sounded bad." His blush returned, brighter than before, and he raked a hand through his hair. "Uh…yeah, I should… I'm going to leave now."

Grimacing, he ducked out of sight. I waited until he was a good distance away before snickering into my quilt.

After zipping up the tent flaps, I looked around my newest lair. I didn't like how flimsy it was, how easily someone could invade. I also wondered if the thin canvas would completely block out the sun when it rose directly overhead. I didn't know if I would wake up if I suddenly burst into flames, or if I would quietly exit the world as my body burned to ash, but it wasn't something that I wanted to find out.

I took out my knife and made a long slit in the floor of the tent, revealing the grassy earth beneath. Now at least I had a quick escape if the sun penetrated my flimsy tent. Or if something unforeseen happened and I needed to get away quickly. Always leave yourself an out; that was the first rule of the Fringe. This group might seem friendly and unassuming, but you couldn't be too careful. Especially around people like Jebbadiah Crosse. And Ruth.

Lying back, I pulled the quilt over my head, hoping no one would disturb my sleep. As darkness closed over me and my thoughts turned slow and sluggish, I realized two things. One, I couldn't keep this up forever, and two, Ezekiel Crosse was far too perfect to survive in this world much longer.

THAT FIRST WEEK was a study in close calls.

Thankfully, I didn't burst into flames sleeping beneath the flimsy canvas tent, though I did wake up feeling uncomfortably warm, and wished I could simply burrow into the cool earth, away from the sun. As for the problem of guard duty, I spoke to Zeke the second night and convinced him to let me have first watch permanently. This meant staying awake a couple hours after dawn, and it was torture at first. My long coat protected me from the worst of the early morning rays, and I survived by staying in shaded areas whenever possible and never facing the direction the sun was coming up. But keeping myself awake was agonizing when my vampire instincts were screaming at me to sleep, to get out of the light. I finally started treating it as an exercise Kanin might have me do; building up my endurance to remain awake and active as long as I could.

My human companions were another issue. Except for Ruth, who continued to be a catty pain in the ass, shooting me poisonous looks if I so much as glanced at Zeke, and Jeb, who treated me with the same harsh aloofness as he did everyone else, the group was pretty friendly. Which I wouldn't have minded, except they were also a curious bunch, always asking me questions about the city, what it was like living there, how I had escaped. I answered as vaguely as I could and finally managed to convince the adults that it was just too painful to remember that life anymore. To my relief, the questions finally stopped, and everyone was very understanding, almost to the point of pity. That was fine with me. Let them think I'd been horribly scarred by my life in New Covington; it made it easier to hide the real reason I got uneasy whenever the word *vampire* came up.

Unfortunately, that wasn't the only problem I ran into.

Eating or, rather, the absence of it, was yet another difficulty. The group stopped twice for meals; once when everyone woke up and again near dawn when they set up camp. Rations were simple: half a can of beans or a few strips of dried meat, whatever they had scavenged or hunted or gathered.

Mealtime was easily the most anticipated part of the day, and after a night of forced marching without a break, everyone was starving.

Except me. And I had to get creative with ways to dump food without anyone noticing. Strips of meat or dried foods were easy; I hid them in my sleeves or pockets until I could toss them later. Canned beans, fruit and stew in bowls were a little trickier. When I could, I gave it away or dumped it into other people's bowls, though I could only do that so many times before people got suspicious. Sometimes I lied, saying I'd already had my share, and once I even ate a few spoonfuls of tomato soup in front of Zeke and Jeb, managing to keep it down long enough to walk calmly behind a tree and puke it back up.

I felt a little guilty, wasting food when it was so precious and scarce. And the Fringer street rat in me *cringed* whenever I threw perfectly good meat into the bushes or dumped half a can of corn down a dark hole, but what could I do? If I didn't keep up the appearance of being human, people would start to suspect. Like Ruth, who already had it in for me. I could hear her, sometimes, talking about me to the rest of the group, spreading suspicion and fear. Most of the adults—Teresa and Silas and Dorothy—paid little attention to her; they had bigger concerns than the jealous accusations of a teenage girl. But some of the others—Matthew, Bethany, even Jake—started eyeing me with distrust. As infuriating as it was, I couldn't do anything about it.

Despite that, it was Jeb who worried me most, the silent judge, whose sharp gray eyes missed nothing. But even though he was the leader, he seemed apart from the rest of the group, separate. He rarely spoke to anyone, and everyone seemed afraid to approach him. In a way, it was a good thing he was so detached from the rest of us; he didn't seem to care what anyone did or said as long as they followed his lead. If it wasn't for Zeke, relaying his orders back and forth, he wouldn't interact with the group at all.

In fact, I would've bet that I knew more about the group than he did. I knew Caleb loved sweets and Ruth was terrified of snakes—something I took great pleasure in when I found a garter snake on the road one night and snuck it into her tent. The memory of her screams made me snicker the rest of the evening. I knew Teresa, the old woman with the bad leg, and Silas, her husband, had been married thirty-nine years and were getting ready to celebrate their anniversary next fall. I knew Jake had lost his wife to a rabid attack three years prior and hadn't spoken a word since. These facts and memories and snippets of their lives trickled in and stayed with me, even though I did my best to remain aloof. I didn't want to know about their pasts, their lives, anything about them. Because with every passing day, I knew I was going to have to pick one of them to feed from, and how could I do that when I knew Dorothy fainted at the sight of blood, and eight-year-old Bethany had nearly died one winter when a fox bit her?

But it was Zeke who continued to fascinate and confuse me. It was clear that everyone adored him; despite being Jebbadiah's second, he was always helping, always making sure people were taken care of. Yet he never asked for anything, never expected any help in return. He was respectful of the adults and patient with the kids, making me wonder how he and Jeb could be so different. Or maybe, Jeb could be that way *because* of Zeke. That hardly seemed fair, to dump so much responsibility on Zeke's shoulders, because Jeb himself didn't want to get involved, but who was I to say anything?

One night, when we made camp a bit earlier than usual, I wandered toward the campfire and was shocked to find Zeke sitting near the flames, *reading* to Bethany and Caleb. Stunned, I crept closer, hardly able to believe it. But he *was* reading, his low, smooth voice reciting passages from the large black book in his lap, the two kids perched on either side.

"'Moses stretched out his hand over the sea,'" Zeke said quietly, scanning the pages before him, "'and at daybreak the sea went back to its place. The Egyptians were fleeing toward it, and the Lord swept them into the sea. The water flowed back and covered the chariots and horsemen—the entire army of Pharaoh that had followed the Israelites into the sea. Not one of them survived.'

"'But the Israelites went through the sea on dry ground, with a wall of water on their right and on their left. That day the Lord saved Israel from the hands of the Egyptians, and Israel saw the Egyptians lying dead on the shore. And when the Israelites saw the mighty hand of the Lord displayed against the Egyptians, the people feared the Lord and put their trust in Him and in Moses, His servant.'"

A bitter lump caught in my throat. For just a moment, I saw myself and Stick, huddled together in the cold shell of my room, an open book between us. Zeke didn't look up, didn't notice me, but I listened to his calm, quiet voice as he read, watched Caleb and Bethany hang on his every word and felt a strange sense of longing pull at my stomach.

"Ezekiel!"

Jebbadiah's voice echoed over the campground, and Zeke raised his head. Seeing the old man waiting for him several yards away, he closed the book and put it in Caleb's arms. "Hang on to it for a second," I heard him murmur, ruffling the boy's hair as he stood. "I'll be right back."

When Zeke left, curiosity drew me closer, wanting to see the book, to hold it in my hands and read the title. Bethany looked up, spotted me, and her eyes got wide. Scrambling to her feet, she ran off after Zeke, leaving Caleb sitting alone by the fire, a vampire looming over him.

Puzzled, Caleb craned his neck, looking back at me, and smiled. "Hi, Allie!" he said as I moved up beside him. "If you're looking for Zee, he just left. He'll be right back, though."

"Can I see that?" I asked, pointing to the leather-bound tome in his arms. Caleb hesitated.

"It's Zee's book," he said uncertainly, holding it tighter. "He told me to watch it for him."

"I won't hurt it," I promised, kneeling in the cool grass. "Please?"

He paused a second more, then brightened.

"Okay, but only if you read me something."

"I…" A part of me recoiled, remembering all those lessons with Stick, and how he stuck a knife in my back for my trouble. But I was still curious, and if this was the only way to see the book without tearing it out of Caleb's hands… "I guess so," I said, and Caleb beamed at me.

Handing it over, he scooted close and perched beside my leg, listening expectantly. Settling back, I gazed down at the leather-bound tome, the first real book I'd seen since fleeing New Covington. It didn't have a title, just the symbol of a gold cross gleaming in the center of the cover, much like the one Zeke wore around his neck. I held the book on its side and saw the edges of the paper were gilded gold, too.

"Read something, Allie," Caleb insisted, bouncing next to me. I rolled my eyes and opened the book with a crackling of pages, turning to where a ribbon bookmarked the middle. It seemed as good a place to start as any.

I read slowly, for the letters were tiny and strange, a style I hadn't seen before, "'Again, I looked and saw all the oppression that was taking place under the sun: I saw the tears of the oppressed—and they have no comforter; power was on the side of their oppressors—and they have no comforter.'"

I felt a chill in my stomach. When was this passage written? *The tears of the oppressed, and the power of their oppressors, with no comfort on either side.* It seemed to be speaking about the entire world, right now. I swallowed hard and continued.

"'And I declared that the dead, who had already died, are happier than the living, who are still alive. But better than both...is the one who has never been born, who has not seen the evil that is done under the sun.'"

I shivered and closed the book. Caleb watched me, a confused frown on his face. "What does that mean?" he asked.

"That *that* particular passage," said a new voice from above us, "was not meant for certain little ears."

Embarrassed, I stood quickly, facing Zeke, who had walked up with a half amused, half concerned look on his face. "Go get dinner, rug rat," he told Caleb, who grinned and scampered off toward Ruth and the crowd that was gathering around her. Zeke looked at me, furrowing his brow, though his expression was more intrigued than upset. "I didn't know you could read," he said in a low voice.

I shrugged, holding out the book. "Kind of a depressing story," I said, unwilling to reveal how much it spooked me. Zeke smiled as he accepted it.

"Some parts of it are," he agreed. "But there are others that can be quite comforting, if you know where to look."

"Like where?"

He paused, then opened the book again, flipping to a certain spot as if he had them memorized. "This one," he said, handing the book back to me, pointing to a certain line. "My favorite quote."

"Zeke!" called another voice, Ruth's this time, echoing shrilly over the campground. "Did you tell Darren he could have your share of the jerky?"

"What? No!" Zeke whirled around as Darren jogged away, laughing. As Zeke took off after him, Darren shouting he'd better catch up before he ate his share of the meal, I bent to the passage Zeke pointed out.

"'Yea,'" I muttered, stumbling over the archaic word, "'though I walk through the valley of the shadow of death, I will fear no evil. For you are with me.'"

A nice thought, I mused, watching the boys chase each other around the campground. But I knew better. Jeb was right; there was no one watching out for us. And the sooner Zeke came to realize that, the longer he would survive this hell.

THE FOLLOWING EVENING, I crawled out of my tent to find Zeke and Darren crouched near the edge of camp, talking in low voices. Both looked as if they were trying to avoid attention, which of course piqued my curiosity. Brushing dirt from my sleeves, I ambled toward them.

"I knew this would happen," Darren muttered in a low voice as I approached. "We should've stocked up when we had the chance. Who knows when we'll come to another town?"

"What's going on?" I asked, squatting beside them. Zeke looked at me and sighed.

"Supplies are running low," he confessed. "At this rate, we'll run out of food in a couple days, even if we cut back the rations." He stabbed a hand through his hair, raking it back. "Darren and I are thinking of going hunting, but Jeb doesn't like the group to separate. Not when there's a chance we could run into rabids. Plus, we're using these," he added and held up a bow and a quiver of arrows. "Which makes it even harder. It's almost impossible to sneak up on deer in the open, but dusk is the best time to try to bring one down."

Across from Zeke, Darren gave me a brief, sudden smile. I blinked and returned it. At least the two boys didn't seem to care about a certain person's gossip-mongering, though I'd never heard Ruth talking about me to Zeke or Jebbadiah. "Why not use guns?" I asked, remembering Zeke's handgun, and the sawed-off shotgun Jeb carried around. Zeke shook his head.

"We're pretty low on ammo," he replied. "The only time we use firearms is for defense, or if it's an emergency. And since we're not quite there yet, it's bows and scavenged arrows for hunting."

I looked down. There was an extra bow lying on the

ground, unstrung and poking out from the square of oiled cloth it was wrapped in. Zeke followed my look and sighed. "Jake usually comes with us," he explained. "But lately, his shoulder's been bothering him and he doesn't have the strength to pull the cord back effectively."

"I'll come with you."

The boys exchanged a look. "I'm a fast learner," I added, ignoring Darren's raised eyebrow. "I'm quiet, and I'm stronger than you think. I'm sure I can get the hang of it."

"It's not that," Zeke said hesitantly. "It's just...I don't want to get you in trouble with Jeb, make him question his decision to let you stay with us." He jerked his thumb at the other boy. "Dare just follows me around like a lost puppy, so it's expected of him—" he dodged the dirt clump lobbed at his face "—but you're new and he won't like it if you wander away from the group. It's probably better if you stay here for now. I'm sorry."

Annoyed, I frowned at them both, vampire pride stinging. *If you only knew. I could bring down a full-grown stag before the pair of you realized it was there.* But I kept my opinions to myself and shrugged. "If you say so."

"Maybe next time, okay?" Darren offered, giving me a wink. "I'll show you how it's done." I bristled, but Zeke grabbed his bow and pushed himself to his feet.

"Let's get moving," he said with a stretch. "Jeb won't leave without me—I hope—so this is on my head if he wants to punish anyone. People have to eat, whether he likes it or not. Allison," he added as I rose as well, "will you let Jeb know what we're doing?" He grinned at me. "After we're a good distance away, of course. Ready, Dare?"

"Sure." Darren sighed, slinging bow and quiver over his shoulder. "Let the exercise in futility begin."

Zeke rolled his eyes and gave the other boy a halfhearted shove as he turned away. Darren swung at him in return, overbalanced as the other dodged, and strode after him as Zeke jogged backward, grinning. I watched their lean forms fade into the darkness, getting smaller and smaller, until they vanished over the rolling hills.

Then I swooped down, grabbed the extra bow and quiver and turned in the other direction.

"What do you think you're doing?"

I sighed and looked over to where Ruth stood, two bowls of the night's dinner steaming in her hands, disapproving scowl firmly in place.

"Sneaking off, are you?" she demanded, narrowing her eyes. "Jeb won't like it. Where are you going?"

"Why don't you just make something up?" I said, taking a step forward, pleased when she hastily backed up. "That's what you've been doing all this time, right?" She flushed, and my smile widened. "I notice you don't talk to Zeke or Jeb when you're spreading your lies. Afraid they'll see the forked tongue come out?"

She looked as if she wanted to slap me, and a part of me hoped she would. I bet she wouldn't be nearly so smug with a missing tooth. For a moment, she struggled to control herself, gripping the bowls of stew so that her delicate knuckles turned white. "I don't know what you're talking about," Ruth said at last, and I snorted. Glancing at the bow in my hand, she sneered at me and raised her chin. "You think you're going to bring something back? What do you know about hunting?

If you think Zeke will notice your pathetic attempt to show off, you're sadly mistaken."

"Yes, shooting a deer so the lot of you won't starve because of the delusional paranoia of a madman is me showing off." I rolled my eyes. "What a brilliant assumption. Why don't you go tell Jeb that?"

"Don't be smart," Ruth hissed back, all subtlety gone. "You think you're so special, just because you're from a vampire city. You think I don't see it? How you sleep away from the rest of us? How you try to be so mysterious, not saying anything about where you came from?" She curled a lip in pure, hateful disgust. "You just want attention—ours and Zeke's. I can see right through your act."

This time I did laugh at her. "Wow, you are a paranoid shrew, aren't you? Does Zeke know what an absolute bitch you can be?" I snickered, and her face flushed bright crimson. "You know, I don't have time for this. Have fun with your theories, spread your poison around as much as you want. I'm going to do something useful now. Maybe you should try it."

"You're a freak, do you hear me?" Ruth called as I turned my back on her. "You're hiding something, and I'm going to find out what!"

I tried not to let her get to me as I jogged away from the camp, already scanning the horizon for moving prey. I tried not to think about turning back around, stalking her to the edge of camp, dragging her kicking and squirming into the night, and tearing out her throat. It wasn't that she was annoying, because she *was,* really, really annoying. It was because she was a threat, and my vampire instincts were telling me to kill, to silence her before she exposed me.

I tried channeling those thoughts of death and violence into my current task, eager to be hunting again. I found a herd of the huge shaggy animals huddled together in a shallow basin but decided they were too big to bother with. Not that I doubted I could kill them; lose enough blood and they'd die just like anything else. But if I went back to camp with one of those giant creatures slung over my back, I might draw suspicion.

Instead, I prowled the rolling hills until I found a herd of small deer, browsing along a grassy ridge. Putting down the bow, I crept forward through the grass, staying downwind, until I could see the gentle rise and fall of their sides, smell the blood pumping hot in their veins.

It was over very quickly. The small buck I'd singled out didn't even know something was wrong until I was nearly right on top of him, and by then it was too late. The rest of the herd scattered as I charged into their midst, but I grabbed the deer's antlers as it was lunging to its feet, wrenched the head around, and quickly snapped its neck, killing it instantly.

As it fell twitching to the ground, I resisted the urge to sink my fangs into its throat, knowing the stag's blood would do nothing for me. Hefting it to my shoulders, I walked back to where I'd left my bow and quiver. Dropping the carcass, I took an arrow from the quiver and drove it into the stag's body, sinking it between the ribs. Maybe I was being paranoid, but explaining to someone why the deer had a broken neck and no arrow wounds could be awkward.

Grabbing it by the horns, I started to drag it away, when a faint yet familiar rumble drifted over the grass, coming from the nearby road. As I froze, wondering where I'd heard it before, two headlights crested a hill and came roaring down the other side. My stomach twisted, and my blood went cold.

Ducking into the grass, I watched the strange machines slow, then pull to a stop on the side of the road. A large bearded man swung off the vehicle, killed the engine and spat into the grass. His companion, a smaller human, pulled his machine to a stop, as well. For a moment, my mind went blank, and I had to kill the urge to flee into the darkness and not look back.

No. It's not possible. I killed them.

"Hang on a second," the larger human muttered, staggering unsteadily to the edge of the pavement. The other man sighed.

"What are you doing, Ed?"

"I'm taking a piss. That okay with you?" The bearded man turned away from his companion, and a moment later there was the sound of falling water hitting the dirt.

Staring at them, I felt myself sag in relief. They weren't the same men. This human had a shaggy brown beard, not yellow, and he was a little broader in the shoulders. But then I saw something else: a tattoo on his left shoulder—a grinning canine, sharp-toothed and pointy.

The same as the ones before.

The other man muttered something and swung himself off the vehicle, digging into his jacket pocket. Pulling out a small white box, he dragged a cigarette out with his lips, lit the end and settled back against his machine, smoking lazily. Ed finished zipping up, turned and caught the box as his friend tossed it to him.

"Any beer left?" he asked, shaking out a cigarette.

"One can."

"Well, let's have it."

"Screw you."

I watched them, my mind racing. From personal experience, I knew these men were bad news: violent, armed and ruthless. If they caught up with the rest of the group…I shivered.

I had to stop them. Or at least get back to warn the others. But, as I crouched there, watching the men pass a silver can back and forth, I knew that—even running my fastest—I wouldn't have enough time. I'd seen how quick those vehicles were. They would reach the group before I was even close. There had to be another way.

Another way. Of course, there was the most obvious choice. The option I couldn't help but think of, no matter how much I tried ignoring it.

Should I…kill them? The thought was tempting, and I felt my fangs lengthen in response. I could kill them, feed on them, hide their bodies and their vehicles, and no one would know. Who would miss them, way out here in the dark? But, as I inched closer to the unsuspecting humans, I remembered the last two I'd met on a lonely road like this one. I remembered their screams, their terror, the panic on their faces. I remembered the glassy eyes and limp bodies, and clenched my fists. I couldn't do it. I was trying not to be that monster. Every death, every life taken by the Hunger, pushed me closer to my demon. If I started killing indiscriminately, it would completely take over, and then what would stop me from stalking Caleb or Zeke into the darkness and ripping out their throats?

Maybe I could creep close enough to damage their vehicles in some way; slash their tires or drain their fuel. But I'd have to get awfully close, and even with my vampire powers, there was the risk of being seen. Even if I did manage to pull it off, they'd probably know someone was here and would be on the lookout for people in the area. That wouldn't be good for the group. I growled in frustration.

Dammit, there had to be something I could do. Something to slow them down, just long enough for me to get back to the others and warn them. I looked up and down the road, searching for ideas, and noticed, in the distance, a large tree on the edge of the pavement.

Breaking away from the humans, I hurried toward the tree and found a thick, gnarled old trunk that looked as if it had been struck by lightning several times. Its branches were twisted and bent, empty of leaves, and it looked more dead than alive.

The roar of engines pierced the silence again. The men had started their vehicles, and were coming, their headlights gliding down the road. I put my shoulder to the trunk and pushed, digging my feet into the slippery grass and dirt, shoving with all my might. The stubborn tree resisted a moment, then with a brittle crack, its trunk split and it toppled slowly to the ground, landing half on and half off the road.

The growl of the vehicles drew closer. If they got past this block, they would reach the group first, and I'd have no time to warn everyone. Cursing, I grabbed the branches and dragged the old tree farther onto the road, expecting the men to come racing over the rise at any second. Bright lights lit up the darkness, illuminating the tree, and I dived into the grass.

"Aw, shit!"

The vehicles skidded to a stop. The men swung off, and one walked to the tree, giving it an angry kick that made the branches rattle. The other scratched his beard and gave it a disgusted look.

"Dammit," he muttered, peering into the darkness. "Think we can go around?"

"I ain't pushing my bike through that," the other snarled, stabbing a finger at the heavy weeds and brambles at the edge of the road, very close to where I was hiding. "Last time I got a flat, and it was a pain in the ass to get it fixed. Besides, the others will be coming through soon."

"Well, then shut up and help me move the thing."

The other let off a string of expletives but moved forward to grab the trunk. I left the men struggling with the old tree, crept silently away and, as soon as I could, took off through the grass.

I raced back to the camp, which was already packed up and on the verge of departure. I saw Darren and Zeke standing near the front with Jebbadiah and Ruth. Darren had a couple of skinny rabbits in one hand, looking uncomfortable, while Zeke seemed to be in an argument with the girl. They were still too far to notice me, but I heard snippets of their conversation, drifting over the wind, and strained my vampire senses to listen.

"I don't care if her tent is empty," Zeke was saying, holding out both hands in a pleading gesture. "Jeb, we can't just leave someone behind. I swear, I saw her just before Darren and I left to go hunting. Ruth, are you sure you didn't see her go after us, or leave the camp?"

"No," Ruth said in a voice that was almost as worried. "Like I said, no one has seen her tonight, and when I realized that, I went to check her tent. It was empty, and all her stuff was gone. You don't think she left for good, do you?"

"Regardless—" Jeb's voice cut in, flat and cold "—we cannot wait for her. I made that clear from the beginning. If she has left us, so be it. If she chooses to flaunt the rules, as you two have done tonight—" he glared at Zeke "—then that is her choice. She can live or die with the consequences."

"Well, it's good to know where I stand," I said, striding into the circle. All four humans whirled on me.

"Allison!" Zeke exhaled with relief, but Ruth looked at me like she had just swallowed a spider. "You're back. Where did you go? We were about to leave—"

"Me behind? I noticed." I looked at Jebbadiah, who gazed back emotionlessly. If he felt anger or guilt that I'd overheard his conversation, he didn't show it. But I couldn't think about that now. "Jeb, I saw men on the road, coming toward us. They're riding strange motorized bicycles, and they have guns."

"Motorized bicycles?" Ruth said, giving Zeke a puzzled frown. Jeb, however, caught on much more quickly.

"Raiders, on motorcycles," he said grimly, and Ruth gasped. Briskly, Jeb turned on me and Zeke. "Get everyone off the road," he snapped, pointing back to the group. "We need to hide. Now!"

No sooner had he spoken than the faint growl of engines echoed down the road, and the glow of headlights appeared in the distance. People gasped, and one of the kids screamed.

Quickly, Ruth, Zeke and I herded everyone away from

the pavement, driving them back into the rolling plains. I snatched up forgotten cans, wrappers and bowls from the ground, flinging them into the tall grass, doing my best to cover the tracks a dozen people left behind.

The raiders drew closer, the hum of engines roaring in the night. Diving behind a log, I flung myself to the ground as the headlights pierced the spot where the group had been. A half second later, Zeke joined me, jumping over the log and dropping to his stomach as the raiders appeared over the hill.

We peeked over the rim, watching the two men on those strange machines cruise past. Again, I was struck with how familiar they looked, how they were very like the two humans I'd met earlier. The two men I'd killed. One of them drove right by, but his companion suddenly pulled to a stop along the side of the road, shutting off his engine. The other turned his machine around and came back, pulling alongside his friend before shutting his off, too.

"Whacha lookin' at?" I heard him growl. Even at this distance, my vampire hearing could make out the words perfectly. The other man shook his head.

"Dunno. I thought I heard something. A scream or something, out there."

"Rabbit, probably. Or coyote." The other man spit on the pavement, then pulled a large machine gun out of a side holster. "Wanna fire a few shots to make sure?"

Beside me, I felt Zeke tense, one hand inching toward his gun, and I put my hand over his. Startled, he looked at me sharply, and I shook my head.

"Nah, don't waste bullets. It's probably nothing." The raider started his engine with a roar, and I caught the last few sentences over the sudden noise. "Jackal is gonna be pissed if we don't find them. He was sure they're somewhere on this stretch."

Jackal. Where had I heard that name before? It was instantly familiar; I knew I'd heard it somewhere. It hit me then—the other raiders I'd met on the road. The dead man had whispered it, right before he died.

Jackal...would've laughed.

I felt a chill run up my spine. It couldn't be coincidence. The tattoos, the bikes, the raiders I'd met before. There was something about this group I didn't know. Someone wasn't telling me something.

"Ain't our fault if they're not here," the other raider shrugged. "Ain't nothing out here. And I'm getting tired of looking for ghosts."

"Derrek and Royce certainly ran into something. Unless you think they just took off without their bikes."

The other said something back, but the reply was drowned in the roar of the bike engines as the two men sped away down the road. I watched them leave, until the rumble of machinery faded into the distance, the lights disappeared, and everything was quiet once more.

Slowly, the group came out of hiding, as if they were scared to make any noise.

"All right!" Jeb's voice cut through the uncertainty. "Listen up! It's no longer safe to use the roads. From now on, we avoid the main stretches. And I want double the guards on every shift! Zeke, you're in charge of that."

"Yes, sir."

"We still have plenty of ground to cover tonight, so let's

move, people!" And Jeb started away through the waving grass, the rest of the group falling in line after him.

I wove my way to the front and fell into step beside Jebbadiah, who marched ahead without looking at me. "What was that?" I asked him. He continued to ignore me, but I wasn't about to let him off the hook. "You knew those men," I continued in a low voice. "Who are they? Why are they after you?"

"You meddle in things you know nothing about."

"Well, yeah. That's why I'm asking here. If I'm going to help you people, I want to know what I'm up against."

"We don't need your help," Jeb said icily. "We didn't ask for your help. This group has been through hell and back, and they have survived this long because they do not question those responsible for their safety."

"Maybe they should," I said, and Jeb fixed me with an unyielding gaze.

"Do not rock this boat, Allison," he warned, raising one long, bony finger to my face. I wondered what would happen if I snapped it off like a twig. "You are here because I permit it, because I turn away none in need, but you are not part of this family. I have come too far, and we have been through too much, for someone like you to endanger that. You have already demonstrated your complete disregard for our way of life. You will not come here and question my authority. And you will not ask questions about things you do not understand." He faced forward again, quickening his pace so that he started to leave me behind. "If you are unhappy with the way we do things, you are free to go," he said without looking back. "But if you wish to remain with this group, you must accept and obey the rules, like everyone else."

I glared after him, falling back with the rest of the sheep. The rules. I'd heard that before. Don't ask questions. Don't draw attention. Keep your head down and your mouth shut. Except I wasn't much of a mindless follower, particularly with rules that made no sense. If Stick-up-the-ass Jebbadiah wasn't going to give me answers, I would have to get them from someone else.

Casually, I lagged behind, letting the others pass me, until I fell back with Zeke, bringing up the rear. He gave me a wary look, as if he knew I was about to ask him something uncomfortable.

"Hey," I said, and he nodded but didn't say anything, as if waiting for the inevitable questions. He'd probably seen me talking with Jeb and knew I hadn't gotten the answers I wanted. Friendly and unassuming as he was, Zeke wasn't stupid.

"Listen," I went on, looking away. "I…uh…wanted to talk to you. I didn't get a chance to before the whole raider thing, so…thanks."

I felt his puzzled frown. "For what?"

"Not leaving me behind." I continued to stare at the horizon, watching a herd of those massive shaggy animals lumber away over a hill. "I heard what you said to Jeb and Ruth, earlier. Thanks for…standing up for me. No one's ever done that before." I fell silent, embarrassed.

Zeke sighed. "Jeb isn't the…easiest…person to understand," he admitted, and I resisted the urge to snort. "He wants to protect everyone, but he knows he's taking us through dangerous territory, and not everyone will make it. He's seen several of us…die, trying to get to Eden. We were a much larger group, once." He hesitated, taking a quick breath. I wondered how much he had seen, how many friends he'd watched die.

"Jeb's only concern now is getting to Eden with as many of us as he can." Zeke gazed at me, unapologetic. "If that means leaving one behind to save the rest, it's a sacrifice he's willing to make. His convictions are much stronger than mine, and sometimes I forget that."

"You're defending him because he's willing to let people die, to leave them behind?"

"Sometimes, to save the many, you must sacrifice the few." He looked away then, a bitter smile crossing his face. "Jeb tells me I'm too soft and that my stubbornness is what keeps me from being a true leader. No, I don't want anyone to die, to be left behind, but that weakness might get the whole group killed."

"Zeke…" I wanted to tell him that was screwed up, that Jebbadiah Crosse was a cold, unreasonable, heartless bastard, but I couldn't. Because, in some sad, twisted way, I agreed with him. Growing up in the Fringe, you came to accept hard truths. Nothing was fair. The world was cold, unforgiving, and people died. It was just the way things were. I didn't like it, but the old man's reasoning wasn't unjustified.

Though I still thought he was a complete bastard.

"Anyway…" Zeke shrugged, giving me a small, embarrassed grin. "You're welcome. And I'm glad you came back. It was a good thing, too—you got us off the road in time. Thank *you* for that."

"Sure." I paused, chewing my lip. Now seemed as good a

time as any, but I wondered how best to bring it up. I opted for my usual dive right in approach. "Zeke...who's Jackal?"

He stumbled, then looked at me sharply, blue eyes narrowing. I knew I had something and hurried on. "The men said Jackal was looking for someone. It's you, isn't it? Or the group." I nodded to the people walking ahead of us. "Who is he, and what does he want from you?"

Zeke took a deep breath, letting it out slowly. Dropping even farther back, he gave the group a wary look, his eyes lingering on Jebbadiah up front. "None of them can know about this," he murmured as I fell back to join him. "They don't know who Jackal is, and it's better that they remain oblivious. I'm the only one, besides Jeb, who knows anything about him, so you can't mention his name to anyone, okay?" He closed his eyes. "And please don't tell Jeb that I told you."

I nodded. "Why the big secret?" I asked, frowning. "Who is this Jackal person, anyway?"

"He's a vampire," Zeke replied, and my stomach clenched. "A very powerful vampire. He leads a group of raiders all across the country, looking for us. The others think we just run into random raider gangs that want to hurt us. They're terrified enough without knowing what he is. But Jackal is their king, and he's been on our trail for a couple years now."

"Why?"

"He hates Jeb," Zeke explained, shrugging. "Jeb nearly killed him once, and he's never forgotten it. So, he hunts him for revenge, but he'll kill us all if he finds us."

That didn't make much sense. "So, you're saying this vampire king is sending his raider army on a wild-goose chase all over the country, looking for one person who could be any-where, all because he's holding a grudge?"

Zeke looked away. I narrowed my eyes. "What aren't you telling me?"

"I can't say." Zeke looked back, eyes pleading. "I promised Jeb that I wouldn't tell anyone. I won't break that promise, no matter what you say. I'm sorry."

I believed him, which was strange. I'd never met a person who couldn't be bought, cajoled or bribed, but Zeke seemed the type that, once he promised something, would take his secrets to the grave. Still, it was frustrating, being left in the dark. Especially if the dark had a powerful vampire king lurk-ing close by.

I cast about for another topic, another way to extract his carefully guarded secrets, but something else he'd said caught my attention. "Wait a minute," I muttered, frowning at him. "You've been wandering around, looking for Eden, for a cou-ple *years?*"

"I think…" Zeke paused a moment, brow furrowed. "I think this summer will be our third year. Or is it our fourth?" He raised one lean shoulder. "It's hard to keep track, any-more."

"And you still think Eden is out there?"

"It has to be," Zeke said in a fervent voice. "If it's not, all the lives we lost, the people who put their trust in us, it'll all be for nothing." His face clouded with pain, before he shook it off, his eyes narrowed in determination. "Every year, we get closer," he said. "Every site we come to and it's not there, that's just one more step closer to finding it. Jackal and his gang, they're out there, looking for us. But they won't find us. We've come too far to be stopped now. We have to keep everyone's faith alive. If they knew a vampire was hunting us, they'd lose hope. And sometimes, hope is the only thing that gets us through the day."

He sounded very tired, and I could suddenly see the terrible burden he carried, the weight of responsibility far beyond his years. I remembered the way his eyes had gone dark when I asked why the group traveled at night, the look on his face as he recalled something terrible. Death had marked him, the lives lost weighed on him; I could tell he remembered each and every one.

"What happened?" I asked. "You said you travel at night for a reason. Why is that?"

He closed his eyes. When he opened them again, he seemed a different person; the bleakness on his face transformed him into someone much, much older. "In the beginning," he said, his eyes dark and far away, "I was the only orphan in the group. There were a lot more of us back then, and we were all so sure we would find Eden before winter set in. Jeb was certain it was along the west coast. When we started out, no one thought that we could be wandering for more than a year." He shook his head, flinging bangs from his eyes. "At first, we traveled during the day, when the monsters were sleeping. At night, we waited a couple hours after the sun went down before making camp, to make sure there were no rabids in the area. We thought that the rabids came out right at sundown, and if we waited an hour or two, we would be safe." His voice faltered, and he shook his head. "We were wrong. Rabids…rabids rise when *they* want to."

Zeke paused, took a quiet breath. "One night," he continued in a low voice, "we made camp as usual, about an hour after sunset. It was at the top of a grassy hill, no trees, no bushes, no places for the rabids to hide or sneak up on us. We posted sentries around the perimeter, per normal, and went to sleep.

"I woke up to screaming," Zeke muttered, gazing at something in the distance, his voice dark and grim. "They came right out of the ground, from the earth under our tents. No warning, nothing. They were just suddenly *there*. We didn't stand a chance."

I shivered in sympathy. I could see the rabids coming out of the ground, right in the middle of the camp of helpless sleepers. "I'm sorry," I offered, knowing how weak that sounded.

"More than half the group was lost," Zeke went on, as if he hadn't heard. "We would've all died if Jeb hadn't been there. I froze—I couldn't move, not even to help the others. Through all that chaos, he managed to get the rest of us together so we could escape. But we left so many behind. Dorothy's husband, Caleb and Ruth's parents." He stopped, his face pinched and tight. "I swore I wouldn't lose anyone else like that," he muttered. "Ever again."

"You were a kid." We had drifted closer, somehow, our shoulders barely touching as we walked side by side. "Jeb couldn't have expected you to face them all on your own."

"Maybe." He didn't sound convinced and kept walking with his head down, watching his feet. "But that's why we can't stop. Even if there's a vampire out there who wants us dead. Even…if there is no Eden." He shuddered. "We have to keep going. Everyone is counting on us to lead them there, and I won't take that away from them. All we have left is our faith." His voice dropped even lower as he looked toward the horizon. "And sometimes, I wonder if that will be enough."

"Zeke!"

Ruth came skipping up to us then, smiling brightly, a tin cup clutched in one hand. "Here," she said, wedging herself between me and Zeke, holding the cup out to him. "I saved a little coffee for you. It's not much, but at least it's warm."

"Thanks." Zeke gave her a tired smile as he took the cup, and she beamed, ignoring me. I looked at her back, at the pale expanse of her neck, and fantasized about sinking my teeth into her smooth white skin.

"By the way," she continued, turning to me with wide, innocent eyes, "why is there a big tear in the floor of your tent? It looks like you purposefully cut it with a knife. What are you doing in there, slaughtering animals?"

Zeke looked at me, raising a puzzled eyebrow. Alarm flickered, but I forced myself to be calm. "There…must've been a hole already," I said, thinking quickly. "I have nightmares sometimes—it could've torn while I was thrashing around."

Zeke nodded and sipped his coffee, but Ruth narrowed her gaze, lips pursed in suspicion. She didn't believe me. A growl rose to my throat, and I swallowed it, before going on the offensive to distract her.

"Besides, why are you snooping around my stuff?" I returned, glaring at her. "Looking for something in particular? I don't have anything you can steal."

Ruth's mouth dropped open, her delicate face contorting in outrage.

"Steal? How dare you! I don't steal!"

"That's good," I went on, smirking at her. "Because, sometimes I kill things in my sleep. Particularly if they come poking around my tent unannounced in the middle of the day. Comes with living in a vampire city—stab first, ask questions later."

She paled and shrank back against Zeke, who gave me a look of mild concern, unsure how to deal with two bickering females.

"Freak," Ruth muttered at last and turned her back on me in blatant dismissal. "Regardless, Zeke, I wanted to ask you about camp rations. We're awfully low—what do you want me to do tonight and tomorrow?"

He gave me an apologetic look. I rolled my eyes and walked away, leaving them to talk, as it was obvious Ruth wouldn't let me get another word in with Zeke. Not that she could've stopped me; I had no issues staying where I was, just to spite her. But watching her with Zeke, hearing her heart beat faster just from being close, her pulse fluttering wildly in her neck, I felt, for the first time since that lonely night on the road, the first stirrings of Hunger.

And I knew I would have to choose one of them, very soon.

CHAPTER 13

"There's something strange about her," Ruth murmured.

I opened my eyes as Ruth's low, sulky voice drifted to me through the tent fabric. According to my internal clock, the sun had just gone down, though the sky overhead was still light. I could hear the camp moving around outside, getting ready to head out, but I stayed there for a moment, picking out bits of conversation, listening to voices drift through the walls.

"Don't you think it's odd," Ruth went on, her voice earnest, "that she showed up in the middle of the night and just happened to stumble upon Zeke and Caleb? What do we know about her? Why was *she* wandering around at night—Zeke never said anything about that. How was she able to survive all that time by herself?"

I felt a prickle of apprehension. The stupid girl was still at it. A growl rose to my throat, and I had to stop myself from fantasizing about dragging her off into the woods.

"I think she's hiding something," Ruth went on. "Worse, I think she's dangerous. If she came from a vampire city, she could be anything. She could be a thief, or a murderer. I wouldn't be surprised if she's killed someone before."

I rolled upright and exited the tent, stepping out into the open. At the fire pit, Ruth fell silent, but I could see her glaring at me over the top of Teresa's head. The old woman looked unconcerned, ladling soup into bowls, but Matthew and Bethany turned to watch me over their shoulders, their eyes wide.

Stifling my anger, I spotted Zeke and Darren standing a few yards away, talking to Teresa's husband, Silas. The old man was pointing a withered hand to the sky, and the boys were nodding solemnly as if it all made sense. Curious, I headed in that direction, trying to ignore the whispers behind me.

"You sure about that, old man?" Darren said as I came up. Zeke smiled at me and nodded, and my gut prickled. Silas snorted through his white beard and glared at Darren.

"My elbow ain't never wrong," he announced, bushy eyebrows bristling. "It only aches like this when there's a storm coming. Considering it feels like it's about to fall off, I'd say there's a big one on the horizon."

The horizon was clear. The first stars glimmered over the trees, and the sky was turning a deep navy blue. I could see why Darren was skeptical, but Zeke studied the sky as if he could see the storm approaching.

"Good," he murmured, as a sudden gust of wind tossed his hair. "It's been a few days since we crossed that stream. Water is running low—this will come at a good time."

"Are we going to stop?" I asked. Darren snorted.

"No," Zeke replied, ignoring his friend. "Unless it becomes truly dangerous, Jeb will want to press on through the storm. Rabids like to hunt during bad weather. You can't hear them coming until they're right up on you. It's not safe to stay put during storms."

I remembered another storm, watching the rabids close in on all sides through the rain, and shuddered.

"If the rain comes at all," Darren put in, making Silas frown. "But I suppose death by lightning is better than death by rabids. At least I won't see it coming."

"Well, if anything, you can finally get a shower," Zeke retorted. "No wonder we can't shoot anything—they can smell your stink coming a mile away."

Darren casually flipped him the finger. Zeke only laughed.

TRUE TO SILAS'S PREDICTION, dark clouds soon billowed on the horizon, blocking out the moon and stars, and the wind picked up rapidly. Lightning flickered, eerie white strands snaking through the clouds, and thunder boomed an answer.

It started to rain, torrential sheets that whipped at faces and exposed skin, drenching everything. The humans pressed forward at a crawl, heads bowed and shoulders hunched against the wind. I hung back, watching for stragglers, not wanting anyone to see that the rain didn't bother me, the cold didn't make my skin prickle with gooseflesh, and the wind didn't make me shiver. The ground quickly became a swamp, and I watched as Zeke pulled Caleb and Bethany through the worst parts of the mud, sometimes hefting them onto his back when it got too deep. The kids were shivering, and Bethany started to cry when she fell into a puddle that nearly swallowed her whole, but Jeb didn't even slow down.

The rain continued. A few hours before dawn, a new sound began to penetrate the constant hiss of falling water. A low roar, faint at first, but growing louder and stronger, until the ground sloped away, and we stood at the banks of a dark, rushing river.

Jebbadiah stood at the edge, arms crossed, lips pressed tight as he glared at the river in annoyance. Turning, he motioned to Zeke, and I edged forward, listening to their voices over the roar of the water.

"Get the rope," Jeb ordered, gesturing to Zeke's pack.

"Sir?"

Jeb frowned and turned away, observing the river again. "Get everyone ready to move. We're crossing now."

I edged closer. Zeke hesitated, gazing at the water in concern. "You don't think we should stop for the night?" he asked. "Wait for the water to go down a little? The current is probably too strong for the kids."

"Then have someone help them." Jeb's voice was ruthlessly calm. "We need to be on the other side, tonight."

"Sir—"

"Ezekiel," Jeb interrupted, turning to stare at him. "Do not make me repeat myself." Zeke held his gaze for a moment, then looked away.

"Make sure everyone is ready soon," Jebbadiah said in a perfectly civil voice that made me want to slug him in the jaw. "Once we're on the other side of the river, we can rest. But I want us safely across before we relax."

Zeke nodded reluctantly. "Yes, sir."

He backed away, shrugging off his pack, as Jeb turned and stared out over the water again. His gaze lingered on something I couldn't see, something down by the water's edge, and his thin mouth tightened.

I waited until he had walked back toward the group, where Zeke and Darren were unraveling coils of rope, before I hurried to the riverbank and looked down.

The water rushed by at breakneck speed, dark and angry. I wondered what Jeb was thinking; was he really that stubborn and heartless to push on through that? Especially when there were kids in the group?

Lightning flickered, and the glare reflected the sudden gleam of dead white eyes.

Jerking around, I gazed downstream, at a boulder lying near the water's edge. Only I could see it wasn't a rock now, but one of those massive horned creatures that roamed the plains in huge herds. This one, bloated and obviously dead, was lying on its side facing me, but its lips were pulled back in an eerie snarl, and its huge white eyes bulged out of their sockets. The wind shifted, and I caught the unmistakable stink of decay and *wrongness* over the water.

My gut twisted, and I hurried over to help Darren and Zeke, unknotting ropes. *So, Jeb wasn't being an evil bastard, after all. Good to know.* Though I wondered why he didn't at least tell Zeke there could be rabids in the area. That might've been important for the second-in-command to know. Maybe he didn't want word to spread and panic the rest of the group. Or maybe the prickly human just didn't feel like his orders needed to be explained. But at least his reasoning to get to the other side of the river made sense now.

Rabids are afraid of deep or fast-moving water, Kanin had told me in the hospital. *No one knows why—it's not like they could drown. Maybe they don't understand why the ground won't hold them up any longer. Or maybe they fear something that is more powerful than they are. But ever since they were created, rabids will not approach deep water. Remember this, for it might save your life one day.*

I watched Zeke, carrying the rope, stride through the mud to a thick tree near the riverbank, and hurried over.

"How are we getting across?" I asked Zeke, who was busy winding one end of the rope around the trunk before knotting it tight. He gave me a rueful smile and held up the rest of the coil.

"We hang on for dear life."

"How?" I asked, glancing at the trunk. "The rope is on this side of the river. It won't help us unless it crosses to the other bank."

"Exactly." Zeke sighed and started tying the other end around his waist. I stared at him, alarmed, and he grimaced. "At least I'm already wet this time."

I looked at the foaming, rushing water and shook my head. "Isn't that a little...dangerous?"

"Exactly." Zeke looked up, meeting my eyes. "Jake can't swim, and I won't ask Darren to take the risk. Or anyone, for that matter. It has to be me."

Before I could answer, he stripped off his boots and jacket, placing them neatly at the top of the rise. Then, with everyone watching, he slipped down the bank, sliding a bit in the mud, and stepped to the edge of the river. A brief pause as he gazed up and down the bank, surveying the current, then plunged into the foaming waters.

The undertow caught him immediately, but he struck out for the far shore, swimming doggedly into the current. I watched his pale form, bobbing along the surface, sometimes getting pulled down. Each time he vanished I bit my cheek and clenched my fists until his head broke the surface once more. He was quite the powerful swimmer, but it was still several tense, breathless moments before he emerged, dripping and panting, on the other side. As the rest of the group cheered, Zeke stumbled over to a tree, tied the rope around the trunk, and then sat down heavily in the mud, apparently exhausted.

He did, however, push himself to his feet as the rest of the group started over, standing at the water's edge to help those who made it across. I hung back, watching, as Ruth crossed first, probably anxious to get over to where Zeke was. After her, Silas and Teresa made their slow, painstaking way across, inching forward, their wrinkled fingers gripping the rope for all they were worth.

Then Darren turned to me.

"Your turn, Allison," he said, holding out a hand. I looked over to where the three kids, Caleb, Bethany and Matthew, stood on the bank, huddled together in the rain.

"What about them?"

"Zeke will be back over to help," Darren replied. "He'll take either Bethany or Caleb across, I'll grab the other one, and Jake will help Matthew. Don't worry, it's not like this is our first crossing. I'll be right behind you." He smiled again and motioned me forward. "Of course, if you need help, I'll be happy to piggyback you to the other side."

"No, thanks." I ignored his hand and made my way down to the rope. "I think I can handle it myself."

The water shocked me. Not the temperature—the freezing cold didn't bother me, of course—but the strength of the undertow as it tried sucking me down was impressive. If I'd still been human, one who didn't swim very well, I might add, I might've been concerned.

The water wasn't very deep, only coming up to my chest, but the current fought me every step of the way. Somewhere behind me, Darren shouted to keep going, his voice nearly lost in the roar of the river. I looked back. Shy little Bethany clung to his back with her arms around his neck, eyes squeezed tightly shut.

As I turned to look at them, something big came hurtling toward us over the water—a broken tree trunk, bouncing on the waves. I shouted to Darren, but the tree was moving fast, and my warning came too late. The trunk slammed into him, tearing him away from the rope, and he vanished into the waves. Bethany screamed once before she was pulled under and lost from view.

I didn't think. I just acted. Releasing the line, I dove into the water. The current sucked at me, dragging me along like a rag doll. It resisted my attempts to thrash my way to the surface, tumbling me along the bottom, until it was hard knowing which way was up. For a few moments, I panicked...until I realized the river couldn't hurt me. I didn't breathe; I was in no danger of drowning.

Once I stopped fighting the current, it was much easier.

The river rushed me along, and I scanned the top of the roiling waves, searching for Bethany and Darren. I caught a split-second glimpse of a blue dress and lunged in that direction.

It was several long minutes before I could grab the limp, bobbing girl and haul her to me, struggling to keep her pale little face above water. Planting my feet on the river bottom, feeling the current rip at my legs as I braced myself, I struck out for shore.

Staggering up the bank, I lay Bethany on her back and sank down beside her, anxiously studying her face for signs of life. The girl looked wholly drowned; eyes closed, mouth slightly open, blond hair tangled and smeared across her face. She didn't seem to be breathing. I put an ear to her chest, listening for a heartbeat, bracing myself to hear only a hollow emptiness.

It was there. Faint, but still beating. Still alive.

I sat up, biting my lip as I stared at the motionless girl. I had an inkling of what I was supposed to do; back in the Fringe, I'd watched as a young boy was dragged out of a flooded storm drain. His rescuer had tried to resuscitate him, breathing in his mouth and pumping his chest, while the crowd looked on. Sadly, the boy failed to revive, and his mother had taken home a limp body. I couldn't help but wonder if Bethany would share the same fate.

Well, she certainly will unless you do something, Allison.

"Dammit," I muttered, gently prying open the girl's mouth, pinching her nose shut. "I have no idea what I'm doing here," I warned her, before lowering my mouth to hers. I had to remember to take a deep breath, drawing air into myself, before releasing it slowly past the girl's lips.

I did this five or six times, breathing for the girl, feeling her stomach expand and contract with each breath. Bethany remained limp, unresponsive. I wondered if I shouldn't shove on her chest, as I'd seen the man do with the boy, but decided against it. I still didn't know my own strength, and the last thing I wanted to do was snap a rib by mistake. It made my stomach crawl just thinking about it.

By the seventh breath, I was about to admit defeat, when Bethany suddenly choked, gagged and started coughing, expelling river water from her mouth and nose. Relieved, I drew back as she struggled upright, bent over and vomited water and mud into the grass.

Shivering, she looked up at me, her small body tense. "Relax," I told her, recalling all the wide-eyed, fearful looks she'd given me whenever I walked by. Ruth's doing, probably. "You fell into the river, but you're safe now. When you're up for it, we can go find the others—"

Bethany lunged forward, throwing her arms around my neck, burying her face in my shoulder. I froze for a second, startled and uncomfortable, not knowing what to do.

She sniffled, mumbling something incoherent, and pressed closer against me, snuggling in. And her little neck was suddenly *right there,* inches from my cheek. We were all alone out here; no Zeke, no Ruth, no Jebbadiah Crosse to find us. It would be so easy, to turn my head…to…

Stop that. I closed my mouth, feeling fangs slip back into my gums, and gently freed myself from the girl's arms. "Let's get back to the group," I said, standing up. "They're probably looking for us."

I hoped. Or had Jebbadiah already given us up for dead and moved on?

Gazing at the foaming river, I winced. *I hope Darren made it out okay,* I thought, trudging along the bank with Bethany close behind. *There's nothing I can do for him now.*

It was a long, muddy walk back up the river. The current had carried us quite a ways, farther than I'd first thought. Bethany whimpered and sniffled a bit, especially when having to walk through deep mud, but I refused to piggyback her through the wet spots, so she eventually sucked it up and trailed doggedly after me.

The rain had finally let up, and dawn was fast approaching when I at last spotted a figure, walking down the bank toward us. It walked with a sense of purpose, scanning the bank and the edge of the water, and spotted me almost at the same time I saw it. As we drew closer to each other, I blinked in surprise. It wasn't Zeke, as I was expecting, or Ruth or even Darren.

It was Jeb.

Bethany suddenly broke away from me, half running, half stumbling toward Jebbadiah who, shockingly, bent down and lifted her in his arms. I watched in amazement as he spoke to her quietly, smoothing back her hair, and wondered if this was perhaps Jeb's long-lost twin brother. The one who wasn't a heartless bastard.

Bethany suddenly pointed back at me, and I stiffened as Jeb's steely gaze turned in my direction. Putting the girl down, he approached, his impassive face giving no hints to what he was thinking.

"I commend you for your bravery, Allison," he said when

he was a few feet away, and I blinked, shocked for the second time that night. "I don't know how or why you did it, but you saved one of our own, and I will not forget that. Thank you." He paused and said, very seriously, "Perhaps I was wrong about you."

"What about Darren?" I asked, not sure if I should trust this unexpected change toward me. "Are there people looking for him? Is he all right?"

"Darren is fine," Jeb replied, no change in his expression. "He managed to grab the trunk when he surfaced, and we were able to pull him to shore when it became lodged between two rocks downstream. We had almost given up hope with you and Bethany." He paused and looked down at the girl, a soft, almost grandfatherly look crossing his face. "You are both very lucky, indeed."

Abruptly, he straightened, brisk and businesslike again. "Come," he ordered. "Dawn is approaching, and we must get back to camp. This delay was unfortunate, and I wish to have an early start tomorrow night. Let us go, quickly."

We followed Jeb back to camp, where Bethany was greeted with hugs and tears of relief, and a few smiles and nods were thrown my way. Teresa even took my hand in both of hers and squeezed with her withered fingers, murmuring how I was a godsend and they were so thankful that I had joined the family. Embarrassed, I excused myself and retreated to the edge of the camp, setting up my tent per normal. When I'd finished, I straightened and turned around, and nearly ran into Zeke.

"Whoops." Zeke put out both hands to steady us. For a half second, we were face-to-face, so close I could see the rings of silver around his pupils, hear the pulse at his throat. The Hunger stirred, and I clamped down on it, hard.

"Sorry," he apologized, taking a step back. His clothes and hair were still slightly damp, and he smelled faintly of the river. "I...just wanted to make sure you were all right," he said and ran his fingers through his bangs, shoving them back. "*Are* you all right? No broken bones, no hidden concussions? No fish swimming around in your lungs?"

I smiled at him tiredly. "There might be a minnow or two, but I'm sure I'll cough them up before tomorrow," I said, and he chuckled. My stomach squirmed weirdly at that laugh, and I eased back toward my tent. "I think I'm done for the night, though. Something about near-death experiences always wears me out." I faked a yawn, covering my mouth just in case fangs were showing. "See you tomorrow, Zeke."

He reached for me before I could turn, taking a strand of my wet hair, running it lightly through his fingers. I froze, my stomach in knots, the Hunger stirring curiously at this newest development.

"Allison." Zeke's smile sent a rush of warmth through me, and I had to stifle the urge to touch him, skin to skin, just to feel that heat. My gums throbbed, fangs aching to break through, and I forced myself to stay put, to not step forward and lean up toward his neck.

"I'm glad you're here," Zeke murmured without a trace of embarrassment or guile. "It's nice, having someone else we can count on. I hope you'll stay, so we can see Eden together."

He gave my hair a final, gentle tug and turned away. I watched him go, Hunger and longing and that strange, squirmy feeling twisting my insides. Crawling into my tent,

I pulled the blanket over my head and tried to sleep, to forget Ezekiel Crosse. His touch. His warmth. And how badly I wanted to sink my fangs into his throat and truly make him mine.

CHAPTER 14

The plains couldn't go on forever. The next night, a scattering of trees appeared on the horizon, growing thicker and more numerous, until it became a proper forest. Trudging through brush and tangled undergrowth, our progress slowed even more. People began to mutter; the forest was more danger-ous than the plains, harder to get through, especially since we weren't following a road. The shadowy trees hid predators like wolves and bears, and of course, the worst fear of all: rabids.

Not surprisingly, Jeb was deaf to these fears and continued to push doggedly through the woods, pausing only to let the little ones rest and to ration out our nearly exhausted supplies. When we finally stopped to camp a few hours before dawn, Zeke and Darren grabbed their bows to go hunting again, and this time I joined them.

"So, do you know how to shoot one of these things?" Darren asked as I followed him and Zeke into the woods. He seemed fully recovered from his tumble into the river, no worse for wear except for a small cut and a purple-green bruise on his forehead. Zeke had teased him about his hard-headedness, and Darren had responded by saying that scars were sexy to the ladies.

I smiled at him, secretly thinking he was making far too much noise for us to be able to sneak up on anything. Ahead of us, Zeke was much quieter. At least Darren was speaking in whispers, though I winced whenever he stepped on a twig or made the leaves crunch.

"I think I've got the general idea," I murmured back. "Point the sharp end at something and pull the string, right?"

"There's a bit more to it than that," Darren said dubiously. "It takes a fair bit of strength to pull the cord effectively, and you have to know how to aim it, too. Are you sure you don't want me to show you how? I'll be happy to teach you."

My annoyance flared. "Tell you what," I said, holding up my bow. "Let's make a bet. If you shoot something before I do, I'll leave the hunting to you and Zeke. If I make a kill first, you let me come hunting with you whenever I want. Deal?"

"Uh." His eyebrows shot up, appraising. "Sure. You're on."

A pebble came sailing through the darkness then, coming from Zeke's direction. I stepped back, but it bounced off Darren's chest, and he turned with a hiss, scowling. Zeke frowned back, then put a finger to his lips and pointed at a clump of bushes ahead.

I was instantly alert. Something was moving in the under-growth about fifty yards away, a large black shape, shuffling low to the ground. Zeke smoothly reached behind him, drew an arrow from the quiver, fit it to the string and raised the bow. As he pulled back the cord, I breathed in slowly, trying to catch the beast's scent.

The stench of blood, rot and general *wrongness* hit me like a hammer, and I gasped. "Zeke, no!" I whispered, throwing out a hand, but it was too late. Zeke released the string, and the arrow shot into the bushes, striking its mark with a muffled *thunk*.

A maddened squeal rose into the air, making my blood run cold. The bushes parted, and a huge boar lunged into the clearing, frothing and shaking its head. Its eyes blazed white, with no pupils or irises, and blood streamed from the sockets, running down its bristly fur. Two yellow tusks curled from its jaw, razor sharp and lethal, as it screamed again and charged at Zeke.

As I lunged forward, Zeke dropped the bow, pulled his gun and his machete at the same time, and fired several shots at the rabid pig. I saw blood erupt from the boar's head, face and shoulders, but the crazed animal didn't slow down. At the last instant, Zeke stepped aside, swinging himself out of the boar's path, and brought his machete slashing down across its flanks.

The boar whirled with frightening speed, but by that time, I had drawn my sword and sliced deep into the animal's back, shearing through flesh and bone. The pig squealed and whirled, gouging at me with those deadly tusks, but its spine had been severed, and its hind legs gave out before it could reach me. Zeke stepped up and hit it again, landing a blow directly behind its skull, opening a gash in its neck, and the boar stumbled. Raising my blade, I brought it down with all my strength, aiming for the gaping wound Zeke already opened. The katana edge sliced cleanly through the pig's burly neck, cutting through spine and flesh and bone and severing the head from its shoulders. The huge body crashed to the ground and rolled over, kicking the air, as the head clenched and unclenched its jaws in helpless rage, before they both, finally, stopped moving.

I slumped against a tree, letting my sword arm drop, watching Zeke as he sank to the ground, gasping. I could see his muscles shaking from adrenaline, the sweat running down his brow and cheeks. And I heard his heart racing a mile a minute, thudding loudly in his chest.

"Oh, my God." Darren staggered forward, shaking as well. There was an arrow fitted to his bowstring, but everything had happened so very fast; he hadn't had time to shoot it. "Are you two all right? I'm sorry, I couldn't...it just came out of nowhere."

Zeke waved it off and stood, grabbing a hanging branch a bit unsteadily. "It's all right," he panted, holstering his gun. "It's done. It's over, and everyone is fine. Allie?" He looked at me. "You're okay, right? It didn't hurt you, did it?"

I shook my head. "I'm fine."

"More than fine." Darren's voice was awed and jealous all at once. "Damn, girl. You cut its head clean off! I take back my side of the bet—you can go hunting with us anytime."

I smirked at him but was suddenly aware of Zeke, watching me now with a thoughtful expression on his face. "You were incredible," he said softly, then seemed to catch himself. "I mean...that sword must be crazy sharp, to cut through a full grown boar. You're not even breathing hard."

Alarm shot through me. I deliberately took a deep, ragged

breath. "It just hasn't hit me yet," I said, trying to sound breathless and shaky. Zeke stepped toward me, looking worried, but my attention suddenly shifted to something else. In that breath, I smelled the foul, rotten carcass of the rabid boar, making me slightly nauseated, but I also caught the hint of blood. Clean, untainted blood. Human blood.

"Hello?" called a weak, unfamiliar voice through the trees. "Is...is anyone there? Are you still alive?"

We all jerked upright, pointing weapons into the darkness. "Where are you?" Zeke demanded, easing back to stand with Darren and me. "Show yourself."

"I can't," the voice answered. "The boar...my leg. I need help...please."

I peered into the forest, tracking the voice by sound, trying to pinpoint its location. "There," I muttered to Zeke, pointing to the branches of an old pine tree. A dark shape huddled among the needles, clinging desperately to the trunk. He smelled of fear and pain. And blood. A lot of blood.

We approached the tree with caution, weapons still out and ready. The dark shape came into focus; a middle-aged man with a short yellow beard and dirty blue overalls. He watched us with glazed eyes, his teeth clenched in a grimace of pain.

"The pig?" he whispered.

"It's dead," Zeke assured him. "You can come down. We're not going to hurt you."

"Thank God." The man slumped in relief and half fell out of the tree, landing with a gasp. The smell of blood was suddenly overwhelming. I bit my lip to keep my fangs retracted.

"Damn pig caught me off guard." The man gasped, sinking back against the trunk, extending one leg with a grimace.

The right pant leg was torn to the knee, stained dark. "I was able to get up the tree and out of reach, but it got me anyway. Stubborn thing was waiting for me to come down. I'd be dead if you hadn't come along."

"Do you have a safe place to go?" Zeke asked, kneeling beside him. He nodded.

"There's several of us living in a compound about two miles west of here." He pointed with a bloodstained hand, and Zeke stood.

"All right," he said. "Darren, go back to the others. Tell Jeb what's happened. Warn them there are probably rabids in the area. Allison," he continued, nodding to the injured man, "help me get him home."

I frowned. Zeke noticed my hesitation and stepped close, lowering his voice to a murmur. "We can't leave him here," he said earnestly. "That wound looks deep, and he's lost a lot of blood."

"Exactly," I hissed back. "He's probably attracted every rabid in a ten-mile radius. Fighting an endless wave of rabids for some random stranger doesn't sound like a good plan to me."

"I'm not leaving him," Zeke said firmly. "Random stranger or not, I'm not going to let another human die out here." His eyes hardened, and he lowered his voice. "I won't leave him to be torn apart by soulless demons. That's not going to happen. So, either help me, or go back to the others with Darren."

"Dammit," I growled as Zeke turned away. The stupid boy didn't know it, but rabids weren't the only thing he had to worry about. The man reeked of blood, and deep within, the Hunger stirred restlessly. My fangs pressed against my gums, and I could almost taste the heat spreading over my tongue. But Zeke was already bending to help the wounded man, shouldering half his weight and lifting him to his feet. The human gasped and leaned on the younger man, keeping his injured leg off the ground, and Zeke staggered under the weight.

"Dammit," I muttered again and stepped to the opposite side, looping the man's arm over my neck. Maybe if I didn't breathe and stopped fantasizing about plunging my teeth into his throat every few seconds, we would be all right.

"Thanks for this," the human panted as we began the agonizingly slow hobble into the dark woods. "The name's Archer—Joe Archer. My family owns these lands, or at least, they did back before the plague."

"What were you doing so far from home, Mr. Archer?" Zeke asked, gritting his teeth as the man stumbled. I braced myself, keeping all of us upright. "Especially at night, when the rabids are roaming around?"

Joe Archer managed a short, embarrassed laugh. "One of our damn goats got through the fence," he admitted, shaking his head. "We keep them outside in the daytime, when the rabids aren't awake. But one of them decided to go roaming the forest, and if we lose even one of the little buggers, that's half our meat and dairy right there. So I went looking for it. I didn't mean to be out so late, but it got dark quicker than I expected."

"You're lucky to be alive," I muttered, wishing they would both move faster. "If that pig had bitten you a few times instead of just gouging your leg, you'd have a lot more to worry about than finding a goat."

I felt him go very still under my arm, and his heart rate sped up. "Yeah," he mumbled, not looking at me. "It was a lucky thing."

MIRACULOUSLY, DESPITE the obvious scent of blood in the air and the conspicuous trail we left behind, we managed to avoid any sudden rabid attacks. Breaking free of the trees, we found ourselves at the edge of a large clearing, encircled with a barbed-wire fence. The remnants of an ancient barn sat rotting within the fence, overgrown with weeds and falling apart, and a rusty tractor sat beside it in the same condition.

In the middle of the clearing, a wall of corrugated metal, wood and cement surrounded a low hill. Bonfires had been set a few feet from the perimeter, lighting the darkness with heat and smoke, and I could see lights and other structures beyond the wall.

We eased Joe through the barbed wire, taking care with his leg, and started across the clearing. Halfway across, a shout came from somewhere up ahead, and someone on the wall shone a flashlight into my eyes. Joe shouted back, waving his arms, and the light disappeared. A few minutes later a rusty groan echoed across the field as the gate opened and three people, two men and a woman, rushed toward us.

I tensed out of habit, and because the younger-looking man did have a rifle, though it wasn't pointed at us. The other man was lanky and rawboned, but it was the woman I paid the most attention to. Her brown hair was in a pony-tail, and though she didn't look very old, a few gray strands poked out from the sides. She might've been pretty once, but her face was lined with creases now, her mouth pinched and severe. And her eyes told me that, without a doubt, this was the person in charge.

"Joe!" cried the woman, flinging herself at us. "Oh, thank goodness! We thought you were dead." And despite her words, she looked as if she would have slapped him if it wasn't for his injuries. "What were you *doing,* going into the forest by yourself, you great damn fool? Never mind! Don't answer that—I'm just relieved you're home. And—" her shrewd brown eyes suddenly fixed on me "—I see I have some strangers to thank for your safe return."

"Be nice to them, Patricia," Joe gasped, making a feeble attempt to smile. "They saved my life. Killed a rabid pig without blinking an eyelash—damndest thing I've ever seen."

"Did they now?" the woman continued coolly as Joe was taken by the two men and limped back into the compound. "You don't say. Well, the Lord works in mysterious ways." Her sharp, no-nonsense gaze fixed on us. "My name is Patricia Archer," she said briskly, "and I don't know who ya'll are, but anyone who takes care of one of mine is welcome here."

"Thank you," Zeke said solemnly. "I'm Zeke, and that's Allison."

"Pleased t' meet you," Patricia shot back, leaning forward and squinting at us. "Let me see you better—my eyes ain't what they used to be. Lord have mercy, you're young. How old are you, boy? Seventeen? Eighteen?"

"Seventeen," Zeke replied. "I think."

"Well, ya'll are extremely lucky, traveling through the forest alone without running into rabids. They're quite the menace 'round these parts."

Menace? I thought. *Like raccoons and rodents are a menace? A rabid boar nearly took off a man's leg.*

"What are y'all doing way out here, anyway?" Patricia continued, but not in a wary, suspicious tone. She just sounded curious. "The pair of you could be my grandchildren. Oh, it doesn't matter." She waved her hand in front of her face. "Stop being nosy, Patricia. Let's get inside afore we attract rabids. I insist you get a hot meal and some sleep. We have a couple of empty rooms. And we can heat a few pots of water for hot baths, as well. You look like you could use one."

A hot bath was a luxury I'd only dreamed about in the Fringe. People said they existed, machines that heated water so that it came out at whatever temperature you wanted. I'd never seen one, myself. But Zeke shook his head.

"Thank you for your kindness," he said politely, "but we should go. We have people waiting for us in the forest."

"There are more of you?" Patricia blinked, looking up toward the trees. "Well, goodness, they can't stay out there, boy. David, Larry!" she called, beckoning two men down to the gate. "There are more people out in the woods," she announced sternly as the men scrambled out, each carrying a rifle. "As soon as the sun comes up, find them and bring them back. In fact, wake Adam and Virgil—tell them to help you, too."

"There's really no need—" Zeke began, but she shushed him.

"Hush, boy. Don't be silly. Ya'll helped one of mine, now I'm going to do the same. It's not like we see other humans around here. Where did you say the rest of your group was?"

Zeke still looked reluctant, unwilling to give up the location of the others or hesitant to accept help from a total stranger. But I glanced over the trees, to where the sky was beginning to lighten, and my nerves jangled a warning. The stars were fading. Dawn was on its way.

"About three miles southeast of here," I said, making Zeke frown at me. I ignored him, meeting Patricia's worried gaze. "There's about a dozen more out there, though half of them are kids. You might need to convince the preacher, though. He can be stubborn."

"A minister?" Patricia's eyes lit up. "Oh, that's wonderful. He can come pray over Joe. And you say there are *children* out there? Lord have mercy. Well, what are you two waiting for?" She scowled fiercely at the two men, who immediately muttered a hasty "Sorry, ma'am" and hurried back into the compound.

"Now." Patricia smiled at us, though her face looked as if she hadn't done it in a long while. "I'm sure you two are exhausted. I'll show you where ya'll can rest, and if you can wait an hour or two, breakfast will be ready." She blinked, as if something just occurred to her. "Oh, goodness, I guess I should go help Martha with the food this morning, shouldn't I? We're going to have a lot of guests. This way, if you would."

"Why did you do that?" Zeke whispered as we followed the tall, bony woman into the compound. "These people don't need more mouths to feed—it's probably hard enough for them to feed themselves."

"I'm tired, Zeke." I didn't look at him as I said it. "It's nearly dawn. I'm hungry, I'm covered in someone else's blood, I don't want to go tromping through the woods again, and for once I'd like to sleep on a bed instead of the cold, hard ground." Well, that last part was a lie, but he didn't need to know that. "You can relax—I don't think they're cannibals or secret vampire worshippers, unless you think the old lady is a devil in disguise."

He gave me an irritated look, then sighed, raking his fingers through his hair. "Jeb isn't going to like this," he muttered, shaking his head.

"Why am I not surprised?"

CHAPTER 15

When I awoke the next evening, I felt…different. Not in a bad way or in a way that nagged at me, like something I had to worry about. But something had definitely changed. Then it hit me. I was actually clean.

I threw back the quilt and sat up, stretching my arms over my head as I remembered the morning before. Soaking in a tub of hot, clean water, the steam rising into the air to fog the windows, was the purest form of bliss I'd felt in a long time. Getting rained on or falling into a muddy, churning river didn't count. And there had been real soap, something I'd only heard about in the Fringe. The Archers made their own soap from lye, sand and goat milk, and I'd used the strange yellow lump to scrub through the caked layers of grime and blood, until I could finally see the pale color of my skin. Sadly, with dawn fast approaching, my bath had been short-lived, but I had stayed in that tub for as long as I dared, until the rising sun had forced me out of the bathroom into the borrowed nightgown left on a pillow, and under the covers of the bed.

I stood, taking in the small room. It had probably been a child's room at one point, if the cheery sun quilt and faded cloud wallpaper were any indication. For a moment, I wondered what became of the child whose room I was borrowing, but quickly abandoned that train of thought.

There was a squeak in the hall outside, movement over the wooden slats, and I froze. Was there someone outside the door? I listened and thought I heard footsteps, moving rapidly away from my room and down the stairs.

Mildly alarmed, I gazed around and spotted my clothes, lying clean and neatly folded atop a dresser. Frowning, I thought back to the previous day. Had I locked my door? Last night, I'd left my clothes in a bloody heap on the floor. Someone had been in my room, if only to wash and fold my clothing, and that made me more than a little nervous. What if they had decided to wake me and couldn't? What if they'd noticed I wasn't breathing? My katana lay on top of the pile, not next to the bed where I'd left it, and that made me even more nervous.

I slipped into my clothes and buckled the sword to my back, vowing not to be separated from it again. I could not afford to be careless, especially when surrounded by even more strange humans. Pulling the coat over my shoulders, I turned to leave when there was a knock at the door.

"Allie?" came a voice from the other side. "You up yet? It's Zeke."

"It's open," I called back. *Though after tonight, that is going to change.*

The door creaked as it swung inward, revealing a very clean, smiling Zeke on the other side, holding a candle. He wore a white shirt and slightly baggy jeans, and his blond hair feathered out over his eyes and collar, looking very soft and touchable. His pistol, machete, hatchet and various weapons were still in place, but he looked more relaxed than I'd ever seen him.

And, though I tried to block it out, I could hear his heart beating, low and contented, in his chest. I could sense the pulse at his throat, echoing it, and the blood flowing through him, hot and powerful.

Cursing myself, I shoved those thoughts away. Maybe it was the overload from last night, being forced to see the wound, smell the blood soaking everything. To be that close, unable to tear into the man's throat, as I'd wanted to do all night, made me crave it even more. I was getting to the point where I'd better feed soon, or I'd go crazy.

Or maybe it was Zeke himself.

That was going to be a problem.

"Oh, wow," Zeke said quietly, his blue eyes dancing with mischief as he held the candle up. "Look at that. There was actually a girl underneath all the blood and dirt. Though you're a bit paler than I expected."

I snorted, hiding my sudden alarm. "Seen yourself?"

He laughed good-naturedly. "Come on. I just got up, but I think Jeb and the others are down in the barn. They arrived a few hours after we went to sleep. At least that's what Martha said—after telling me she was washing my unmentionables and I could have them back tomorrow." He wrinkled his nose. "I think the old woman was trying to come on to me."

"Okay, I'm just going to erase that image from my brain now." I gave him a mock-horrified look as we started down the corridor. "For the record, the words *old woman* and *unmentionables* should never be used in the same sentence."

He grinned as we made our way down the stairs and through the shadowy halls of the ancient farmhouse. It was a truly monstrous old building, two stories tall, with high windows, wooden floors and a roof that had been patched numerous times. Over the years, it had been expanded and built upon, and the back part of the house didn't quite match the first half, but it served its purpose I supposed, keeping a roof over the Archer clan's heads.

"Where is everyone?" I asked as we hit the ground floor without running into any of the clan's numerous members. Last night, Patricia had proudly told us that they had three generations of Archers living under one roof: brothers, sisters, aunts, uncles, cousins, in-laws, grandmothers, grandfathers, the whole family tree. I'd seen at least a half dozen people taking care of Joe when we'd followed Patricia into the house, and I'd suspected even more had been sleeping in their rooms. Where was everyone now? I heard banging noises coming from the kitchen, but other than that the old farmhouse was silent.

Zeke shrugged. "I think most everyone is outside, taking care of the animals, finishing work in the fields, and making sure the wall is safe. Martha told me they keep goats and sheep out in the pasture during the day, but they have to bring them in at night. Otherwise the rabids will get them."

"Zeke?" A frail, reedy voice came from the kitchen. "Is that you?"

Zeke grimaced and ducked behind a wall, blowing out the candle as a small white-haired old woman came out of the kitchen with a frying pan in one bony claw. She blinked when she saw me, thick glasses and toothless gums making her look like a lizard.

"Oh," she said, not able to hide her disappointment. "It's you. The girl."

"Allison," I provided.

"Yes, of course." Martha wasn't even looking at me anymore, rheumy eyes scanning the candlelit room. "I thought I heard that boy out here. Is Zeke with you?"

"No," I said firmly, not glancing at the corner where Zeke was vigorously shaking his head. "I haven't seen him."

"Oh. Pity." Martha sighed. "He must be in the barn with the others. Such a handsome lad, that one." She sniffed and peered at me, narrowing her eyes behind her glasses. "Oh, good. You found your clothes. I was going to tell you I had washed them, but you were sleeping so soundly, I couldn't even rouse you. You sleep like the dead!"

"Yeah." I shifted uncomfortably. *I am so definitely locking my door tonight. That, or I'll nail the damn thing shut.* "I guess I was tired. We—our group—we sleep during the day and travel at night. I'm not used to being up in the afternoon."

"Sleeping is one thing." Martha nodded her wrinkled head sagely. "You, my girl, were out like a log." I started to reply, but she appeared to lose interest now that Zeke wasn't around. "Well, if you see that boy, tell him I'm making a pie just for him. Boys like pie. Dinner will be ready in an hour. Be sure to tell your people."

"I will," I muttered as she vanished back into the kitchen. I glanced at Zeke, hoping he hadn't picked up on my unease. He just shrugged, and I raised an eyebrow.

"The mighty hunter," I quipped as we snuck out the back door, escaping into the yard. "He can take down vicious rabids and rampaging boars, but one old lady can make him flee in terror."

"One *scary* old lady," he corrected me, looking relieved to be out of the house. "You didn't hear what she told me when I got up—*you're so cute I could put you in a pie.* Tell me that's not the creepiest thing you've ever heard." His voice climbed a few octaves, turning shrill and breathy. "Today for dessert, we have apple pie, blueberry pie and Ezekiel pie."

We laughed together, our voices bouncing off the farmhouse walls. Outside, the twilight air was cool and hazy, and when I took a breath, I could smell smoke, dirt, livestock and manure. It was a clean smell, much cleaner than the Fringe and the city streets. Chickens milled about the yard, scattering before us, and a shaggy black-and-white dog watched us from a rusty tractor. It growled at me, curling its lips back as I met its gaze, but Zeke didn't notice.

"Now it's my turn," Zeke said, watching his feet as we walked down the muddy path to the barn. I glanced at him, frowning, and he kicked a pebble into the grass, following it with his gaze. "To thank you," he elaborated. "For helping me with Joe, and for killing that pig…basically for saving our lives. I don't think… I mean, if you hadn't been there…"

I shrugged. "Don't worry about it," I said, embarrassed.

"You would've done the same and so would Darren, and I think we both got really lucky that night. No one got hurt, so it's over."

"It almost got me," Zeke muttered, almost to himself. "I felt its teeth catch my leg as it went by. Thank God it didn't break the skin. If Jeb were to find out…" He trailed off.

"What?" I prodded.

He shook himself. "Nothing. Never mind. I would just… he would lecture my ear off, that's all." I watched him intently, but he wouldn't meet my eyes. "Anyway, I just wanted to say thanks." He shrugged. "And you're welcome to tag along with me and Darren whenever you want."

"Tag along?"

"You know what I mean."

We had reached the barn, a faded gray building that smelled of straw and goat poop. A warm yellow glow came from inside, along with the murmurs of people and the bleating of livestock. Slipping through the large double doors, we found Jeb near the front, talking to Patricia, while the rest of the group had sprawled around them, sitting on bales or leaning against fence railings. Matthew sat in the corner, holding a bottle for the baby goat in his lap, while Caleb and Bethany looked on in delight.

"Thank you for your hospitality," Jeb was saying as Zeke and I eased inside. "We appreciate you offering your home to us, but we don't want to be a bother."

"Oh, Jebbadiah, stop it," Patricia said, overruling him. "It's no bother at all. Y'all are welcome here, for as long as you need. We have enough food, and if you don't mind sleeping in the barn, there's more than enough space to go around. I must say, it's a mite strange that y'all sleep during the day, but I'm not here to judge, no I'm not." She cast her gaze over the rest of the group, smiling at Matthew, Caleb and the baby goat. "I know it's too soon to decide," she continued in an almost wistful voice, "but if ya'll decide to stay on a more permanent basis, we can always extend the house. We done it before, we can do it again."

"We cannot stay long," Jeb said firmly. "And I do ask that our sleep cycles not be interrupted, but perhaps we can find other ways to repay your hospitality."

"Just you prayin' over our man Joe, that's enough, preacher," Patricia said, her face turning somber and grim. "And maybe, if you really wanted to help, you could spare a couple of your men to help us watch the wall at night, keep the fires going and keep an eye on the critters. Since ya'll are night folk, anyway."

"Yes." Jebbadiah nodded and suddenly caught sight of Zeke and me, standing by the front doors, watching. "Yes, we can do that," he continued and beckoned to Zeke, clapping him on the shoulder as he came up. "You've met my son," he said with a trace of pride. "Ezekiel will be in charge of the night watches and anything else you need done."

"It'll be nice to have more people on the watch," Patricia mused and gave Jeb a tight smile. "Very well, preacher, we accept your offer. I'll have David and Larry show your boys the way we do things here at night."

They nodded at each other, two rigid, no-nonsense leaders finding something they appreciated in each other. For a second, I had the absurd thought that they would make a pretty good, although terrifying, couple, and snickered out loud at the image.

Three pairs of eyes turned to me. "And this is Allison," Jeb said blankly, with none of the pride he showed for Zeke. "She is the newest member of our little family, though Ezekiel tells me she's quite dangerous with that sword. Apparently she took down the rampaging wild boar very nearly by herself." The words were hollow, stiff. He might not be condemning me, but he sure wasn't praising me, either.

So much for our little heart-to-heart by the river. I guess he still has to keep the cranky-bastard appearance going for the rest of the group.

"We've met," Patricia said with a small approving smile. "Joe said he watched you two from the tree. Said you moved faster than anyone he's ever seen."

I shrugged, uneasy, but thankfully Zeke stepped in. "How is he?" he asked, a note of genuine concern in his voice. It still surprised me how worried he could be for a complete stranger.

Patricia's face fell, growing dark. "Alive," she murmured, and her voice dropped to nearly a whisper. "He's in the Lord's hands now."

DAVID AND LARRY, the two older farmhands, showed up later that night and explained what needed to be done. First, and most important, was guarding the wall, the barrier that surrounded the compound and kept the rabids away. Platforms and walkways had been constructed along the inside of the wall, giving the watch a clear view over the open field of anything coming out of the woods. Not only did the platforms need to be manned, but the bonfires that burned just outside the wall needed to be continuously fed. And someone needed to stay in the barn with the animals, for they would panic if they so much as smelled a rabid outside.

Zeke, Darren, Jake and I were drafted to help with the night watch. Ruth also volunteered, hoping to be close to Zeke, but the job required that you knew how to shoot a rifle, and delicate little Ruth was scared of guns. So she was put in charge of watching the sheep and goats, while I was shown how to use a hunting rifle. I tried not to act smug at the look on Ruth's face when they passed me the gun without hesitation, but it was hard.

"Nice," Zeke muttered, gazing down the barrel of the rifle, sweeping it over the fields below. We had taken the platform closest to the forest, where we had come out with Joe the previous night, and Zeke was kneeling with his elbows resting against the railing. "I used to have a rifle like this. Scoped, too. It made shooting game a lot easier, till I dropped it from a tree and cracked the stock." He grimaced and lowered the gun. "Jeb...was not happy with me."

I winced in sympathy. "How long do you think we'll be here?" I asked, leaning against the railing, hoping the rickety planks would support me. "It's not like Jeb to stop like this. Why is he even considering staying here a few nights?"

"He told me he wants to stay until the 'Joe thing' is resolved," Zeke replied. "Patricia asked him to pray for Joe, but I think it's more than that. I think he wants to be certain that we're not leaving a demon behind."

A demon? I thought, but movement out in the field caught

my attention. "Zeke," I muttered, pointing toward the woods. "Rabids."

Zeke straightened, bringing up the rifle, while I watched the monsters creep closer, their awful, rotten stench drifting over the breeze. There were three of them, pale and emaciated, moving across the field, straight toward the wall. They moved unnaturally, sometimes on all fours, sometimes hunched over, their jerky, spastic gait making my skin crawl. Two of them were completely naked, but one still had the remnants of a tattered dress clinging to its body, dragging it through the mud.

"Rabids!" Zeke called, his voice echoing through the compound. Instantly, Darren and Larry scrambled down from the platform opposite ours and hurried toward us. They clambered up, the platform creaking under their weight, and I stepped back to make room. Zeke dropped to a knee and leveled his gun at the rabids, but Larry held up a hand.

"No, don't waste ammo," he warned, eyes narrowed as he peered past the smoke and flames from below. "They're too far out still, and it's nearly impossible to kill them in one shot. Let 'em come closer, get a good bead on them, before you start firing. We might not need to shoot at all."

The rabids suddenly jerked to a halt, gazing at the wall with blank, hungry expressions. Zeke and Darren kept their guns trained on them, but it seemed the rabids knew just how close they could be without getting fired on. They skirted the edge of the field, keeping just out of reach, ducking behind trees and into bushes, never getting close enough for a clean shot.

Beside me, Zeke made a noise that was almost a growl. I stared at him in amazement. His shoulders were stiff, tense, and his eyes glittered with hate. "Come on," he muttered, and the cold rage in his voice shocked me. "Come a little closer, just a few more steps."

"Easy, boy," Larry soothed. "Don't be too eager. We don't want to attract more with the commotion."

Zeke didn't answer, his entire focus on the rabids below. He seemed different now; the smiling, easygoing boy I knew was gone. In his place stood a dark stranger with cold, ruthless eyes, his expression frozen into a flinty mask. Watching him, I felt a stab of apprehension. In that moment, he looked very much like Jeb.

"They've gotten wise to us," Larry muttered, squinting to see past the flames into the darkness. "A few years ago, there were a whole lotta them, and they'd come rushing up to the walls, searching for a way in, all night. We picked off several—damn things are hard to kill—before we got the fire idea. They still hang around—" he jerked his thumb toward the edge of the forest "—but they very rarely come close anymore. Mostly, they check to see if we have the fire going, and then they leave. Look, there they go."

I watched the rabids melt back into the woods, disappearing into the trees. The tension left Zeke and Darren's shoulders, and they straightened, lowering their guns, though Zeke looked disappointed.

"They'll come back," Larry said, not weary or resigned. Just a statement, a simple fact. "They always do." He tapped Darren's shoulder. "Come on, then, Darren was it? Let's get back to our post. Sometimes the monsters creep around and come at us again from the other side, sneaky bastards."

Darren and Larry climbed down from the platform and

shuffled back to their own, Larry already pointing out more rabid "strategies," if you could call them that. Zeke set down his rifle and leaned next to me against the railing, our shoulders barely touching as we gazed out over the fields.

"They have a nice life here," he said, and his voice wasn't mocking or sarcastic. It was almost wistful, envious. I snorted and crossed my arms, hiding the unease of a moment before.

"What, you mean with the wall and being penned in like sheep, and the constant threat of rabid invasion? It's like a miniature New Covington, except there are no vampires here."

Except one.

"They have a home," Zeke said, giving me a sideways look. "They have a family. They've carved out their own lives, and yeah, it might not be completely perfect or safe, but at least they have something that belongs to them." He sighed and scrubbed his fingers through his hair. "Not like us, constantly wandering around, never knowing what we'll find or what comes next. Not having a home to go back to."

The longing in his voice was palpable. I felt his shoulder against mine, our arms brushing together, the heat radiating from him. We didn't look at each other, keeping our gazes on the looming forest. "What was home for you?" I asked softly. "Before all this, before you started looking for Eden. Where did you live?"

"A little yellow house," Zeke murmured, his voice sounding distant. "With a tire swing in the front yard." He blinked, giving me an embarrassed look. "Ah, you don't want to hear about it, do you? It's pretty boring. Nothing special."

I gave him a puzzled look. My whole life, I thought there was nothing beyond the vampire cities but wilderness and rabids. The fact that there were other settlements out there, other towns, no matter how scattered, gave me hope. Maybe the world wasn't as empty as I'd first thought.

But I didn't tell him that. I just shrugged and said, "Tell me about it."

He nodded, paused a moment, as if gathering memories. "I don't remember much," he began, gazing out into the darkness. "There was a community down in the hollow of a mountain range. It was fairly small, everyone knew each other. We were so isolated, we didn't even think about rabids and vampires and things happening on the outside. So when the rabids did come, no one was prepared for it. Except Jeb."

Zeke stopped and took a quiet breath, his eyes far away and dark. "They came to our house first," he mused. "I remember them scratching at the windows, tearing down the walls to get in. My mom or my dad hid me in a closet, and I listened to their screams through the door." He shivered, but his voice was calm, as if this had happened to someone else, and he was detached from the boy in the story.

"The next thing I clearly remember was the door opening and Jeb standing there, staring down at me. He took me in, and we lived there for several years."

"Is that where the rest of the group came from?"

"Mostly." Zeke gave me a sideways glance. "There were more of us at first, and some like Darren we picked up along the way. But, yes, the majority of us came from that town. After the rabid attack, people were scared. They didn't know what to do. So they started listening to Jeb, coming to him for help, pleading for his advice. In time, it became a weekly thing, where we met in the old church for an hour or so and listened to him talk. Jeb didn't want to be a preacher again, he told everyone that. But people kept coming. And after a while, he sort of…gained a following."

"But…Jeb believes God has abandoned the world, that He's not here anymore." I gave Zeke a confused look. "I can't imagine that went over well."

"You'd be surprised." Zeke shrugged. "People were desperate for some sort of guidance, and it wasn't as bleak as you might think. Jeb believes that, even though God is no longer watching us, we have to keep fighting the evil while we're here. That we can't let ourselves become tainted by the demons. That it's the only way to have a shot at eternity when we die."

"How cheerful."

He smiled faintly. "He did have some rather strong opposition, but it didn't seem to bother him. Jeb was never really attached to the town, not like me. Now that I think about it, I don't think he ever meant to stay long. Not with what he was teaching me."

"What did he teach you?"

"Everything I know—how to shoot, how to fight. We would go out to the hills behind the town, in the daylight, of course, and he would show me how to survive in the wilderness. I shot my first rabbit at the age of six. And I cried all the way through cleaning it.

"But," he continued, "that evening, our neighbor took that skinny carcass and made a stew out of it, and we sat around our kitchen table and ate it all. And Jeb was so proud." Zeke chuckled, self-conscious, and shook his head. "That was home to me, crazy as it sounds. Not this endless wandering. Not a faceless city that we might never find." He sighed heavily, glancing back toward the barn, and the burden on his face was almost overwhelming. "So, anyway," he finished, shaking off his melancholy as he looked back to the woods, "that's why I think the Archers have a good thing here. Rabids and walls and fire and everything." He finally looked at me then, smirking and defiant. "So, go ahead—tell me I'm a sentimental idiot if you want, but that's my story and I'm sticking to it."

"You're not," I replied. "I think you're too hard on yourself, and that Jeb shouldn't expect you to keep everyone alive and safe and happy, but I don't think you're an idiot."

He smiled, a real one this time, though his voice remained teasing. "So, what *do* you think I am?"

Naive, I thought at once. *Naive, brave, selfless, incredible— and much too kind to survive this world. It'll break you in the end, if you keep going like this. Good things never last.*

I didn't say any of these things, of course. I just shrugged and muttered, "It doesn't matter what I think."

Zeke's voice was soft, almost a whisper. "It matters to me."

I looked at him. His eyes were stormy blue in the moonlight, his hair a pale silver-blond. The cross glimmered against his chest, winking metallically as if in warning, but I couldn't tear my eyes from his face. Slowly, he let go of the railing and leaned in, reaching up to brush a strand of hair from my cheek.

His fingers grazed my skin, and warmth shot through me like an electrical jolt. I heard his heart thudding in his chest, the pulse throbbing beneath his jaw. His scent was everywhere, overwhelming; heat and blood and life, and a distinct, earthy smell that was uniquely him. I imagined kissing him, trailing my lips down to his throat, a rush of hot blood flooding my mouth. I felt my fangs lengthen, even as I leaned in.

"Zeke!"

Ruth's voice shattered the stillness, jerking us apart and bringing me to my senses. Horrified, I rose and stepped to the edge of the platform, facing the wind. What the hell was I doing, playing with fire like this? Biting the preacher's son was an excellent way to get myself excommunicated and hunted down. Jeb was ruthless when it came to moving on, but I had the feeling he would make an exception for me. Even worse, Zeke would know what I was—and he would hate me for it.

And, a dark little corner of my mind whispered, *what if you had bitten him and couldn't stop? What if you had drawn every bit of light and warmth into yourself, and when you were done, nothing was left of him?*

I shuddered and willed my fangs to retract, stifling the desire and the Hunger that came with it. I thought back to our almost kiss and had to wonder: would I have kissed him, or would I have leaned in those final inches to tear out his throat?

"Zeke!" Ruth called again, oblivious to the scene up top, "Miss Archer wants me to remind you that the fire outside the wall needs to be fed. The woodpile is back behind the water cistern. I can show you where it is if you want to come down."

"I'll go," I said quickly as Zeke leaned over the railing to call back to Ruth. He stopped and gave me a puzzled look, but I turned away toward the ladder before he could say anything. If Ruth wanted alone time with Zeke, so be it. She could have her chance. Right now, I had to get away from him, before we both did something we'd regret.

"Allison," Zeke said softly, stopping me. I glanced up at him from the ladder, and found him looking at me with a sad, confused expression. "I'm sorry," he murmured. "I shouldn't have...I thought..." He trailed off with a sigh, raked a hand through his hair. "Don't go?" he pleaded, giving me a hopeful smile. "I'll behave, I promise."

But I can't. I shook my head and climbed down, leaving my rifle up top against the rails. I felt Zeke's eyes on me as I left, but I didn't look at him.

Naturally Ruth glared at me as I descended, but I ignored her, too, continuing toward the water cistern at the far corner of the lot. Her shoes clumped against the ladder as she climbed up to join Zeke, and I forced myself to keep walking. Hopefully, Ruth's single-minded adoration would distract Zeke from coming after me, though a part of me wished he would.

It's better this way, I told myself, passing the barn. Soft murmurs and contented bleats came from within; the rest of the group was taking advantage of the unexpected stop, probably relieved not to be hiking through rabid-infested woods. *That was way too close,* I continued, hurrying past before anyone could see me. *What would you have done if Zeke found out? You think he could like you, if he knew what you really were?* A mental snort. *You saw how he was with the rabids. He'd put a stake in your heart or a bullet in your skull without thinking twice about it. He'd sell you out, just like Stick.*

I came to the tiny woodshed in the shadow of the gravity-fed cistern, really nothing more than a three-sided wooden shelter with a tin roof. It was stacked high with split logs, and I loaded several into the rusty wheelbarrow sitting nearby, when I heard a soft moan.

Warily, I put a hand on my sword and waited, unmoving. It came again, the soft, hopeless sound of a human in pain. From the other side of the woodshed.

Still keeping a hand on the hilt, I edged around the building, ready to draw my weapon if necessary. When I saw what was making the noise, however, I dropped my arm. There was no need.

A large iron cage stood at the back of the woodshed. The bars were thick and close together, though far enough apart to see inside. The door was barred in two places from the outside, padlocked shut and wrapped in chains. Even the floor of the cage had iron bars running across it, separating the prisoner from the natural earth. A thin layer of straw had been spread over the ground, partially absorbing the smell of urine, iodine and blood.

Huddled under a blanket, curled up in the corner closest to the woodshed, a familiar, bearded face raised its head to stare at me.

I blinked. "Joe?" I whispered, recognizing the man Zeke and I had dragged back from the woods. "What are you doing in there?" I asked, appalled. I could smell the blood on him, the torn flesh under the bandages. He was still badly hurt and needed to be in a bed, or at least a room where he could be looked after. "Who put you in here?" I demanded, wrapping a fist around the bars. He stared at me with bleary eyes, and

I backed away, fuming. "I'll get Patricia," I told him. "She'll let you out. Just hang in there."

"No," Joe wheezed, holding out a hand. I stared at him, and he coughed, shuddering beneath his quilt. "No, it's all right," he continued when the spell had passed. "The boar savaged my leg pretty bad. I have to be locked up till they can be sure I don't Turn."

"They did this to you *on purpose?*" I came back, gripping the bars as I peered at him. "And you let them? What about your leg?"

"It's been looked after as well as can be expected," Joe replied, shrugging. "In the morning, someone will come and rebandage it. And it's not as bad as it looks. I think I have a good chance of pulling through this one."

I looked at his sallow, sweaty face, the pain glazing his eyes, and shook my head. "I still can't believe they'd leave you in here like an animal. I'd be screaming and tearing the walls down, trying to get out."

"I want to be here," Joe insisted. "What if I die in the house and Turn before anyone notices? When everyone is asleep? I could kill my whole family. No." He leaned back, drawing his blanket closer. "This is necessary. I'm not a danger to anyone here, and the family is safe. That's all I care about."

"Good man," said a voice over my shoulder.

I whirled. Jeb stood at a corner of the cage, looking in, his sharp face impassive. The man moved like a vampire himself; I hadn't even heard him approach.

"You see, Allison," Jeb mused, though he wasn't looking at me. "This is a man who is more concerned about the safety of his family, rather than his own short existence. In fact, everyone here understands what must be done to protect the whole, rather than a few individuals. That is how they have survived here so long."

"You think locking an injured man up like a dog, with no treatment or help or medicine, is the best thing for him?"

Jeb's steely eyes turned to me. "If that man's soul is in danger of corruption, and his body is in danger of succumbing to the darkness, then he is no longer a man but a demon. And when the demon emerges, it is best to have it contained. For the safety of the untainted humans, yes, I do believe that is the best thing." I opened my mouth to protest, but he overrode me. "What would *you* do differently?"

"I—" Jeb raised his eyebrows expectantly, and I glared at him. "I don't know."

"You and Ezekiel." The old man shook his head. "Both of you refuse to see the world as it is. But that is not my problem. If you'll excuse me, I must get to praying for this man's soul. Perhaps it can yet be saved."

He turned from me and bowed his head, speaking quietly. Inside the cage, Joe did the same. I retreated back to the woodshed, grabbing the wheelbarrow and filling it with wood, making sure to fling the logs so they clattered around in the noisiest way possible.

I knew, in a sick, twisted way, that Jeb was right. Any human bitten by a rabid, whether it was a dog or skunk or a rabid person, was in danger of Turning. It was different from becoming a vampire, where you had to drink your sire's blood to become one. In my case, Kanin's Master vampire blood had made me strong enough to overcome the disease, and he'd gotten to me immediately after I'd been attacked. Even then, I had been very lucky; most vampires still created rabids when they tried to make new offspring.

Rabidism, however, was much more potent and certain. Every case was different, Kanin had told me—usually it depended on the severity of the wound and the victim's fortitude and will to fight off the infection. The virus spread quickly, accompanied by raging fever and a great deal of pain, before it finally killed the host. If left undisturbed, the body would rise again completely changed; a rabid, carrying the same deadly virus that had Turned it.

I knew the precautions the Archers had taken were necessary; even with one of their own, they could not afford the risk of him going rabid. But it still made my skin crawl, the thought of being locked in a cage, alone, waiting to die. I wondered what Zeke would think of it. Would he be as shocked and disturbed as I was? Or would he side with Jeb, claiming it was the right thing to do?

Zeke. I pushed the thought of him from my mind, hurling a log into the wheelbarrow so forcefully it bounced out and hit the wall of the shed. That moment we'd shared up on the platform, that couldn't happen again. No matter how much I wanted it. I couldn't allow him to get that close ever again. For both our sakes.

Ruth and Zeke were still up on the platform, sitting side by side, when I returned with the wheelbarrow full of logs and branches. I didn't go back to the tower but watched as Larry demonstrated how to feed the fires by dropping the wood down several chutes that led straight into the flames, all without leaving the safety of the compound. I was impressed. Rather than stupidly scurrying outside to toss logs onto the flames and tempt any number of rabid hordes watching from the forest, they'd worked out an ingenious way of dealing with the problem in the least dangerous way possible. You had to admire their creativity.

After feeding the bonfires, I wandered back to the barn, wanting to avoid Zeke and Ruth on the platform. Maybe he could show her how to hold and shoot my rifle—she'd love that—and I could take over guarding the livestock. Whatever it took to stay away from him.

The barn was musty and warm as I opened the door and slipped inside, the livestock dozing contentedly. Most of the group was outside or in the farmhouse, helping with the watch or doing various chores around the compound. But Teresa, Silas and the youngest of the kids remained in the barn with the animals. Old Silas dozed in a corner, covered in blankets, snores coming from his open mouth. Teresa sat nearby, mending a quilt and humming softly to herself. She smiled and nodded at me when I came in.

"Allison." Caleb emerged from one of the stalls and walked up to me, shy little Bethany trailing behind him, clutching a bottle in a grubby fist. Caleb held a spotted baby goat in his arms, and it was almost too much for him to handle, bleating and struggling weakly. Quickly, I knelt and took the animal from him, holding it against my chest. It calmed somewhat but still cried out pitifully.

"It doesn't have a mommy." Caleb sounded close to tears, wiping his face and leaving a streak of mud across one cheek. "We have to feed it, but it won't drink its bottle. It keeps crying, but it doesn't want the milk, and I don't know what it wants."

"Here," I said, holding out my hand, and Bethany gave me the bottle. Sitting against the wall, I settled the tiny creature in my lap, as the two human kids watched anxiously. For a moment, I felt a prick of irritation that Ruth should be here doing this, not me, but then I focused on the task at hand. I had only a vague idea of what to do, having never seen a goat before, much less held one, but I'd have to make it work.

I pinched a drop of milk onto the nipple and waited until the goat bleated again before sliding it into its mouth. The first two times, the stubborn kid shook its head and cried louder than ever, but the third time, it finally realized what I was offering. Clamping its jaws around the bottle, it started drinking in earnest, gurgling through the milk, and my audience clapped in relief.

Before I knew what was happening, Caleb sat down on one side of me, Bethany on the other, and leaned against my arm. I stiffened, holding myself rigid, but they didn't seem to notice my discomfort, and the kid on my lap cried greedily when I didn't hold the bottle up far enough. Resigned, I leaned back, watching the three young creatures around me, trying not to breathe in their scent or listen to their hearts. Teresa looked over at me and smiled, and I shrugged helplessly.

"You know," I muttered, mostly to keep my mind distracted, so I wouldn't think of blood or hearts or how hungry I was getting, "I think this little guy needs a name, if he doesn't have one already What do you think?"

Caleb and Bethany agreed. "What about Princess?" Bethany suggested.

"Stupid," Caleb said instantly. "That's a girl's name."

She stuck out her tongue, and Caleb returned the gesture. I

watched the kid suckle at the bottle, milk dribbling down his chin. He was mostly white, except for a few black splotches on his back legs and one large circle over his eye. It made him look like a bandit or a pirate.

"What about Patch?" I mused.

They clapped in delight. Both thought this was a perfect name, and Bethany even kissed Patch on his furry head, which the goat ignored. After a moment of watching him guzzle milk, Caleb suddenly let out an explosive sigh and slumped against me.

"I don't want to leave," he muttered, sounding tired and world-weary even for one so young. "I don't want to keep looking for Eden anymore. I'd rather stay here."

"Me, too," Bethany mumbled, but she was half asleep now, curled up into my side.

Caleb reached up and scratched Patch on the shoulder, making its skin twitch as if it was shooing off a fly. "Allie, do you think there'll be goats in Eden?" he mused.

"I'm sure there will be," I answered, holding up the bottle so the kid could get the last drops. "Maybe you could even have a few of your own."

"I'd like that," Caleb murmured. "I hope we get there soon, then."

Not long after, the bottle was empty, and all three were asleep, curled up on my lap or leaning against my ribs. Teresa had also dozed off, her head against her chin, the quilt fallen beside her. It was very quiet in the barn, except for the live-stock shifting in their sleep, and the beating of the three hearts surrounding me.

Bethany suddenly slumped over, her head falling to my

leg, her golden hair spilling over my thigh. I stared at her. Flickering lamplight danced along her pale little neck, as she sighed and pressed closer, murmuring in her dreams.

My fangs slid out. Her heartbeat was suddenly very loud in my ears; I could hear it, pulsing in her wrist, her throat. My stomach felt hollow, empty, and her skin was warm on my leg.

Brushing her hair aside, I slowly leaned forward.

CHAPTER 16

No! Closing my eyes, I jerked back, thumping my head against the wall. The baby goat let out a startled bleat, then tucked its nose beneath its hindquarters with a sigh. Caleb and Bethany slept on, unaware how close they had come to being food.

Horrified, I looked around for an escape route. I couldn't keep this up. The Hunger was slowly taking over, and it wouldn't be long before I gave in to temptation. I needed to feed, before it grew too strong to ignore.

Gently, I extracted myself from the sleeping kids and returned the newly christened Patch to his pen, where he promptly fell asleep. Once free, I slipped outside and leaned against the barn, pondering the inevitable question. It was time. That had been way too close. Who was I going to feed from?

Not the kids. Never. I was not so inhuman that I would draw blood from a sleeping child. Teresa and Silas were so old, though, too weak to lose any blood, and I was *not* going

to bite them in front of two sleeping children. Jake and Darren were on guard duty, and Ruth was with Zeke.

Zeke was definitely out of the question.

That left Dorothy the crazy woman, who was in the farmhouse gossiping with Martha, who didn't go to bed until midnight, apparently, and Jebbadiah Crosse.

Yeah, right. I might as well just shoot myself in the face
than go anywhere near Jeb.

I growled in frustration. This wasn't getting me anywhere.
When had I gotten so close to the people I was supposed to
be feeding from?

It always starts out that way. Kanin's voice echoed in my
mind, quietly knowing. *Noble intentions, honor among new vampires. Vows to not harm humans, to take only what is needed, to not
hunt them like sheep through the night. But it becomes harder and
harder to remain on their level, to hold on to your humanity, when
all you can see them as is food.*

"Dammit," I whispered, covering my eyes with a hand.
How did Kanin do it? I tried to remember, thinking back to
our time in the Fringe. He had some sort of code, a type of
moral honor system, that he used when feeding off unsuspecting victims. He left something behind—like the shoes—
payment for the harm his actions would bring.

I couldn't do that now. I didn't have anything I could give.
True, I was helping out, taking the night watch and all, but
that was more of a group effort. We were all pitching in to
help.

But, I did save that man's life…

Guilt and disgust stabbed at me. How could I even think
about preying on a weak, caged human? Earlier tonight, I'd

been horrified to see him locked up like a beast, and now I was thinking of feeding off him? Maybe Kanin was right. Maybe I was a monster, just like he said.

I could hear him now, his deep voice echoing in my head, as clearly as if he were standing beside me. *Make your choice, Allison,* he would say, calm and unruffled. *Will you prey on those you consider friends and companions, or a stranger who already owes you his life? Know that each path is evil; you must decide which one is the lesser of the two.*

"Damn you," I muttered to the empty air. Figment Kanin didn't reply, shimmering into nothingness; he already knew what path I was going to choose.

I WATCHED JEBBADIAH CROSSE finish praying over the wounded man, watched him stride back to the farmhouse, his severe form cutting a rigid path through the darkness. I watched the man in the cage, waited for his coughing and shifting to stop, for his raspy breathing to slow, becoming heavy and deep.

When he was snoring quietly, I glided from the shadows along the wall, walking quickly to the woodshed and snatching the key from where it hung on its nail. Silently, I removed the iron bar across the door, unlocked the padlock and removed the chains, being careful not to clink them against the bars. Carefully, being cautious that the door didn't creak, I eased it open.

Joe Archer lay slumped in the corner, covered in blankets, his body curled into itself to conserve heat. His leg, heavily bandaged and reeking of blood and alcohol, lay at an awkward angle.

Are you really going to do this?

I shoved the voice aside, burying my feelings of horror, guilt and disgust. I didn't want to, but it was necessary. I didn't dare go into the farmhouse; with so many people under one roof, I didn't want to creep into a room only to be discovered by a light sleeper or someone getting up to use the bathroom. I thought of Caleb and Bethany, Zeke and Darren. If I didn't do this, they might be the ones in my sights next. I could kill them if I didn't feed soon. The cage was isolated, out of the way, and no one would be coming to check on him for a while. Better a stranger than someone I knew, someone I actually cared about.

Besides, he owed me for saving his life.

If that's what you want to tell yourself. Let's get this over with, then.

Joe stirred in his sleep and coughed, his snores faltering. Quickly, before I had more second thoughts, I stepped up beside him and knelt, easing the collar of his coat aside. His throat, bared to the moonlight, pulsed softly. My fangs lengthened, the Hunger rising up like a dark tide. As the human groaned, eyelids fluttering, I leaned forward and sank my teeth into his neck, right below his jaw.

He jerked, but relaxed instantly, succumbing to the near delirium of a vampire's bite. As blood began flowing into my mouth, the Hunger drank it greedily, demanding more, always more. I kept a tight leash on it this time, fighting to keep my senses, to not lose myself to the heat and power flowing into me.

Three swallows. That was all I'd allow myself to take, though my Hunger was raging at me for more. Reluctantly,

I drew my fangs from the human's skin, sealing the wounds before stepping back. He groaned, half asleep and dead to the world, and I slipped out of the cage, replacing the locks and chains as quickly as I could.

"Allison?"

Just as I was replacing the last bar, footsteps crunched behind me and Zeke's familiar voice floated over my shoulder. I turned, and he stood a few paces behind me, a thermos in one hand, a metal cup in the other.

"Here you are," he said, not accusingly, though he seemed puzzled. "You never came back after Ruth left. Are you still angry with me?"

"What are you doing here?" I asked, ignoring the question. I wasn't angry, of course, but maybe it was better if he thought I was. He nodded to himself, as if expecting it.

"They're getting dinner ready in the barn," he continued, holding up the mug. "If you want something, I'd head over soon, before Caleb and Matthew eat all the soup."

I nodded and turned away, watching Joe sleep through the bars of the cage. "Did you know about this?" I asked, hearing him move up beside me.

"Jeb told me." Zeke knelt close to the bars and reached through, shaking the unconscious man. He stirred with a groan, opening his eyes blearily, and Zeke held up the thermos. "Hey," he murmured, unscrewing the top and pouring out a dark, steaming liquid. "Thought you could use this. It's black, but it's better than nothing."

"Thanks, boy," Joe wheezed, reaching for the mug. His hands shook, and he nearly dropped it. "Damn, I'm worse off than I thought. How long until morning?"

"A couple hours," Zeke replied gently, handing the cup of soup through the bars, as well. "This will be over soon. How are you holding up?"

"Oh, I'll live." Joe sipped at the coffee and smiled. "At least for another day."

Zeke smiled back, like he really believed it, and suddenly I had to get out of there. Spinning on my heel, I hurried away—away from the caged, doomed human who had been prey to me moments before. Away from the boy who showed me just how monstrous I truly was.

"Hey! Allison, wait!"

I heard Zeke jogging after me and I whirled on him, suddenly furious. *"Go away,"* I snarled, managing, barely, not to show fangs. "Why do you keep hanging around? What are you trying to prove, preacher boy? Do you think you can save me, too?"

He blinked, utterly bewildered. "What?"

"Why do you try so hard?" I continued, glaring disdainfully, holding on to my anger through sheer force of will. "You're always giving things away, putting yourself at risk, making sure others are happy. It's stupid and dangerous. People aren't worth saving, Ezekiel. Someday that person you help is going to stick a knife in your back or slit your throat from behind, and you won't even see it coming."

His blue eyes flashed. "How ignorant do you think I am?" he demanded. "Yeah, the world's an awful place, and it's full of people who would as soon put a knife in my back as shake my hand. Yeah, I could stick my neck out for them, and they'd throw me to the rabids without a second thought. Don't think I haven't seen it before, Allison. I'm not *that* stupid."

"Then why keep trying? If Jeb thinks this is hell, why even bother?"

"Because there has to be more than this!" Zeke paused, ran both hands through his hair, and looked at me sadly. "Jeb has pretty much given up on humanity," he said in a soft voice. "He sees corruption and vampires and rabids, and thinks that this world is done. The only thing he cares about is getting to Eden, saving the few lives he can. Anyone else—" he shrugged "—they're on their own. Even people like Joe." He nodded back toward the woodshed. "He'll pray for him, but he keeps himself distant, detached."

"But you don't believe that."

"No, I don't." Zeke looked me straight in the eye as he said it, unembarrassed and unshakable. "Jeb might've lost faith, but I haven't. Maybe I'm wrong," he continued with a shrug, "but I'm going to keep trying. It's what keeps me human. It's what separates me from them, all of them, rabids, demons, vampires, everything."

Vampires. That stung a lot more than I thought it would. "That's great for you," I said bitterly. "But I'm not like that. I don't believe in God, and I don't believe humans have anything good in them. Maybe you have a nice little family here, but I've been on my own too long to trust anyone."

Zeke's expression softened, which was not what I wanted to see. I wanted to hurt him, make him angry, but he just watched me with those solemn blue eyes and took a step forward. "I don't know what you've gone through," he said, holding my gaze, "and I can't speak for everyone, but I promise you're safe here. I would never hurt you."

"Stop it," I hissed, backing away. "You don't know me. You don't know anything about me."

"I would if you'd let me," Zeke shot back, then crossed the space between us in two long strides, gripping my upper arms. Not hard; I could've jerked back if I wanted, but I was so shocked that I froze, looking up into his face.

"I will if you give me a chance," he murmured. "And you're wrong—I know a few things about you. I know you and Ruth don't get along, I know Caleb adores you, and I know you can handle a sword better than anyone I've seen before." He smiled then, achingly handsome, his eyes liquid blue pools as he gazed into mine. "You're a fighter, you question everything you don't agree with, and you're probably the only one here who's not terrified of Jeb. And I've never met anyone like you. Ever."

"Let go," I whispered. I could hear his heartbeat, thudding loud in his chest, and was suddenly terrified he would hear my lack of one. He complied, sliding his hands down my arms, holding the tips of my fingers before dropping them. But his eyes never left my face.

"I know you're scared," he continued in a quiet voice, still close enough that I could feel his breath on my cheek. The Hunger stirred, but it was weaker this time, sated for now. "I know we just met, and we're all strangers, and you keep yourself apart for your own reasons. But I also know I haven't... felt this way about anyone before. And I think...I hope...you feel the same, because that was really hard for me to say. So..." He reached out again, taking my hand. "I'm asking you to trust me."

I wanted to. For the second time that night, I wanted to

kiss him, standing there so openly in the moonlight, his bangs falling jaggedly into his eyes. Zeke leaned forward, and for just a moment, I allowed him to step close, to cup the back of my head as his lips moved down toward mine. His pulse throbbed, his scent surrounding me, but this time, I only saw his face.

No, this can't happen! I shoved him, hard. He staggered backward and fell, landing on his back in the dirt. I heard his sharp intake of breath, saw the shocked, wounded look in his eyes, and almost turned to flee.

I didn't. Against my will, against everything screaming at me not to do this, I drew my sword and stepped up beside him, pointing it at his chest. Zeke's eyes went wide at the blade, gleaming inches from his heart, and he froze.

"Let me make this as clear as I can," I told him, holding the hilt tightly so my hands wouldn't shake. "Don't do that again. I don't trust you, preacher boy. I don't trust anyone. And I've been stabbed in the back too many times for that to change, do you understand?"

Zeke's eyes were angry, wounded stars, but he nodded. I sheathed my blade, turned and walked back to the farmhouse, feeling his gaze on me all the way. But he didn't follow.

Dawn wasn't far. I went back to the empty room and closed the door, being sure to latch it this time. My eyes burned, and I clamped down on my emotions before they spilled over my cheeks.

In the bathroom, I splashed icy water on my face, gazing at my cracked reflection in the mirror. Unlike the stories said, we actually did cast a reflection, and mine looked awful: a pale, dark-haired girl with traces of blood running from her eyes, and someone else's blood flowing in her veins. I bared my fangs, and the image of the girl disappeared, revealing a snarling, hollow-eyed vampire in the glass. If Zeke only knew what I really was...

"I'm sorry," I whispered, remembering the way he'd looked when I'd shoved him, when I'd pointed my sword at his chest. Shocked, betrayed, heartbroken. "It's better like this. It really is. You have no idea what you're getting into."

I couldn't keep this up. It was too hard, seeing Zeke, keeping my distance, pretending I didn't care. It was also getting harder and harder to keep my secret. Sooner or later, I'd slip up, or someone would put the pieces together and realize what had been lurking in their midst. And then Jeb or Zeke would put a sharp wooden stick through my chest or cut off my head. Zeke had watched rabids kill his friends and family, and he was the protégé of Jebbadiah Crosse. I could not believe he would accept a vampire hanging around the group, no matter what he said about trust.

Maybe it was time to leave. Not tonight—dawn was too close—but soon. When they left the compound, that would be a good time to go. I knew Jeb didn't want to stay much longer; he was already anxious to get on the road. I would see them through the woods, protect them from any rabids that might be lurking around, and then I would slip away before anyone realized I was gone.

Where will you go? my reflection seemed to ask. I swallowed the lump in my throat and shrugged. "I don't know," I muttered. "Does it matter? As long as I get far away from Zeke and Caleb and Darren and everyone, it doesn't matter where I go."

They'll miss you. Zeke will miss you.

"They'll get over it." I left the bathroom, my mind churning with conflicting emotions. I didn't want to leave. I had grown attached to Caleb and Bethany and Darren. Even Dorothy had her strange charm. The rest I barely spoke to, and some—Ruth and Jebbadiah—I would be perfectly happy if I never saw again, but I would definitely miss the others.

Especially a certain boy with starry eyes and an open smile, who saw nothing but good inside me. Who didn't know... what I really was.

I slept with my sword close that day, the covers pulled over my head. No one disturbed me, or at least, when I woke again the following evening, the room was as I'd left it. Lightning flickered outside, searingly bright for a split second, and thunder rumbled in the distance. If Jeb wanted to leave tonight, it would be a long, wet walk out.

Voices echoed through the stairwell, and I found the entire group downstairs, milling around the enormous wooden table that dominated one side of the kitchen. Ruth and Martha were ladling stew into bowls and passing them around, and a large bowl of corn muffins sat on the table within easy reach of everyone. Despite the feast, the mood around the table was somber and grim; even the kids ate silently with their eyes downcast. I wondered what was going on. Jeb wasn't here, and neither was Patricia, but I glanced up and met Zeke's eyes on the other side of the table.

As soon as our gazes met, he turned, grabbed a muffin from the bowl and walked out of the room without looking back.

My chest constricted. I wanted to go after him, to apologize for last night, but I didn't. It was better that he hate me now; I'd be gone from his life soon enough.

Instead, I wandered over to where Darren stood, leaning against a corner and dunking his bread in his stew. He glanced at me, nodded and went back to eating. But he didn't seem openly hostile, so maybe he hadn't spoken to Zeke about what happened.

"What's going on?" I asked, leaning beside him. He gave me a sideways look and swallowed a mouthful of food.

"We're leaving soon," he muttered, gesturing to the back door, where all our packs lay, stacked in a neat pile. "Probably in a couple hours, after everyone has eaten. Hopefully, we can get underway before the storm hits, and then the rain will hide our noise and our scent from any rabids in the woods. Jeb is talking to Patricia right now—she's trying to get him to stay for another night or two, but I don't think she'll get very far. Jeb already gave us the order to move out."

"Now? Tonight?" I frowned, but Darren nodded. "I thought we were staying until Joe got better."

"He died," Darren said softly, and my throat clenched in horror. "This afternoon. Larry went out to check on him, and he was gone."

He's dead? "No," I whispered, as a growl of distant thunder drowned my voice. *No, he can't be dead. Not after…* Breaking away, I ducked out the back door and headed toward the woodshed.

Outside, a few drops of rain had begun to fall, making pattering sounds on the tin roof. As I passed the barn, the animals inside were bleating and crying, and I heard thumps of bodies hitting each other and the walls, the scuffle of hooves

on the floor. In the twilight, the woodshed was dark and silent. Several logs had already been taken to feed tonight's
fires, though the rain would drench the flames soon enough.
I wondered if the rabids got excited every time it stormed.

As I rounded the shed, I saw the cage, and the body huddled in the corner, shaking. Relief swept through me. Darren had been wrong. Joe was still alive.

"Hey," I greeted softly, stepping up to the bars. "You sure
gave me a scare. Everyone thought you were de—"

Joe looked up, eyes blazing, and lunged at me with a scream.

I jerked back, and the body struck the cage with a chilling shriek, grabbing at me through the bars, its skin pale and
bloodless. The rabid howled, shaking the bars of the cage,
biting and clawing at the iron, its mad eyes fixed on me.

Sickened, I stared at the thing that had once been Joe Archer, at the once familiar face, now gaunt and wasted. His
beard was covered in blood and froth, his eyes glazed and
glassy as they stared at me, nothing in them except hunger.
And my stomach twisted so hard I thought I might throw up.

Did I do this? Is this my fault? I thought back to the previous
night, when Joe had spoken to me, had accepted coffee from
Zeke and even made a joke. He had been fine then. Had I
taken too much that he had died, succumbed to the infection? Would he still be alive, if I hadn't fed from him?

I heard the crunch of gravel behind me and turned, hoping and fearing it was Zeke. But it was only Larry, come to
return the empty wheelbarrow to the woodshed. He set it
aside and stared at the rabid a few moments, his weathered
face crumpled with grief.

"Damn," he muttered in a choked voice. "Damn damn

dammit! I was hoping he wouldn't…" He sucked in a breath, swallowing hard. "I'll have to let Patricia know," he whispered, sounding on the verge of a breakdown. "Aw, Joe. You were a good man. You didn't deserve this."

"What will happen to him now?" I asked.

Larry didn't look at me, continuing to stare at the rabid as he answered. "Joe is gone," he said in a flat, dull voice. "We would've buried the body if he hadn't Turned, but there's nothing left of him anymore. The sun will take care of the rest tomorrow."

He shuffled away, back toward the farmhouse, leaving me to stare at the monster that had been Joe and feel completely and utterly sick.

My eyes burned, and I felt something hot slide down my cheek. I didn't wipe it away this time, and more followed, burning crimson paths down my skin. The rabid watched me, cold and calculating. It had stopped throwing itself against the bars and now huddled against the back corner, unnaturally still, a coiled spring ready to be unleashed.

"I'm sorry," I whispered to it, and it bared its fangs at the sound of my voice. "I did this. You'd still be alive if I hadn't bitten you. I'm so sorry, Joe."

"I knew it," someone hissed behind me.

I whirled. Ruth peered at me from around the corner of the woodshed, her brown eyes wide with shock.

CHAPTER 17

We stared at each other, frozen in time. As our eyes met, I became aware of the small things happening around us: the drip of rabid drool hitting the ground, the lines of blood smeared across my cheek.

Then Ruth stepped back and took a breath.

"Vampire!"

The cry echoed off the woodshed, carrying over the rain, as Ruth turned to flee. Behind me, the rabid shrieked in response, and my vampire nature surged up with a roar. I lunged forward on instinct. Before the girl could take a single step, I was in front of her, slamming her back into the wall, fangs bared to their fullest. Ruth screamed.

"Shut up!" I snarled, even as I caught myself from lunging forward, from driving my fangs into her slender throat. The vampire within howled a protest, urging me to bite, to kill. Shaking from holding myself back, I glared at her, curling my lips from my teeth. "That was you by my room last night, wasn't it?" I demanded. "I thought I heard someone on the stairs. You've been snooping around me all this time, just waiting for something to happen."

"I knew it," Ruth panted, shrinking back from me, her expression caught between defiance and terror. "I *knew* there was something wrong about you. No one believed me, but I knew. Zeke will put your heart on a platter when he finds out, vampire bitch."

I hissed, leaning close, baring my fangs in her face. "You're awfully smug for someone who's about to die."

She turned white. "You can't!"

I smiled, showing teeth, unsure if I was serious or not. "Why not?"

"Zeke will know!" Ruth cringed, panicked now, throwing up her arms to protect herself. "And so will Jeb! You can't kill me."

"I'm a *vampire!*" I snarled, on the verge of losing it. *"Why wouldn't I?"*

"Allison!"

I froze, feeling the world stop for a fraction of a second. In that heartbeat, a torrent of emotion rushed through me, almost too fast to recognize. Horror, anger, guilt, regret. What was I doing? What the hell had come over me? I looked at Ruth in a daze, dismay and revulsion spreading through me. Another second, and I might have killed her.

But worst of all…

Dropping my hands, I turned slowly…to face Zeke standing a few yards away. His gun was drawn, angled at my heart.

We stared at each other, silent in the falling rain. For another surreal moment, I felt a stab of déjà vu, flashing back to our first meeting in the abandoned town. But unlike that first time, Zeke's eyes were stony, his mouth pulled into a grim line. This time, he was serious.

"Let her go, vampire."

My insides cringed, hearing that word from him, cold, hard and unyielding. "Why should I?" I challenged. "You'll shoot me as soon as she's clear."

He didn't deny it, just continued to watch me, eyes glittering through the rain. I waited a moment longer, then slumped in resignation.

"Get out of here," I told Ruth without looking at her, and she didn't pause. Scrambling away from the woodshed, she fled to Zeke's side, glaring back at me with wide, hate-filled eyes.

"Go get Jeb," Zeke ordered in a calm voice, never taking his gaze off me. "Alert the rest of the house, but don't come back to help, Ruth. Stay inside, keep the kids close, and lock the doors, understand?"

She nodded and fled back toward the house, already screaming. I tensed as her shrill voice echoed over the rain. In a few minutes, every male in the compound would be rushing at me with axes and pitchforks and firearms. I had to get out of here, but first, I had to deal with Zeke.

I drew my sword, and he stiffened, pulling his machete as well, still keeping the pistol trained unwaveringly at my center. I gazed at him and fought the despair threatening to crush me. I was going to have to fight him. Zeke wasn't going to let me go, not after what I'd done to Ruth. *I'm sorry,* I wanted to tell him, knowing he wouldn't care. *I'm sorry it ended this way. But you're not going to let me walk out, and I'm not going to stand here and die, even for you.*

"That's not going to stop me," I told him, shifting to a better stance, so I could lunge out of the way if needed. "I'm much faster than you. Even if you empty that clip into my heart, it's not going to kill me. I'm already dead."

"It'll slow you down," Zeke replied, twirling his machete in a graceful arc, the razor edges glinting in the darkness, "and that's all the time I need." He eased to the side, a slow, cautious movement, and I stepped with him, moving off line. We circled one another, weapons held at the ready, eyes trained on each other, while the rabid hissed and growled from its cage.

"How many?" Zeke demanded, his face hard. I frowned in confusion. "How many of us did you bite?" he elaborated in a cold voice. "Who did you feed from? Caleb? Darren? Should I be worried *they're* going to turn into rabids or vampires?"

"I never bit any of you," I shot back, angry that he would think that, knowing I had no right to be. Of course, what else would he believe? "I never fed off anyone," I said in a more reasonable voice. "And it doesn't work that way. I would have to kill someone to turn them into a rabid."

"Like Joe."

My stomach clenched, but I tried keeping my voice and expression neutral. "I...I didn't mean for that to happen," I said, willing him to believe me. "And it might not have mattered. He could've already been infected by the boar." But it was a weak excuse, one I didn't really believe, and I knew Zeke didn't, either. In his mind, I had Turned that rabid all on my own.

Zeke shook his head. "You were just using us," he muttered, as if it pained him to say it. "This whole time. It makes sense now—you never believed in Eden, you never believed in any of this. All you wanted was an easy food source. And I fell for it." He clenched his jaw. "God, I left Caleb and Bethany alone with a vampire."

My heart sank, even as betrayal burned hot and fierce in my chest. This Zeke was different, the student of Jebbadiah Crosse, the boy who had been trained his whole life to hate vampires and everything about them. His eyes were cold, his expression closed off, unyielding. I was no longer Allison to him but a nameless demon, the enemy, a creature that needed to be slain.

So this is it. I tightened my grip on my weapon, and I saw him do the same. We circled slowly, each looking for an opening. He had range with that gun, but I was betting Zeke didn't know how quickly a real vampire could move. Getting shot was going to *hurt,* but after the first round I could close the distance and...

My steps faltered. And...what? Kill him? Cut him down, like I did with the raiders or the rabid boar? I could already feel the bloodlust, humming in my veins, eager for violence. Even if I disarmed him, I couldn't trust myself, my demon, not to pounce on him and tear him apart.

Zeke's eyes followed me, never wavering. I could almost see his finger tightening on the gun, when I straightened and slid my weapon back in its sheath. His brow furrowed, confusion crossing his face, as I shook my head.

"I can't do this." Facing him fully, I raised my empty hands, before letting them drop to my sides. "Shoot me if you have to, but I'm not fighting you, Zeke."

He didn't move, a war of different emotions raging in his eyes, though the gun didn't waver. In the distance, toward the house, shouts echoed over the rain, the sound of footsteps sloshing through the mud.

I eased back a step, away from him, toward the outer wall and the forest that lay beyond. "I'm leaving now," I said quietly, and Zeke raised the pistol a fraction of an inch, pressing his lips together. "You won't see me again, and I won't talk to anyone on my way out. Feel free to put a bullet in my back, but one way or another, I'm walking out of here."

I half turned then, bracing myself, waiting for the pop of gunfire, for the explosion of pain across my shoulders. Zeke stood with the gun trained on me a moment longer, then dropped his arm with a sigh.

"Just go," he whispered, not looking at me. "Get out of here, and don't come back. I don't want to see you again, ever."

I didn't answer. I turned my back on him fully and crossed the final steps to the wall, gazing up at the rim.

"Allison."

I turned. Zeke stood in the same spot with his back to me, the gun still dangling at his side. "We're even now," he murmured. "But...this is the last favor I'll grant. If I see you again, I'll kill you."

I faced the wall again, not wanting to reveal how much that hurt, or how much I wanted to spin around, knock him over and let him see how much of a demon I really was. My throat burned, but I swallowed the tears and the anger, burying it under cold indifference. I'd known, eventually, it would come to this.

Crouching slightly, I leaped for the top of the wall, finding cracks and handholds to scale the fifteen feet of rusty metal and iron. Landing on the other side, I jumped as gunshots rang out behind me, four in rapid succession, from Zeke's pistol. I whirled to see a handful of bullet holes in a square of sheet metal, several yards from where I stood. Zeke hadn't been aiming for me, only making sure Jeb knew he drove me off. That he hadn't let the vampire go without a fight.

The fields stretched out before me, and beyond them, the dark woods beckoned. Behind me, I heard Zeke pause for a long moment, then his footsteps walked away, back to Jebbadiah and his family, where he belonged.

I began walking as well, away from the fence and the humans and the safe haven that was only a lie. I imagined myself and Zeke, the gap between us widening as we drew farther and farther away, each of us vanishing into our own world where the other could not survive. By the time I neared the edge of the woods, where the rabids and the demons and the other horrors waited, the chasm had become so vast I couldn't see the other side anymore.

PART IV

WANDERER

CHAPTER 18

They were waiting at the edge of the woods, blank eyes shining through the rain, watching me with the unblinking stare of death. Four of them, including the woman in the tattered dress, crouched among the trees and dripping branches of the forest. I watched them, and they did the same, none of us moving; five statues in the darkness, water streaming down our pale skin, trickling off the blade in my hand.

And we waited. Monsters in the night, sizing each other up. The storm flickered around us, reflecting in the rabids' eyes, revealing the deadness behind them, but none of us so much as flinched.

Then the woman in the dress hissed softly, showing jagged fangs, and backed away, retreating from me into the darkness. After a moment, the other rabids did the same, creeping back without a fight, recognizing another predator.

I watched them, feeling cold and detached, watched as they eased around me and slipped out of the woods toward the compound I'd just left. I wasn't prey. I was a corpse, a creature whose heart didn't race, who didn't breathe or sweat or smell of fear. I was dead.

Just like them.

You are a vampire, Kanin had told me, so long ago it seemed. *You are a wolf to their sheep—stronger, faster, more savage than they could ever be. They are food, Allison Sekemoto. And deep down, your demon will always see them as such.*

Lightning flashed through the trees. The Archer compound stood behind me over the fields, outlined by weak fires that smoldered in the storm. Fewer people would be manning those platforms now, their frail human vision blinded by rain and smoke.

"You're a vampire," Stick whispered, *his eyes huge and terrified. "A vampire."*

The rabids reached the edge of the trees and stopped, four pale, motionless killers, staring at the compound on the hill. I wondered how many more rabids lurked in the darkness just beyond the fields, watching their prey with the patience of the dead. If Jebbadiah led his people away from the compound tonight, they could walk right into an ambush. Even if they managed to kill them or drive them off, someone would probably die.

So what? Sheathing my sword, I turned my back on the rabids, on the people still hiding behind the wall. I'd tried to fit in, and they had driven me away. Let them be slaughtered by rabids, what did I care? I was Vampire, and humans were no longer my concern.

"This is the last favor I'll grant," Zeke said, *his voice cold and hard. "If I see you again, I'll kill you."*

My chest felt tight. Of all the lies and treachery and knives
in the back, his hurt the worst. It was different from Stick's
betrayal; though we had been friends for years and years, I'd
known, deep down, that Stick was using me. That he was
more than capable of selling me out if something better came
along. Zeke was different. He did things because he truly
cared, not because he expected anything in return. It was such
an alien philosophy. On the streets, in the Fringe, it didn't
matter where you were—it was every human for himself. I'd
learned that nothing was free, and everyone had an angle. It
was just how things were.

Except Zeke. Zeke had treated me like a human, like an
equal. He'd stood up for me, helped me, given me things as
if it was the most natural thing in the world. He cared, because it was his nature.

Which made it all the more painful to find out he'd lied
when he'd said I could trust him, when his eyes had gone
hard and cold, and he'd turned on me as if I was a monster.

"You are a monster." Kanin's deep voice droned in my head
again, as I forced myself to move, to walk away. *"You will
always be a monster—there is no turning back from it. But what
type of monster you become is entirely up to you."*

I bit my lip. I'd forgotten that part. For a moment, I stood
there, struggling with myself. The wind whipped around
me, tossing my hair and clothes, rattling the branches above.
Across the fields, the bonfires smoldered, burning low, and
the rabids shifted restlessly at the edge of the trees.

Zeke betrayed you, a small, furious voice whispered in my
head. *He's no better than Jebbadiah, no better than any of them.*

You're just another demon to be hunted down and shot. Why should you care if he makes it to his Eden? Why care about any of them?

Because...

Because I did care, I realized. I cared that this small, stubborn band of human beings would challenge everything in their search for a better life. I cared that they would risk rabids and starvation and horrible conditions to follow that dream and cling to hope, even if they knew, somewhere deep down, that it was impossible. I thought of Caleb and Bethany. I'd told them there would be goats in Eden. They couldn't die now, dying of hunger or torn apart by rabids. I wanted them to succeed, to defy all odds and to make it to the end. Could I abandon them to the very monsters that had killed me?

"No."

The rabids hissed, glancing back at the sound of my voice. Slowly, I turned to face them, and we glared at each other once more, the wind swirling around us.

"No," I said again, and the rabids curled their lips back, showing fangs. "I'm not like you. I'm not like the vampires in the city. I might be a monster, but I can be human, too. I can *choose* to be human." Reaching back, I gripped my sword and drew it out, a bright flash of steel in the darkness. The rabids snarled and crouched down, their eyes fixed on the blade. Stepping forward, I bared my fangs and snarled back. "So, come on, you bastards," I challenged. "If you want them, you'll have to get through me first!"

The rabids screamed, baring and gnashing their fangs. I roared a battle cry, feeling my demon erupt, tasting violence, and this time I welcomed its arrival. Brandishing my weapon, I lunged into their midst.

I hardly knew what I was doing; everything was screaming fangs and slashing claws, rabids hurling through the air,
my blade singing as we danced and spun and cut at the monsters around us. Their tainted, foul-smelling blood soaked the
ground and the trees, their shrieks rising into the wind. More
rabids came at me, drawn by the sounds of battle, leaping into
the fray. I cut them down, too, growling my hate and fury
and vengeance. They were too slow, too mindless, flinging
themselves on my sword with vicious animal fury. I whirled
from one attack to the next, ripping my blade through pale,
shrieking bodies, feeling the sword dance in my hands.

When it was over, I stood in the center of a massacre,
scratched, bleeding and surrounded by pale, dismembered
bodies. Hunger flickered, always there, but I pushed it down.
I was a vampire. Nothing would change that. But I didn't
have to be a monster.

Wiping rabid blood off my sword, I sheathed it and turned
to gaze over the fields. The compound sat silent and dark on
the hill, clouds of smoke billowing up through the rain. Settling against a tree, I watched it, waiting for the iron gates to
swing open, listening for the creak and groan of metal. But
as the hours passed and the storm moved on, sweeping off
toward the east, the gates still did not budge.

*I guess Jeb doesn't want to leave the safety of the compound when
there could be a vampire lurking outside,* I mused, glancing nervously at the sky. Only an hour or so before dawn; they probably wouldn't go anywhere tonight. *I guess some things are
enough to give him pause, after all.*

Forty minutes later, with sunlight threatening the horizon

and the birds chirping in the trees, I rose to find a place to sleep just as the groan of metal caught my attention.

They're leaving? Now? Stunned, I watched as the gates swung open, and the small group of humans filed out into the grass. I counted them all: Jeb and Darren, both carrying shotguns pointed into the woods. Ruth and Dorothy. Caleb, Bethany and Matthew huddled together in the center. Silent Jake, now carrying a rifle. Old Teresa and Silas. And finally, bringing up the rear, making sure everyone got out okay, the boy who'd driven me off, who had turned his back on the vampire but still let it walk away without a fight.

So, Jeb had decided to move them out during the day, obviously trying to outrun the vampire by traveling when she could not. A smart choice, I had to admit. I wouldn't be able to follow them far, not with the sun minutes away from breaking over the horizon. Still, Jeb didn't know vampires. And he didn't know me. He could lead his people as fast and as far as he liked. I was very, very persistent.

Zeke swept his pistol over the fields as he left the compound, his eyes narrowed in concentration. Looking for a vampire, but he wouldn't find it. He couldn't see me here in the trees and darkness, the woods still cloaked in shadow. Part of me still wondered why I was doing this, why I would bother. Jeb would kill me if I was discovered, and Zeke would do his best to help. But as they started across the field, I couldn't help but think how vulnerable they looked, how easily a rabid horde could tear them apart, even with Zeke and Jeb's protection. And I remembered the look in Zeke's eyes when he spoke of how many they had lost, the torment on his face because he blamed himself. I would not let that happen. Not to Caleb or Bethany or Darren or Zeke. I wouldn't let anyone die.

As the last human passed through the gate, it closed behind them with a loud, final bang that echoed across the empty fields. With Jebbadiah Crosse at the front and Zeke bringing up the rear, the group shuffled quietly into the dark woods, inching toward their mythical city somewhere beyond the horizon.

A small smile played across my lips. *Okay, Zeke,* I thought, drawing back into the shadows, preparing to sink into the earth. *Run if you want. I'll see you all soon, even if you don't see me. I'll make sure you get to your Eden, whether you like it or not. Stop me if you can.*

THE NEXT EVENING, I pushed myself out of the ground with a sense of purpose. The night was clear, the moon and stars bright overhead. It wasn't hard to find the tracks of a dozen humans, making their way through the woods. I could see their footsteps in the soft earth and mud. I could trace their passing in the snapped twigs and crushed grass, blatant signs they left behind.

They're not even bothering to hide their tracks, I mused, stepping over a low spot on the trail, churned to mud from several boots and feet. It made me a little nervous. If my vampire senses could pick them up this easily, so could any number of rabids or wild animals lurking about. *I guess Jeb is more concerned with speed now. Good thing rabids aren't smart enough to track their prey, otherwise they'd be in a lot of trouble.*

I followed the trail for most of the night, slipping easily through the dark woods, having no need to rest or slow down.

I found a few empty cans tossed into the bushes, crawling with ants, and knew I was on the right path. When dawn arrived, I buried myself in the earth, frustrated that I had to stop, but feeling I was closing the distance.

Two hours past midnight on the second night, I finally heard voices, drifting ahead of me through the trunks and branches, and my heart leaped. As silently as I could, I eased closer, listening to snippets of conversation echo over the breeze. Stepping around a boulder, I finally spotted two familiar figures, standing on the edge of a narrow cracked road that snaked into the darkness.

Jebbadiah and Zeke hovered beside the pavement, facing each other. Jeb's mouth was stretched into a thin, severe line, while Zeke's face looked earnest, his expression intent.

"We'll make less noise if we're walking on pavement," Zeke was saying, sounding exasperated but trying not to show it. A few yards away, the rest of the group huddled beneath the trees as Jeb and his pupil argued. I leaned against the rock, concealed in shadow, and listened. "It'll be easier on Teresa and the kids, and we'll make better time, too."

"If Jackal and his thugs come around any of those bends, we won't know it until they're right on top of us," Jeb argued in a low voice, glaring at Zeke with cold, angry eyes. "You've seen how fast they can move—by the time we hear them coming, it'll be too late. Will you sacrifice the safety of this group just because walking through forest is a little harder?"

To his credit, Zeke didn't back off.

"Sir," Zeke said quietly, "please. We can't keep going like this. Everyone is exhausted. Walking all day and all night—

we need a rest. If things don't get easier, we'll have people lagging behind and making mistakes. And if anyone is following us, we'll just be that much easier to pick off." Jeb's jaw tightened, eyes narrowing, and Zeke hurried on. "We're going to need supplies soon," he said. "And Larry told me this road eventually leads to a town. Sir, we need food, ammo and a proper rest. I think we'd rather deal with the possibility of raiders than have to watch our backs for rabids and vampires in the woods."

Jeb stared at him, and for a moment, I thought he would refuse just on the principle of never agreeing with anyone. But then he blew out a short, irritated breath, and turned to the road.

"Keep everyone together," he snapped, as Zeke straightened quickly. "And I want two people hanging back at least twenty feet from the rest of us. If they hear or see anything at all, I want to know about it immediately, do you understand?"

"Yes, sir."

He gave his pupil one last baleful glare, then strode purposefully onto the pavement, while Zeke turned to signal everyone to keep moving. They shuffled forward, clearly relieved to be out of the tangled woods and dark, grasping trees. The road, crumbling and full of holes, was still treacherous, but it was easier than hacking through brush and tripping over rocks and branches.

I stayed off the pavement, however, slipping through brush and trees at the edge. Though it was still dark as pitch, it might've been too easy for Zeke to look back and see a silhouette following them down the open road. I could still hear

him, though, as he and Darren dropped back the required
twenty feet from the group to guard the rear. They were
quiet at first, the only sounds being their feet on the uneven
pavement, then Darren's low voice drifted to me through the
darkness.

"Your old man is sure kicking your ass lately," he muttered. "That's the first time since the Archers that he's actually talked to you like a human being."

"He was angry." Zeke shrugged halfheartedly. "I endan-
gered the entire group. If anything had happened, it would've
been my fault."

"You can't blame yourself, Zeke. We all saw her, talked to
her. She had us all fooled."

My gut twisted and I narrowed my eyes, zeroing in on the
conversation. The sound of the wind and creaking branches
faded away as I concentrated solely on the boys in front of
me. I heard Zeke's sigh, imagined him stabbing his fingers
through his hair.

"I should've seen it," he muttered, dark loathing rolling off
his voice. "There were so many signs, so many little things,
now that I think about it. I just didn't put it together. I never
thought…she could be a vampire." Zeke suddenly kicked a
chunk of pavement, sending it crashing into the bushes. "God,
Dare," he muttered through clenched teeth, "what if she bit
someone? Like Caleb. What if she had been feeding on those
kids the whole time? If she had killed someone, if anything
happened to them…because I was…" He trailed off, nearly
choking on disgust, before murmuring, "I could never forgive myself."

I felt cold and clenched my fists to stifle the anger rising up like a storm. Zeke should know me better, he should know I would have never...

I stopped, uncurling my hands. No, he shouldn't. Why should he? I was a vampire, and those kids were the easiest form of prey. In his position, I would think the same.

Still, it hurt. To hear, again, what they really thought of me: a monster who preyed indiscriminately on the smallest and weakest. It hurt a lot more than I'd thought it would. I had struggled hard not to feed on any of them, especially Caleb and Bethany, and it was all for nothing.

But then, I had also sacrificed someone else, a stranger, in order not to feed on those I knew. So, maybe their fears were justified.

"Zeke." Darren's voice came again, hesitant, as if he feared people were listening. "You know I have no reason to doubt you. If you say she was a vampire, then I believe it. But...but she didn't seem...that bad to me, you know?" He paused, as if shocked that he could have voiced such a thing, but continued. "I mean, I know what Jeb's told us. I know he says they're demons and there's nothing human about them, but... I've never seen one before Allison. What if we're wrong?"

"Stop it." Zeke's voice sent ice into my stomach. It was hard, dangerous, the same tone he'd used when facing down a vampire that night in the rain. "If Jeb heard you say that he'd kick you out before you could blink. If we start questioning everything we know, we're lost, and I am not going to start doubting now. She was a vampire, and that was all I needed to know. I'm not going to put everyone in danger just because you became somewhat attached."

Look who's talking, I thought, just as Darren muttered the exact same thing. Zeke scowled at him. "What?"

"Look who's talking," Darren repeated, angrier this time. "I might've welcomed her along in hunts, but I wasn't tripping over myself to talk to her every night. Everyone could see the way you looked at the girl. You weren't exactly subtle, you know. Ruth nearly had kittens every time the two of you went off to do something. So don't lecture me about getting attached, Zeke. You were falling for that vampire—we all knew it. Maybe you'd better check your own neck before you go pointing fingers at other people. Seems to me the vampire could've bitten you anytime she wanted—"

Zeke turned and punched Darren in the jaw, sending him sprawling to the pavement. I froze in shock. Darren staggered upright, wiping his mouth, and tackled Zeke with a yell, knocking them both down. Shouts and cries rose from the group as the two boys struggled and kicked, fists flying, in the middle of the road. Darren was older and slightly taller than Zeke, but Zeke had been trained to fight and managed to straddle Darren's chest, pounding his face. The smell of blood trickled through the air.

It was over in seconds, though the actual fight seemed much longer. Jake and Silas descended on the boys, prying them apart, and the two fighters glared at each other, panting and wiping at their mouths. Blood streamed from Darren's nose, and Zeke's lip had been split open, dripping red onto the pavement. They didn't struggle against their captors, though both seemed ready to fly at the other once more if they were released.

"What is the meaning of this?"

You had to give Jeb props. He didn't shout or even raise his voice, but the tension between the two boys diffused instantly. Jeb waved the men aside and stood between the former combatants, looking grim. I watched their faces closely. Darren looked pale and terrified, but the expression on Zeke's face was one of shame.

"Disappointing, Ezekiel." Jeb's tone couldn't be any flatter if he'd dropped it from a thirty-story building, but Zeke winced as if he'd been given a death sentence.

"I'm sorry, sir."

"It is not me you should apologize to." Jeb eyed them both with his steely gaze, then stepped back. "I do not know the cause of your fight, nor do I care. But we do not raise our hands in anger to anyone in this community—you both know that."

"Yes, sir," both Zeke and Darren muttered.

"Since both of you have energy enough to fight, tonight you will give your rations to someone who is in better need of them than you."

"Yes, sir."

"Jake," Jeb called, motioning the older man forward. "Take up the rear guard with Darren. Zeke—" he turned to Zeke, who flinched ever so slightly "—you will join me up front."

Zeke and Darren exchanged a glance, then Zeke turned away, following Jebbadiah to the head of the group. But I saw the unspoken apology flash between them and suddenly realized that Darren was afraid, not for himself, but for Zeke.

I FOUND OUT WHY SEVERAL HOURS later, when we stumbled upon the small town Larry had been talking about. It had the same empty, desiccated feel of most dead communities: cracked streets, rusting cars, structures falling apart and overgrown with weeds. A herd of deer scattered through a parking lot, leaping over vehicles and rusty carts. Darren watched them bound away with a hungry, regretful look on his face, but Zeke, walking stiffly beside Jebbadiah, didn't even glance up.

I followed them through the town, hugging buildings and easing around cars, until they came to a small building on the corner of the street. At one point, it had been white, with a sharp black steeple and windows of colored glass. Now the siding was peeling off, showing rotten boards underneath, and the windows had been smashed into tiny razor fragments that glinted in the moonlight. A wooden cross balanced precariously atop the roof, leaning forward as if it might topple at any moment.

This must be a church. I hadn't actually ever seen one standing; the vampires had razed all the ones they could find. No wonder the group would be attracted to this building; it probably gave them a sense of security. Jebbadiah escorted them in, pushing through the rotting door, and I looked around for a place to hole up, too.

The statue of an angel, broken and corroding away, poked out of the weeds at the edge of the lot next to the church. Curious, I examined it and found several chipped, broken gravestones buried under the long grass.

This must be a graveyard or a cemetery. I'd heard of them before in New Covington, places where families used to bury their dead. In New Covington, bodies were usually burned to prevent the spread of disease. This place, like the church itself, was a relic of another time.

Dawn was about an hour away. Crouching, I was about to burrow into the cool, rich earth that lay beneath the grass and weeds when approaching footsteps made me look up.

Zeke's bright, tall form cut through the grass several yards away, followed by Jebbadiah, close on his heels. I froze, becoming vampire-still, as motionless as the gravestones around me. They passed very close, close enough for me to see Zeke's cross, glimmering on his chest, and the smooth white scar tissue on Jebbadiah's face. Zeke walked stiffly in front of the older man, staring straight ahead, like a prisoner on his way to the gallows.

"Stop," Jeb said quietly, and Zeke stopped. The older man held something long and metallic, tapping it against his leg.

A car antenna.

"Let's get on with it, Ezekiel," he murmured.

I flicked my gaze to Zeke, who stood motionless for a heartbeat, his hands clenched at his sides. Then, slowly, methodically, he turned and removed his shirt, tossing it to the ground. I bit the inside of my cheek. His skin was a map of old, pale scars, crisscrossing his back and shoulders. Turning stiffly, he placed his palms against one of the gravestones poking out of the grass and bowed his head. I saw his shoulders tremble, once, but his face remained impassive.

"You know why I do this," Jeb said softly, moving up behind him.

"Yes," Zeke muttered. His knuckles were white from gripping the headstone.

Don't move, I told myself, closing my fists in the dirt. *Do not move. Do not go out there to help him. Stay where you are.*

"You are a leader," Jebbadiah continued and, without warning, struck Zeke's exposed back with the strip of metal. I cringed, fighting the impulse to snarl, as Zeke tightened his jaw. Blood, bright and vivid, seeped crimson down his scarred back.

"I expect more of you," Jebbadiah continued in that same calm, unruffled voice, striking him again, this time across the shoulders. Zeke bowed his head, panting. "If I fall, you must lead them in my place." Two more vicious blows in rapid succession. "You must not be weak. You must not succumb to emotion or the desires of the flesh. If you are to become a true leader, you must kill everything that tempts you, everything that makes you question your morals or your faith. If we are to survive this world, if we are to save the human race, we must be ruthlessly diligent. If we fall, the sacrifices of those before us will be for nothing. Do you understand, Ezekiel?"

The last question was delivered with such a vicious blow that Zeke finally gasped and buckled against the headstone. I crouched in the grass, shaking with fury, my fangs fully extended, fighting the urge to leap out and rip Jebbadiah open from sternum to groin.

Jeb stepped back, his face smooth and blank once more. "Do you understand?" he asked again in a quiet voice.

"Yes," Zeke answered in a surprisingly steady voice as he pulled himself up. His back was a mess of blood, angry slashes over his already numerous scars. "I understand. I'm sorry, sir."

The older man tossed the antenna into the weeds. "Have you apologized to Darren yet?" he asked, and when Zeke nodded, he stepped up and grasped his shoulder. Zeke flinched.

"Come, then. Let's get you cleaned up before the blood attracts anything dangerous."

I sank my fingers into the dirt, watching Zeke stoop slowly, painfully, to retrieve his shirt and follow Jebbadiah out of the cemetery. My muscles ached from holding myself back. The scent of blood, the violence, the furious rage toward Jebbadiah, was almost too much to handle. I watched Zeke stumble, wincing as he braced himself against a headstone, and a low growl slipped out before I could stop it.

Zeke straightened, glancing back toward the cemetery, a wary frown crossing his face. I bit my tongue, cursing myself, and thought motionless thoughts. I was a tree, a stone, a part of the landscape and the night. Zeke's gaze swept through the cemetery, peering into the shadows. At one point, he looked right at me, our eyes meeting through the darkness, but then his slid away and continued on without recognition.

"Ezekiel." Jebbadiah turned to frown at his pupil, impatient. "What are you looking at?"

Zeke took a step back. "Nothing, sir. I thought I heard…" He shook his head. "Never mind. It was probably a raccoon."

"Then why are we still standing here?"

Zeke murmured an apology and turned away. They disappeared around the corner, back into the church, and I slumped to the ground, fury and the Hunger buzzing through my veins.

The smell of Zeke's blood still hung in the air, though not as strong as when he was present. I had to get away; the longer I stayed, the more I wanted it. And if Zeke, or worse, Jebbadiah, came through the cemetery again, I might not be able to resist attacking either of them.

The sky overhead showed a faint pink light on the belly of the clouds, and the sun wouldn't be far behind. I burrowed into the cold cemetery ground, trying not to imagine what else was buried here, beneath the grass and tombstones. The earth closed around me, dark and comforting, and I slipped into the waiting blackness of sleep.

And, for the first time since I left New Covington, I dreamed.

A DARK, EMPTY CITY.

Skyscrapers leaning against each other like fallen trees.

Memories tinted with anger. Shouldn't have let my guard down. Should've seen that trap. I was careless.

Lightning flickered, turning the world white for a split second. And in the stillness between the flash and the next boom of thunder, I saw him.

Smiling at me.

CHAPTER 19

I jerked awake in the darkness and immediately knew something was wrong. Everything was completely black, but I could hear muffled booms topside, feel vibrations through the earth, like being underwater while something raged overhead.

I clawed my way through the dirt, breaking through the cemetery grounds, and a wave of heat blasted my face, making me snarl and cringe back.

The church was on fire. Red and orange flames leaped out of the windows and slithered up the walls. The cross on the roof burned, wreathed in fire like a man with outstretched arms, welcoming the agony as it consumed him.

The vampire in me recoiled, hissing, wanting to run, to burrow back into the earth where the flames could not touch me. I fought the urge and scrambled upright, scanning the grounds frantically for Zeke or any sign of the others.

The roar of engines echoed over the flames, and gunfire exploded somewhere down the street, four shots in rapid succession. I took off, leaping over tombstones, drawing my sword as I passed the doomed church and sprinted into an alley. As I followed it around a corner, something flashed by the mouth of the corridor; something that roared and coughed smoke and glinted metallic in the dim red light. Bikes, men and guns.

Raiders. My stomach contracted into a tight knot.

Jackal's gang was here.

I shot out of the alley, sword and fangs bared, to see another raider bearing down on me, the roar of his bike pounding off the buildings. He gave a shout as I leaped aside, barely clearing the tires, and brought my sword across the handlebars as he passed. The raider swerved aside, the blade missing him by inches, and careened into a wall. I heard the crunch of metal and bones, and the raider crumpled to the pavement with the bike on top of him.

A shout rang out behind me, and I spun. Through a maze of dead cars, a trio of humans looked up from the center of the lot, eyes widening as they saw me. Two of them were struggling with a body they had slammed across the hood of a car, arms pinned behind him, binding his wrists with rough cord. His pale hair gleamed in the darkness, his face tight with pain as they pressed it to the metal.

"Zeke!" I cried, starting forward, and the two raiders scrambled into action. One grabbed the assault rifle that lay on the car roof and the other dragged the prisoner behind a van and out of sight.

I roared, baring fangs, and went for the raider with the gun. Without hesitation, he raised the long muzzle to shoot at me, though his eyes were wide with shock and fear; he knew what I was and didn't pause as he sighted down the barrel and pulled the trigger.

The gun chattered on full automatic, sending out a hail of bullets, striking the rusty cars around me and sparking off the metal. Windows shattered as I ducked and wove around cars, the roar of gunfire and breaking glass nearly deafening. But I could sense my prey, smell his fear and desperation. Crouched behind a vehicle, I waited until the stream of gunfire paused, heard a frantic curse from the raider as he fumbled to reload.

I leaped atop the car, bounding over the roofs, and the human's eyes went wide with terror. He raised his gun, fired three wild shots, and then I was on him, slamming him against a door, breaking the window. Something bright flashed in his hand as he plunged a knife into my neck, right above the collarbone, and pain shot through me like a bullet. I screamed, wrenched his head down to my level, and sank my fangs into his throat.

My neck burned, I could feel my own blood running down my collar into my shirt. The Hunger was a gaping hole inside, dark and ravenous. Blood filled my mouth, flooding my senses. This time, I didn't hold back.

The raider shuddered and eventually went limp in my arms. Dropping the body, letting it slump to the cement, I gazed around the lot for Zeke and the other raider. They couldn't have gone far, especially if Zeke was resisting. I caught a glimpse of two bodies vanishing between buildings, the smaller one being shoved into the alley with a gun at his back, and leaped after them.

Coming out of the alley, I spotted the raider dragging Zeke toward a gray van parked on the sidewalk, doors open and engine running. The van had been modified into a lethal weapon. Metal spikes bristled from the doors and hood, and iron slats ran across the windows. Even the hubcaps were sharp and pointed.

The raider turned and spotted me coming for him. His face went pale. Zeke was still struggling with his captor, trying to yank out of his grasp. I bared my fangs and roared, and the raider made a decision. Turning, he shoved his captive toward me, but as Zeke stumbled forward, he raised his gun and pointed it at Zeke's unprotected back.

Two gunshots rang out. Zeke fell, striking his head on the pavement. I gasped and rushed toward him as the raider leaped into the van, slammed the door and screeched off.

"Zeke!"

Flinging myself down beside him, I ripped the cord from his wrists and rolled him onto his side. His skin was pale, blood trickling from his nose and mouth, and his eyes were closed. I shook him, feeling sick as his head flopped limply, then I forced myself to be still and listen. For a heartbeat, a pulse, anything. Relief coursed through me. It was there, loud and frantic. He was alive.

"Zeke." I touched his face, and this time he stirred, opening his eyes with a gasp. Pain-filled blue eyes flicked up to mine.

"You!" he gasped through clenched teeth and jerked away from me. "What are you doing here? How—" He gasped again, curling into himself, his expression tight with agony.

"Lie still," I told him. "You've been shot. We have to get you out of here."

"No," Zeke rasped, trying to get up. "The others. Get

away from me! I have to help them." His leg buckled, and he crumpled to the pavement again.

"Lie still, idiot, or you're going to bleed to death, and then you won't be able to help anyone!" I glared fiercely, and he finally relented. "Where are you hit?"

He winced. "My leg," he panted, gritting his teeth.

There was a nasty chunk taken out of Zeke's calf, which was bleeding all over the place, but thankfully, the bone seemed intact. Still, the amount of blood oozing from the gash both tempted and worried me. I bandaged him up as best I could, using strips from my coat to make a tourniquet, trying to ignore the smell and feel of the blood on my hands, on his skin.

Zeke set his jaw and didn't make a sound through the first part of the process, but a few minutes in, he reached out and stopped my hand.

"I can do the rest," he panted. "Go help the others." He hesitated a moment, then added: "Please."

I met his gaze. Desperation and worry shone from his eyes, overshadowing the pain I knew he was in. "I'll be all right," he said, struggling to keep his voice steady. "The others, though. They're after them. You have to stop them."

I nodded and stood, gazing into the shadows, listening for sounds of pursuit. "Where?"

He pointed down the street. "Last I saw, Jeb was leading part of the group in that direction. We split up when we heard them coming, to throw them off." His face darkened. "They already have Ruth and Jake—you have to stop them from getting anyone else."

I grabbed him under the arms and, ignoring his protests

and gasps of pain, dragged him off the road. "Stay here," I said, setting him down behind a clump of weeds, higher than our heads. "I don't want you getting caught again while I'm searching for the others. I'll be back as soon as I can. Don't move."

He nodded wearily. I retrieved my sword from where it lay on the sidewalk and sprinted down the road, looking for the people who had cast me out.

It didn't take long. I could hear the roar of bike engines, and the pop of distant gunfire over the tops of the buildings. The boom of Jeb's shotgun echoed off the roofs, and I began to run. But the buildings masked the direction of the shots, and the streets wound confusingly through the small town, dead-ending or going nowhere.

I leaped over a moss-eaten wall just as two vans, armored and spiked like the previous one, roared past me, trailing plumes of smoke. Sprinting into the road, I watched them tear away, the hoots and laughter of the raiders echoing behind.

A face appeared in the back window, frightened and pale, pressed against the glass. Ruth's eyes met mine, terrified, before she was yanked back into the darkness, and the van screeched around a corner out of sight.

In the split second that I thought about pursuing them, headlights pierced the road at my back, and the roar of engines echoed down the street. I turned to see the rest of the gang, at least thirty or forty armed bikers, turn a corner and come swooping at me.

I dived behind a car as the gang passed, laughing and howling, some firing their weapons into the air. I gripped my sword, torn between attack and self-preservation. I could've leaped out and sliced down two or three raiders before the rest even knew what was happening. But then I'd be facing the rest of the gang, who would probably turn and spray me with bullets. And even though I was a vampire, I would not survive that, not from so many. My body was tough but not invincible.

So I waited and listened until the sounds of their voices disappeared, until the roar of engines and the pop of gunfire faded into the darkness, and silence settled over the town once more.

Just to be certain, I checked the surrounding area for survivors. I found the spot behind a warehouse where an obvious battle had taken place; skid marks on the pavement, bullet holes in the walls, lining the sides of dead cars. Jeb's shotgun lay in a puddle next to an overturned truck, and a pair of raider corpses lay sprawled in the weeds close by, indicating the old man had not gone quietly. But others had not escaped the chaos, either. Dorothy sat crumpled against a cement ramp, two small holes seeping crimson below her collarbone, her puzzled eyes staring off into nothing.

I looked at her body, feeling hollow and numb. I hadn't known her long, and she had been a little on the crazy side, but even with her talk of angels and vampire-devils, Dorothy had been kind to me.

Now she was gone. As were the others.

In a daze, I wandered back to the spot I'd left Zeke, almost fearful of what I would find. When I turned down the correct street, however, I saw a familiar form leaning against

a stop sign, one hand clutching a machete while the other
clung to the pole, trying to pull himself up. Or keep himself
from falling. A speckled trail of blood followed him down
the sidewalk.

"Zeke!" Sprinting over, I reached for his arm, but he jerked
away with a hiss, raising his weapon. I saw anger and uncertainty flash through his eyes before they glazed over with
pain once more, and he slumped forward.

I took his weight again, trying not to breathe in his scent,
the blood soaking his clothes. Fear and worry made my voice
sharp as we hobbled down the sidewalk. "What are you doing,
you idiot? You want to get yourself killed? I thought I told
you to stay down."

"I heard…gunshots." Zeke panted, his face and hair damp
with sweat. I could feel him shaking, his skin cold and
clammy. Dammit, he couldn't keep going like this. I looked
around for shelter and decided that house across the street
would work just fine.

"I wanted to help," Zeke continued as we limped across
the road. "I couldn't sit there and do nothing. I had to try.
To see…if anyone escaped." He clamped his lips together as
I kicked the fence open and pulled him through the yard up
the weed-eaten porch steps. "*Did*…anyone escape?"

I ignored that question, nudging open the door and peering inside. This, at least, was somewhat familiar. The plaster
walls were cracked and peeling, the floor strewn with rubble
and trash. There were a couple holes in the roof and broken
shingles scattered throughout the living room, but the struc-
ture appeared fairly sound. Against the wall was a very moldy

but remarkably intact yellow sofa, and I carefully steered Zeke across the uneven floor until we reached it.

He collapsed on the sofa with a barely concealed groan, closing his eyes for just a moment before jerking them open again, as if he feared taking his gaze off me. I felt a prick of hurt as I stared down at him, lying helpless on the couch. He didn't trust me at all.

"You're bleeding again," I said, catching sight of fresh blood seeping through the makeshift bandage. He stiffened, and I had to stifle the urge to point out that if I'd wanted to bite him, I would've done it by now. "Wait here. I'll try to find something we can clean that up with."

Turning away to hide my anger, I walked out of the room, going farther into the darkened building. Zeke didn't say anything, so I rummaged through the house in silence, looking for bandages, food or anything that could help us. The rooms, though filthy and covered in dust and mold, were remarkably intact, as though the owners had just left without taking anything. The kitchen held a scattered collection of broken plates and mugs, and inside the refrigerator I found what had to be a hundred-year-old milk carton sitting on the top shelf. The bedrooms were mostly empty, stripped of sheets and clothes, though by the stench of feces and urine, I suspected a fox or maybe a whole family of raccoons had made its home under the bed.

I ducked into the hall and found the bathroom. The mirror over the sink was shattered and broken, but inside the cabinet I found a box of gauze pads and a dusty bandage roll. Beneath them sat a small bottle of pills and a larger brown bottle half full of liquid. I squinted at the faded label, mentally thanking Kanin for insisting that I learn to read better: the brown bottle contained something desperately needed. *Hydrogen peroxide—topical disinfectant for surface cuts and minor wounds.*

A little wary of the white pills, I left them in the cabinet but took the gauze and the peroxide and grabbed a dusty towel from the rack nearby, bringing it all out to Zeke. He was sitting straighter on the couch, trying to unwrap the tourniquet from his leg. But by his set jaw and sweaty, furrowed forehead, it wasn't going well.

"Stop that," I ordered, crouching beside him, setting the items on the floor. "You're going to make it worse. Let me do it."

He eyed me warily, but exhaustion and pain won out in the end, and he lay back down. I set to work on his leg again, cleaning the blood with the towel, then pouring the disinfectant liberally over the wound. Zeke hissed through his teeth as the clear liquid touched the gash, bubbling into white foam.

"Sorry," I muttered, and he blew out a short breath. Cleaning away the last of the blood, I pressed the bandage to his leg and started wrapping the gauze around it.

"Allison."

I didn't look up from my task, and my voice came out stiff and flat. "What?"

Zeke hesitated, perhaps sensing my mood, then asked, very quietly, "The others? Did you...did anyone...?"

I set my jaw, wishing he hadn't brought it up just yet. "No," I told him. "They're gone. Jackal's men took them all."

"Everyone?"

I considered lying, or at least glossing over the truth, but

Zeke had always been honest with me. I had to tell him, even if I hated it. "Not everyone," I admitted. "Dorothy is dead."

He didn't say anything to that. I finished wrapping his leg and looked up to find him with his head bowed and one hand over his eyes. I gathered the first-aid supplies and stood, watching uncomfortably as he struggled with his grief. But he didn't make any noise: no words, no short sobbing breaths, nothing. And when he dropped his hand, his eyes were clear, his voice hard.

"I'm going after them."

"Not alone, you're not," I said, putting the peroxide and bandages on a rotting table. "Unless you think you can take on forty raiders by yourself, wounded as you are. I'm coming with you."

He glared at me, blue eyes flashing in the darkness and shadows, the cross glimmering on his chest. I could see the struggle within; I was a vampire, still the enemy and something that couldn't be trusted—but at the same time, I'd just saved his life, and I was his best hope of rescuing the others. I remembered the scars across his back and shoulders, the beliefs that had, quite literally, been beaten into him and wondered how deep Jeb's indoctrination ran.

Finally, he nodded, a reluctant, painful gesture that seemed to take all his resolve. "All right," he muttered at last. "I'll take all the help I can get. But..." He sat up straighter, eyes narrowed into those cold blue slits I'd seen at the Archer compound. "If you try to bite me, or feed off any of the group, I swear I'll kill you."

I resisted the urge to bare my fangs. "So nice to know where we stand, especially after I just saved your life."

A shadow of guilt crossed his face, and his shoulders slumped. "Sorry," he muttered, raking a hand through his hair. "I just… Never mind. I'm grateful that you showed up when you did. Thank you."

The words were stiff, uncomfortable, and I shrugged them off. "It's fine." Not much of an apology, but at least he wasn't trying to put a machete through my neck. "On to the raiders, then. Do you know where they went?"

Zeke leaned back against the couch. "No," he said, his voice cracking just a tiny bit. It was clear he was trying to hold back his emotions. "I don't know where they are. Or where they took them. Or even *why* they took them. Jeb never said much about it, only that Jackal and his men were looking for him, and we had to find Eden before they caught up."

"So we don't even know what direction they've gone," I muttered, looking out the door. Zeke shook his head and slammed a fist into the armrest with a hollow thump. I looked out the door at the faint red glow over the rooftops, the remains of the church burning to the ground. The streets were silent now. Except for the dying flames, there was nothing left to show they had come at all. Jackal's men had known what they were doing. The attack had been quick, efficient and deadly, with the marauders fading into the night without a trace.

Or, most of them had.

"Wait here," I told Zeke. "I'll be right back."

Chapter 20

"Well, it's a good thing you were wearing a helmet, isn't it?"

Pinned under his bike, the raider looked up at me, eyes wide with pain and fear. I heard his heart racing in his chest, smelled the blood that dripped somewhere beneath the motorcycle. He was tough for a human, I'd give him that. Given how hard he'd slammed into the wall that evening, I'd half expected to find a corpse with a broken neck lying here. Which would've put a rather large dent in my plans.

I smiled at him, showing fangs. "Too bad your leg is broken, though. That's going to make things difficult for you, isn't it? I must admit, I'm a little sad it ended this way. The chase can be just as thrilling as the kill."

"Oh, shit." The raider panted, his face pale under a sheen of sweat. "What do you want, vampire?"

How interesting. He was terrified of the vampire but not shocked or surprised to see one. "Well, here's the thing," I went on conversationally. "I've heard rumors that your boss isn't quite human. That he's a lot like me." I crouched down, smiling at him at eye level. "I want to know where he is, where his lair is located, what his territory is like. I don't meet many vampires wandering about outside the cities these days. This 'raider king' has me curious. And you're going to tell me about him."

"Why?" the raider challenged, which took balls, I had to admit. "You lookin' to join the ranks, bloodsucker? Become queen to his king?"

"What if I am?"

"Jackal don't like to share."

"Well, that's not your problem now, is it?" I said and narrowed my eyes. "Where is he?"

"If I tell you, you won't kill me?"

"No." I smiled again, baring my fangs. "If you tell me, I won't use you as my personal canteen until we reach Jackal's territory. If you tell me, I won't snap both your arms and other leg like twigs, drag you around until you're a limp sack and dump you on the road for the rabids to find. If you tell me, the worst I'll do is leave you here to die as you please. Actually, I'm feeling kind of hungry now…"

"Old Chicago!" the raider burst out. "Jackal staked his territory in the ruins of Old Chicago." He pointed in a random direction. "Just keep following the highway east. The road ends at a city on the edge of a huge lake. You can't miss it."

"How far?"

"About a day if you're riding. I dunno how fast you vamps can walk, but you'll get there tomorrow by evening if you ride through the night."

"Thank you," I said, standing up. A quick glance at the

raider's bike showed the left side crumpled and dinged up pretty bad, but otherwise it seemed fine. "Now, I just need you to show me one more thing."

ZEKE HAD FALLEN ASLEEP on the couch when I returned, lying on his back in an ungainly sprawl, one arm dangling off the side. In sleep, he looked younger than I remembered, the pain smoothed out of his face, his expression unguarded. It made me reluctant to wake him, but he stirred as soon as I entered the room, and his eyes shot open.

"I fell asleep?" he gasped and sat upright with a grimace, swinging his feet off the couch. "Why didn't you wake me? How long was I out?"

"It's a little past midnight," I told him and tossed a backpack onto the couch, raising a cloud of dust. "That's yours. There's food, drink, medicine and other supplies, enough for several days. How's the leg?"

"Hurts," Zeke said, gritting his teeth as he rose, slowly, to his feet. "But I'll live. I can walk out of here, anyway." He drew the pack gingerly over his shoulders. "Did you find out where they took everyone?"

"Yeah." I smiled faintly as he glanced up, his eyes flaring with hope. "Jackal's territory is in the ruins of a city a day or two east of here. Old Chicago. That's where they took the others."

"A couple days east," Zeke muttered, limping toward the door. I went to help him, but he stiffened and shook his head, so I backed off. "Then it'll probably take us several days to get there. I don't think I'll be going very fast."

"Not necessarily," I said and pushed open the door. Zeke's eyebrows shot up, and I grinned.

The motorcycle sat humming at the edge of the sidewalk, a little crumpled and dinged but none the worse for wear. "Took me a while to learn how to work the stupid thing," I said as we hobbled down the steps and onto the street, "but I think I got it, more or less. Nice of our raider friends to let us borrow it, right?"

Zeke glanced up at me, relief and gratitude chasing away the hard-eyed suspicion, at least for the moment. In that breath, he looked like the Zeke I knew. Embarrassed, I plucked the helmet off the seat and tossed it at him, making him blink as he caught it.

"I don't need it," I said as he frowned in confusion. "But you might want to put it on—I'm still getting the hang of this. Hopefully I won't run into any more walls."

I swung a leg over the bike, gripping the handlebars, feeling the power that rumbled through the machine. I could definitely get used to this. Zeke hesitated, still holding the helmet, eyeing the motorcycle as if it might bite him. Then I realized it wasn't the bike he was wary of.

It was me.

I squeezed the lever on the handlebars, making the bike snarl loudly, and Zeke jumped. "Do you want to do this or not?" I asked as he glared at me. His jaw tightened, and he gingerly swung his bad leg over the seat, sliding in against my back. I felt the warmth of his body, even though he tried to hold himself away, and felt the pounding of his heart in his chest. It made me thankful I didn't have a heartbeat, or mine would be doing the same.

"Hold on tight," I muttered as he strapped on the helmet. "This thing has some kick to it."

I gunned the engine, probably a little harder than I should have, and the bike jumped forward. Zeke yelped and grabbed my shoulders. "Sorry," I called back to him, as he reluctantly slid his arms around my waist. "Still getting the hang of this."

I tried again, a bit slower this time, and the bike eased forward as I maneuvered it down the streets. Once we reached the main road, I stopped and glanced over my shoulder. Zeke's face was tight, his arms and back stiff, whether from discomfort or pain or both.

"Ready for this?" I asked, and he nodded. "Then hang on. I'm going to see how fast we can really go."

His arms tightened around me, his heart thudding against my back. I turned the bike east, kicked it into motion, and the engine roared to life as it surged forward. We gained speed, the wind shrieking in my ears as we went faster and faster, nothing between us but empty road. I felt Zeke's arms squeezing my ribs, pressing his face to my back, but I raised my head to the wind and howled.

Above us, the full moon shone huge and bright on the flat prairie, lighting our way as we sped east, toward the end of the road.

I COULD'VE RIDDEN FOREVER. The wind in my hair, the open highway ahead of me, flying down the road at this crazy speed; it never got old. Unfortunately, the approaching dawn and Zeke's condition forced us to stop a couple hours before sunrise, pulling up to a crumbling farmhouse to rest and re-bandage Zeke's leg. After clearing out the colony of rats that had made their nest in the dilapidated kitchen, I sat Zeke down at the table to check his wound. The gash didn't look infected, but I poured liberal amounts of peroxide on it before wrapping it in clean bandages. The strong odor of chemicals, mixed with the scent of Zeke's blood, made me a tad nauseated, which I took as a blessing in disguise. I had no desire to bite him when he smelled so strongly of disinfectant.

"Thanks," he muttered as I rose, gathering up the old bandages to bury outside. I didn't think there were rabids nearby, but you could never be too careful. Rabids probably had no issues drinking peroxide-scented blood.

"Allison."

I turned warily. From the tone of his voice, I knew he was just as uncomfortable as me. Zeke was silent for a moment, as if debating whether or not he should say something, then he dropped his shoulders with a sigh.

"Why did you come back?"

I shrugged. "I was bored? I had nowhere else to go? It seemed a good idea at the time? Take your pick."

"I would've shot you," Zeke went on softly, staring at the ground. "If I'd seen you, hanging around? I would've done my best to kill you."

"Well, you didn't," I said, sharper than I intended. "And it doesn't matter now—though next time, if you don't want me saving your life, just say so." Turning away, I started to leave.

"Wait," Zeke called and sighed, running his hands through his hair. "I'm sorry," he said, finally looking up at me. "I'm trying, Allison, I am. It's just…you're a *vampire,* and…" He made a frustrated, helpless gesture. "And I wasn't expecting...any of this."

"I didn't bite anyone," I told him quietly. "That's the truth, Zeke. I didn't feed from anyone in the group."

"I know," he said. "I just thought—"

"But I wanted to."

He looked up sharply. I faced him, my voice and expression calm. "There were a lot of times," I continued, "where I could have fed off you, Caleb, Darren, Bethany. And it was hard, not to bite them, not to feed from them. The Hunger, it's constantly with you. That's what being a vampire is, unfortunately. You can't be around humans for long and not want to bite them."

"And, you're telling me this...why?"

"Because you need to know," I said simply. "Because this is what I am, and you should know what that is, before we go any further."

His voice was cold again. "So, you're saying...none of us will ever really be safe around you."

"I can't promise that I will never bite any of you." I shrugged helplessly. "The Hunger makes it impossible not to crave human blood. We can't survive without it. And maybe you were right to drive me off that night. But I can promise you this—I will keep fighting it. That's the best I can offer. And if that's not enough, well..." I shrugged again. "We can worry about that after we've rescued the others."

Zeke didn't answer. He appeared to be deep in thought, so I left the room without another word, heading outside to dispose of the bloody wrappings.

In the yard, I buried the rags quickly, then stood to gaze

down the road. Old Chicago waited at the end of the highway, along with a whole raider army and a mysterious vampire king. Who ruled a vampire city. I found it ironic; the very thing I'd been running from all this time was the place I'd return to in the end.

The sky in the east was lightening. I returned inside to find Zeke still at the table, the open backpack beside him, munching from a bag of pretzels I'd scavenged in town. He glanced up as I came in but didn't stop eating, an instinct I recognized from my Fringer days. No matter what the situation, no matter how awful you felt or how inappropriate it was, you still ate when you could. You never knew when your next meal would be, or if your current meal would be your last.

I also noted he had his gun out, lying on the table within easy reach, and decided to ignore it.

"Dawn is almost here," I told him, and he nodded. "There's painkillers in there if you need them, and some water. The bandages and peroxide are in the front pocket."

"What about ammo?"

I shook my head. "I couldn't find any back in town, and I didn't have much time to look around." I deliberately did not look at the pistol close to his hand. "How many bullets do you have left?"

"Two."

"Then we'll have to make them count." Glancing through the window, I winced. "I have to go. Take it easy on that leg, okay? If something happens, I can't help you until the sun goes down. I'll see you this evening."

He nodded without looking up. I wandered down the hall, weaving through cobwebs and scattered rubble, until I reached the bedroom at the end. The door was still on its hinges, and I pushed it open with a squeak.

A large bed sat against the wall beneath a broken window, curtains waving gently in the breeze. On the worm-eaten mattress, two adult skeletons lay side by side, the remains of their clothes rotted away. Between them was a much smaller skeleton, being held in the arms of one of the adults, cradling it to its chest.

I gazed at the skeletons, feeling an odd sense of surrealism. I'd heard stories of the plague, of course, when my mother had told me tales of life before. Sometimes it struck so fast, so suddenly, that entire families would get sick and die within a couple days. These bones, this family, were of another age, another era, before our time. What had it been like, to live here before the plague, when there were no rabids and vampires and silent, empty cities?

I shook those thoughts away. No use in wondering about the past, it wasn't going to do *me* any good. I backed out of the room and crossed the hall, pushing open the door opposite the bedroom. The space here was smaller, with a single twin bed against the wall, but it was dark, the windows were shuttered closed against the sun, and it didn't have any skeletons.

I lay down on my back, keeping my sword within easy reach on the mattress. Of course, if anyone wanted to sneak up on me during the day, I'd be easy pickings, lying here like the dead, unable to wake up.

I glanced at the closed door, and a thought came to me that turned my insides to ice. Zeke was still out there, awake, mobile and armed. While I slept, would he come creeping into my room to cut off my head? Would he kill me as I lay here, helpless, following the principles that Jeb had instilled in him? Did he hate vampires that much?

Or would he simply take the bike and drive off to confront the raiders alone?

I suddenly wished I'd chosen to sleep outside, buried in the deep earth, away from vengeful demon slayers. But gray bars of light were slanting in beneath the shutters, and I could feel my limbs getting heavy and sluggish. I would have to trust that Zeke was smart enough to know he couldn't rescue the others alone, that his principles weren't nearly as strict as his mentor's, and that even though I was a vampire, he would realize that I was still the person he had known before.

My eyes closed, and just before I lost consciousness, I was almost certain I heard the door creak open.

THE WORLD WAS UPSIDE DOWN.

I couldn't move my arms from behind my back, couldn't move anything. A soft breeze slithered across my naked shoulders. My arms felt broken. Or bound. Or both. Strange that I felt no pain.

The floor, a few feet from my head, was concrete. The walls around me were concrete. It had the feeling of being deep underground, though I remembered nothing of how I came to be here. I turned my head and saw, upside down, a table a few feet away, covered in instruments that glinted at me from the shadows.

Footsteps. And then a pair of boots stepped in front of me, the glowing end of a poker suddenly inches from my face, blindingly hot. I jerked away as a voice slithered down from the haze above.

"Welcome to my home, old friend. I hope you like it—you're going to be here for a while, I think. Maybe forever, won't that be exciting?

Oh, but before you say anything, let me first give you your official welcome to hell."

And the point of the poker was suddenly rammed through my stomach, exploding out my back, the smell of blood and seared flesh misting on the air.

And then the pain began.

I JERKED AWAKE WITH A SNARL, lashed out at the unfamiliar shadows above me and toppled out of bed. Hissing, I leaped upright, glaring at my surroundings as the phantom pain of a steel bar through my gut ebbed away into reality.

I relaxed, retracting my fangs. Again with the strange nightmares. Only this one was infinitely more awful than the one before. It had felt so real, as if I was right there, hanging from the ceiling, a white-hot poker jammed through my body. I shuddered, remembering that cold, slithering voice. It seemed familiar, as if I'd heard it before...

"Allison." A knock came at the door. "You all right? I thought I heard a yell."

"I'm fine," I called back, as relief swept in and drowned everything else. *He's still here. He didn't leave, or cut off my head in my sleep.* "I'll be right out."

Zeke raised his eyebrows as I opened the door and emerged into the hall, feeling rumpled and tired. "Bad dreams?" he asked, and I glared at him. "I didn't think vampires had nightmares."

"There are a lot of things you don't know about us," I muttered, shuffling past him into the kitchen. A candle flickered on the table amid opened cans of beans and empty jerky wrappers. He must've discovered a stash of food. "Come on, it's probably a good idea to check the bandages one more time before we head out."

"Actually, I've been thinking," Zeke admitted, limping as we went into the living room. He definitely looked better this evening; food, rest and painkillers were finally doing their job. "About what you said last night. I want to know more about vampires...from you. The only things I've heard are what Jeb has told me."

I snorted, grabbed the backpack off the floor. "That we're vicious soulless demons whose only purpose is drinking blood and turning humans into monsters?" I joked, rummaging around for the bandages and gauze.

"Yes," Zeke answered seriously.

I looked at him, and he shrugged. "You were honest with me last night," he said. "You didn't tell me what I wanted to hear, what I expected you to say. So, I thought I could... listen to your side of the story. Hear you out, if you wanted to tell it. Why you became a vampire. What made you want to..." He paused.

"Become undead? Drink the blood of the living?" I pulled out the peroxide, the bandages and the gauze, setting them on the floor in front of the couch. "Never have to worry about sunburns again? Well, maybe once more."

He gave me an exasperated frown. "If you don't want to tell me, that's fine, too."

I gestured to the couch, and he sat down, resting his elbows on his knees. I knelt and started unwinding the gauze from his leg. "What do you want to know?"

"How old are you?" Zeke asked. "I mean, how long have you been...a vampire?"

"Not long. A few months, at most."

"Months?"

He sounded shocked, and I raised my head to meet his gaze. "Yeah. How old did you think I was?"

"Not...months." He shook his head. "Vampires are immortal, so I thought...maybe..."

"That, what? I'm hundreds of years old?" I smirked at the thought, bending over his leg again. 'Believe it or not, this is all very new to me, Zeke. I'm still trying to figure everything out."

"I didn't know." Zeke's voice was soft. "So, you really are just as old as me." He paused a moment, digesting that fact, then shook his head. "What happened to you?"

I hesitated. I didn't like discussing or remembering anything about my life before; the past was past—why dwell on something you couldn't change? Still, Zeke was trying to understand me; I felt I owed him an explanation, at least. The truth.

"I didn't lie when I said I was born in a vampire city," I began, focused on my task so I didn't have to look at him. "My mother and I...we lived in a small house in one of the sectors. She was Registered, so that meant twice a month she had to go to the clinic to get 'blooded.' It was all very civilized— or that's what the vampires wanted us to believe. No forced feedings, no violent, messy deaths." I snorted. "Except people still disappeared from the streets all the time. Vampires are hunters. You can never take that out of them—out of us—no matter how civilized things are."

I felt Zeke's discomfort, his sudden unease at me admitting that all vampires were, more or less, killers. Well, he wanted the truth. No more lies, no more illusions. I was a vampire, and this was how things were. I only hoped he could accept it.

"Anyway," I continued, peeling back the gauze to reveal the wound. It looked angry and deep, but not infected. "Mom got sick one day. She wasn't able to get out of bed, so she missed her scheduled bloodletting. Two days later, the pets came and took the required amount by force, even though she was still too weak to move, or even eat." I paused, remembering a tiny, cold bedroom, and my mother lying beneath the thin blankets, pale as snow. "She never recovered," I finished, pushing the image away, back to the darkest part of my memories. "It wasn't long before she just...faded away."

"I'm sorry," Zeke murmured. And sounded as if he actually meant it.

"I hated the vampires after that." I soaked a rag in peroxide and pressed it to the wound, feeling him stiffen, gritting his teeth. "I swore I would never be Registered, that they wouldn't brand me like some piece of meat, that I wouldn't give them even one drop of blood. I found others like me, other Unregistereds, and we scraped out an existence as best we could, stealing, scavenging, begging, anything to survive. We almost starved, especially in the winter, but it was better than being a vampire's bloodcow."

"What changed?" Zeke asked softly.

I picked up the bandages, unwinding the roll without seeing it. Memories flickered again, dark and terrifying. The rain and the blood and the rabids, lying in Kanin's arms, feeling the world fade around me.

"I was attacked by rabids," I finally said. "They killed my friends and tore me up pretty bad, outside the city walls. I was dying. A vampire found me that night, gave me the choice of a quick death, or to become one of them. I still hated the vampires, and I knew, deep down, what I would become, but I also knew I didn't want to die. So I chose this."

Zeke was silent for several minutes. "Do you regret it?" he asked finally. "Becoming a vampire? Choosing this life?"

I shrugged. "Sometimes." I tied off the gauze and met his gaze, searching for reproach. "But if the choice was being dead—really dead—and being alive, I would probably do the same thing." Zeke nodded thoughtfully. "What about you?" I challenged. "If you were dying and someone offered you a way out, wouldn't you take it?"

He shook his head. "I'm not afraid to die," he said in a voice that was neither boastful or condemning, just quietly confident. "I know…I have faith, that something better is waiting for me, after I'm done here. I just have to wait, and do my best, until it's time for me to go."

"That's a nice sentiment," I said honestly. "But I'm going to keep living for as long as I can, which will be forever if I'm lucky." Gathering up the supplies, I stood, staring down at him. "So tell me, what happens to vampires when they finally kick it? According to Jeb, we don't have souls anymore. What happens when we die?"

"I don't know," Zeke murmured.

"Don't know, or don't want to tell me?"

"I don't know," Zeke said a little more firmly, and exhaled. "Do you want me to tell you what Jeb would say, or do you want my own opinion?"

"I thought Jeb taught you everything he knew."

"He did," Zeke replied, holding my gaze. "And he's tried

very hard to mold me into the leader he wants me to be."
He sighed, looking evasive, defiant and ashamed all at once.
"But, if you haven't noticed, we don't always see eye to eye.
Jeb says I'm stubborn and intractable, but I have my own
opinions about certain things, no matter what he believes."

"Oh?" I raised an eyebrow. "Like what?"

"He was wrong about you. I…was wrong about you."

I blinked. Abruptly, Zeke rose, his face troubled, as if he
really hadn't meant to say that. "We should get going," he
said, avoiding my gaze. "We're not far from Old Chicago
now, right? I want to find the others as fast as we can."

Outside, the stars were just beginning to show. I noticed
three piles of fresh, overturned earth in the front yard, a pile
of stones at the head of each one, and glanced at Zeke ques-
tioningly.

"They needed to be buried," he said, gazing down at the
new graves. His blue eyes grew haunted, and he sighed. "I
just hope they're the only ones I'll have to lay to rest."

I didn't want to give him false hope, so I didn't reply.
Mounting the bike, I waited until he slid in behind me and
wrapped his arms around my waist, without hesitation this
time. Easing the bike from the dirt onto the pavement, I
opened it up, and we sped off toward the vampire city waiting at the end of the road.

IF I THOUGHT NEW COVINGTON was big, it was nothing compared to Old Chicago.

The wind whipped at my hair, blowing in from the biggest
body of water I'd ever seen. The lake stretched away until it

met the sky, and dark waves rose and fell, breaking against the rocks.

On the edge of the lake, rising into the clouds, the city of Old Chicago loomed over everything. Back in New Covington, the three vampire towers were the most prominent buildings in the city, standing proudly over the rest. But the Chicago skyline had buildings that dwarfed even the vampire towers, and there were a lot more of them, even shattered and crumbling as they were. It reminded me of a mouthful of broken teeth, grinning madly against the night sky.

Behind me, Zeke blew out a short breath, tickling my ear. "Wow, it's huge," he said. "How are we supposed to find anything in that?"

"We'll find them," I said, hoping I wasn't making empty promises. "Just look for the huge band of raiders led by a vampire. How hard can it be?"

I ate my words a few minutes later.

Old Chicago was even more sprawling and massive up close than viewed from afar. It felt as if it went on forever, miles of broken pavement, dead cars and empty buildings. Cruising through the rubble-filled streets, the monstrous skyscrapers looming above us, I wondered what the city had been like when it was alive. How many people had lived here to justify so many buildings packed this close, reaching up to the sky? I couldn't even imagine.

We followed the road until we turned a corner and found the path blocked by the remains of a huge skyscraper. I pulled the bike to a stop and gazed around, trying to get my bearings.

"This is hopeless," Zeke said, looking past me at the collapsed building. "It's too big. We could be searching this place for weeks, months even. And by then who knows what they'll do to everyone?"

"We can't give up, Zeke," I said, turning the bike around. "They're here somewhere. We just have to keep—"

I stopped then, because something else had turned that corner and was coming toward us. A pair of raiders on long, sleek bikes, their handlebars sweeping up like horns, roared out of the shadows, catching us in their headlights. I stiffened, and Zeke tensed as the men pulled to a stop a few yards away, regarding us curiously. One of them had a woman sitting behind him, her frizzy hair tangled by the wind.

One biker jerked his head at us. "Heading to the Floating Pit, huh? Guess you heard the news."

The what? "Um…yeah," I replied, shrugging. "We did. Is that where you're going?"

"Yep." He turned and spit on the pavement. "Should be a good show tonight." He eyed us then, forehead creasing. "Haven't seen you two around before," he said. "You new to the Pit, little girl?"

Zeke's arms around me tightened. I hoped he wouldn't lose it. I was about to make up something about being new to Old Chicago, when the woman on the other bike slapped her driver's shoulder. "We're going to be late," she whined, and the man rolled his eyes. "Jackal promised us a show, and I don't wanna miss it. Let's go, already."

"Shut up, Irene." Her raider scowled but jerked his head at the man who'd spoken to us. "Come on, Mike. Talk to the rookies later. Let's go." He gunned his engine, drove the bike up a ramp that went through the skeletal skyscraper, and was gone. The other raider rolled his eyes and started to follow.

"Mind if we follow you into the Pit?" I asked pleasantly. He glanced at me, surprised, but shrugged.

"Shit, I don't care, rookie. Just try to keep up."

THE FLOATING PIT, I quickly learned, lived up to its name.

We followed the raiders through the streets of Old Chicago, zooming around dead cars, rubble and more fallen skyscrapers, going faster than we probably needed to. The roar of the engines echoed off the buildings, and sometimes we barely cleared a wall, a tunnel or an overturned vehicle, passing so close I could've reached out and touched it. I loved this, though Zeke wasn't quite as thrilled. His cheek pressed into my back and his arms were locked tightly around my waist, making me glad I didn't have to take a breath.

Finally, we rolled to a stop on the back of another fallen giant, looking over what I guessed had been downtown Chicago, once upon a time. The skyscrapers here defied belief, even skeletal and crumbling as they were. One tower had lurched to the side and was now leaning precariously against another, shortening the lifespan of both. There were several gaps in the skyline where it looked as if buildings had already fallen, but it was impressive nonetheless.

From where we stood, I could make out a long stretch of elevated tracks, looping around the buildings like a huge snake. I remembered, from my mother's stories, a certain type of vehicle had run on those tracks in the days before, shuttling people back and forth at high speed. Below the tracks, a series of platforms, bridges and catwalks had been cobbled together, stretching between buildings and crisscrossing the streets like a giant web. Which was necessary, because everything at ground level was underwater.

Humans crowded the narrow platforms and walkways like ants, making their way over the dark, turbulent waters. There were swarms of them, more than I'd expected. This wasn't just a raider hideout; this was a city, a real city like New Covington or any other vampire territory. It didn't have a wall—I assumed the deep water kept out the rabids—and the humans here were free to come and go as they pleased, but there was no question that we were stepping into the lair of a vampire king. On the bright side, from the number of humans wandering about, getting through unnoticed would be much easier than I'd feared.

The raiders we'd followed didn't pause to look at the city; I watched their headlights cruise down a ramp, over a ramshackle bridge and onto an enormous barge sitting at the water's edge. Dozens of bikes were parked there in messy rows, along with a couple of the armored vans I'd seen earlier. I guessed the raiders couldn't take their bikes onto the narrow walkways of the flooded city.

I felt Zeke peering over my shoulder, felt him take a deep breath, and glanced back at him. "Ready for this?"

He nodded, eyes grim. "Let's go."

We followed the same path as the others, down the ramp, over the bridge and onto the barge. Finding a free corner, I killed the engine and stepped away, a little sad that I'd have to leave the bike behind. I wondered if I would get the chance to come back for it.

Probably not.

I turned slowly, gazing at the vast expanse of water on either side. It felt odd, being on top of the water. The ground felt unstable, as if it could suddenly sink into the black depths. A cold wind hissed through the rows of bikes, and the boat bobbed gently on the waves, making Zeke stumble as he stepped up beside me.

Worried, I grabbed his elbow. "How's the leg?" I asked, noticing he kept his weight off it. "Can you do this? Will you be all right?"

"I'm fine." He pulled his arm out of my grip, standing on his own. But his face was pale and clammy with sweat, even in the chill. "Don't worry about me. I can keep up."

The growl of bike engines distracted us. More raiders were arriving, several of them this time, laughing and shouting over the noise of their bikes. Zeke and I ducked behind a stack of crates, watching as they killed their engines and swaggered toward another bridge on the other side, pointing into the city.

Zeke and I exchanged a glance. "Sure you don't want to wait?" I asked, and he scowled at me. I frowned back. "You're still hurt, Zeke. I can find the others on my own if I have to."

"No." His voice was rough, final. "It's my family. I have to do this. Don't ask me again."

"Fine." I glared at him and shook my head. Stubborn idiot. "But at least try to look a little more raider-ish, okay? We don't want to attract attention."

Zeke's snort sounded suspiciously like laughter. "Allie, you're a beautiful, exotic-looking vampire girl with a katana. Trust me, if anyone is going to attract attention, it's not going be me."

I didn't answer as we crossed the flimsy, creaking bridge into the lair of the vampire king. We didn't talk to each other for several minutes. If Zeke had asked, I would've said that I was thinking of how to find everyone, but that wasn't entirely true. I *was* thinking of the others and how I was going to get them out alive...but I kept being distracted by the thought that Zeke had called me beautiful.

THE CITY WAS LIKE A MAZE, a labyrinth of walkways, bridges and catwalks, all strung together in the most confusing way possible. A catwalk would lead to a platform, which led to a bridge, which led to the roof of a sunken building, which led right back to the same catwalk we'd already been on. After wandering in circles a couple times, I was ready to jump into the dark water and swim my way out. Torches and steel drums burned along ramps and walkways, the flickering lights reflecting in the dark water and only adding to the sense of disorder.

People hurried by on the narrow walkways, bumping us, jostling us out of the way, sometimes on purpose. Sometimes they would snicker or bark curses as they shoved me aside. I kept my head down and clenched my teeth every time someone hit me, fighting the urge to snap at them. There was no law here, no pets to keep order, no guards to contain an outbreak of violence. A fight erupted once, with two raiders throwing punches atop a narrow platform, until one pulled out a knife and stabbed the other in the neck. Choking, the man toppled off the platform, hit the water and sank from view. After a cursory glance, everyone went about their business.

"This is crazy," Zeke muttered, pressing close. His blue eyes swept nervously over the crowd. "Jeb told me about places like this. We have to find the others and get them out now, before someone shoots us in the back for no reason."

I nodded. "The raiders said something about Jackal 'putting on a show' at the Floating Pit," I mused. "He's the one we want. If we find him, we'll probably find the others."

"Right. So, we have to find the Floating Pit." Zeke looked around, noticed a dark, wild-haired woman walking toward us, and sighed.

"Excuse me," he said, reaching out to stop her. "Would you help us, please?" She jerked back, eyes narrowing as she raked Zeke up and down, then her thin lips curved into a smile.

"Excuse me?" she mocked, her voice high and nasal. "Excuse me, the boy says. Oh, well, how polite and proper. Makes me feel like a lady again." The grin grew wider, showing missing teeth. "How can I help you, polite boy?"

"We're looking for the Floating Pit," Zeke said calmly, ignoring the way she leered at him, her tongue flicking through the spaces in her teeth. "Can you tell us where it is?"

"I could." The woman stepped closer. "Or I could show you where it is. How 'bout it, boy? I wasn't going myself—Jackal's little shows are a bit much for me—but for you, I'd make an exception, hey?"

I stepped up beside Zeke, resisting the urge to growl. "Just directions, if you don't mind," I said pleasantly, with an undertone that warned *get away from him or I'll tear your throat out.* The woman snickered and drew back.

"Ah, well, that's too bad. I would've made it worth your

while." She sniffed and pointed down a catwalk, where a group of people were already headed. "Just follow that path till you reach the Pit. It'll be all lit up this time of night. You really can't miss it."

"Thank you," Zeke said, and the woman cackled, holding her hand to her heart.

"Such manners," she said, pretending to wipe away a tear. "If only my slug of a man spouted that poetry, I might actually want to stay with him. Well, have fun, you two. This is your first show, eh?" She snickered again and brushed past us, shaking her head, calling back over her shoulder. "You might want to bring something to throw up in."

Zeke and I exchanged a worried glance.

"That sounds ominous," I muttered.

THE WOMAN WAS RIGHT, the Floating Pit was impossible to miss. Standing on a street corner, the square stone building wasn't as tall as the skyscrapers around it, but the towering, neon red CHI AGO sign next to the entrance glowed brilliantly against the darkness. Besides missing its letter *C,* the sign was full of holes and cracks. But despite the damage, it still functioned. For what purpose, I had no idea.

"I guess that's the Floating Pit?" Zeke muttered, watching raiders crowd through the door. Since the first floor was underwater, the walkway connected to a wooden platform that led inside the building. "Doesn't look like a pit to me. And the sign says *Chicago.* You'd think they'd call it something different."

"I'm guessing literacy isn't high on a raider's priority list," I murmured as we approached the building, craning my neck to gaze up at the sign. Looking down, I saw an overhang shimmering beneath the water, probably where the original doors would be. The entrance into the building was an arched stone frame with no hinges or doors, making me think it must've been a window at one point.

More walkways and bridges covered the flooded front hall of the building. I couldn't see the first level, but stairwells rose out of the water and ran up to second story balconies, where the crowd was headed. We followed them up the stairs and through the doors into a dimly lit arena, where anticipation hung thick on the air and in the crowds milling about the room.

"And this is why it's called the Pit," I said, looking around in amazement.

The chamber we'd stepped into was huge, an enormous domed room that soared majestically overhead. A balcony stretched around the room, lined with moldy seats that folded into themselves. On the left side, part of the balcony had fallen away, leaving a jagged, gaping hole, but there were still enough seats here to hold every raider in the city. Narrow aisles led down to the edge of the overhang, where it dropped away into the dark waters below.

Below us, an enormous red curtain stretched across the back wall, dropping down until it touched a floating wooden stage. A cage covered most of the platform, twenty feet high, with wire mesh covering the top so nothing could escape. The back half of the stage was hidden by the curtain, and I wondered what they were keeping back there.

Then Zeke touched my arm, pointing to something inside the cage.

A steel kennel had been shoved against a wall, with only tiny barred slits for windows. Every so often, the box would shake as whatever was inside moved around, but it was too dark to see through the slits. The wooden floor was stained with old blood.

"Blood sport," Zeke muttered as we hovered near the back. "This must be Jackal's idea of entertainment. They place bets to see which animal comes out of it alive." He looked around at the excited mob and shivered. "I don't particularly want to see two dogs rip each other to pieces. We should look for the others."

Before I could reply, a spotlight flicked on, shining down on the arena. I blinked. The stage had been empty a few seconds ago, I was sure of it. But a man now stood at the front, smiling at the crowd. He was tall, lean but muscular as well; I could see the cut of his chest beneath his shirt and faded leather duster. Thick black hair had been pulled into a ponytail, accenting a young, handsome face and smooth, pale skin. His eyes, sweeping over the crowd, were a lazy gold.

The man raised his arms as if to embrace us all, and the crowd went wild, roaring, beating on the floor, even firing their weapons into the air. And I suddenly knew. We had found him. This was Jackal, the vampire raider king.

"Good evening, minions!" Jackal bellowed, to a chorus of hoots and howls and screams. "I am in a fabulous mood tonight. What about you?" His voice carried easily over the noisy room, clear, confident and magnetic. Even the roughest bandit was hanging on his every word. "Never mind! I don't really care how you feel, but thank you all for coming to this little spectacle. As you might've heard, we have some exciting news! For the past three-and-a-half years, we've been searching for something, haven't we? Something important! Something that could change not only our world, but the entire world as we know it. You know what I'm talking about, don't you?"

I didn't, but listening to the raider king speak, I felt a glimmer of recognition. Like I should know him from...somewhere, though I didn't know why I felt that way. I was positive I'd never seen him before.

"Anyway," Jackal continued, "I wanted to let everyone know that a few nights ago, our search finally came to an end. We have found what we've been looking for all this time."

Zeke stiffened beside me. Behind Jackal, a pair of raiders pushed aside the curtain and shoved someone onto the stage. Jackal spun with shocking grace, grabbed the figure by the collar and dragged him forward, into the light.

Jebbadiah. His wrists were bound, and dark bruises covered his face and eyes, but he stood tall and proud next to the raider king, glaring at the mob with icy contempt. I put a warning hand on Zeke's arm, in case he forgot where he was. With a few hundred raiders and only two of us, now was not the time for a suicide rescue.

The crowd booed and jeered as Jeb regarded them coldly, but Jackal smiled and threw an arm around his shoulders, patting his chest.

"Now, now," he chided. "Be polite, all of you. You'll make him think we don't want him here." Jackal grinned, looking entirely animalistic. "After all, this is the man who holds the key to your immortality. This is the man who will be responsible for our rise to glory. This is the man who is going to cure Rabidism for us!"

The crowd erupted into chaos, but I still heard Zeke draw in a sharp breath. Stunned, I turned to him, seeing him pale, as if he already knew. And suddenly, everything made a lot more sense.

"That's why he's been after you," I hissed, leaning close to be heard over the howling mob. "He thinks Jeb can cure the virus, that's why he's hunted you for so long. *Anyone* would want that." Zeke looked away, but I grabbed his arm, pulling him back. "*Does* Jeb have the cure? Is that what you've been hiding, this whole time?"

"No," Zeke rasped, finally turning to face me. "No, he doesn't have the cure. There *is* no cure. But—"

I held up my hand, silencing him. The mob had finally quieted down. Jackal waited until the last few revelers had stopped, then turned to pat Jeb on the shoulder. "Unfortunately," he went on in a sorrowful voice, "our good friend here is somewhat reluctant to share what he knows! Can you believe it? I have a lovely lab all set up, waiting for him for *three years,* with everything he needs or could possibly want, and he doesn't seem to appreciate it."

A chorus of loud boos and insults. Jackal held up a hand again.

"I know, I know. But we can't force him to work, can we? I mean, it's not like I can break his fingers or bash his head in to get him to do what I want, right?" He laughed good-naturedly, and it sent a chill down my spine. "Which is why we're here tonight," he went on. "I've set up a bit of entertainment for our guest of honor, but I hope the rest of you enjoy it, too. Hopefully, it won't be over *too* quickly, but we do have a whole troop of new faces we can toss in if things get dull." He turned and stared directly at Jeb as he said this, lips pulled into a demonic smile, before turning back to the crowd. "So, I guess I don't have anything else to say except— on with the show!"

He exited the stage to a cacophony of cheers and howls, pulling Jebbadiah out with him. Zeke reached down and took my hand, squeezing tightly, as if to anchor himself for what was to come.

The curtains parted, and two more raiders marched out with another figure between them, his head covered with a dark bag. Opening the cage, they jerked the bag off, shoved him inside the cage, and slammed the door.

"Darren," Zeke moaned, starting forward. I tightened my grip on his hand and grabbed his arm, holding him back.

"Zeke, don't." He gave me a desperate look, but I held firm. "Go out there and you'll just get yourself caught or killed," I said, meeting his tortured gaze. "There's nothing we can do for him now."

A chilling screech drew my attention back to the ring. Darren, standing fearfully in the center of the cage, glanced at the kennel on the far wall. A rope that I hadn't noticed earlier had been tied to the door, drawn through the cage bars, and was now in the hands of a raider, bracing himself to yank on it. And I suddenly knew, with terrible certainty, what was in that kennel.

For a split second, the whole room was silent, voices fading away as the onlookers held their breath. Darren, alone in the arena, looked around desperately for an escape route, but there was nothing, nowhere he could run. Zeke was rigid; I could feel him shaking beneath my hands, unable to look away. For just a moment, Darren looked up, and their gazes met...

Then the hollow clang of the kennel door opening echoed in the silence, and Darren didn't even have time to turn before the rabid slammed into him, pulling him down with a screech.

The crowd roared and surged to their feet, and for a moment Darren was lost in the swell, though his screams could be heard even over the crowd. Zeke let out a breathless sob and turned away, wrenching himself from my grip, but I forced myself to watch, searing the images into my brain. It was the least I could do for Darren, to remember his last moments and to remind myself of what I could become. Not a rabid but something worse; something ruthless and savage and power-hungry, a true monster, like the raider king. Jackal had abandoned his humanity long ago, but I would not forget. I would remember this moment, and Darren's life would not go to waste.

Thankfully, it was over very quickly. Darren's limbs hadn't even stopped twitching when Jackal sauntered up to a bench and stood on it, raising his arms to the cheers of the crowd. Jeb stood behind him, his face white, shaking with grief and fury. "How's that for entertainment?" Jackal called, and the mob roared approval. I found myself hating all of them, wishing I could fly down and start ripping their jeering mouths off their faces. "And, good news—there's plenty more where that came from!" He whirled on Jeb, eyes gleaming. "So, what'dya say, old man? I think the next one in the cage should be that pretty girl. Or maybe one of the kids? It really makes no difference to me. Or...did you have something else in mind?"

I couldn't hear Jebbadiah, over the crowd, but I saw his lips move as he stared at Jackal, fear and hatred lining every part of his body. "I have no choice," I thought he said, and Jackal nodded, smiling. "I will do as you ask."

"There, that wasn't so hard, was it?" Jackal motioned to one of his raiders, and they took Jeb away. Turning back toward the crowd, the vampire grinned, showing a pair of extremely long, deadly fangs. "Minions, I promised you immortality, and I'm going to deliver! Now, the only thing left to choose is who I'll Turn first once we find the cure. Who is going to have that prestigious honor? Hmm." He snapped his fingers. "Maybe we'll just hold a huge free-for-all, and whoever comes out alive gets to be immortal, what'dya say?"

The crowd roared again, beating the seats, pumping fists and weapons into the air, screaming his name. Jackal raised his arms again, accepting the applause, the adoration, while behind him, Darren's blood pooled over the side of the cage and dripped into the water.

Zeke made a strangled noise and walked away, staggering toward the doors as if he was drunk. No one noticed him; their attention was riveted on Jackal and the show he'd put on in the center. But as I drew back, preparing to hurry after Zeke, Jackal raised gleaming yellow eyes over the crowd and caught my stare. He blinked as our eyes met, a puzzled expression crossing his face, and then I was out the door, following Zeke into the dark corridor.

CHAPTER 21

"Zeke!"

I caught him and yanked him around a corner just as a pair of rough-looking men came down the hall, laughing and swearing at each other. The raiders continued into the main room, where the echo of the crowd could still be heard through the open doors. I wondered what Jackal was doing and hoped he didn't have any more "entertainment" planned for the night.

Zeke was leaning with his back against the wall, but, as I approached, he slid down until he was sitting in the corner, gazing straight ahead at nothing. For a few heartbeats, he stayed like that, his expression glazed and dead. Then a shudder racked his frame, and he slowly hunched over, bending his head to his knees, as he sobbed quietly into his hands.

I watched him silently, my own throat suspiciously tight. I wished I knew what to say, the right words to comfort him, but sympathy was never my strong suit, and besides, anything

I said would probably end up sounding forced. Especially after the horrible scene we'd just witnessed.

Guessing he wanted a moment alone, I drew back and left him at the back of the hall, letting him mourn the death of his friend. Truthfully, I needed a few minutes by myself, as well.

My eyes stung, and I let a bloody tear slide down my cheek before swiping it away. First Dorothy and now Darren. Darren, who had joked around with me, who had stood up for me, even to Zeke. Who had been a good hunter, a companion, maybe even a friend. I would miss his company, I realized. He hadn't deserved that death, to come so far only to be torn apart by a rabid in the end. I clenched my fists, feeling the nails bite into my palms. Jackal would pay for this. He would pay for everything.

I turned and walked back to Zeke, trying to formulate some kind of plan, hoping he was clearheaded enough to help me out. He was still sitting in the corner, staring at the wall, but his face and eyes were clear.

I crouched beside him. "You okay?" Not the most brilliant or comforting question ever, but there was nothing else I could think of.

He shook his head. "We have to find the rest of them," he whispered, struggling to his feet. Leaning against the wall again, he took a deep breath and looked at me, his voice growing stronger. "Where do you think Jackal is keeping everyone?"

"I have no idea," I muttered. "But I'm guessing it's nearby. With everything underwater, it's probably not easy to transport prisoners back and forth. He'll want to keep them close."

"We should search the building," Zeke said, nodding, "once everyone has cleared out—"

A cheer from the open doors to the main hall drew our attention. Either Jackal was on a roll, or someone else was being torn apart. I shuddered and hoped it wasn't the latter.

Zeke and I glanced at each other, thinking the same thing. There was no time. For every minute we waited, another person could die, shoved into a cage and ripped apart for the crowd's entertainment. Jackal was ruthless, and I had no doubt he would sacrifice Caleb or even Bethany to get what he wanted. We had to find our people now.

"Backstage," Zeke whispered, his eyes hard. "They brought Jeb and Darren out through the curtain. Maybe they're keeping the others back there, as well."

I nodded. "Makes sense. It's a good place to start looking anyway."

But there were two hundred raiders and thirty feet of water between us and the stage, not to mention Jackal himself. I had no clue how powerful the raider king was and no desire to find out. "There has to be a back door," I muttered. "A way to get in from behind."

"There are plenty of windows," Zeke pointed out.

"Yeah," I said, turning away. "I hope you're up for a swim."

IN THE SHADOWS of the outside wall, we made our way through the black, grimy water, easing around the side of the building. I wasn't the best swimmer, not like Zeke, but there were plenty of handholds as we clung to the side of the wall. And of course, I didn't have to worry about drowning. Every so often, my leg would brush something beneath the surface of the water, a branch or a pole or the roof of a car, making me wonder what else was down there. Hopefully nothing alive. Or, if it was alive, hopefully nothing that wanted to eat us. I imagined huge rabid fish, gliding silently through the black waters, circling our legs, and decided not to voice that worry to Zeke.

"There," I said, pointing to a rusty metal staircase against the wall. Twisted and bent, it zigzagged up the outside wall to a platform on the top floor. Maneuvering around rubble, pipes and rusty beams, I made my way through the murky black water until I could grab the lowest rung. Heaving myself up, I turned to help Zeke, grabbing his arm as he pulled himself onto the first step. He was shivering, teeth clacking together, and I was reminded that he was only human. The water here was colder than the river had been, far colder. It didn't bother me, but Zeke was in danger of freezing to death if we weren't careful.

"You all right?" I asked as he crossed his arms, shivering in the wind. His pale hair lay plastered to his forehead, and his shirt clung to his chest, emphasizing his leanness. His face was tight. "Do you need to wait here? I can go on alone, if you want."

"I'm fine," he gritted out, clenching his jaw. "Let's keep moving."

The metal staircase creaked horribly as we made our way up the steps, and I could feel it swaying under our weight. But it held until we reached the top platform and crawled in through the broken window.

"I can't see a thing," muttered Zeke, pressing close to my back.

I could. The room here had the same crumbling, gutted feel of most other city buildings; cracked ceiling, peeling walls, floor strewn with rubble and trash. Looking closer, I had to fight the urge to hiss. Blank-eyed humans stared at me from the shadows of the room, some draped in rotted costumes, arms and legs missing or lying scattered on the floor. It took me a moment to realize they weren't real. Just plastic figures made to resemble humans.

Zeke gave a start, one hand dropping to his gun. He'd seen the creepy plastic figures, too, and in the dark, with normal human vision, it might freak anyone out.

"Relax," I told him. "They're not real. They're statues or something."

Zeke shuddered and took his hand away. "I've seen a lot of weird things," he muttered, shaking his head, "but I think this takes the prize. Let's get out of here before I start seeing them in my dreams…or before they start moving."

I glimpsed a dismembered arm on the floor, and a remark about needing a hand sprang to mind, but this wasn't the time for jokes. We carefully picked our way across the room and opened the door into another dark, narrow hallway.

The door creaked shut behind us, plunging the corridor into darkness thicker than ink. In complete blackness, the world looked shadowy gray to my vampire sight. But at least I could still see. Zeke was edging forward with one hand outstretched, the other on the wall beside him.

"Here," I said quietly, and took his hand. He stiffened, muscles coiled to pull back, but then relaxed with a tight nod. "Just follow my lead," I told him, ignoring the pulse at his wrist, the beat of life through his veins. "I won't let you fall."

We crept through the lightless hallway, passing rooms filled with dusty boxes, racks of rotting clothes and furniture covered in plastic sheets. It was obvious the raiders didn't use this part of the building; the dirt and plaster dust lining these hallways hadn't been disturbed in years—except for the countless rats and mice that went scurrying away, vanishing into the walls and floor. At one point, I stepped in something soft, like mud, and looked up to see the ceiling crawling with what looked like hundreds of winged mice. I didn't mention this to Zeke as we hurried forward, though for some bizarre reason I felt a strange kinship with the tiny grotesque creatures.

The back of the building was like a maze, with endless rooms, hallways and scattered rubble. Some of the walls had fallen in, and sometimes we had to pick our way over a section of ceiling or edge around a floor that had collapsed. Zeke kept a tight grip on my hand as we maneuvered the labyrinth, occasionally stumbling as his wounded leg gave out but for the most part keeping up with me.

As we stepped over a fallen girder, a splintering crack rang out like a gunshot, and a section of floor gave way beneath us. I grabbed wildly for the beam with one hand, keeping a tight grip on Zeke with the other, as we plummeted straight down. My fingers hit the rusty edge of the girder, latching on desperately, as the weight of Zeke's body nearly tore my arm out of the socket.

For a moment, we dangled over empty blackness. I could hear Zeke's panting, feel his pulse racing under my fingers.

Overhead, the floorboards groaned threateningly, showering me with dust, but the girder itself didn't move.

The weight on the end of my arm gave a strangled gasp, hand tightening around my wrist. My fingers digging into the girder slipped a fraction of an inch. "Zeke," I gritted out, "there's a beam right above us. If I pull you up, can you grab it?"

"I...can't see anything," Zeke replied, his voice tight with suppressed fear, "so you'll have to be my eyes. Just tell me when I'm getting close."

I half swung, half lifted him to the edge of the hole, feeling my shoulders scream in protest. "Now," I muttered, and Zeke lashed out with his free arm, hitting the girder on his first try. The weight dragging me down vanished as Zeke grabbed the beam like a lifeline and hauled himself up.

I followed, crawling out of the hole and rolling onto my back next to Zeke, who had done the same. He was breathing hard, shaking with adrenaline, his heart crashing in his chest. I felt nothing. No pounding heartbeat, no gasping breaths, nothing. A near-death experience, and I didn't feel a thing.

Wait, scratch that. I did feel something. Relief. I was relieved that Zeke was alive and still with me. And now that the excitement was fading somewhat, I felt a stirring of real fear in my stomach, not for me, but for what could've happened. I'd almost lost him. If I had let him fall, he would be dead.

Zeke stirred, shifting to his elbow, squinting into the darkness. "Allie?" His voice was hesitant, probing the black. "You still there?"

"Yeah," I muttered and felt him relax. "Still here."

He shifted to his knees, one hand reaching out tentatively. "Where are you?" he murmured, frowning. In the dark, I watched his face, seeing his gaze pass over me without seeing. "You're so quiet—it's like you're not even here. You're not even breathing hard."

I sighed, deliberately, just to make some kind of noise. "That's what happens when you're dead," I murmured and rolled to my knees to face him. "That whole breathing thing isn't so important anymore."

I reached for his hand, but he suddenly leaned in, and his fingers brushed my cheek. Warmth flooded my skin, and I froze, waiting for him to pull back.

He didn't. The tips of his fingers lingered on my cheek for a moment. Then, very slowly, his hand slipped forward, the palm brushing my skin. Frozen, I stared at him, watching his face as his fingers moved from my cheek to my forehead to my chin, like a blind man tracing someone's features to see them in his mind.

"What are you doing to me?" he whispered, as his hand moved down to my neck, tracing my collarbone. I couldn't answer even if I wanted to. "You make me question everything I've learned, everything I know. Truths I've believed since I was a kid, gone." He sighed, and I felt a shiver go through him, but he didn't pull his hand back. "What's wrong with me?" he groaned, low and anguished. "I shouldn't be feeling any of this. Not for a..."

He trailed off, but the word hung between us, raw and painful. I could sense Zeke's struggle with himself, perhaps trying to find the will to pull away, perhaps to do something that went against everything he'd been taught. I wanted, desperately, to lean forward, to respond to his touch, but I was afraid that if I moved, he would pull back and the moment would shatter. So I remained still, passive and unthreatening, letting him decide what he wanted. Silence stretched between us, but his hand, his gentle fingers, never left my skin.

"Say something," he murmured at last, cupping my cheek like he couldn't bear to pull back. "I can't see you, so...I don't know what you're thinking. Talk to me."

"And say what?" I whispered.

"I don't know. Just..." Zeke bowed his head, his voice quietly desperate. "Just...tell me I'm not crazy," he whispered. "That this...isn't as insane as I think it is."

His heartbeat stuttered, racing in my ears. The Hunger stirred curiously, always eager, but I could ignore it this time. I wasn't thinking of his blood, rushing just below the skin. I wasn't thinking of his heartbeat or his touch or the pulse at his throat. Right now, all I was thinking of was Zeke.

"I don't know," I told him softly as he shifted closer, radiating warmth even through his wet clothes. I knew I should pull away, but what was the point? I was tired of fighting. In this absolute darkness, with no one to see or judge, our secret seemed safe. "Maybe we're both a little crazy."

"I can live with that," Zeke murmured and finally did what I'd been fearing and hoping and dreaming he'd do from the very start. His other hand reached up, framing my face, as he leaned in and kissed me.

His lips were warm and soft, and his scent was everywhere, surrounding me. I gripped his arms, kissing him back...and the Hunger rose up, as powerful as ever, yet different from before. I didn't just want to bite him and drink his blood;

I wanted to draw him in slowly, make him a part of me. And I wanted to share a part of myself with him, so that we became one.

I could feel my fangs against my gums, aching to slip out. To drop to the hollow at Zeke's throat, where his pulse beat the hardest against his skin, and sink below the surface. I felt the urge to tip my head back as well, baring my throat so that he could do the same.

And that scared me back to my senses.

I pulled away, breaking the kiss, an instant before my fangs lengthened and slipped through my gums. Zeke watched me with a puzzled expression, but in the darkness he couldn't see the monster kneeling not six inches from his throat.

"Zeke," I began, once I had firm control over myself. But before I could say anything else, a guilty expression crossed his face, and he sat back on his heels.

"Sorry," he whispered, sounding horrified with himself. He stood quickly, and I did the same, almost relieved for the distraction. "God, what am I thinking? I'm sorry, I shouldn't be stalling us like this. We have to find the others."

"This way," I said, and this time I didn't have to reach back for his arm. His hand sought my own and gripped it tightly, twining our fingers together. Treading lightly, we picked our way over the floor and continued into the ruin of the old building.

We slipped through more hallways, more crumbling steps, being extremely careful now as we made our way down to the lower floors. Finally, I saw a sign painted in faded red letters that said Backstage, with an arrow pointing down a flight of stairs. As we made our way down the musty staircase, I started to hear the noise from the auditorium; the ruckus of the crowd still had not died down.

"I hope they're all right," Zeke muttered behind me. "I hope no one else ended up like...like Darren."

His voice caught, and when I glanced back at him, I pretended not to see the glimmer in his eyes.

The stairwell ended in a swath of jet-black water, lapping against the metal steps. That meant we had reached the ground level of the theater. Another Backstage arrow lay half submerged against the wall, pointing downward.

"I think we're going to have to swim again," I muttered, releasing Zeke's hand. He nodded bravely, just as I caught a faint shimmer of light somewhere in the depths. "Wait a second," I cautioned as he stepped forward. "I think there's a door down there. I'll see if I can get it open."

"All right," Zeke said. "I'll wait here for you. Be careful."

He sank down onto one of the steps, arms around himself, and leaned forward, shivering. For a moment, I wanted to bend down and kiss him, to reassure him that it would be all right. I didn't. I walked down the stairs, straight into the murky depths, and continued downward as the water closed over my head.

The steps went down another flight and a half, ending at a rusty metal door. A faint orange glow trickled out between the cracks, but pushing on it revealed the door was locked or stuck. It was difficult to find the leverage I needed to force it open, but vampire strength, plus the handy benefit of not having to breathe while underwater, won out in the end. After bashing my shoulder against the surface repeatedly, it finally gave way.

Orange light flooded the stairwell, coming from somewhere beyond the door. I turned and swam back up the steps to Zeke, waiting anxiously at the edge of the water.

"Got it open," I said, unnecessarily. The stairwell was no longer pitch-black. Though it was still plenty dark, Zeke was no longer blind. He nodded and gazed past me, into the water.

"Did you see anyone?"

"Not yet. But there's light coming from that room, so I'm guessing we're backstage, behind the curtain." I gestured back to the exit, making a small splash. "The door is underwater, but it's not far. Follow me and you'll be fine."

Zeke nodded and, without hesitation, plunged into the icy waters. Pulling ourselves down by the railings, we swam through the flooded stairwell, through the door, and surfaced cautiously. Treading water, I gazed around the small lake, trying to get my bearings.

We were definitely backstage. The floating platform bobbed on the water's surface about fifty feet away, each corner lit by flickering oil lamps, sputtering on their posts. The massive red curtain hung across the center, moldy and tattered, but still a barrier separating the backstage from the auditorium. A raucous cheer came from the other side; the raider audience was still out there and getting rowdier.

Puzzled, I gazed around the room, wondering where everyone was. Chairs floated or lay half submerged in the murky water, which was also choked with floating black wires and bits of rope. A plastic arm bobbed past my face, and I could see the remains of a couch, bloated and falling apart, beneath me. But, except for the floating stage and the huge red curtain, the room appeared empty.

Then I heard voices above me, and looked up.

A maze of catwalks and platforms stretched above the room, dangling twenty or so feet above the water. They crisscrossed their way through the open air, between coils of ropes and pulleys, surrounding a pair of cages hanging from the rafters. The cages, made of rusty iron and steel, hung a little below the catwalks, each suspended by a single thick rope that swayed gently in the open air. Soft sobbing noises came from inside, as a group of people huddled together behind the bars.

Zeke drew in a sharp breath. He'd seen them, too. We started forward, but the beam of a flashlight suddenly pierced the gloom above the catwalks as a raider stalked out of the darkness, shining the light into the cage.

"Hey, shut up in there!" he ordered, aiming the beam into the face of a terrified Caleb, who cringed back and clung to Ruth. I felt Zeke's fury, the tight coil of his muscles under his shirt, and put a warning hand on his shoulder.

"You little shits should be thankful," the raider continued, as two more guards emerged from the shadows, ambling along the catwalk. "No more 'spectacles,' at least for tonight. Let's hope the old man can do what Jackal says he can, otherwise we might have to feed one of you to the rabids for inspiration, hey? Chew on that for a while, ha!"

He spat over the railing and sauntered off, joining his friend on another platform. I turned to see Zeke draw his gun, aiming it at the raider's back, and grabbed his arm.

"Zeke, don't!" I forced his wrist underwater, and he glared at me. "You'll alert the whole compound," I whispered, gesturing back toward the curtain. "Let me go first. I can take them out quietly. Even if they see me, it won't matter if I get shot."

He hesitated but gave a tight nod. Silently, we made our way to the floating platform, and I started up the ladder to the catwalks above.

I landed over the railings in a crouch, searching for my targets. I could hear their footsteps, sense their beating hearts. One was very close. I crept along the walk, weaving through thick tangles of rope, until I found him, leaning against the railing smoking a cigarette.

He didn't see the arms that reached through the ropes until it was too late. I snaked one arm around his neck, one hand against his mouth, and yanked him back into the coils. He let out a muffled yelp, but then my fangs were already in his throat.

That was easy, I mused, pushing the ropes aside as I stepped out, smiling. *Now, where are the other two?*

There was another one, standing at the edge of a platform, smoking. His friend was wandering away, back toward the far wall, leaving the other alone. His back was to me, but I'd have to creep around the cages to get to him. And I'd have to do it before he could alert his friend.

Crouching down, I started forward. I'd just have to be quick—

"Allie!"

The shrill cry echoed through the room, making me jump, and the guard's attention snapped to the cage. Caleb's small form was pressed against the bars, his wide eyes fastened on me, one hand outstretched. The raiders followed his gaze and jerked upright as they saw me.

Damn. So much for the element of surprise. As the guards went for their guns, I took two running steps toward the edge of the platform and hurled myself into space. My coat snapped out behind me as I flew over the water, and the raiders' eyes bulged as I soared from one side of the catwalks to the other. At the last second, one tried bringing up his gun, but I was already on top of him, slamming my knee into his chest. We hit the platform with a ringing clang, and the back of his skull hit the metal edge. He slumped off the platform, hitting the water with a loud splash. The other raider screamed a curse.

I whirled with a snarl, showing fangs, but the guard was already fleeing down the maze of catwalks. Ducking behind the cages, he paused to look back and paled when he saw me running toward him with my sword drawn.

Caleb cried out again, and the guard's gaze snapped eerily to the child, a chilling look crossing his face. Pulling a huge knife from his belt, he leaned out and slashed at the thick ropes holding the cages above the water. The first snapped, and the cage with Caleb, Ruth, Bethany and Teresa plummeted to a chorus of screams into the icy water.

As the second rope frayed, and the raider raised an arm to hack at it again, a shot rang out from behind. The man jerked. Blood exploded from his chest in a thin spray, and he fell backward. Still clutching the smoking pistol, Zeke rushed onto the platform just as the second rope snapped and the cage joined the first one in the waters below.

I leaped over the edge, plummeting into the foaming water. The second cage had, miraculously, fallen skewed on an underwater table, so a corner still stuck out above the surface. Jake, Silas and Matthew were clinging to the bars, struggling to keep their faces above water. But the other cage, lying on the wooden floor, was fully submerged, and bubbles foamed up where it had fallen.

I dove to where the cage landed, searching frantically for the door. The bodies within were thrashing about, shaking the iron bars, their eyes wide with terror. I found the door padlocked shut and yanked on it. It wouldn't budge. Snarling under my breath, I yanked harder, straining at the metal, but it stubbornly refused to give.

Looking through the bars, I saw Teresa's limp body, floating toward the top, and Caleb's frantic expression as he tried squeezing through.

One last time, I wrenched at the iron door and finally felt it give way. Pulling it open, I grabbed Ruth and Bethany, shoving them through the door, then went after Caleb and Teresa. Caleb was so frantic he refused to let go of the bars at first, and I had to pry him off and shove him out of the cage. Grabbing Teresa's limp form, I swam for the surface, hoping I wasn't too late.

I broke the surface of the water to chaos. The kids were screaming, flailing in the water. Ruth was trying desperately to lead them to the stage, but it was obvious Bethany couldn't swim and Caleb was hysterical. A few feet away, Zeke was at the other cage, trying to work it open. I saw the flash of keys in his hand—taken from the dead raider, probably—a second before he pried the door open, letting the captives swim out.

As I hauled Teresa's unconscious body onto the stage, the curtain behind me parted, and a raider came through, probably drawn by the racket of the kids and gunfire and falling cages. For just a moment, he stared at us in shock, then turned to shout a warning. But that second was all the time I needed to lunge in and drive a sword between his ribs. His shout turned into a startled gurgle, and he dropped to the stage with a thud.

But other raiders would soon be arriving. I could see them through the holes in the curtain, clambering over the seats toward the stage. I glanced back, seeing Zeke emerge from the water with a shaking, hiccuping Bethany, Caleb clinging to his neck from behind. Near my feet, Teresa began to cough up water.

Ruth pulled herself up to the platform and, as Zeke set Caleb and Bethany on solid ground, flung herself into his arms. "You're alive!" she sobbed into his chest, as he held her close and the kids plastered themselves to his waist. "We were sure you were dead! Oh, God, it's been horrible, what they did to us. Darren—"

"I know," Zeke said, his face tightening. "And I'm so sorry I couldn't…" He closed his eyes. "I'm sorry," he whispered. "That won't happen again, I swear."

"Zeke," I warned, and his eyes flickered to me. "No time for this. The men are coming. We have to get them out of here."

He nodded, composed and businesslike again, but Ruth turned on me, eyes blazing with suspicion and fear.

"What is *she* doing here?" Ruth hissed, still clinging to Zeke, one delicate hand on his chest. "She's a vampire! Jeb told us to kill her if she came poking around again."

"Stop it, Ruth." Zeke's voice was hard, and we both blinked at him in shock. "She saved my life," he continued in a calmer voice. "And yours, too, in case you didn't notice. I wouldn't have gotten this far if she hadn't come back."

"But...Jeb said—"

"Save it," I barked at her, and she cringed back, eyes wide. "We're not out of here, yet. And, now that you mention it, where is Jeb? He's not here, that's for sure. Where did they take him?"

"I'm not telling you, vampire!" Ruth shrieked, on the verge of hysterics. "I'm not telling you anything!"

I snarled, ready to smack some sense into her, but Zeke held up a hand, stopping me. "Ruth." He shook her gently, bringing her attention back to him. "Where is Jeb? Did they say where they took him, where he's being held?"

The girl nodded, clinging to his shirt. "Jackal's tower," she whispered. "They said he's being taken to Jackal's tower."

The words were barely out of her mouth when Bethany screamed and another raider came through the curtain, followed by a friend. I spun, blade flashing, and quickly beheaded one, making Bethany and Ruth scream again, but the other got off a yell before I could silence him. As their bodies hit the stage, I spun toward Zeke.

"Move! Get them out of here!" I swept a hand toward the catwalks, to the door the guards had used. "Don't wait for me—I'll catch up when I can. Just get them out of the city and don't look back."

"Catch up?" Zeke had started ushering the group up the ladder to the catwalks but now turned back with a frown. "You're not coming with us?"

"No." I shot a quick glance at the curtain, hearing the

crowd rushing the stage, the splashes as the raiders plunged into the water. "I'm going back for Jeb."

He stared at me. "You? But...no, I should be the one. He's family. It should be me."

"You're still hurt, Zeke. Besides—" I nodded to the group as the last of them scrambled up the ladder, peering down at us "—you have to lead them out of here. I'll have the best chance to find Jeb if I'm alone."

"But..." Zeke hesitated, torn. "Even if you find him, he might not go with you. Allie, he might...try to kill you."

"I know." I stepped away from him, toward the curtain. The raiders were climbing the stage now, hauling themselves out of the water. "But if I don't do this, I'll *be* the monster he thinks I am." Spinning, I slashed at a raider who charged through the curtain, splitting him open to the shrieks of the kids. As he staggered and fell into the water, I whirled back on Zeke. "If Jeb is alive, I swear I'll find him! But you need to get them out of here, Zeke! Go, now! If I'm not back by dawn, don't wait for us, because we'll be dead. Go!"

With one last tortured look, Zeke turned and fled up the ladder. I spun toward the stage, slashing at another raider, and grabbed the oil lamp from the post. As the mob outside drew close, I raised the lamp over my head and smashed it to the floor, shattering glass and sending flaming oil over the red fabric.

The old curtain caught fire instantly, and tongues of orange flame sprang up with a roar, engulfing the cloth and spreading to the wood beside it. As a pair of raiders came through, I snatched the second lantern and did the same to the other side, flinching away as the oil splattered everywhere, catching the two men in the spray. They howled, flailing their arms as their clothes caught fire, and fled back the way they had come.

The inferno roared, eating rapidly at the old curtain, licking at the wooden frame around it. I stumbled back, clutching the last lantern, fighting the instinct to run as the flames snapped and reached for me, blistering and lethal. For the first time, I felt an almost primal terror, facing down one of a vampire's greatest fears. Fire could destroy me. The wind, rushing in from the roof and shattered windows, blew clouds of embers and burning cloth into the air; one landed on my coat sleeve, and I hissed as I slapped it away.

I smashed the final lantern at the base of the stage, turned and fled up the ladder, feeling the heat sizzle against my back. Cries of alarm echoed over the roar of the fire as the raiders scattered back and forth, not knowing what to do. Some jumped into the water to flee and some tried dousing the flames with whatever they could find, but the inferno was licking at the walls and ceiling now, spreading to the oiled wood without any sign of slowing down.

At the top of the ladder, I looked over to see Zeke usher the last of the group through a door at the end of the catwalk. He glanced back, and our gazes met. For just a moment, we stared at each other, as the wind and flames shrieked around us, snapping at hair and clothes. I saw regret that he wasn't able to come with me, a fierce determination to get the rest of them out alive…and a trust that hadn't been there before. I gave him a brief nod, and he returned it solemnly before vanishing through the doorway.

I turned. The flames were spreading faster than I thought

possible, tearing at the walls, the wind carrying burning embers to the plush seats to catch fire. I faced part of the outer wall that had collapsed, seeing crumbled buildings through the gaping hole, the dark outline of the city through the smoke.

I sprinted for the end of the catwalk and leaped, hurling myself over the water, grabbing rough wood and plaster as I hit the wall. A section gave way beneath my hand, plummeting down with a splash as I pulled myself up. Finding handholds along the outer wall, I easily climbed up to the roof and gazed out on the city.

Skeletal buildings loomed above me, dark and crumbling, brushing the sky. I turned, scanning the towers, looking for anything that might indicate Jackal's lair. They all looked the same, broken and empty, and I spat out a curse. How was I going to find that old man in such an enormous...

I stopped, blinking. A light suddenly glimmered against the darkness like a stray star, a glow at the very top of a massive black tower.

The tower of a vampire king. If I was lucky, I would find Jebbadiah waiting there, alive and unharmed. If my luck held, I would *not* find a certain raider king waiting for me, as well. And if I was *really* lucky, I could rescue the old man and bring him back without being killed, by Jackal *or* Jebbadiah Crosse.

CHAPTER 22

I didn't encounter any resistance as I made my way to Jackal's tower, probably because everyone was preoccupied with the burning building. I hoped that it would be enough of a distraction to cover Zeke's escape, and that he'd be able to get everyone out safely.

I could still see the glow of the inferno as I approached the tower. Clouds of burning embers billowed over the wind, and several smaller fires had already sprung up in adjoining buildings. It surprised me how far a fire could spread, even through a city that was so completely waterlogged.

The steps and first floor of Jackal's tower were underwater, but a series of bridges led from the elevated tracks into the lobby. The water here was only waist deep, and it lapped against the platforms and rotting front desk as I snuck into the dark, open room. Pausing on a swaying walkway over the desk, I looked around. How did one get to the top floor of this place? Did they take the stairs all the way up? Did the vampire king know how to fly?

A loud clanking, grinding noise drew my attention to one wall, where a pair of elevator doors sat half open in their frames, flaking with rust. I slipped from the walkway into the water, ducking behind the huge desk as a hand appeared between the doors and shoved one of them aside. Two armed raiders emerged from the elevator, hurried over the walkways and out into the flooded street. I watched them head toward the glow of the burning building and quickly waded over to the elevator.

Shouldering the doors back, I observed the tube cautiously. The whole thing had obviously been jerry-built by Jackal's men, and if I hadn't just seen it in action I'd have doubted it could get off the ground. A simple steel frame encircled with wooden railings and wrapped with chain-link dangled from the thick cable. The floor was nothing but a few rotting planks, and I could see water sloshing underneath the wood. Some kind of lever had been welded to the corner, eaten with rust and sitting in a tangled nest of exposed wires. A few sparks jumped out to sizzle into nothingness, doing nothing for my skepticism.

Easing into the box, which creaked and swayed in protest, I stepped over the gaping holes in the floor and wrenched the lever up.

The lift shuddered, sparking furiously, and then began a slow but steady climb up into the blackness. I gripped the metal frame hard enough to leave impressions in the rust, gritted my teeth with every jolt or clang against the wall, and wondered how the people from before could stand being in a tiny box dangling hundreds of feet in the air.

Finally, the thing came to a screeching, lurching stop at another pair of doors, these in slightly better condition. They still had to be pried open, and I shouldered my way through, relieved to be on solid ground again.

Or…maybe not.

The first thing I saw, coming out of the elevator, was sky. Twenty feet from the doors, a wall of windows stretched away down the hall, showing the dark, gleaming, decayed glory of the city below. Much of the glass had blown out, and a sharp wind hissed through the frames, whipping at my hair, smelling of water and smoke.

The next thing I saw was a guard at the end of the corridor. He stood in front of the windows, gazing down at the streets, but turned as I stepped out of the elevator. He blinked, no doubt startled to see a vampire girl at the end of the hall.

Too bad for him. I lunged across the floor and hit him hard, and he didn't make a sound as he slumped down the wall. Stepping around his body, I reached for the door.

Light spilled from beneath, and a faint, nearly inaudible hum came from beyond the wall. Hoping I wouldn't find a grinning raider king on the other side, I eased the door open and peered through the crack.

Searing light blinded me, and I flinched away. Shielding my eyes, I tried again, squinting through the haze. The room beyond was painfully bright; light came from every corner, every nook and cranny, leaving no shadows whatsoever. Countertops and shelves lined the walls, some holding books, some holding odd machines and glass tubes that reflected the light. How was it so bright? Not even a hundred torches or flashlights could light up a room like this. I pushed the door open a little farther, scanning the room cautiously.

More oddities. Across the room, a strange green board hung on the wall, one half scrawled with white letters and numbers that meant nothing to me. A map had been taped to the other half, showing "The United States of America," as it was before the plague. It, too, had been marked up and scrawled on with red ink, things circled and crossed out in what looked like frustration.

Movement caught my attention. In the corner, opposite the wall of glass running the length of the room, sat a monstrous old desk. A blinking screen sat on one side, showing lists of words I couldn't make out. I stared at it, mystified. A real computer, from an age where such technology could be found in every household. I'd never seen a working one before, though rumors in the Fringe had said they existed, if you had an external power source. Jackal had put a lot of thought and time into creating this place. What exactly did he expect to do here?

I continued to scan the room, moving my gaze along the far wall, and finally found what I was looking for.

A man stood at the window, silhouetted against the night sky, gazing down on the city. A faint glow flickered over the sharp features of Jebbadiah Crosse, casting his face in red light. And it might've been my imagination, but I thought I saw a glimmering wetness down one hollow cheek. The look on his face was one of devastation, of a man who had lost everything and had nothing left to live for.

I opened the door fully and stepped into the room. "Jeb-badiah."

He turned, and for a moment surprise crossed his harsh features. "You," he said, frowning. "The vampire girl. How... Why are you here?" He paused, gave a bitter smile. "Ah, yes. You followed us, didn't you? You wouldn't just let us go. It makes sense now. Revenge comes so easily for your kind." His voice changed, becoming cold and steely, filled with hate. "This is the perfect place for you. A lost city, filled with demons and sinners, ruled by a devil. Have you come to gloat, then? See the old man who has lost everything?"

"I'm not here to gloat," I said, moving toward him. "I came to get you out of here."

"Lies," Jeb said without emotion. "I wouldn't go anywhere with you, devil, even if I could. But it doesn't matter now." He turned back to the window, watching the smoke rising on the wind. "They're gone now. They're free of this world. I will join them soon."

"They're not dead." I stepped up behind him. "Zeke and I got them out. They're waiting for us outside the city, but we have to go now before Jackal finds us."

"Are you afraid of death, vampire?" Jeb asked quietly, still gazing out the window. "You should know that there is nothing more dangerous than a man who is not afraid to die. I have lost everything, but that frees me. The vampire king will never use me to achieve his goals. And you—you will not threaten anyone again."

"Jeb." I moved closer, reaching for his arm. "Jackal might be here any second. We have to get out of here, no—"

Jeb turned, stepped forward and very calmly stabbed me in the gut.

I gasped and jerked, hunching over, as pain shot through my stomach, a blinding, crippling flood. Snarling, fangs bared, I staggered away from Jebbadiah, who watched impassively with his fingers smeared bright red.

My hands went to my stomach, feeling the weapon still jammed into my flesh, sharp-edged and torturous. Blood pooled around the object, making it slick, but I grasped the end and drew it out, clenching my teeth to keep from screaming. A glass shard, nearly six inches long, slid out of my gut in a blaze of agony, and I dropped it with a gasping cry, before my legs gave out and I crumpled to my knees.

Jebbadiah stepped across my field of vision, moving away toward one of the many shelves, his face expressionless. I was healing, the wound knitting together, but not quickly enough. "Jeb," I gritted out, trying to get to my feet, sinking back with a grimace, "I swear...I came here to get you out. The others are alive, waiting for you—"

He opened a drawer, drew out a scalpel and walked back with it gleaming in his hand, his eyes hard as stone. He didn't seem to have heard me. "Let this be my final penance," he murmured, almost in a daze, as I desperately struggled to my feet, grabbing a counter to pull myself up. "Eden is lost. Ezekiel is lost. The cure for the human race is lost. I failed, but at least I will bring one devil back to hell with me. I can still do that much."

I staggered away from him, holding my stomach. The urge to draw my sword was overpowering, but I forced myself to face the old man. "Cure?" I said, putting a counter between us. "What cure?" He didn't answer, following me calmly around the obstacle, scalpel held in front of him. "So, Jackal was right," I guessed. "You do know the cure for Rabidism. You've been keeping it from everyone all this time."

"Do not speak of matters you do not understand, vampire," Jeb shot back, with a little more emotion than he'd previously shown. "There is no cure, not yet. All that exists are fragments, pieces of information, results of failed experiments from decades ago."

"You knew about the vampire experiments," I guessed. Jeb stared at me over the glass and the beakers, hands at his side. "How? Were you there? Did you live in New Covington before it became vampire territory? You're not *that* old."

"My grandfather was part of the team searching for the cure," Jebbadiah said flatly. "He was the head scientist, a brilliant man of his field. It was he who discovered vampire blood might be the key to finding the cure for Red Lung. It was he who decided they needed live specimens to experiment on. And it was he who finally convinced the others to let a vampire help them with the project."

I leaned against the counter, the pain in my middle slowly ebbing away. But the Hunger was growing strong now. I needed blood, and there was no one around but Jeb. I clutched the edges of the counter, trying to concentrate on what the old man was saying, not the pounding of his heart.

"That decision destroyed them," Jeb continued in that same flat voice, his eyes blank and mirrorlike. "Because of one man's pride, the rabids were born. Because one man consorted with a demon. Nothing good can come out of pure evil, and it came back to haunt them in the end. The demons they created escaped, killed everyone and the lab burned to the ground. But, before he died, the head scientist made sure to copy all his research, everything they had learned, and pass it on to his son."

"Your father. Who passed it on to you." I suddenly remembered Kanin, sifting through the ruins of the old hospital, searching for something he would never find. Jeb didn't answer, which spoke volumes, and I nodded slowly. "That's the real reason you want to find Eden. You want a place to study that research, to find the cure."

"If I died, it would have gone to Ezekiel," Jeb murmured, a pained expression briefly crossing his face. "But he is gone, and there is no one left. And so, it will die with me. I will not allow it to fall into the hands of a devil."

"Jeb, *Zeke is still alive.* They all are!" Frustrated, I glared at him, wishing I could pound the truth into his skull by force. "Listen to me! Zeke and I followed Jackal's men here together. We rescued the others and set a building on fire for a distraction. By now, they're probably out of the city. You can still get to Eden, if you stop being so damned stubborn and pay attention to what I'm telling you!"

Jeb blinked, his glassy expression cracking just a little. "Ezekiel is…alive?" he murmured, then shook his head almost desperately. "No. No, you lie, demon. Ezekiel was my son, though he was not my blood. He would never consort with the likes of you. I taught him better than that."

My anger boiled over, and with it, the Hunger that had been building as my wound slowly knit itself closed. "Zeke cared more about his people than you ever did, preacher!" I snarled at Jebbadiah, whose face tightened at the sight of my fangs. "He would do anything to save them, anything! Even get himself killed trying to rescue them. Even team up with a vampire who, I have to point out, is still trying to save your stubborn ass! I might be a demon, but Zeke is far more human than you or me or anyone, and if you can't see that, then you don't know him as well as you should."

Jebbadiah stared at me a moment longer, then slowly shook his head, closing his eyes. "How can I trust it?" he whispered, and he wasn't speaking to me. "Should I believe what it tells me, that my son is alive, that the others have been spared?" He opened his eyes, his face tormented by indecision. "I am too old to turn from my path," he said, staring at something I could not see. "I cannot believe a demon has a soul, that it can be saved. This I will not believe. I will be lost if I begin to doubt..." His gaze flicked to mine, still anguished, and he finally spoke directly to me. "Why have you come, vampire? Why do you hesitate? I know you wish to kill me, I can see it in your eyes. What is stopping you?"

I paused a moment to control myself, so my voice would be steady when I answered. "I promised Zeke I would find you. Believe what you want, but that's the truth." Carefully, I stepped around the counter, keeping a wary eye on the hand that still held the blade. "I said I would bring you back safe, and I will. If you won't do this for me, do it for Zeke and Caleb and Bethany. They deserve better than this, don't you think?" I gestured out the window, then turned back to him, glaring. "But you can't stop now. You can't let them down. Get that damned cure to Eden, so they can have *some* kind of future. Do that for them, at least."

The color drained from Jeb's face. The scalpel suddenly dropped from his hand, clattering to the floor.

"You shame me, vampire," he whispered in a voice almost too soft to hear. "All this time, I was so concerned about getting my people to Eden, I forgot my duty to protect them on the journey. I let Ezekiel handle what I should have from the beginning. And now, look where we are." He turned from me, gazing out the window. "I killed Dorothy," he murmured, "and Darren. And all the others. I brought us here. Their deaths are on my head."

"Not everyone is gone," I reminded him, struggling to contain the Hunger, which had emerged with a vengeance now that I was healed. I badly wanted to fly at this human and sink my teeth into his throat, but I shoved down the urge and stomped on it. I had been hungry my entire life, on the brink of starvation many times in the Fringe; it would not control me now. "Zeke is waiting for you, along with the rest of them. You can still save lives, Jeb. You can still get to Eden. We just have to go *now.*"

"Yes." Jeb nodded, though he still wasn't looking at me. "Yes, I will make it up to them. Even if I must sell my soul to a demon, I will bring them home."

A slow clapping came from the doorway, and my stomach dropped to my toes.

"Bravo," drawled the tall, smirking form of the vampire raider king, leaning in the doorway. "Bravo. What a touching performance. I think I shed a tear."

CHAPTER 23

"Well, well," Jackal purred, smiling as he came into the room, shutting the door behind him. "What do we have here? Another vampire has snuck into my little kingdom, I see. I thought I felt something odd tonight. Suddenly, all the craziness outside makes sense." He *tsked* at me and shook his head. "Did you burn down my theater? That wasn't very civilized of you. Now I'm going to have to find another spot to hold the ritual dismemberments."

He stopped, folding his arms and watching me with a patronizing look, maybe because I had drawn my sword and had sunk into a ready stance, waiting for him to make the first move. That weird feeling of familiarity, of déjà vu, crept up again.

"Well, this is awkward," Jackal continued, not looking the slightest bit concerned with the appearance of weapons. "It seems we have different ideas of what's going to happen tonight. You see, *I* don't want to fight you. I don't get many of my kin through here, especially the beautiful, sword-wielding variety. But I must have pissed you off in the past, because I feel I know you from somewhere, I just can't remember where or how."

"I don't want a fight, either," I said and nodded to Jeb. "I'm just here for him. Let him go, and we'll get out of your city right now."

"Ah, well, that's going to be a problem." Jackal sighed, rubbing his chin. "See, I've been looking for the old man for quite some time now, ever since I heard about the scientists and their project. I need him to develop the cure. He says the information is incomplete, so I've given him everything he needs to finish it. I'm doing a good thing here." The raider king smiled, charming and handsome. "All I want is to end the curse of Rabidism. That's not such a horrible thing, is it? Wouldn't you do the same, if given the opportunity?"

I didn't trust him. That couldn't be the whole reason. "Where did you hear about the cure?" I asked. Jackal shrugged.

"My sire told me about it."

"Sire?" I suddenly felt weak. No, it couldn't be. That feeling of recognition, the instant connection, the sudden knowledge that he wasn't just a random vampire. I knew, beyond a doubt, what he was going to say next, and wanted to scream at him to stop.

"Creator? Father figure?" Jackal made an offhand gesture. "The one who Turned me. He found me in the desert, dying of exposure after bandits killed my family, and made me what I am. I'll always be grateful to the stuck-up prick, but we never saw eye to eye on a lot of things. A few months after he

Turned me you could say we…parted ways. He called himself—"

"Kanin," I whispered.

Jackal narrowed his eyes.

"How did you…" He paused, staring at me, as if seeing me
for the first time. Then he threw back his head and laughed.
"Oh, of course! That's the connection! I *knew* I knew you
from somewhere. Kanin, you lying bastard. What happened
to that vow that you wouldn't Turn anyone after me?"

I stared at Jackal, trying to process it. Kanin was our sire.
He'd Turned Jackal, same as me, so that meant we were…
siblings? Was he my brother? I didn't know how this worked
in vampire society. This was the one thing Kanin had ne-
glected to teach me.

"What a shock, huh, sister?" Jackal grinned, utterly de-
lighted. I started, unused to hearing that word. *Sister* implied
we were related. Family. "Well, this is too perfect, isn't it? You
can't turn on me now, right? Not your dear older brother."

"You are not my brother," I growled, coming to a decision.
Jackal raised his eyebrows in mock surprise. "I want nothing
to do with you, not after what you've done." I remembered
Darren, pleading and frightened, right before the rabid pulled
him down. I remembered Dorothy's sightless gaze, staring up
at the sky. "You killed my friends, and I will not forgive you
for that."

"Friends?" The raider king snorted, crossing his arms. "Humans aren't friends, sister. Humans are pets. Food. Minions.
Not friends." He gave me an easy smile. "Oh, they have their
uses, I suppose. They're entertaining sometimes. But even
they realize that we vampires are the superior race. That's

why, deep down, they all want to be like us. Take the minions out there." He jerked his thumb at the window. "I give them freedom, let them come and go and kill as they please, but do they stay away?" He shook his head. "No. They always come back, because they hope that someday, if the curse is lifted, I will reward their service and make them just like me."

"And that is why you want the cure, demon," Jebbadiah said, his body a coiled wire as he faced the vampire lord. "You want to turn your own people into vampires, to make more like yourself. An army of demons, with you at the head."

"I might have offered my people immortality." Jackal shrugged, still talking to me. "What of it? It's a gift I would offer gladly. Our race has lost just as much as theirs, perhaps more." He raised his empty hands and took a step toward me, ignoring Jeb. "Come on, sister, why are you so concerned about one human? They're food, bloodbags. We were meant to rule over the human race, that's why we're superior in every way. Stop fighting your instincts. If Kanin truly sired you, then you have the potential to be a Master, same as me. And I'm not above sharing everything with you. I don't tolerate other vamps in my kingdom, but for you, I'd make an exception." His voice became low, soothing. "Think of what we could create, the two of us. We could have our own little paradise, with our armies and servants and human cattle. We could offer our faithful the gift of immortality, and we would rule this world till the end of time. Our own vampire Eden."

"Never!" Jeb cried and snatched the scalpel from the floor. "Never!" he said again, his face wild. "Blasphemy! I will die before I let that happen!" And he flew at the raider king with the scalpel held high.

Jackal turned as the human lunged, easily grabbing Jeb's wrist and wrenching the blade from his grasp. "Now, now," he growled, baring his fangs as he lifted Jeb off his feet. "You can't die yet. I need you to finish that cure. However, I have no qualms about torturing you a bit to get it."

He flung Jeb backward, and the human crashed into the counter, smashing vials and beakers on his way down. He collapsed amid a rain of glass, and the sweet scent of blood rose up like a geyser.

The Hunger roared. I hurried over to Jeb, who was struggling upright amid the sea of glass, not knowing for sure whether I would help him or attack. Blood trickled down his arms and face, running into his eyes, and he slumped against the counter, his head falling limply to his chest.

"Jeb." I crouched in front of him, desperately trying to ignore the pulse pounding in his throat, the crimson spreading over his shirt. He reached one hand inside his torn coat. Off to the side, I could see Jackal in the same spot, arms folded to his chest, watching us with a smirk on his face.

"Vampire," Jeb whispered through gritted teeth and shoved his hand at me. I caught it, and something small, a tiny strip of dark plastic, dropped from his palm into my hand. I stared at it, frowning. It was about the length of my middle finger, and about as wide.

"For Ezekiel," Jeb murmured, dropping his arm weakly. "Tell him...to take care of our people."

"Jeb—"

"Well, that was entertaining," Jackal said, dusting off his

hands. "But I believe I've run out of patience for the night. So now, my dear sister, I need an answer from you. Will you join me? Will you help me find the cure and populate our world again? Think of what the vampire lords would give us for this information. We could rule them all, if we wanted. What do you say?"

I looked at Jeb, slumped against the counter. I could smell his blood, hear his heart in his chest, feel his cold eyes on me. Judging, hating. Even now, I was still a demon. He would never see me as anything else.

I faced Jackal again. "No," I said, and his eyebrows shot up. I walked around the counter and stood between him and the human, raising my sword. "I'm taking Jeb out of here, whether you like it or not. So get out of my way."

Jackal shook his head sadly. "Pity," he muttered. "We could've had something extraordinary, you know. Two siblings, united by fate, join forces to change their world. What can I say—I'm a romantic at heart, though this story wasn't meant to be." He took a breath and gave a dramatic sigh, smiling at me. "I'm going to have to kill you now."

"Then stop talking," I challenged, sinking into a ready stance, "and get on with it. The sun is going to be up soon."

Jackal bared his fangs, and his golden eyes flashed. "Oh, trust me, sister. This won't take long at all."

Reaching into his duster, he drew forth a long wooden stick, one end coming to a deadly point. My stomach twisted in raw, primal fear, and I stumbled back.

"I thought you might appreciate this," he said, smiling evilly as he stalked forward. "Kanin was the one who taught me, you know. To master my fear, to use it to my advantage." He twirled the stake between his fingers, grinning. "What's the matter, sister? Didn't he teach you the same? Or was your education cut short by our kin who want his head on a platter? How much practice did you get with dear old Kanin, anyway? I'm guessing less than me. I've known our sire a long time."

"Did he teach you how to bore your opponents to sleep? Because I think I missed that lesson."

Jackal roared with laughter. "Oh, I like her," he mused, shaking his head. "It's going to be such a shame to kill you. Are you certain you won't reconsider? These humans can get so dull sometimes."

"No." I glared at him, shaking my head. "I won't let you hurt anyone else."

"Very well." The vampire king shrugged, flipping the stake in his hand. "I gave you the chance. Are you ready, then, sister? Here I come!"

He lunged forward, covering the room in a blink, moving faster than I could see. I slashed at him wildly, but Jackal ducked and stepped into my guard. His hand shot out, grabbing my throat, lifting me off my feet. Before I could react, he slammed me hard onto the counter. Glass flew everywhere again, like a crystal blizzard, and the back of my skull struck the marble edge. Stunned, I lay there for a half second, before Jackal raised his fist and slammed the wooden stake through my stomach.

I arched up, screaming. My sword fell from my hand, clattering to the floor. The pain was unlike anything I had felt before; waves of fire shooting through my body, centered on that point where the wood entered my flesh. I could *feel* the stake inside me, like a fist clenching my intestines, twisting and squeezing. I went to yank it out, but Jackal grabbed my wrist, slamming it back onto the counter, pinning me down.

"Hurts, doesn't it?" he whispered, bending over me, yellow eyes gleaming. "Incredible that a piece of wood shoved through your gut could hurt so bad. I'd rather have a hot poker jammed through my eye into my brain." My body convulsed, and I clenched my jaw to keep back another scream. Jackal continued to hold me down, smiling. "Oh, and if you're wondering why it's getting hard to move, let me enlighten you. Your body is going into shock—it's shutting down, trying to repair itself. A few minutes of this, and you'll be begging me to cut off your head and end it."

I struggled, but my limbs felt sluggish. Jackal had one arm pinned, and though the other was free, the blinding agony in my middle made it impossible to shove him off. I was literally staked to the counter, speared like an animal. Jackal grinned down at me and sadistically twisted the wooden spike in deeper, and this time I couldn't hold back a shriek.

"Bet you wish you'd taken my offer now, huh, sister?" I could barely focus on what he was saying. "Such a pity. I was imagining all the things we could've done, together. But you had to side with the bloodbags, didn't you? Just like Kanin. And now look where he is—captured and tortured by that psychotic freak, Sarren. You must be so proud to have followed the same road as our sire."

I reached back with my free hand, desperately searching for something, anything, to free myself. I forced myself to talk, to keep him distracted. "H-how...did you..."

"Know about Kanin?" Jackal twisted the stake again, and

I arched in helpless agony. "You've been having the same dreams, right? Intense emotion can sometimes be carried to those who share our blood. So Kanin might even be experiencing your pain right now. Isn't that an interesting thought?" He leaned in, smiling. "Hey, Kanin, can you hear me? Do you see what I'm doing to your newest little spawn? What's that?" He tilted his head to one side. "Give her another chance, you say? Don't kill her, like you did your brothers? What an interesting thought. Do you think if I offered again, she would agree?"

My groping fingers found the edge of a beaker, miraculously unbroken, and curled around the neck. With Jackal still leaning in, I brought it forward with all my strength, smashing it against the side of his face. The glass shattered, knocking his head to the side, and Jackal roared.

Spinning back, he yanked me off the counter and swung me over his head. The next thing I knew, I was hurling through the air, and had a split-second glance of the windows, rushing at me, before I struck the glass with a splintering cacophony. Cold Chicago wind hit my face as I hovered in empty air for a moment, then started to plummet.

I twisted desperately, lashing out with both hands, seeking anything solid. My fingers scraped against the wall, and I hit the side of the building, one hand clinging to the ledge below the windows.

I looked up. Jackal loomed above me, the side of his face webbed in crimson, yellow eyes blazing as he glared down. But he was still grinning, his own blood trickling into his mouth, turning his fangs red.

"That," he said in a conversational tone completely different from his expression, "wasn't very smart. Ballsy, but not smart. And after I just offered you a way out, too. Any real vampire would have jumped at the chance. But not you. No, you're still hung up on the humans."

It was difficult to listen to him. The stake was still lodged in my stomach, a constant, throbbing agony, making my limbs weak and unresponsive. My fingers slipped, and I clawed frantically at the ledge.

Jackal reached down and grabbed a large chunk of broken concrete, nearly the size of a human skull, and tossed it easily in one hand. "If you're so fond of these walking bloodbags," he smiled, raising the stone over his head, "then you can join them in hell."

I braced myself, knowing I was about to die. But then, I heard footsteps behind Jackal an instant before Jebbadiah Crosse slammed into the raider king from behind. Howling, Jackal toppled over my head, thrashing and flailing, with the old human clinging doggedly to his back. They both sailed into open air, one screaming and one grimly silent, and dropped away into the darkness.

Stunned, I dangled on the ledge, barely coherent, my mind reeling. In a daze, I reached down and grabbed the stake, yanking it free with a scream. It tumbled from my limp fingers and spun end over end, clinking off the building, until it was lost to the dark waters far below.

Trembling, I was able to pull myself into the building again before my limbs gave out, and I sprawled on the tile in front of the smashed window, staring at the ceiling.

I couldn't move. Pain and Hunger raged within, but I felt hollow, completely drained of life. I was tapped out, done.

There was nothing left to repair the damage done to my body, and I could feel myself fading, wanting to slip into the blackness of hibernation, away from the pain.

I wasn't sure how long I lay there. Somewhere deep within, my body knew it had to move, find shelter. Dawn was coming, and it wouldn't be long before the first rays of the sun peeled the skin from my bones and turned me into a bonfire. I tried to crawl away, to make my limbs respond, but they were so heavy, and I was so tired. Angry now, I struggled to stay awake, raging against the darkness pulling me under, fighting to move. But as the sun crept closer, it seemed inevitable that my time was finally up.

I slumped, exhausted. This was it. I had nothing left. Dawn was less than an hour away, and it would find me here in the open, helpless to resist. Fitting that I should burn as I left this world for good.

"Allison."

The voice came out of nowhere, cutting through the layers of darkness. I stirred weakly, not quite believing. Maybe I was dreaming. Maybe I was already dead. Then someone knelt beside me and pulled me into their lap, cradling me gently. I wanted to pull away, to struggle, but my body simply wasn't listening anymore, and I gave up trying to fight it.

"Oh, God," whispered the voice, familiar and tormented, and I felt something brush the gaping hole in my middle. "Allison, can you hear me? Wake up. Come on, we have to get out of here."

Zeke? I thought, dazed. No, that couldn't be right. Zeke was gone; I'd told him to get out of the city with the others. He should be far away by now. But it *was* his voice, urging me to get up, to open my eyes. I wanted to, but hibernation was pulling at me, drawing me under, and his voice was growing faint. I couldn't answer him. He shifted me in his arms, and I heard a hiss of pain, as the hot scent of blood suddenly filled the air.

"Please let this work," he whispered and pressed something to my mouth.

Warm liquid trickled past my lips. Instinctively, I bit down hard and heard a gasp somewhere above me. I barely noticed it, nor did I care. This was life, and I snatched at it greedily, feeling strength returning to my body, shaking off the sluggishness. The Hunger surged up with a roar, as if realizing how close to death we had come, and I bit down savagely, driving my fangs in deep. There was a stifled cry, and the flesh and muscles against my mouth tightened. It drove me crazy with desire. The blood wasn't flowing fast enough; I wanted to rip and tear the veins open, releasing it in a hot flood. I could feel the pulse at the wrist, throbbing in time with a heartbeat, and wanted to drink and drink until they both faltered and finally stopped.

With a roar, I released the arm and lunged up to the prey's throat, where the blood pumped the hardest and life flowed just below the surface. Baring my fangs, I was about to sink them into his neck, to release that glorious surge of heat and power, when the body went rigid against mine. I heard a heartbeat quicken, thudding loudly in his chest, and I realized.

Zeke! No, I can't do this. Trembling with need and Hunger, I paused, a breath away from his throat, so close I could feel the heat radiating from his skin. Zeke was frozen, his breath coming in gasps, his whole body tense with anticipation and fear. A tiny part of me wanted to draw back, but I couldn't make myself move. Not with his pulse fluttering an inch from my lips, and the sweet, heady scent of blood filling every part of my senses. I leaned closer, and my lips brushed his skin, a soft, featherlight touch, and Zeke gasped.

And then, as I knelt there shaking, trying to find the will-power to pull away, Zeke moved. Just a fraction, a tiny shift that might've gone unnoticed. Except he shivered, took a deep breath and tilted his head back, exposing his throat. Offering it to me. And I couldn't stop myself.

I lunged, sinking my fangs into his neck, driving them deep. Stifling a cry, Zeke stiffened and gripped my arms, arching his back. His blood coursed hot and sweet into my mouth, spreading through me, a slow-moving fire. It tasted of earth and smoke, of heat and passion and strength, of all things Zeke. He breathed my name, a sigh of benediction and long-ing, and I couldn't get close enough, never close enough. His heartbeat roared in my ears, pounding out a savage rhythm, and I lost myself in the moment, cocooned in ecstasy, feeling the essence of this remarkable human swirl through me.

No! Through the Hunger and bloodlust, a tiny, sane part of me emerged, gasping in horror. *This is Zeke!* it cried out. *This is Zeke you're feeding from, Zeke's heartbeat you're listening to. His blood is saving your life, and you're going to kill him if you don't stop now!*

The Hunger roared; it wasn't satisfied, not nearly sated enough. I had nearly been killed and needed more blood to heal completely. But I could not take any more without risk-ing Zeke's life. Zeke was in no position to push me off; I had to control myself. *Stop,* I told myself firmly, clamping down on my Hunger once more. *No more. That is enough!*

With a monumental effort, I pulled away, forcing my fangs to retract. I felt Zeke shudder as my fangs slid from his throat, felt his whole body slump against mine.

For a moment, neither of us moved, and I looked down in horror. Under my assault, Zeke had fallen back and was now resting on his elbows, breathing hard, with me straddling his waist. Blood still oozed from two tiny holes in his neck. He still wore a dazed expression, but when he finally raised his head and looked at me, his eyes were clear.

I froze. He had seen. He had seen me at my worst, a vampire in a snarling, foaming blood frenzy. A monster who had almost killed him on instinct. Until now, even though he'd known what I was, I had at least appeared more or less human. I could only imagine what he thought of me now.

Zeke stared at me, and under his intense gaze I wanted to crawl into a deep hole, but also to pounce on him again, to drive him back to the floor and finish what I'd started. I could feel him shaking underneath me, his heart thudding against my palms.

"Zeke...I..." I didn't know what to say. What *could* I say? Sorry I almost killed you? That I couldn't control the demon? That I wanted to keep drinking until you were an empty, lifeless husk? *I didn't want you to see me like this,* I thought despairingly, closing my eyes. *Out of everyone, I didn't want you to see the monster.*

"Just..." Zeke paused, letting out a breath, as if his body had seized up, and he could just now breathe again. "Just answer me this one question," he said in a shaky voice. "Does this mean...will I...this doesn't mean I'm going to Turn, does it?"

I immediately shook my head. "No," I whispered, glad for something to say. "The process is different. You would have to take some of my blood to become a vampire." *I would also have to nearly kill you.*

He sighed, and some of the tension left his body. "Then... I'm glad I came back."

I rose, scrambling away from him, and Zeke rolled upright and faced me, pale from cold and pain and blood loss. I turned away, staring at the shattered windows, watching embers from the fires dance on the wind. I felt his gaze on my back, and shame burned through me like the hottest fire.

"Why did you come back?" I whispered. "I told you to keep going. You shouldn't have..."

"I couldn't leave you," Zeke said. "Not after everything you did for us. For me. I had to come back." I heard his footsteps, felt him step up beside me. From the corner of my eye, I watched him gaze at the city, watching the flames. "The others are safe," he announced. "They're at the edge of the city, waiting for us. We should go. I guess..." And his voice faltered, suspiciously close to breaking, and he swallowed hard. "I guess Jeb won't be coming back with us."

Jeb. I felt a blinding stab of guilt. And a hollow emptiness, knowing I had failed them both. "Zeke," I said, finally turning to face him. "Jeb is..."

"I saw," he whispered, gesturing to the broken glass, his face tight. "I saw...what he did, when you were beneath the window. I was coming up to the building when the bodies... fell."

My stomach felt cold. "Did…did Jeb…"

"No." He shook his head and closed his eyes, as if trying to squeeze out the memory. "There was nothing I could do for him."

"I'm so sorry." Words were inadequate. I looked at his trembling shoulders, the fists clenched at his sides, and wished I dared to pull him close for just a moment. "I tried."

"Not your fault." His voice broke at the end, and he took a deep breath. "It was his decision. He chose to end it that way, even if it meant saving a…" He paused, raked a hand through his hair. "You must've done something to make an impression," he finished softly. "I knew him for fourteen years, and he never once changed his mind."

You're wrong, I thought. *It wasn't me he was thinking of tonight, it was you.* Reaching into my pocket, I drew out the small plastic strip Jebbadiah had given me. "He wanted you to have this," I said, and Zeke turned. "He said you would know what to do with it."

He took it gently, almost reverently, staring as he held it up. "Do you know what it is?" I asked after a moment.

"Yes." Looking around the room, he hurried over to the desk in the opposite corner and shoved the plastic strip into a slot on the side of the computer. I was amazed that he knew how to use it, even more so when he fiddled around with the keyboard and pulled up several files on the screen.

"Yes," Zeke muttered, blue eyes flickering across the screen. "This is all their research. All the information they had on the plague and the rabids and the virus. It lists everything—their methods, the tests they ran on the vampires, everything. If we can get this to Eden, there might be a real chance of finding a cure." He sighed and yanked the strip out of the computer, raking a hand through his hair again. "If we can ever find it. We still have no idea where it is."

I looked at the green board, the one with the dusty white letters scrawled across its surface, and the map on the other side. Frowning, I walked up and ripped the map from the board, narrowing my eyes. Cities had been circled and crossed out, notes scrawled along the edges in what was probably Jackal's handwriting. But one place stood out, one area had been circled several times, a question mark hovering beside it.

"I think we do."

CHAPTER 24

The Floating Pit was in full blazing glory when Zeke and I left Jackal's tower, a huge fireball burning against the night. Several smaller fires burned around it as the wind carried live embers to empty rooftops and through shattered windows, setting them aflame. We met no resistance on our way down; the flooded streets and walkways were remarkably clear as we hurried through the city, all attention being diverted to the huge inferno that lit up the sky.

Zeke was silent as we fled Jackal's tower, brooding and drawn into himself. In a single day, he'd lost a best friend and a father and was now expected to lead in Jeb's place. I wished I could talk to him, but there'd be time for that later. Right now, we had to escape the city and get everyone to safety. If such a thing existed.

The Hunger still raged within, gnawing at my insides, urging me to pounce on the human in front of me and tear him open. Zeke's blood had helped with the worst of the damage, but I was still starving. Worse, the sky over the buildings was growing lighter. The sun would be up soon, and we had to be clear of Jackal's city before then or I'd be toast.

However, as we hurried along the bridges and catwalks, I realized we had another problem. The Floating Pit sat between us and our exit, and right now it was surrounded by a horde of Jackal's men, not to mention the firestorm sweeping through the buildings around it.

"Where are the others?" I asked Zeke as we crouched inside a half-crumbled building, watching long streamers of fire snap in the wind. My vampire instincts were screaming at me to go the other direction, but the only way out was through that firestorm.

Next time, try burning your bridges after *you've crossed them, Allison.*

"They're just over the bridge," Zeke replied, observing the flames worriedly. "At least, that's where I left them. I hope they're still okay."

"How did you get them out?"

Zeke pointed to the elevated tracks circling the district, passing, I noticed, right next to the theater. "We followed the tracks," he said, sweeping his finger around. "It takes you right out of the city, like you said. Once we got to the barge, we sort of…hijacked one of the vans." A shadow crossed his face, guilt that he'd had to kill yet again. "The others are waiting just outside the city," he continued, "hidden, and safe. If we can get to them, we're home free."

"Well," I muttered, turning back to the fire, feeling the heat from the flames, even here, "we're going to have to get through that. Ready for another swim?"

Zeke nodded solemnly. "Lead the way."

Entering the water, we swam through the flooded streets, passing between the burning buildings. The air was thick with smoke, and flaming rubble toppled into the waters around us, hissing as it struck the surface. I concentrated on moving forward, ignoring the canyons of fire around me, ignoring the Hunger that still cramped my stomach, and the warm body next to mine.

As we passed under a walkway, Zeke hanging a little behind, footsteps echoed above us, and a raider peered over the railing.

"You!" he shouted, pulling the gun from his belt. "I saw you in the Pit! You're the bitch who set it on fire!"

A shot rang out, and pain exploded through my chest with a spray of blood. I heard Zeke cry out as the water closed over my head.

Anger and Hunger roared to life. I was sick of being shot, stabbed, burned, gutted, staked and thrown out windows. Snarling, I exploded back to the surface, grabbed the raider by the belt and dragged him over the edge. We hit the water with a splash and sank like a rock, the human thrashing frantically in my grip. He stiffened as I plunged my fangs into his throat and stopped moving by the time we hit the bottom.

I finished feeding and hesitated, tempted to leave him for the fishes and the worms. But Zeke would be waiting up top, and he had seen me pull the raider into the water. With a growl, I grabbed the limp body and struck back for the surface. He might still succumb to hypothermia and blood loss, but at least I wouldn't leave him to drown.

Zeke gaped as I broke the surface, shaking water from my

ears. "You're alive," he gasped, teeth chattering with cold. "But...you took a shot right to the chest. I was right there and I saw..."

"It takes a lot to kill me," I muttered. "Well, scratch that. It takes a lot to kill me again. I'm already dead, remember?"

Swimming beneath the walkway, I heaved the raider's limp body out of the water onto the edge of the platform. His head lolled to the side, revealing two oozing bite marks that I hadn't sealed. Zeke's gaze followed mine, and his face tightened, but he didn't say anything.

I could feel him thinking, however, as we swam through the streets and finally reached the elevated tracks leading out of Jackal's territory. Dripping, shivering, he followed me up the framework to the top, grabbing my hand as I pulled him onto the planks. An icy wind rushed along the surface, and I was struck by how miserable he looked, wounded, wet and freezing, with his hair and clothes plastered to his body. Yet his eyes still gleamed with iron determination as he gazed across the bridge, only looking forward. Unlike me, who turned and glanced back toward the city and the fires that raged through it.

So many gone. So many lives lost. People I had known, talked to. Dorothy, Darren, Jeb...I hadn't been able to save them. I swallowed hard and rubbed my eyes. When had I started caring so much? Before Kanin Turned me, death was something I faced every day. People died, often; it was just how the world worked. I thought that, after the deaths of my old gang and Stick's betrayal, I wouldn't worry about anyone else. And yet, here I was, a vampire, wishing I could have saved the very person who hated me most.

"Allison." Zeke's voice made me turn around. He shivered in the cold wind but stood tall and unbowed at the edge of the tracks. "The sun is coming up," he said, nodding to the tops of the buildings. "We have to get you and everyone else to shelter soon. Come on."

I nodded and wordlessly followed him, sprinting down the tracks, over the bridge leading out of the city and into the ruins of Old Chicago, leaving Jackal's territory behind to burn.

"HELLO, OLD FRIEND," Sarren crooned, bringing his scarred face very close, so that I could see the madness raging in his black eyes. "You can't go to sleep yet, I'm afraid. What fun would that be? I have the whole night planned out." He chuckled and stepped back, watching me hang limply from the chains. At least I was no longer upside down, though I suspected one of my arms was still broken. It was difficult to tell; my body had been broken, healed and systematically broken again; the only thing I was aware of now was the Hunger.

Sarren smiled. "Hungry, are you? I can't imagine how that feels— it's been four days. Oh, wait. Yes, I can. They used to starve us before an experiment, so we would attack whatever beast they put in our rooms. Did you know that?"

I did not answer. I had not spoken for the entire length of my captivity, and I would not begin now. Nothing I said would sway this madman; he was only looking for ways to torment me further, to break me. And I would not give him that, not as long as my mind was my own.

Tonight, however, he might torture me all he wanted; it would not come close to the pain that I had endured earlier, the visions of my two offspring killing each other far from my reach. Two children that I had failed.

Allison. Forgive me, I wish I could have prepared you better. What were the odds that you would meet your blood brother so far from your origins?

"You seem distracted tonight, old friend." Sarren smiled and picked up a scalpel, holding it up to his face. His tongue flicked out, sliding along the surface. *"Let us see if we can't bring your mind back to where it's supposed to be. I've heard blood tastes the best straight off the blade. Why don't we see if that is true?"*

I closed my eyes, preparing myself. I would not survive much longer; already I could feel my sanity slipping, succumbing to pain and madness. My only comfort was that at least Sarren had found me first, that I was taking the brunt of his hate, and that my offspring were safe from his demented clutches.

Then the blade found my skin, and all thoughts melted away and turned to pain.

"KANIN!"

Sand flooded my mouth, clogging my nose and the back of my throat. Spitting and choking, I bolted upright, clawing through layers of dirt until I reached the surface.

Zeke rose quickly from where he sat against a half-buried rail. Bewildered, I gazed around, trying to remember where we were. A few yards away, waves rose and fell against a strip of white sand, making hissing noises as they returned to the lake. Behind us, Chicago's ruined skyscrapers crowded the skyline, threatening to topple into the sand.

Pieces of the night came back to me. Zeke and I had found the others across the bridge where he'd left them, sitting in one of the very same vans used to kidnap them. With only minutes till sunrise, we had torn off down the streets, putting as much distance as we could between ourselves and the

raiders, until we hit the coast. With nothing on my mind
except getting out of the sun, I'd buried myself in the sand
moments before the light peeked over the water and instantly
blacked out.

"You all right?" Zeke asked, his hair whipping about in
the wind. He looked stronger this evening, not quite as pale,
wearing a heavier jacket over his tattered clothes. "More
nightmares?"

"Yeah," I muttered, though I knew it wasn't a dream. It
was Kanin. In trouble. "Where are the others?" I asked. "Are
they all right?"

Zeke gestured to the building behind us, where the truck
had been parked near the door, sand piling around its tires.
Every so often, the wind scoured away the dusty coating,
showing spots of pavement beneath. "Caleb is sick and Teresa
sprained her ankle," he replied, "but other than that, they
seem fine. Healthwise, anyway. It's amazing, really. That no
one else was seriously hurt."

A slender figure appeared in the doorway, watching Zeke
and me. When she saw me gazing at her, however, she quickly
vanished back inside.

"They're afraid of me, aren't they?"

Zeke sighed, scrubbing a hand through his hair. "They've
been taught their whole lives that vampires are predators and
demons," he said, not apologetic, or defensive, just matter-
of-fact. "Yes. They're afraid of you, despite everything I told
them. And Ruth…"

"Hates me," I finished, shrugging. "Not much of a change,
there."

"She kept insisting I dig up your body and kill you while

you were sleeping." Zeke frowned, shaking his head. "She even tried to get Jake to do it when I refused. We had to have...a talk." His face fell, and he looked away. "She's scared. They all are. After what they've been through, I don't blame them. But she won't get in your way or cause trouble," he continued in a firm voice. "And the others have accepted that you'll be traveling with us for now. You're still coming, right? You'll still see us there?"

"To Eden?" I shrugged again and looked away, toward the water, so I didn't see his face. Looking at him would make it that much harder. "I don't know, Zeke. I don't think Eden is the type of place that will welcome someone like me." Kanin's face swam across my mind again, tortured and in agony. "And I have...something I have to do. Someone to find." *I owe him that.*

"They'll be all right with you now." I finally gave Zeke a sideways glance. "You can get them there. According to Jackal's map, Eden isn't far."

"Forget the others then." Zeke stepped toward me, not touching, but close. "*I'm* asking you. Please. Will you see us through the final stretch?"

I looked at him, at his pale, earnest face, at his blue eyes, quietly pleading, and felt my resolve crumble. Kanin needed me, but...Zeke needed me, too. I wanted to stay with him, despite knowing that this—whatever we had—would only end in tragedy. I was a vampire, and he was still very much human. Whatever my feelings, I couldn't separate them from the Hunger. Being around Zeke put him in danger, and yet, I was willing to risk it, even his life, just to be close to him.

And that—that dependency—scared me more than anything I'd ever faced. Allie the Fringer knew all too well: the closer you got to someone, the more it would destroy you when they were inevitably gone.

But we'd come so far; it didn't feel right, not seeing this through to the end. "All right," I murmured, hoping Kanin could hang on a little longer. *I'll be there soon, Kanin, I swear.* "To Eden, then. Let's finish what we started."

Zeke smiled, and I returned it. Together, we walked up the beach, to where the group waited for us in the shadow of the building.

SEVEN PEOPLE HUDDLED in the back of the van, silent, terrified. Two young adults, two older people and three kids, one who kept coughing and sniffling into his sleeve. Zeke drove, and I sat next to him in the passenger's seat, gazing out the window. Nobody spoke much. I offered to switch seats once, to let someone else sit up front, but was met with horrified silence. Nobody wanted the vampire in the back with them. So Zeke and I remained up front, the weight of words unsaid lingering between us.

We drove east along the seemingly endless lake, following the road and Jackal's map, keeping a wary eye on the city fading behind us. I kept glancing at the side mirrors, waiting for headlights to break over the road and come swarming toward us. It didn't happen. The road remained dark and empty, the landscape silent except for the hiss of falling waves, as if we were the only people alive.

"We're getting low on fuel," Zeke muttered after several hours of driving. He tapped the dashboard of the van, frowning, then sighed. "How far from Eden do you think we are?"

"I don't know," I replied, gazing at the map again. "All I know is we have to follow the road east until we get there."

"God, I hope it's really there," Zeke whispered, gripping the steering wheel, his eyes hard. "Please, please, let it be there. This time, let it be real."

We drove through another dead city on the edge of a lake, passing crumbling skyscrapers, the ruins of old buildings and an endless number of cars clogging the cracked streets. Weaving through a choked sea of rusting vehicles, I wondered how chaotic it would've been in the time before, how people ever got anywhere without crashing into each other.

Zeke suddenly pulled the van to a stop alongside a faded red truck and shut off the engine. I blinked at him. "Why are we stopping?"

"We're almost out of gas. There's a hose and a gas container in the back—I saw them when we hijacked the van. I figure I can siphon something from a few cars, at least. Watch my back?"

I nodded. Zeke half turned, poking his head toward the back as the other passengers stirred and muttered uneasily. "Everyone, stay put. We're just stopping for fuel. We'll be on our way soon, okay?"

"I'm hungry," muttered Caleb, sniffling. Zeke smiled at him.

"We'll take a break soon, I promise. Let's just get out of the city first."

I watched Zeke, fascinated, as he opened a lid on the side of a vehicle, stuck the hose in, and sucked on the end. The first two cars yielded nothing, but on the third try, Zeke suddenly choked, turned and spit out a mouthful of clear liquid, before sticking the hose into the plastic container. Wiping his mouth, he leaned against another car and watched the gas trickle into the canister.

I walked up beside him and leaned back against the car door, our shoulders barely touching. "How're you holding up?"

He shrugged. "All right, I guess." He sighed, rubbing his arm. "It still hasn't hit me yet, you know? I keep expecting Jeb to give me directions, tell me where we're going next, when we should stop." He sighed again, heavily, looking out toward the city. "But he's gone. And it's all up to me now."

I hesitated, then reached down and took his hand, lightly weaving our fingers together. He squeezed them gratefully.

"Thank you," he murmured, so soft I barely caught it. "I wouldn't...be doing nearly so well if you weren't here."

"We're almost there," I told him. "Just a few more miles, I think. And you can relax. No more vampires, no more rabids, no more raider kings hunting you down. You'll finally be able to breathe."

"If Eden really exists." He sounded so melancholy I turned to stare at him.

"What's this?" I asked, giving him a challenging smile. "Don't tell me you're losing your faith, Ezekiel Crosse."

His mouth twitched into a smirk. "You're right," he said, pushing himself off the car. "We can't give up now. Let's get there first, and see what happens next." He bent down and picked up the container, peering at the contents. "That's... what, about three gallons? Two and a half? Think we can get a few more before we leave?"

"Zeke," I growled, gazing down the road. Zeke's gaze followed mine, and he went perfectly still.

A spindly, emaciated creature crouched atop a dead car about a hundred yards away, its white skin pale in the moonlight. It hadn't seen us yet, but I saw another rabid skitter behind a truck, and the one atop the car snarled and hopped down after it, vanishing into the sea of vehicles.

"Let's get out of here," Zeke murmured, and we hurried back toward the van. Grimly, Zeke poured the gas into the fuel tank, while I scanned the darkness and ocean of cars for rabids. Nothing moved, but I heard scuttling noises between the vehicles, and knew they were out there. It was only a matter of time before they saw us.

"Done," he muttered, slamming the lid shut. Tossing me the gas can, we moved toward the front, but suddenly, the side door slid open and Caleb stumbled out, rubbing his eyes.

"I'm tired of sitting," he announced. "When can we stop to eat?"

"Caleb, get inside," Zeke ordered, but at that moment, a piercing shriek rent the air as a rabid hurled itself over a nearby car and lunged for him.

I dived forward, grabbed Caleb around the waist and spun, hugging him to my body. The rabid hit me hard, ripping at me with its claws, sinking jagged fangs into my neck. I hissed in pain, hunching my shoulders to protect Caleb as the rabid clawed frantically at my back.

Ruth suddenly shot out of the van, screaming, clutching a rusty tire iron. She swung it wildly, striking the rabid in the arm, and the monster whirled on her with a hiss.

"Get away from my brother!" Ruth shrieked and hit its

cheek with a satisfying crack. The rabid staggered, roared and lashed out, curved talons catching the girl in the stomach, ripping through cloth and skin, tearing her open. Blood spattered the side of the van. As she fell back, gasping, Zeke lunged over the hood of the van, swung his machete and buried it in the rabid's neck.

The monster collapsed, mouth working frantically, as howls and wails began to rise around us. I tossed Caleb in the van, ignoring his frantic cries, as Zeke scooped up Ruth and dived inside with her. Slamming the side door, I leaped over the hood and swung into the driver's seat, yanking the door shut just as a rabid bounced off the glass, leaving a bloody spiderweb of cracks.

Another rabid leaped on the hood, hissing, as I turned the keys Zeke had left in the ignition and threw the van into Drive. The rabid smacked into the windshield, rolled off, and suddenly I had a clear shot at the open road. As I slammed my foot onto the pedal, the van leaped forward and screeched away down the sidewalk, striking a few rabids, as we escaped the city and fled into the night.

WE BURIED RUTH just before dawn, on a small strip of farmland about an hour outside the city. She was conscious up until the end, surrounded by her family, cradled gently in Zeke's arms the whole time. I concentrated on driving the van, trying to ignore the smell of blood soaking everything, and the soft, hopeless sobs coming from the back. Sometime near the end, I heard her whisper to Zeke that she loved him, and I listened to her heartbeat as it grew softer and softer, and finally stopped altogether.

"Allison," Zeke called a few minutes later, over Caleb's hysterical sobbing and pleas for his sister to wake up, "it'll be dawn soon. Look for a place to stop."

I pulled to a stop in front of an abandoned farmhouse, and even though dawn was close, I helped Zeke dig the grave in the hard clay outside the building. And with everyone gathered silently, Zeke said a few words for everyone we'd lost: Ruth and Dorothy, Darren and Jeb. His voice broke a few times, but he remained calm and matter-of-fact, even with the tears streaming down his face.

I couldn't stay for the whole thing. With the sun threatening to peek over the horizon, I met Zeke's eyes over the mound of earth, and he nodded. Drawing away from the much smaller group, I found a bare patch of soil behind the farmhouse and sank into the earth as Zeke's quiet, grief-stricken voice followed me down into the darkness.

CHAPTER 25

Blissfully, my sleep was free of nightmares this time. But that didn't quell my sense of urgency as I pushed myself free of the earth the next night, shaking dust from my hair and clothes. Kanin was still out there, somewhere. In trouble. Maybe he couldn't be saved. Maybe the eerie silence in my dreams meant he was already dead. But I couldn't leave him. I had to try to find him, at least.

Soon.

Picking a clump of clay from my hair, I turned and found Caleb staring up at me.

His eyes were red and swollen, his face dirty and streaked with old tears, smudges where he'd wiped at his face. But he stood there, watching me with dry, hooded eyes, solemn and unafraid.

"They put Ruth in the ground," he said at last, as a faint growl of thunder echoed somewhere in the distance. Behind him, lightning flickered, showing a storm was on its way.

I nodded, wondering what he was getting at.

"But you came out," Caleb said, his gaze flicking to the disturbed earth behind me. He padded up, staring into my face, his eyes hopeful. "You came out, so maybe…Ruth will come back, too? We could wait. We could wait until she comes back, just like you."

"No, Caleb." I shook my head sadly. "I'm different. I'm a vampire." I paused, to see if that frightened him. It didn't. Kneeling, I took his hand, staring at the grubby fingers. "Ruth was human," I whispered. "Just like you. And Zeke. And everyone. She isn't coming back."

Caleb's lip trembled. Without warning, he lunged at me, striking me with his small fists, beating on my shoulders. "Then make her a vampire!" he sobbed, as tears began welling in his eyes again. I flinched, more startled than anything, not knowing what to do. "Make her come back!" he screamed at me. "Bring her back right now!"

"Hey, hey! Caleb!" And Zeke was there, grabbing the boy's wrist, swinging him into his arms. Caleb wailed and buried his face in Zeke's shoulder, still pounding his chest weakly.

Zeke held him until the tantrum quieted, then lowered his head and murmured something in his ear. Caleb sniffled.

"I'm not hungry," he mumbled.

"You should go eat something," Zeke insisted, brushing back Caleb's hair. His own eyes were red, and dark circles crouched beneath them, as if he hadn't slept at all. Caleb sniffled and shook his head, sticking out his bottom lip. "No?" Zeke asked, smiling faintly. "You know, Teresa found apple jelly in the basement. And peach jam. It's really sweet."

A tiny gleam of interest from Caleb. "What's apple jelly?"

"Go ask her to give you some," Zeke said, putting him down. "Everyone is in the kitchen. Better hurry, or Matthew might eat it all."

Caleb padded off, sullen, but at least his outburst seemed to have run its course. Zeke watched until he vanished around the corner, then sighed, rubbing a hand over his eyes.

"Have you slept at all?" I asked.

"Maybe an hour." Zeke lowered his arm, not looking at me, gazing over the tangled, choked fields beyond the fence. "Found some fuel in the garage," he said, "and there's about a dozen cans of preserves in the cellar, so we should be good for another night." He sighed, bowing his head. "You told Caleb that Ruth wasn't coming back?"

I stiffened, then nodded. "He needed to hear it. I didn't want to give him false hope, that his sister could still be alive. That would just be cruel."

"I know." Zeke finally turned, and the bleakness on his face shocked me. He looked years older, lines and circles around his eyes and mouth that weren't there before. "I was trying to tell him earlier, but…" He shrugged. "I guess he needed to hear it from you."

"You know this wasn't your fault."

"Everyone keeps telling me that." Zeke hunched his shoulders against the rising wind. "I wish I could believe it." He raked his hair out of his face, shaking his head. "I wish I could believe…that we're going to make it. That Eden is still out there, waiting, after all this time. That there's *anywhere* on this godforsaken earth that is safe." He turned and kicked a bottle lying in the weeds, sending it smashing into the side of the house. Green shards exploded, flying everywhere, and I blinked, watching him sadly.

Zeke tilted his head back, glaring up at the clouds. "Give me a sign," he whispered, closing his eyes. "A hint. Anything. Anything to tell me I'm doing the right thing. That I shouldn't give up and stop looking for the impossible, before everyone around me is dead!"

As expected, there was no answer except the wind and the approaching storm. Zeke sighed, dropping his head, and turned to me with eyes that had gone completely blank. "Let's go," he muttered, starting forward. "We should get on the road before the storm hits."

I glanced back at the wall of clouds rolling in off the lake. Something glimmered against the black, a brief flash of movement, and I squinted, waiting for it to reappear. "Zeke," I whispered, gazing over the fence. "Look."

He turned, narrowing his eyes. For a moment, we stood there, the wind rising around us, forks of lightning slashing across the horizon. Thunder growled threateningly, and the first drops of rain began to fall.

Then, far in the distance, a beacon cut through the darkness, a beam of light, scuttling across the clouds. It vanished momentarily, only to reappear again a few seconds later, a spotlight turned toward the sky.

Zeke blinked. "What is that?"

"I don't know," I murmured, stepping up behind him. "But—and I could be wrong—it looks like it's coming from the east."

"Where Eden is supposed to be," Zeke finished in a near whisper and took off, jogging around the side of the house without looking back. I heard him calling for the others and joined them, feeling the excitement and nervousness as everyone scrambled to leave. And I hoped, desperately, that at the end of this road, they would find what they were looking for.

WE FOLLOWED THE LAKE EDGE, keeping our eyes on the faint beam of light over the trees. No one spoke, but the excitement from several rapidly beating hearts was easy to hear. Rain pounded the windows, and Zeke squinted through the glass, his gaze focused and intent. Though it was difficult to see through the storm, the light never stopped, a sliver of hope glimmering through the rain, urging us on.

The road narrowed, weaving its way through overgrown forest and woods, sometimes vanishing altogether as grass, dirt and brush crowded the edges and broke through the pavement. Dead vehicles began appearing through the trees, scattered on the side of the road or abandoned in the ditch. Uneasiness stirred, and my instincts jangled a warning. It seemed to me that these cars could have belonged to others drawn to that light, following the same promises of hope and safety. Only, they never made it. Something had stopped them before they reached their Eden. Something that was probably waiting for us, as well.

Rabids are always drawn to places that have lots of people. Kanin's voice echoed in my head. *That's why the ruins just outside vampire cities are so dangerous. Because the rabids have discovered where their prey is, and though they can't get over the walls, they never stop trying. Of course, they're not intelligent enough to set up complex*

traps, but they have been known to ambush people or even vehicles,
if they know where their prey is going.

Zeke suddenly slammed on the brakes. Caleb and Bethany
cried out as the van skidded a few feet in the road, then came
to a lurching halt, still in the center of the pavement. Peering
through the glass, my blood ran cold.

A tree lay across the road, huge and thick and gnarled, much
too big to go around, over or through. From the storm and
the amount of rain and wind, it might've fallen on its own. It
might've been uprooted and had crashed from entirely natural causes.

And yet…I knew it had not.

Zeke looked at me, his face pale. "They're out there, aren't
they?"

I nodded.

"How long until sunrise?"

I checked my internal clock. "It's not even midnight."

He swallowed. "If we sit here…"

"They'll tear the van apart, trying to get at us." I looked
down the road, searching for the light. It shone above the
branches, tantalizingly close. "We're going to have to make
a run for it."

Zeke closed his eyes. I could see he was shaking. Opening them, he stole a quick glance at the back, at Caleb and
Bethany, Silas, Teresa, Matthew and Jake. The last of our
party. The only ones left. Leaning in close, he lowered his
voice. "They'll never make it," he whispered. "Teresa has a
bad leg, and the kids…they can't outrun those things. I can't
leave them."

I glanced out the window. Beyond the headlights was only

rain and darkness, but I knew they were out there, watching us. *Leave them,* my survival instincts whispered. *They're lost. Get Zeke out of there and forget the others; there's no saving them, not this time.*

I growled, deep in my throat. We had come this far. We just had to go a little farther. "Don't worry about the rabids," I muttered, grabbing the door handle. "Just concentrate on the others. Get them to safety as quickly as you can and don't look back."

"Allison—"

I put my hand over his, feeling him tremble under my fingers. "Trust me."

He met my gaze. Then, not caring of our audience or the gasps that echoed from the back, he leaned forward and pressed his lips to mine. It was a desperate kiss, full of longing and sorrow, as if he was saying goodbye. "Be careful," he whispered, pulling away. And I suddenly wished we could've had more time, that the world didn't consume every bit of light and goodness it found, that people like Zeke and I could somehow find our Eden.

I turned, opened the car door and stepped out into the rain.

Hopping the tree, I drew my sword, seeing my shadow stretch out before me in the headlights. *All right, monsters,* I thought, walking forward. *I know you're there. Let's get on with it.*

The storm swirled around me, pelting me with rain, whipping at my coat and hair. Lightning flashed, turning the world white, revealing nothing but empty woods and shadows.

It flickered again, and suddenly, the trees were full of them, hundreds of dead white eyes glaring at me as they shuffled forward. There were so many; like ants swarming out of a nest, and the air filled with their eerie wails and cries.

I gripped my blade and took one deliberate step forward.

With piercing shrieks, the rabids flung themselves at me, a pale, chaotic swarm. Howling a battle cry, I lunged to the edge of the road and met the first wave with flashing steel, cutting through limbs and splitting bodies in two. Claws slashed at me, tearing through my coat, into my skin. Blood misted on the damp air, both mine and the tainted blood of the monsters, but I didn't feel any pain. Roaring, I bared my fangs and surged into the wave, splitting them apart. Everything dissolved into a chaotic blur of blood and fangs and slashing limbs, and I lost myself in complete, savage destruction.

A scream drew my attention to the van. Zeke was pulling Caleb out the side door, when a rabid clawed its way out of the earth next to the van and slashed at them with curved talons. With one arm, Zeke swung Caleb out of its reach, bringing the machete down with the other. The blade struck the monster's skull, burying deep, and the rabid jerked away, twitching. I started toward them when suddenly, through the trees, the earth roiled, and another wave of monsters erupted from the ground. Eyes blazing, they gave chilling wails and flung themselves at the van.

"Zeke!" I screamed, cutting a rabid's head from its neck, even as the claws ripped a gash in my sleeve, "get them out of there now!"

"Go!" Zeke bellowed, and the tiny group of six humans scrambled over the tree and took off down the road. Silent Jake led them, clutching the ax he'd picked up from our last stop, but the others were either too small or too old to carry weapons. Zeke hovered by the van, waiting until everyone was gone, before turning to flee, as well.

A rabid came hurling out of nowhere, slamming into him before he could move, pinning him to the hood of the van. Jaws snapping, it lunged for Zeke's throat, but Zeke's hand shot out, clamping around its neck, holding the teeth away. The rabid hissed in fury and ripped at him with its claws, tearing at his chest, and for a horrible moment, I flashed back to that night in the rain, where I had died, holding the monster away from my throat while its claws tore my life away.

"Zeke!" Breaking away from the horde, I started toward him. But Zeke brought his foot up, kicking the rabid in the chest, hurling it away. His blue eyes met mine through the rain.

"Help the others!" he spat, as the rabid bounced to its feet with a hiss and sprang at him again. It met the blade of a machete, slashing across its face, and lurched back with a shriek, blood pouring across its eyes. "Allison!" Zeke spared me a split-second glance. "Forget about me—help the others! Please!"

I watched Zeke bring his weapon up, the front of his shirt drenched with blood, watched the rabid close on him, and made my decision.

Whirling, I sprang after the rest of the group, catching up to them just as a pair of rabids lunged for Bethany, cutting them down before they touched her. But the circle was closing in; everywhere I looked, rabids were coming at us, leaping through the trees and rising out of the ground. Several jumped forward, but I sliced them apart before they reached the rest of the group. Still, it was only a matter of time before numbers overwhelmed us.

From the corner of my eye, I could see them, huddled together. Teresa and Silas had the kids between them, sobbing, and Jake stood behind me with his ax, silent and grim. Zeke was gone. The rabids were coming, wave upon wave of them. There was nowhere left to go.

Run, my vampire instincts whispered. *The rabids don't want you; they want the humans. You can still get out of this alive. Run now!*

The circle of rabids closed in, hissing and snarling. I glanced behind me at the small group of humans, then turned to face the sea of death, edging forward from all sides.

Zeke, I thought, swinging my blade up one last time, *this is for you.*

Baring my fangs, I roared a battle cry and lunged forward.

Light pierced the darkness, sudden and blinding. The rabids froze, whirling around, as a monstrous vehicle roared through the crowds, crushing bodies and flinging them aside. It skidded to a halt a few feet away, and several uniformed humans leaned out over the top and sent a hail of machinegun fire into the mob.

Rabids shrieked and howled as the roar of bullets joined the deafening cacophony, tearing through flesh, shattering concrete and making dirt and trees explode. I cringed back with the others, huddled as close to the truck as I could, hoping a stray bullet wouldn't hit anyone by mistake. Rabids pounced toward the vehicle but were cut down before they reached the massive tires, twitching as they were riddled with holes. There was a shout, and something small flew through the air, thrown by one of the humans. A few seconds later an explosion rocked the ground, sending rabids flying.

Snarling, the rest of the pack turned and fled, bounding back into the forest or burying themselves into the earth. In a few seconds, the whole pack had disappeared, and the night was still except for the rain.

I tensed as a human leaped from the top of the truck and stalked toward us. He was big and muscular, dressed in a uniform of black and green, and held a very, very large gun in both hands.

"We saw your lights down the road," he said, matter-of-factly. "Sorry we couldn't get here sooner. Is anyone hurt?"

Dazed, I stared at him. Other soldiers were springing down from the vehicle now, wrapping the group in blankets, leading them back to the truck. One of them picked Bethany up after throwing a blanket around her, and another helped Teresa hobble over the pavement. The lead soldier watched them a moment, then turned back to me.

"Is this everyone?" he asked briskly. "Once we leave, we're not coming back if we can help it. Is this your whole party?"

"No!" I gasped and whirled around, scanning the road behind us. "No, there's one more. We left him by the van—he could still be alive."

I started forward, but he grabbed my arm.

"He's dead, girl." The soldier's eyes were sympathetic, as I turned on him furiously. "If he fell behind with the rabids, he's dead. I'm sorry. But we should get those who are alive to Eden."

"I'm not leaving him," I snarled, yanking my arm out of his grip. My throat burned with anger at the unfairness of it all. That Zeke could come so far, get this close, only to fall at the end. I thought of the data he was carrying, the precious information that could save the human race, and backed away from the soldier. "You don't know him—he could still be alive. If he's dead—" I clenched my fists, my voice breaking a little. "I still have to know. But I'm not leaving him behind. We've come too far for that."

"I know it's hard—" the soldier began but was interrupted.

"Sarge?" One of the soldiers peered down from the truck. "Sergeant Keller, I think you'd better see this."

I whirled around. A lone figure was walking steadily down the road toward us, one hand holding his shoulder, the other gripping a machete at his side. He was covered in blood, clothes torn, and every step looked painful, but he was alive.

Relief shot through me. Breaking away from Keller, I ran to him, catching him just as he staggered, dropping his weapon to the pavement. He was shaking, his skin cold, and he reeked of blood, both his own and the rabids'. I felt his heartbeat, thumping frantically in his chest, the most beautiful sound I'd ever heard. One arm snaked around me, holding us together, and he rested his forehead against mine.

"Zeke," I whispered, feeling his shaky breath on my skin, the tension lining his back and shoulders. He said nothing, only held me tighter, but I pulled back a little to glare at him. "Dammit, don't you ever do that to me again."

"I'm sorry," he whispered, his voice reedy with pain. "But...the others? Is everyone okay?" I framed his face with both hands, wanting to laugh and cry and slap him all at once.

"Everyone is fine," I told him, and felt him relax. "We made it, Zeke. Eden is right around the corner."

He blew out a ragged breath, and sagged against me. "Thank you," he whispered, just as the soldiers swarmed around us. We were safe now. I released him and stepped back, letting the humans throw a blanket around his shoulders, shine a flashlight over his wounds and ask him a ton of questions.

"They're just scratches," I heard Zeke say, as Sergeant Keller peered down at him, frowning. "I'm not bitten."

"Get him on the truck," Keller ordered, waving his arm. "They can check him out once we're behind the wall. Let's move, people."

Moments later, I sat beside Zeke in back of the monstrous truck, both of us wrapped in blankets, his hand clutched tightly in mine. Surrounded by so many humans, the Hunger stirred restlessly as the scratches beneath my coat slowly healed, but I ignored it. Caleb and Bethany clung to the adults they knew, eyeing the soldiers warily, but the rest of them were dazed with relief. As the rain slowly let up, I peered over the top of the truck and saw it approaching a pair of enormous iron gates at the end of the road. A fence stretched out on either side of it, reminding me of the Wall in New Covington, dark and massive and bristling with razor wire on top. The white beam of a spotlight spun slowly around just inside one corner of the wall, piercing the sky.

There were shouts from inside the fence, and the massive gates slowly swung open, allowing the truck to pass through. More armed, uniformed humans lined the path beyond the gate, jogging after the truck as it cruised into a tiny compound with muddy roads and a few long cement buildings in the distance. Watchtowers rose along the wall every hundred feet or so, and the humans here seemed to be all military.

Caleb peered over the rim with wide eyes. "Is this Eden?" he asked plaintively. One of the soldiers laughed.

"No, little guy, not yet. Look." He pointed to where a dock stretched out over the dark waters of the huge lake. "Eden is on an island in the middle of Lake Eerie. There's a boat that will arrive to take you there tomorrow morning."

So Jeb had been right. Eden *was* on an island. This place was just a checkpoint, the last stop before getting to the city.

"How far?" Zeke murmured from my shoulder, his voice tight with pain. Sergeant Keller glanced down at him, frowning.

"Not far. About an hour by boat. But first, we have to make sure you're not infected. You've all been in contact with the rabids. Everyone will get a thorough examination here, before you're allowed into the city."

Uh-oh. That didn't sound good for me. And Zeke's hand tightened on mine, showing he felt the same. The truck pulled through the camp and finally stopped at one of the long cement buildings near the edge of the lake.

A bald man in a long white coat waited for us near the back door and spoke urgently to Sergeant Keller as we piled off the truck. I saw the sergeant point to Zeke and myself, and the bald man glanced over anxiously.

A bed on wheels was brought out, pushed by two more men in white coats, and Zeke was loaded onto it despite his protests. In the end, he relented but still kept a tight hold of my hand as we swept through the doors into a sterile white room. Cots lined the walls, and men and women in white rushed toward us, ushering the others to different parts of the room. Caleb resisted a little, clinging to Jake, but was won over when the man pulled something tiny and bright out of his coat pocket. It looked like a green button on a white stick, but when Caleb put it in his mouth, his eyes widened, and he crunched down on it with a smile. The man held out a hand, and Caleb allowed him to lead him toward a counter.

"Excuse me."

I glanced up. We had reached a pair of double doors at the end of the room, and the small bald man was looking at me apologetically.

"I'm sorry," he said. "But we have to take this one into surgery now. Some of his wounds are quite severe, and we still don't know if he's been bitten. You need to let him go."

I didn't know what "surgery" was, but I didn't want to let Zeke go, suddenly afraid that if he went through those doors without me, I'd never see him again. "I can't be there with him?"

"I'm sorry," the man said again, blinking behind his glasses. "I'm afraid it's not allowed. Too dangerous, you see, both for the patient, and yourself. But I swear we'll do everything we can for him. He'll be in good hands, I assure you."

I looked at Zeke again. He lay there, pale and bloody under the harsh lights, eyes closed. One of the women had stuck his arm with a needle earlier, and it had put him out completely. His fingers around mine were limp.

"You can wait outside the room, if you want." The bald man gave me a tired, understanding smile. "And we'll let you know how he is as soon as we're done. But you need to let him go now. Let him go."

Gently, he took my wrist, easing it away from Zeke's hand.
I resisted a moment, then let it drop. The bald man smiled
again and patted my arm.

They wheeled Zeke through the doors, and I followed them
down a narrow, dimly lit hall until they vanished through
another pair of doors with no windows, a bright No Entry
painted on the metal in vivid red. I caught a whiff of old
blood through the doors as they swung shut, and my stomach turned in both fear and Hunger.

I stayed in the hallway, staring at the doors, feeling the
hours tick away. I wondered how the others were doing. I
wondered if Zeke was all right, if he would pull through.
There had been so much blood. If he had been bitten…if he
turned into one of those monsters…

I shook my head, abandoning that thought. Leaning back
against the wall, I looked up at the ceiling and let my eyes
slip shut.

I don't know if you can hear me, I thought in the general direction of the sky, *or if you're even listening. But, if you have any
sense of justice at all, you won't let Zeke die in there. Not when
he's this close. Not when he's sacrificed everything to see the others
here alive. I know you're probably anxious to get him home, but he's
needed down here a little more. Just let him stay a little longer.*

The hall remained empty, silent. I bowed my head, letting
my thoughts drift. I wondered, suddenly, where Kanin was,
if he was still alive. If he could sense me, feel where I was, or
if he even cared. If he was still sane enough to care. I wondered if he was sorry that one of his offspring had killed the
other.

I felt it then. A flash of rage and hate so strong, I jerked my head up, bashing my skull into the wall. Wincing, I stared down the corridor, feeling my fangs poking through my gums, growling softly. For a split second, I'd felt him, seen his face. I felt his anger, directed right at me. Not Kanin. Not psycho vamp.

Jackal. He was alive.

The doors at the end of the hall swung open. I leaped upright as the bald man emerged looking very tired, smears of blood on his white coat.

"Your friend is going to be fine," he said, smiling, and I collapsed against the wall in relief. "He's lost a lot of blood, has a slight concussion, and there was an old gunshot wound on his leg, but he isn't infected. I expect him to make a full recovery."

"Can I see him?"

"He's sleeping now." The bald man gave me a severe look. "You can visit him later, but I believe *you* need stitches, too, young lady. Judging from those rips in your clothes, I'm surprised you're not in worse shape. Has someone examined you? Hold still a moment." He swung a strange device off his neck and stuck the ends in his ears. "This won't hurt," he promised, holding up the shiny, metallic circle on the end of the tube. "I'm just going to listen to your heart, check your breathing—"

He moved the device toward my chest...and my hand shot out, grabbing his wrist before either of us knew what was happening.

He jumped, startled by how fast I moved, and looked up at me with huge round eyes behind his glasses. I met his gaze sadly.

"You won't find anything there," I murmured, and he frowned a moment, confused. Then his face drained of color, and he stared at me, frozen. I heard his heartbeat speed up, and a sheen of sweat glistened on his brow.

"Oh," he whispered in a tiny, breathy voice. "You're a... Please don't kill me."

I released his wrist, letting mine drop to my side. "Go on," I muttered, turning away. "Do what you have to do." He hesitated, as if fearing a trick, that I would turn and pounce on him the second his back was turned. Then I heard his footsteps, sprinting off down the hall, running to spread the word about vampires in the hallways. I didn't have a lot of time. Hurrying to the surgery doors, I pushed my way inside.

The room was dark, save for a single bright light that shone down on a bed in the middle of the room, surrounded by beeping machines and shelves of metal instruments. Zeke lay on his back, clean gauze wrapping his chest, one arm in a sling, breathing peacefully. His pale hair gleamed under the lights.

I approached the bed and leaned close, smoothing the hair from his eyes, listening to the sound of his heart. "Hey," I whispered, knowing he probably couldn't hear me, unconscious as he was. "Listen, Zeke, I have to go. There's something I have to do, someone I have to find. I owe him a lot, and he's in trouble now. I just wanted to say goodbye."

Zeke slept on. I put my hand on his uninjured arm, squeezing gently. My eyes burned, but I ignored them. "You probably won't see me again," I murmured, feeling something hot slide down my cheek. "I got you here, like I promised I would. I wish...I wish I could've seen your Eden, but this place isn't for me. It never was. I have to find my own place in the world."

Bending down, I brushed my lips to his. "Goodbye, Ezekiel," I whispered. "Take care of the others. They'll be looking to you now."

He stirred in his sleep, but didn't wake. Releasing him, I turned and walked away, out of the room and through the doors. As they swung shut behind me, I thought I heard him murmur my name, but I did not look back.

WALKING BACK THROUGH the main hall was a much more hostile journey than when I'd arrived. The men and women in white coats either glared or cringed back from me, huddled along the wall, watching as I strode through the room. No one from our original group was there to say goodbye. Probably better that way. Caleb would make a fuss, and the others might want to know where I was going. But I didn't know where I was going. All I knew was Kanin, and now Jackal, were out there. I had to find my sire, see if I could still help him. I owed him that much. As for my "blood brother," I was pretty sure he would find me, eventually. And I didn't want to be around those I cared about when he did.

Outside, the storm had moved on, and the stars glimmered brightly through the clouds. A breeze cooled my skin, smelling of sand and fish and lake water, and a new beginning. Just not for me.

A squad of soldiers came rushing up to me, led by Sergeant Keller. I raised my hands as they surrounded me, leveling their guns at my chest, their faces hard with suspicion and fear.

The sergeant stepped forward, his previously smiling mouth

pulled into a grim line. "Is it true?" he asked, narrowing his eyes. "Are you a bloodsucker, like the doc says?" When I didn't reply, his face hardened. "Answer me, before we start pumping you full of holes to see if you die or not."

"I don't want any trouble," I said calmly, keeping my hands where he could see them. "I was just leaving, in fact. Let me walk out of here, and you'll never see me again."

Sergeant Keller hesitated. The other soldiers kept their guns trained on my heart. From the corner of my eye, I saw movement on the waters of the lake; a faded white ferry pulling up to the dock. The boat that would take everyone but me to Eden.

"Sarge," one of the men growled. "We should kill it. Now, before anyone hears we let a vampire through the gates. If the mayor finds out, there'll be a citywide panic."

I met Keller's eyes, keeping my expression calm, even though I felt my body tense, ready to explode into violence if needed. I didn't want to hurt these men, but if they started firing, I would have no choice but to tear them apart. And hope they didn't shoot me full of holes before I could escape.

"You'll leave?" Keller asked gravely. "You'll walk away and not come back?"

"You have my word."

He sighed and lowered his gun. "All right," he stated, as a few of his men started to protest. "We'll escort you to the gates."

"Sarge!"

"Enough, Jenkins!" Keller glared at the man who had spoken. "She hasn't hurt anyone here, and I'm not about to start a fight with a vampire if there's no need. Shut up and stand down."

The soldiers relented, but I felt their glares on my back as they led me across the muddy yard, back to the huge iron gates guarding the entrance. Keller yelled a command, and one of the gates creaked open, just enough for one person to walk through.

"All right, vampire," Keller said, nodding to the gate. I heard the click of their weapons behind me, a half dozen barrels leveled in my direction. "There's the door. Get out and don't come back."

I didn't say anything. I didn't look back. I walked to the gates and slipped through, feeling them grind shut behind me, sealing me off from humanity, Eden and Zeke.

We are vampires, Kanin had told me, on one of our last nights together. *It makes no difference who we are, where we came from. Princes, Masters and rabids alike, we are monsters, cut off from humanity. They will never trust us. They will never accept us. We hide in their midst and walk among them, but we are forever separate. Damned. Alone. You don't understand now, but you will. There will come a time when the road before you splits, and you must decide your path. Will you choose to become a demon with a human face, or will you fight your demon until the end of time, knowing you will forever struggle alone?*

A silent road stretched before me, damp with rain and littered with cars. As I watched, pale figures began to slip through the trees or claw their way out of the earth. Rabids edged onto the pavement, filling the road, their hisses and snarls rising into the air. Their empty white eyes blazed with madness and Hunger, and they began to sprint forward.

Reaching back, I drew my blade, feeling it rasp free, gleaming as it came into the light. Looking up at the approaching rabids, I smiled.

★ ★ ★ ★ ★

ACKNOWLEDGMENTS

Funny story, back at the beginning of my writing career, I remember telling myself that I wouldn't write a vampire book. That there were already so many books about our favorite bloodsuckers, I didn't have anything new to add to the masses. Obviously, *that* plan went by the wayside, and I am so thankful it did. I've loved every moment of writing this book, and I have many people to thank for that. My wonderful agent, Laurie McLean, who convinced me to give this whole "write a vampire book" a go. My editor Natashya Wilson for all her encouragement, hard work and little smiley faces next to the passages that she really likes. I live for those smiley faces. The fabulous people at Harlequin TEEN for awesome covers, awesome support and all-around awesomeness.

As always, my gratitude goes to my family, and especially to my husband, Nick, who continues to point out obvious logic-holes in the plot when I'm being stubborn and want it to work out "because I say so."

QUESTIONS FOR DISCUSSION

1. Allison claims she hates vampires and believes they are monsters. Yet when faced with a choice to die or become one, she chooses to be a vampire. Given a choice between death and becoming something you hate, what would you do? How did Allison's choice make you feel about her character?

2. *The Immortal Rules* takes place about sixty years after a virus has killed off most of the world's human population. What do you think the biggest challenges would be for the remaining population if that happened today?

3. Kanin warns Allison that the longer she lives as a vampire, the more her humanity will slip away. What traits do you think are essential to humanity? Does Allison continue to display these traits? How does she change as the story progresses?

4. Allison's decision to contact Stick compromises her and Kanin's hiding place. Would Allison have been better off letting go of her past, or was she right to approach him? What would you have done, and why?

5. As a vampire, Allison believes she must try not to form a romantic attachment with Zeke. Do you believe they have a chance at a future together, or are their differences too great? What do you believe makes a relationship work?

6. Jebbadiah continually emphasizes that he is willing to leave one person behind for the good of the group, yet he comes searching for Bethany and Allison when they are swept away by the river. What do you think makes someone a strong leader? Would you follow Jeb in this situation?

7. Zeke, Jeb and the group cast Allison out when they discover what she is. Yet when they are attacked, Allison jumps in to help them. How did her actions make you feel? What do you think makes someone heroic?

8. Allison feels loyalty toward Kanin and decides to try to find and help him. But before she does that, she agrees to stay with Zeke and the group until they reach Eden. Do you think her loyalty to the group was misguided? What do you think makes someone deserving of loyalty?

Julie Kagawa's *Iron Fey* series has been praised as unique, innovative, entertaining, romantic and much, much more. We're pleased to share with you a special excerpt from Book One of a new *Iron Fey* trilogy, featuring Meghan Chase's brother, Ethan....

THE LOST PRINCE

CHAPTER ONE
New Kid

My name is Ethan Chase.

And I doubt I'll live to see my eighteenth birthday.

That's not me being dramatic; it just is. I just wish I hadn't pulled so many people into this mess. They shouldn't have to suffer because of me. Especially...her. God, if I could take back anything in my life, I would never have shown her my world—the hidden world all around us. I *knew* better than to let her in. Once you see Them, they'll never leave you alone. They'll never let you go. Maybe if I'd been strong, she wouldn't be here with me as our seconds tick away, waiting to die.

It all started the day I transferred to a new school. Again.

THE ALARM CLOCK WENT OFF at 6:00 a.m., but I had been awake for an hour, getting ready for another day in my weird, screwed-up life. I wish I was one of those guys who can roll out of bed, throw on a shirt and be ready to go, but sadly, my life isn't that normal. For instance, today I'd filled the side pockets of my backpack with dried Saint-John's-wort and stuffed a canister of salt in with my pens and notebook. I'd also driven three nails into the heels of the new boots Mom had bought me for the semester. I wore an iron cross on a chain beneath my shirt, and just last summer I'd gotten my ears pierced with metal studs. Originally, I'd gotten a lip ring and an eyebrow bar, too, but Dad had thrown a roof-shaking fit when I came home like that, and the studs were the only things I'd been allowed to keep.

Sighing, I spared a quick glance at myself in the mirror, making sure I looked as unapproachable as possible. Sometimes, I catch Mom looking at me sadly, as if she wonders where her little boy went. I used to have curly brown hair like Dad, until I took a pair of scissors and hacked it into jagged, uneven spikes. I used to have bright blue eyes like Mom and, apparently, like my sister. But over the years, my eyes have become darker, changing to a smoky blue-gray—from constant glaring, Dad jokes. I never used to sleep with a knife under my mattress, salt around my windows and a horseshoe over my door. I never used to be "brooding" and "hostile" and "impossible." I used to smile more and laugh. I rarely do any of that now.

I know Mom worries about me. Dad says it's normal teenage rebellion, that I'm going through a "phase" and that I'll grow out of it. Sorry, Dad. But my life is far from normal. And I'm dealing with it the only way I know how.

"Ethan?" Mom's voice drifted into the room from beyond the door, soft and hesitant. "It's past six. Are you up?"

"I'm up." I grabbed my backpack and swung it over my white shirt, which was inside out, the tag poking up from the collar. Another small quirk my parents have gotten used to. "I'll be right out."

Grabbing my keys, I left my room with that familiar sense of resignation and dread stealing over me. *Okay, then. Let's get this day over with.*

I have a weird family.

You'd never know it by looking at us. We seem perfectly normal; a nice American family living in a nice suburban neighborhood, with nice clean streets and nice neighbors on either side. Ten years ago we lived in the swamps, raising pigs. Ten years ago we were poor, backwater folk, and we were happy. That was before we moved into the city, before we joined civilization again. My dad didn't like it at first; he'd spent his whole life as a farmer. It was hard for him to adjust, but he did, eventually. Mom finally convinced him that we needed to be closer to people, that *I* needed to be closer to people, that the constant isolation was bad for me. That was what she told Dad, of course, but I knew the real reason. She was afraid. She was afraid of Them, that They would take me away again, that I would be kidnapped by faeries and taken into the Nevernever.

Yeah, I told you, my family is weird. And that's not even the worst of it.

Somewhere out there, I have a sister. A half sister I haven't seen in years, and not because she's busy or married or across the ocean in some other country.

No, it's because she's a queen. A faery queen, one of Them, and she can't ever come home.

Tell me *that's* not messed up.

Of course, I can't ever tell anyone. To normal humans, the fey world is hidden—glamoured and invisible. Most people wouldn't see a goblin if it sauntered up and bit them on the nose. There are very few mortals cursed with the Sight, who can see invisible faeries lurking in dark corners and under beds. Who know that the creepy feeling of being watched isn't just their imagination, and that the noises in the cellar or the attic aren't really the house settling.

Lucky me. I happen to be one of them.

My parents worry, of course, Mom especially. People already think I'm weird, dangerous, maybe a little crazy. Seeing faeries everywhere will do that to you. Because if the fey *know* you can see them, they tend to make your life a living hell. Last year, I was kicked out of school for setting fire to the library. What could I tell them? I was innocent, because I was trying to escape a redcap motley that followed me in from the street? That wasn't the first time the fey had gotten me into trouble. I was the "bad kid," the one the teachers spoke about in hushed voices, the quiet, dangerous kid whom everyone expected would end up on the evening news for some awful, shocking crime. Sometimes, it was infuriating. I didn't really care what they thought of me, but it was hard on Mom, so I tried to be good, futile as it was.

This semester, I'd be going to a new school, a new location. A place I could "start clean," but it wouldn't matter. As long as I could see the fey, they would never leave me alone. All I could do was protect myself and my family, and hope I wouldn't end up hurting anyone else.

When I came out, Mom was at the kitchen table, waiting for me. Dad wasn't around. He worked the graveyard shift at UPS, and often slept till the middle of the afternoon. Usually, I'd see him only at dinner and on weekends. That's not to say he was happily oblivious when it came to my life; Mom might know me better, but Dad had no problem dol- ing out punishments if he thought I was slacking or if Mom complained. I'd gotten one *D* in science two years ago, and it was the last bad grade I'd ever received.

"Big day," Mom said as I tossed my backpack on the counter and opened the fridge, reaching for the orange juice. "Are you sure you know the way to your new school?"

I nodded. "I've got it set to my phone's GPS. It's not that far. I'll be fine."

She hesitated. I knew she didn't want me driving there alone, even though I'd worked my butt off saving up for a car. The rusty, gray-green pickup sitting next to Dad's truck in the driveway represented an entire summer of work—flip- ping burgers, washing dishes, mopping up spilled drinks and food and vomit. It represented weekends spent working late, watching other kids my age hanging out, kissing girlfriends, tossing away money as if it fell from the sky. I'd *earned* that truck, and I wasn't going to take the freaking bus to school.

But, because Mom was watching me with that sad, almost fearful look on her face, I sighed and muttered, "Do you want me to call you when I get there?"

"No, honey." Mom straightened, waving it off. "It's all right, you don't have to do that. Just...please be careful."

I heard the unspoken words in her voice. *Be careful of* Them. *Don't attract Their attention. Don't let Them get you into trouble. Try to stay in school this time.*

"I will."

She hovered a moment longer, then placed a quick peck on my cheek and wandered into the living room, pretending to be busy. I drained my juice, poured another glass and opened the fridge to put the container back.

As I closed the door, a magnet slipped loose and pinged to the floor, and the note it was holding came free, fluttering to the ground. *Kali demonstration, Sat,* I read as I picked it up, and I let myself feel a tiny bit nervous. I'd started taking Kali, a Filipino martial art, several years ago, to better protect myself from the things I knew were out there. I was drawn to Kali because not only did it teach how to defend yourself empty-handed, it also taught stick, knife and sword work, too. And in a world of dagger-toting goblins and sword-wielding gentry, I wanted to be ready for anything. This weekend, our class was putting on a demonstration at a martial arts tournament, and I was part of the show.

If I could stay out of trouble that long, anyway. With me, it was always harder than it looked.

Starting a new school in the middle of the fall semester sucks.

I should know. I've done all this before. The struggle to find your locker, the curious stares in the hallway, the walk of shame to your desk in your new classroom, twenty or so pairs of eyes following you down the aisle.

Maybe third time's the charm. Slumped into my seat, which thankfully was in the far corner. The heat from two dozen stares blazed on the top of my head, and I deliberately ignored them all. *Maybe this time I can make it through a semester without*

*getting expelled. One more year, just give me one more year and then
I'm free.* At least the teacher didn't stand me up at the front of
the room and introduce me to everyone; that would've been
awkward. For the life of me, I couldn't understand why they
thought such humiliation was necessary. It was hard enough
to fit in without having a spotlight turned on you the first
day.

Not that I'd be doing any "fitting in."

I continued to feel curious glances directed at my corner
the rest of the class, and I concentrated on not looking up,
not making eye contact with anyone. I heard people whispering and hunched down even farther, studying the cover
of my English book.

Something landed on my desk: a half sheet of notebook
paper, folded into a square. I didn't look up, not wanting to
know who'd lobbed it at me. Slipping it beneath the desk, I
opened it in my lap and looked down.

U the kid who burned down his school? it read in messy handwriting.

Sighing, I crumpled the note in my fist. So they'd already
heard the rumors. Perfect. Apparently, I'd been in the local
paper, a juvenile thug who was seen fleeing the scene of the
crime. But because no one had actually *witnessed* me setting
the library on fire, I was able to avoid being sent to jail. Barely.

I caught giggles and whispers somewhere to my right, and
then another folded-up piece of paper hit my arm. I was going
to trash the note without reading it this time, but curiosity
got the better of me, and I peeked quickly.

Did u really knife that guy in Juvie?

"Mr. Chase."

Miss Singer was stalking down the aisle toward me, her severe expression making her face look pinched and tight behind her glasses. Or maybe that was just the dark, tight bun pulling at her skin, making her eyes narrow. Her bracelets clinked as she extended her hand, waggling her fingers at me. Her tone was firm. "Let's have it, Mr. Chase."

I held up the note in two fingers, not looking at her. She snatched it from me. After a moment, she murmured, "See me after class."

Damn. Thirty minutes into a new semester and I was already in trouble. This didn't bode well for the rest of the year. I slumped farther, hunching my shoulders against all prying eyes, as Miss Singer returned to the front and continued the lesson.

I REMAINED IN MY SEAT after class was dismissed, listening to the sounds of scraping chairs and shuffling bodies, bags being tossed over shoulders. Voices surged around me, students talking and laughing with each other, gelling into their own little groups. As they began to file out, I finally looked up, letting my gaze wander over the few still lingering. A blond boy with glasses stood at Miss Singer's desk, rambling on while she listened with calm amusement. From the eager, puppy-dog look in his eyes, it was clear he was either suffering from major infatuation or was campaigning for the position of teacher's pet.

A group of girls stood by the door, clustered together like pigeons, cooing and giggling. I saw several of the guys staring as they left, hoping to catch the girls' eye, only to be disappointed. I snorted softly. Good luck with that. At least three of the girls were blond, slender and beautiful, and a couple wore extremely short skirts that gave a fantastic view of their long, tanned legs. This was obviously the school's pom squad, and guys like me—or anyone who wasn't a jock, rich or politically inclined—had no chance.

And then, one of the girls turned and looked right at me.

I glanced away, hoping that no one noticed. Cheerleaders, I'd discovered, usually dated large, overly protective football stars whose policy was punch first, ask questions later. I did not want to find myself pressed up against my locker or a bathroom stall on my first day, about to get my face smashed in, because I had the gall to look at the quarterback's girlfriend. I heard more whispers, imagined fingers pointed my way, and then a chorus of shocked squeaks and gasps reached my corner.

"She's really going to do it," someone hissed, and then footsteps padded across the room. One of the girls had broken away from the pack and was approaching me. Wonderful.

Go away. I shifted farther toward the wall. *I have nothing you want or need. I'm not here so you can prove that you're not scared of the tough new kid, and I do not want to get in a fight with your meathead boyfriend. Leave me alone.*

"Hi."

Resigned, I turned and stared into the face of a girl.

She was shorter than the others, more perky and cute than graceful and beautiful. Her long, straight hair was inky black, though she had dyed a few strands around her face a brilliant sapphire. She wore sneakers and dark jeans, tight enough to hug her slender legs, but not looking as if she'd painted them on. Warm brown eyes peered down at me as she stood with her hands clasped in front of her, shifting from foot to foot, as if it was impossible for her to stay still.

"Sorry about the note," she continued, as I shifted back to eye her warily. "I told Regan not to do it—Miss Singer has eyes like a hawk. We didn't mean to get you in trouble." She smiled, and it lit up the room. "I'm Kenzie. Well, *Mackenzie* is my full name, but everyone calls me Kenzie. *Don't* call me Mac or I'll slug you."

Behind her, the rest of the girls gaped and whispered to each other, shooting us furtive glances. I felt like some kind of exhibit at the zoo. Resentment simmered. I was just a curiosity to them, the dangerous new kid, to be stared at and gossiped about.

"And...you are...?" Kenzie prompted.

I looked away. "Not interested."

"Okay. Wow." She sounded surprised but not angry, not yet. "That's...not what I was expecting."

"Get used to it." Inwardly, I cringed at the sound of my own voice. I was being a dick; I was fully aware of that. I was also fully aware that I was murdering any hope for acceptance in this place. You didn't talk this way to a cute, popular cheerleader without becoming a social pariah. She would go back to her friends, and they would gossip, and more rumors would spread, and I'd be shunned for the rest of the year.

Good, I thought, trying to convince myself. *That's what I want. No one gets hurt this way. Everyone can just leave me alone.*

Except...the girl wasn't leaving. From the corner of my eye, I saw her lean back and cross her arms, still with that lopsided grin on her face. "No need to be nasty," she said, unconcerned with my aggressiveness. "I'm not asking for a date, tough guy, just your name."

Why was she still talking to me? Wasn't I making myself clear? I didn't want to talk. I didn't want to answer her questions. The longer I spoke to anyone, the greater the chance that *They* would notice, and then the nightmare would begin again. "It's Ethan," I muttered, still staring at the wall. I forced the next words out. "Now piss off."

"Huh. Well, aren't we hostile." Though her words were sharp, she still seemed more amused than anything. I resisted the urge to glance at her, though I still felt that smile, directed at me. "I was just trying to be nice, seeing as it's your first day and all. But, if you want to be a jackass…"

"Miss St. James." Our teacher's voice cut across the room. Kenzie turned to look, and I snuck a peek at her. "I need to speak with Mr. Chase," Miss Singer continued, smiling at Kenzie. "Go to your next class, please."

Kenzie nodded. "Sure, Miss Singer." Glancing back, she caught me staring at her and grinned before I could look away. "See ya around, tough guy."

I watched her bounce back to her friends, who surrounded her, giggling and whispering. Sneaking unsubtle glances at me, they filed through the door into the hall, leaving me alone with the teacher.

"Come here, Mr. Chase, if you would. I don't want to shout at you over the classroom."

Pulling myself to my feet, I walked down the aisle and slouched into a front-row desk. Miss Singer's sharp black eyes watched me over her glasses, then she launched into a lecture about her no-tolerance policy for horseplay, and how she understood my situation, and how I could make something of myself if I just focused. As if that was all there was to it.

Thanks, but you might as well save your breath, I thought. *I've heard this all before. How difficult it must be, moving to a new school, starting over. How bad my life at home must be. Don't act as if you know what I'm going through. You don't know me. You don't know anything about my life. No one does.*

And, if I had any say in it, no one ever would.